Carol Drinkwater trained at the Drama [...]
has had an extensive theatre career. She [...]
National Theatre under the direction of Lord Laurence Olivier,
was awarded the Edinburgh Festival First Fringe Award for
her work with a young experimental group and has starred in
London's West End on many occasions. Her most recent stage
appearance was in Harold Pinter's *Old Times*. Carol's television
credits are numerous and she is most famous for her award-
winning role as Helen Herriot in the series *All Creatures Great
and Small*, which was voted Britain's top drama series of all
time. Her many cinema appearances include Stanley Kubrik's
A Clockwork Orange. Alongside her acting career Carol has a
flourishing career as a novelist and screenwriter. Her first
novel, *The Haunted School*, was made into a family mini series
and won The Chicago Film Festival Gold Award for Children's
Films. As well as her children's books Carol has had published
several novels. Her books are translated into many languages.
She lives in London and the South of France where she has an
olive farm.

BY THE SAME AUTHOR
PUBLISHED BY HOUSE OF STRATUS

FICTION:
AN ABUNDANCE OF RAIN
AKIN TO LOVE
MAPPING THE HEART

CHILDREN'S FICTION:
THE HAUNTED SCHOOL

OTHER BOOKS BY CAROL DRINKWATER

NON-FICTION:
CROSSING THE LINE: YOUNG WOMEN AND THE LAW
THE OLIVE FARM

CHILDREN'S FICTION:
THE HUNGER: THE DIARY OF PHYLLIS MCCORMACK, IRELAND 1845–1847
MOLLY
MOLLY ON THE RUN
TWENTIETH CENTURY GIRL: THE DIARY OF FLORA BONNINGTON, LONDON 1899–1900

CAROL DRINKWATER

Because You're Mine

HOUSE OF
STRATUS

This edition published in 2001 by House of Stratus, an imprint of
Stratus Holdings plc, 24c Old Burlington Street, London, W1X 1RL, UK.
Also at: Suite 210, 1270 Avenue of the Americas, New York, NY 10020, USA.

www.houseofstratus.com

Typeset, printed and bound by House of Stratus.

A catalogue record for this book is available from the British Library
and the Library of Congress.

ISBN 0-7551-0287-8

'Real life is an affair of broken threads and loose ends'

Points of View, W Somerset Maugham

For Michel and for my ever-expanding family
in Ireland, England, France and Germany. As well as for my father
who loved life with a passion and a crazy sense of humour.

Acknowledgements

Enormous thanks to a few special people: Sophie Hicks, Patrick de Maré, Maggie Phillips, Chris Brown, Bridget Anderson, David Graham, the late and much-missed George Tee, Doraine Tee, Otto and Jill Wolff. Thank you, each of you, for offering support through the toughest of storms.

Also thanks to everyone at House of Stratus particularly my lovely editor, Sarah Fergusson.

1

Lyndsay Potter shot bolt upright in her bed, revealing her nakedness.

'Oh, my God! Stephen, wake up!'

Their lovely house was in darkness. Upstairs, the windows in their bedroom were wide open. Lyndsay had been asleep, tossing and turning in her dreams. Suddenly, in the distance, a screech had exploded across the navy sky. It had grabbed silence by the throat and ripped it apart with savage force. In the space of seconds, all peace had been sundered.

'Stephen, wake up!' Lyndsay was shivering, concentrating, trying to gather her thoughts together. Something had woken her. She was confused. A scream? Yes. Sharp and vicious. Was someone hurt? Or had a dream disturbed her? Petrified, she reached out for her husband, flailing around for the comfort of him, the heat of his body, but he was not there. She was alone. She had forgotten. Their bed, Stephen's half of it, was stone-cold empty. Her husband had not returned from Paris. There was no one, only the silence once more. But now it was an awesome silence, drifting through the mocking night. The bloodcurdling cry echoed through her mind.

At the reminder of it, an unreasonable terror gripped Lyndsay and left her so breathless she feared she was suffocating. She cast about amongst the disordered sheets, gasping for breath. Fresh air. She needed air. Throwing off the covers she stumbled to the open window, sucking in lungfuls of oxygen.

Leaning out over the casement, Lyndsay Potter's breathing began to steady. Slowly, as she surveyed the expanse of moonlit gardens beneath her – softly undulating acres cultivated with lavish vegetation – the palpitations of her heart calmed. These grounds were Lyndsay's domain, her paradise, and the sight and perfumes of their lustrous growth always reassured her.

She returned her attention to the bedroom. Due to the scare she'd had, the elegantly furnished space had grown menacing. Her and Stephen's four-poster, Anglo-Indian bed of darkly polished rosewood cast sinister shadows across the refurbished wooden floor. The earthy-toned arras tapestry had turned a lurid, blood red while the discreetly silent leather-cased alarm clock, its pearly hands reading twenty minutes to four, ticked too loudly on the antique console table.

Lyndsay shuddered and ran her fingers through her fine sandy hair. Had that horrible screeching been real? Judging by the state of the starched linen bedding it had been a nightmare, a violent one at that. Strange, though, that she had no recollection of it. She picked up her dressing gown and returned to the window, perched on the sill and gazed up at crisply outlined stars and a handful of ragged clouds until the stillness grew friendly again.

But all too soon her reverie was broken by a chorus of barkings that subsided as quickly as it began. It was her two dogs in the kitchen below. Lyndsay crossed back to the bed and poured a tumbler of mineral water. As she lifted it to drink she heard the click of a door, a creaking on the stairs, and she froze. The light on the landing went on. Oh, Christ, someone was in the house! That's what had alerted the dogs.

Rigid with fear she listened to the ascent of footsteps followed by coughing, then more footsteps and the wheezing cough again. It was Matthew. Her eldest son, Matt. How could she have been so foolish? Matt was home for half-term. She had forgotten. She made for the landing, opened the door and discovered him climbing the stairs.

'What are you doing out of bed?' she hissed, then realised the enquiry was way too sharp. She had no idea why she was chastising him. The sight of him was such a blessed relief. Nor could she have explained her whispers because, aside from the pair of them, the big house was empty. Paul, her youngest son, had opted for spending his week's break with a school friend's family on the south coast.

Matthew stared at his mother nervously. 'Nothing,' he replied.

'You must've been doing something, Matt. Why aren't you in bed?'

He stared blankly. These questions were an intrusion. 'I was getting a drink,' he muttered, lifting both hands to scratch his tousled hair and rub his exhausted face.

'That horrible sound.'

'What?'

'Didn't you hear it?'

Matthew shook his head.

'A screeching. Like pain.' He averted his eyes. This interrogation in the middle of the night challenged and oppressed him. He had reached the landing and was turning his back on his mother, necessary in his trek along the corridor to his own room, when she stopped him. 'Matt!'

The grandfather clock in the hall struck four.

'What?' He spoke without looking back.

'It woke me. You must have heard?'

'I didn't. 'Night, Mum.'

'Goodnight, Matt.'

So, it must have been a dream after all. The cry that had so alarmed her. Demons from her own subconscious.

Back in her room, Lyndsay hauled the bedding back into some semblance of a sleeping arrangement and settled into it. Her drowsing thoughts were of Matt. She blessed him for being in the house. Something, though, about his appearance was puzzling her. Why had it seemed bizarre? Then it struck her that he hadn't

3

been carrying a glass. He must have drunk his water in the kitchen. As Lyndsay drifted off into waves of sleep, she was still contemplating her son and his teenage habits. It was late May, and warm. She was sleeping naked with the windows open, but Matt, who couldn't abide fresh air and always moaned about the cold, had been wearing an anorak over his pyjamas. He was such a peculiar boy!

Later, a week or more later, when Lyndsay was to recall this exchange, she struggled to bring to mind every last detail of this night as well as all the other days and nights which followed on from it because every minute of every one of those days were to take on a horrifying life-and-death significance, and what she recalled above all else about this encounter was that Matt's face was damp. As he ascended the stairs, moving into the spill of light shining from the ceiling above her, she had noticed, though without registering it at the time, that he was clammy with sweat, shiny from physical exertion.

2

'Do you want this note, Mrs Potter, or shall I chuck it?' It was Denise, the branch manageress, enquiring.

Lyndsay was in the dry-cleaners in Tonbridge, rummaging through her handbag for her cheque-book to pay for the shirts she was collecting.

'What is it?' she asked, frowning. A thumping headache was making her irritable. She had slept badly – had never got back to sleep properly after a dream which had woken her and left disquieting doubts swirling about in her mind.

Plump, kind Denise was brandishing a fax retrieved from Stephen's blazer pocket. Lyndsay took it from her and glanced at it. Its content, instantly clear, knocked her for six.

'Are you all right, love?'

'Mmm? I...better keep it. Thanks.'

Working her way through the tightly crowded, noisy shopping precinct towards the car park, Lyndsay, laden with laundry, grappled in her pocket for the curled sheet of paper and paused among the busy shoppers to stare at the message once more. Two lines. A memo from Stephen's personal assistant, Amanda, it read:

Stephen,
I have confirmed the Hôtel Crillon for this coming weekend. They are holding the suite you requested. And, as requested, the booking is in the name of Mr and Mrs Potter.
A.

The fax was dated the previous Monday. Today was Saturday, Whitsun weekend.

Less than an hour later, Lyndsay was driving home along the lanes of the Kentish Weald as the sun shone brightly on the softly sweeping hillsides. As a rule she loved nature, particularly in Kent, where the hedgerows blossomed hawthorns and the richly textured, exposed countryside was scented with fresh, young growth, but on this particular May morning she was oblivious to the fine weather and the flourishing plants.

For sixteen years, Lyndsay and Stephen had been married. She knew, always had, that she had married a man who guarded his privacy jealously. It had been a strong part of her attraction towards him. From the beginning, she had recognised that there were areas for both of them that neither chose to divulge and the other never enquired after. They had discovered their points of contact. They had found their mutual interests, and it was upon these that they had built their relationship. Theirs was a secure marriage, not a passionate one. Unlike some couples, they did not live in one another's pockets. So, if, during Stephen's countless trips away from home, he had occasionally strayed into the arms of some passing female, Lyndsay hadn't felt hurt or threatened because she had never been made aware of it. Thankfully, above all else, Stephen had always been discreet.

As a father, she considered him too strict, too tough on the boys. This, as well as his busy schedule, meant that he was frequently distanced from them but they were amply provided for. Both boys were receiving the finest education so, all in all, Lyndsay had never had cause for complaints.

But on this particular Saturday morning, she felt insecure and wretched. The discretion that Stephen had always shown towards her had been thoughtlessly cast aside. She was livid that it hadn't occurred to him that she checked all his pockets before sending anything to the cleaners.

Braking now at the crossroads, in front of the signpost for Churdle Heath, Lyndsay decided to make a short detour to the local store and pick up some dried fruits for baking. She needed time to compose herself before returning to the house.

The village of Churdle Heath was situated in the heart of the Weald of Kent. It was a half-timbered, Tudor hamlet, which boasted a well-maintained medieval church and a fine sixteenth-century coaching house. The coaching house, known as the Lamb and Flag, was renowned for its courtyard, splendid gardens, delicious lunches – recommended in *The Good Food Guide* – and its oak-beamed restaurant. Alongside the pub and across the street from the thirteenth-century church was the post office-cum-general store, where Lyndsay was now heading. It had recently been taken over by an Indian couple.

As Lyndsay turned the corner onto the main street, the only street running through the village, she caught sight of Raj Bharjee on the pavement outside his shop. He was fiddling with a display of postcards. At the sound of the motor, Bharjee tossed his cigarette into the gutter and glanced round.

The arrival of an Indian couple in the village had been regarded by a certain section of the local community as an unwelcome intrusion. It had caused whispers of disapproval and resentment. Lyndsay had been shocked. She was fully aware that the majority in Churdles – the name affectionately bestowed on the village – believed in 'solid English values', but she had never expected to hear even the most conservative of them voice such blatantly racist remarks.

Through the window of her car, Lyndsay nodded to Mr Bharjee who barely seemed to register her. She had to admit that his rather surly disposition did nothing to improve relations with his neighbours. As she switched off the engine she asked herself if Stephen's liaison was with a woman she knew, a resident of Churdle Heath, perhaps? Unlikely. They were old biddies most of them, carping and moaning about Britain belonging to the British and Indians being an affront to this beautiful unspoilt village. Nobody sprang to mind.

So taken up was she with her own thoughts, she had not noticed that she had parked directly behind two police cars and that standing alongside her four-wheel drive, leaning against the stone wall which surrounded the church grounds, was a tall man in his mid-thirties. He was in conversation with four uniformed bobbies two of whom she recognised from the police station in Tonbridge. Churdle Heath had no station of its own; there had never been need of one. It was little more than a backwater. Events of great excitement never took place here. Spring was the only exception. Not a mile from the village was a nature reserve, and within it, a magnificent bird sanctuary. Each spring rare species of birds from all over the world migrated here. Some stayed to lay their eggs while others merely rested, breaking their journey, en route to nesting grounds in the more northerly reaches of Britain.

The osprey eagles were the local boast. They were annual visitors, arriving in early April and usually departing after several weeks, but this spring ornithological history was being made because, for the first time in a century, the eagles were nesting at the bird sanctuary. Every year tall platforms had been constructed to encourage them to stay south but they had never been seduced by them until now. This season the local sanctuary claimed two breeding pairs.

The stranger turned his attention towards Lyndsay as she stepped from her car. He smiled broadly and said hello. Lyndsay nodded in response. She couldn't recall ever having seen him before but it was not unusual hereabouts for neighbours to acknowledge a person even if they couldn't put a name to the face. He was dressed in faded denims and an anorak, most likely a thirsty hiker waiting for the pub to open, or a tourist visiting the church or bird sanctuary. But why the police? Intrigued by him, Lyndsay glanced his way once more before crossing the street. It was then she noticed he was carrying a shotgun.

The bell clanged as she opened the door. Inside, the shop was cool and deserted. It smelt pleasantly of rice and tapioca, of capsicum and other, less familiar spices. Even the sombre lighting seemed to hint at a distant oriental past. Young Mrs Bharjee rose from a stool set in a darkened corner of the store and shuffled obliquely towards the counter.

'Hello, Mrs Bharjee.'

The Indian woman nodded, eyes downcast. She was little more than a girl, probably even younger than Lyndsay had been when she'd first met Stephen, and so timid. Lyndsay smiled encouragingly. At twenty, Lyndsay had been equally timorous. It had been one of the traits Stephen claimed to have been attracted to. Evidently, no longer!

'Two packets of raisins, please.'

Mrs Bharjee's long, raven hair was swathed in a soft, forest-green sari. It fell loosely, concealing the left side of her face. Even partially visible she was lovely, Lyndsay had often thought it. Did she ever venture out from this post office? Lyndsay had never seen her in the street. She wasn't even sure if the young woman spoke more than a smattering of English. Was she lonely in this isolated Kentish village? Life here must be so alien to everything she was used to.

'Seems to be an invasion of police outside, any idea why?' Lyndsay, only partially curious, was attempting to engage the young shopkeeper in conversation, but Mrs Bharjee made no response. She simply turned to the shelves behind her in search of Lyndsay's order. Lyndsay watched her, trying not to torment herself with a mental picture of Stephen arm in arm with another woman masquerading as Mrs Potter. Mrs Bharjee handed Lyndsay the dried fruit without a word. As she did this a multitude of golden bracelets on her dark wrists jangled sweetly.

They drew Lyndsay's attention to a shocking bruise that covered the back of her left hand. Lyndsay shot her a solicitous look.

'What...?'

Registering Lyndsay's concern, the young woman abruptly withdrew her arm and gathered the sari closer about her face.

Back outside, Lyndsay paused uncertainly before crossing the street. Mr Bharjee, who was hanging cards of local National Trust properties, eyed her without interest. Attempting a smile, she wished him a fine weekend and went on her way. The stranger and police officers had disappeared. Aside from the hollow ring of a steel barrel being rolled along the cobbled lane beside the Lamb and Flag, Churdle Heath felt chillingly quiet for a warm Saturday. Suddenly, the strident screeching Lyndsay had heard in the night reverberated in her mind and sent a shiver down her spine. This stillness unsettled her. She hurried to her car.

A mile or so further down the road at the T-junction, Lyndsay signalled to the right and swung into Quigley Lane. Her thoughts were still with Stephen. She resolved not to mention the fax when he returned later; nor would she confront him with its contents.

A hundred metres along the leafy lane, she crossed the river by the old brick bridge and, once again, steered her navy-blue jeep to the right. She was approaching a secluded access protected by a magnificent pair of wrought-iron gates. The electric gates, which slid silently apart at the press of her remote command, bore two signs: 'Churdle Bridge Farm' and 'Year-round daffodils for sale: £2.25p including terracotta pot'. Lyndsay had painted this second sign herself. Her nursery and its plants were her pride and joy.

The gravel crunched and spun beneath the sturdy tyres as Lyndsay pressed open her window and motored slowly up the long winding drive. Banks of azaleas, yesterday's freshly mown grass and a carpet of bluebells perfumed the air. Lawns fringed with well-pruned box bushes, flowering irises and white and purple lilac fanned out either side of her, disappearing into the distance. Rhododendrons and an assortment of other flowering shrubs, collected from every corner of the world, created pockets of blazing colour in amongst the impressive lawns. Lyndsay adored this place. She bit into her lip, smarting at the pain, aggrieved by her husband's infidelity.

Even though it was Whitsun and Matthew was home, Stephen hadn't troubled to return. He was in Paris. In a foolishly adolescent way Lyndsay still considered Paris 'their city'. Silly, after sixteen years. Still, the fact that his affair was taking place in Paris sharpened its sting.

Ahead was their home, a red brick, sixteenth-century manor house. Until their arrival it had been known as Churdle Bridge Estate. Lyndsay had judged estate too grand and unwelcoming an address for a family home and had promptly rechristened it Churdle Bridge Farm.

She pulled up in the forecourt alongside Stephen's Porsche. Was it significant that he hadn't driven to Gatwick? Had he travelled to the airport with his mistress? Lyndsay, irritated by the advent of suspicion, unloaded her few bits of shopping and strode across the pebbled ground calling to her son as she went. There was no response. She continued on round to the back of the house, along the path lined with terracotta pots planted with ringlets of geraniums.

'Matt!' she called again.

Still no response. She had hoped to find him sitting by the pool, playing with the dogs, but there was no sign of him in the garden. No sign of the dogs either, which meant they were probably still shut up in the kitchen where she had left them and Matthew was still in bed.

'Matt!' she yelled. It wasn't healthy for a boy to be forever buried away in his room.

As she shoved open the kitchen door the dogs bolted past her, leaving her staring at the mess on the table: boxes of cereals, a dirty mug and bowl, coffee beans scattered like dice and two open cartons of milk.

'Matt!' she cried. 'Why can't you ever clean up after yourself?'

She flung her bags onto a chair, kicked off her driving shoes and, in stockinged feet, headed for the hall. The bass thud of unfamiliar music shook the walls and did nothing to alleviate her increasing headache.

'Matt!' she shouted, climbing the stairs. Music hailing from a stereo system or a synthesizer drowned her thump on his door. She was on the point of bursting in when he appeared.

'What?'

'It's nearly midday. You're not dressed, the kitchen looks like an army invaded it and the noise is insufferable!'

'I'm recording. Can you lend me a fiver, please?'

'You know what your father says about borrowing money.'

'Well, Dad's not here, is he? Anyway, it's not borrowing. He forgot to leave me my allowance.'

'Perhaps he's got other things on his mind,' she snapped. 'When you've cleaned up the mess you've made in the kitchen, we'll talk about it. I'll be in the greenhouses. And for heaven's sake, get dressed!'

'What mess?' sighed Matthew, closing his door.

Why was she being ratty with Matt? He might be an alarmingly reclusive teenager, but he wasn't to blame for his father's absence. She so looked forward to the boys coming home from boarding school and now she was being a nag. Lyndsay, bound for the lower slopes of the garden where her splendidly lush nurseries had been constructed, cursed her darkening mood. Her two beloved dogs, Sambo, the Labrador, and Rita, the Golden Retriever, hared across the lawns to accompany her and she paused to caress them. It was then that she noticed a silhouette moving amongst the tropical plants in the nearest of her clutch of greenhouses. A customer perhaps? She hurried down the slopes to attend to them but as she drew near she hesitated, recognising Dennis Carter, her gardener's son. Dennis was fifteen and not very bright. What was he doing in the greenhouses? Whatever it was, she would send him straight home. Vexed, she broke into a trot. Lyndsay hated herself for thinking such thoughts because he seemed such a lonely boy but Dennis made her uncomfortable. She disliked it when he hung around the place, which he was doing more and more frequently. There was something about the way he stared at her, and how he so rarely answered when she spoke to him.

She found him with his back to her. In his right hand was a green plastic plant spray. She waited by the door, cautiously observing Dennis who was spraying the leaves of a fruiting banana tree with water. His movements were sharp and fast and nervous.

'Dennis?' She entered gingerly.

He appeared not to have heard her, or he was choosing to ignore her as he so often did. As Lyndsay drew closer she saw that he wasn't spraying the plant at all, but the palms of his hands and his front torso. He sprayed the fine mists of water as though he were a girl covering herself in sweet-smelling cologne.

Lyndsay hung back, puzzled by his behaviour. He was humming. No, it was a tuneless high-pitched exhalation punctuated by the tender hiss of water.

'It's hot,' he said by way of an explanation but without turning.

It was suffocatingly hot. Lyndsay, suddenly aware of the thick heat, glanced around her. All the windows had been closed. Angrily, she stepped forward and began to shove them open. 'Did you do this, Dennis?' She moved towards him and snatched the plastic spray from out of his hand. He shoved his hands behind his back like a guilty child and stared at her with unblinking disbelief.

13

'But it's hot,' he repeated, pinning a glazed gaze upon her.

'Because you closed the windows! Have you messed with the thermostats as well? What are you doing in here? I've told you before, I don't want you in the greenhouses!'

A flicker of fear crossed his pasty, freckled face. 'Why?'

Lyndsay sighed at her own unkindness. 'Is there something you want, Dennis?' she asked in a softer, more patient tone.

'To go swimming,' he murmured. His T-shirt clung to him damply.

'Not today, Dennis.'

'But I'm hot,' he wailed.

'It's hot in here because you've closed the windows. It's not hot outside. Please, Dennis, go home.' Lyndsay turned her back on the wild-haired boy and strode the length of the greenhouse, clearing dead leaves as she went. She wanted to check the thermostats and she wanted to get away from Dennis. When she glanced back, he had disappeared and she was in a thoroughly bad mood.

Outside, as she pulled the door firmly behind her, she heard someone calling, 'Coo-ee!' Up, behind the house, a loudly dressed woman in her mid-fifties was stalking the stone paths.

'Oh, no!' Lyndsay recognised the caller at once. 'Get down!' The dogs were gambolling about her heels. One of the disadvantages of leaving the gates open for nursery customers was that she was prey to uninvited visitors, such as Dennis Carter and Marion Finch.

Marion Finch and her husband Arthur were longstanding residents of Churdle Heath. Marion was a notorious gossip and drove Lyndsay to distraction with her asinine twitterings and her determination to root out every piece of scandal.

'I can't deal with her now!' Lyndsay muttered to Sambo and Rita and ducked swiftly, heading for the strawberry beds where she grabbed a fork standing upright in the earth.

Arthur Finch had bought over 400 acres of arable farmland, a short drive east of Churdle Heath, and constructed a housing estate, thus securing what he described as his 'nest egg'. Local environmentalists had lobbied against it but, due to Arthur's connections within the local council, he had been granted planning permission, in spite of insufficient schools and facilities to cater for the influx. The arguments and debates, the letters to the local press still continued, even now, four years after the estate had been completed and occupied. Many who had moved there had never found work and local unemployment figures had soared. Dennis' father, Tom Carter, who worked part-time for Lyndsay, was amongst them.

Marion, craning and turning like an inquisitive, brightly plumed bird, peered past the orchard towards the fruit gardens and spotted Lyndsay digging vigorously. 'Leave that and come and say hello. Your vegetable beds are sprucer than most of our living-rooms.' Her voice carried like a hunting horn.

Lyndsay plunged her fork into the ground and strode towards the house. She needed an aspirin. Several aspirins.

Marion stepped from path to grass. Beneath a wild, white cherry in glorious blossom was a teak table with matching chairs. She staggered towards them.

'These are new.'

'Hello, Marion.'

'I need a drink.'

'Lemonade?' Lyndsay swung an arc and bee-lined for the kitchen, removing gardening gloves as she disappeared. The dogs padded after her. Lyndsay pressed two tall glasses against the ice crusher and poured home-made lemonade from a jug standing on the table. Then she reached into one of the cupboards for the first-aid kit and dug out the aspirin bottle. 'Matt!' she called, 'Tidy up this kitchen, please!'

She replenished the water in the dogs' bowls and sighed, swallowing two tablets. *If Marion starts prying about Stephen...* She emerged from the kitchen, smiling dutifully.

'You make me feel dull. Your home. You and Stephen. It's all so fucking "Mazon and Jardan". Excuse my French.' Marion's speech was noticeably slurred.

Lyndsay approached the table. 'Here, lemonade.' The air smelt sweet, gravid with blossom. She inhaled it appreciatively and sipped her squash wondering why, aside from insatiable curiosity or boredom, Marion had turned up here on a Saturday, sloshed.

Marion fell unsteadily into one of the chairs. 'I need the deadliest weedkiller you've got. I'm going to poison Arthur.'

Lyndsay nearly choked on her glass, trying not to laugh. 'Why?'

'Fucking bastard hasn't been here since Tuesday. In London "on business", he said. Takes me for a bloody fool. So, I drove up, and...'

'What?' Lyndsay felt a knot tighten in her stomach.

'I walked in on them. If it hadn't been my husband, I'd have died laughing. Caught with his pants down. Not a pretty sight.'

Lyndsay rested her glass on the table and warily eyed the woman seated alongside her. This was the first time Marion had ever narrated her personal life as scandal. She sympathised, but, frankly, she hadn't the slightest notion how she was going to handle her own marital difficulties, let alone Marion's. The two women sat in awkward silence.

'You're very tense, Lyndsay. Everything all right?'

'Fine.'

'Just fighting the fight against smelly old compost and rogue dandelions. I wish my life was so wholesome.'

Lyndsay bit back the need to remind Marion that less than a year ago she had lost her father. Did Marion imagine that such a loss just went away? And that Stephen, in Paris also 'on business', was actually with another woman. She had no desire to share her mourning or her marital concerns with Marion Finch though. Nor did she wish to dwell upon the army of emotions rising within her.

Marion lifted her lemonade. 'Any chance of a gin?' With a woman less brittle or garrulous Lyndsay might have been more willing to listen but she would never return the intimacy. She was incapable of sororal instincts, of sisterhood. In truth, unbosoming herself to anyone terrified her. 'Don't worry, darling, one stiff one and I'll be gone. Oh, did you hear,' Marion called after her, 'someone broke into the bird sanctuary last night and attacked the eagles?'

3

Stephen Potter stood outside the Hôtel Crillon, searching for a taxi. He ventured a few steps into the square and looked about. The Paris traffic was surprisingly congested for noon on a Saturday. Almost as bad as the bottleneck he had encountered coming in from Roissy airport the afternoon before. It had been hair-raising and had left him just short of late for his meeting. Stephen loathed arriving anywhere at breakneck speed with only nanoseconds to spare. As a rule, the taxis parked directly in front of the hotel but not today and there were no passing ones. Where the hell was the doorman? Stephen glanced left, along the rue de Rivoli, past the French Marine base, in the hope of hailing one himself. It was Whitsun weekend; that must be the explanation.

And then he remembered, the Clintons were in town and the Crillon was slap alongside the American Embassy. Hillary had been inaugurating something or other the evening before, hence the swarms of police vans and plain-clothes security everywhere. What a hullabaloo, what a heap of chaos inflicted on a city by the presence of one fairly ordinary couple. The Clintons did not impress Stephen. He had met Bill years earlier at some bash in Oxford, soon after he, Stephen, had returned from his stint at Harvard. At the time, he had dismissed the American as flaccid. Now, he judged him to be foolish.

An empty taxi rounded the corner approaching from the direction of the rue Royale. Stephen stepped forward and flagged it.

'Rue Elzévir, please, but not directly. I want to take a particular route. *Faire un petit tour*. I'll show you.'

Stephen's business was wrapped up for this trip and his flight back to Gatwick was not until early evening. He could have opted for an earlier plane but he had decided against it. His plan was to spend an hour at the Musée Picasso and then take himself off to a restaurant for a splendid lunch. He had intended bringing Lyndsay along. Or rather, suggesting that she fly in that morning and spend the bank holiday with him in Paris. It had been a while since they'd taken a trip together, since they'd frittered away time on hedonistic pursuits, a long while since sex had been on the agenda and, as far as Stephen was concerned, their marriage was at an end. He had marked out this weekend to tell her, to break it to her gently in surroundings where she could feel good about herself.

He was forty-six and he felt an urgent need to re-experience some of his old boyish impulses, to rediscover his romanticism. He wanted time to himself now. He had business concerns that he could not share. It was – had been for a while – time to cut loose, and go it alone. Life with Lyndsay suffocated him. She was the mother of his sons and that would never change but for the rest, he felt nothing.

Amanda Graeme, Stephen's personal assistant, had done as he'd requested and booked him his favourite suite at the Crillon facing directly onto the square. The pleasure he had accrued from preparing an elegant exit from his marriage had relaxed him. He had kept everything from Lyndsay, not wanting to upset her at home. After all, he had no desire to hurt her, only a need to be free of her. He had intended to hand her the air ticket as he set out for Gatwick, but then at the eleventh hour he had changed his mind.

Things had become very tense between them these last months. Since her father's death, Lyndsay's moods had grown dark and strange. This should have given them an incentive, a bond, but it had not and now Stephen had lost all interest in the marriage. When Matthew had telephoned from college to say that he would not be spending Whitsun with his chum, Rupert, as arranged, that he wanted to come home, Lyndsay had started worrying that something was wrong. 'Matthew is spending an inordinate amount of time at home,' she'd said. 'It's curious that a boy verging on sixteen wants to be with his parents all the time.' And what made matters worse, according to Lyndsay, was that whatever Matt's problem might be – if there was a problem, which Stephen doubted – Matthew was not confiding in his mother. Stephen had refrained from pointing out that although Matt was spending a great deal of time under the same roof as his parents, precious little of it was actually spent in their company. The boy usually incarcerated himself in his room, writing music. Since the death of Lyndsay's father, Matthew had spent most of his time home from college alone. Before that, he had whiled away a fair proportion of his weekends with his grandfather in the cottage in the grounds. Music had been a strong bond between them. No doubt he was pining for the old boy. Conventional adolescent behaviour, Stephen felt sure. Nothing to fret about.

Stephen had thought better of the weekend in Paris. The timing was wrong. His plan had been dropped without a mention. Instead, he had settled on extending his own visit. He had already visited two luxury apartments not far from the Crillon and had decided to rent one of them. Now, he was stealing a few hours of leisure in the city he loved so well, before hopping on a plane that would deliver him home in time for dinner. If the weather was fine on Sunday he would drive mother and son to the boat and take them sailing. Then, in the evening, when Lyndsay was in a receptive mood he would break the news to her.

'I want to go to the Picasso Museum, but first I'd like us to drive along the Left Bank,' Stephen informed the driver in impeccable French.

Modern art was one of Stephen's passions but he was not a man to go to a gallery and wander doggedly from room to room cramming in every piece on display. He selected carefully the works he wished to view, and not always the same set of canvasses. However, amongst the Impressionists, the Post-Impressionists and the paintings of Picasso or Matisse, he had his perennial favourites. These he looked up, as he might a longstanding mistress, whenever he chanced to be in the particular city where they were exhibited. There was one particular period of Picasso's work, from the late 1920s, early 1930s, amongst which were a collection of drawings – sketchbook stuff and a handful of oil paintings – which fascinated him; the Minotaur works and the bull oeuvres. All of them were compositions of duality: man and beast, victim and aggressor, love and death. Stephen was fascinated by the concept of duality, he always had been. Twin personalities. Double lives, double standards.

The taxi crossed the river. It travelled the length of Saint Germain as far as Place Maubert, turned left into rue Lagrange and drove along the Left Bank quay. Motoring alongside the Seine on a fine day elated Stephen. Following further instructions the cab crossed north over the Pont Neuf, east alongside the Right Bank and deposited him in the heart of the Marais, the ancient swampland of Paris.

The taxi left him in the rue Vieille du Temple. Because there were too many pedestrians in the narrow streets gazing in the shop windows and holding up the flow of traffic, Stephen decided to walk from there. He strolled to the third *arrondissement*, which was not in his opinion a very salubrious area, and arrived at the Hôtel Salé where the Picasso exhibition was on permanent display.

He was allocating three-quarters of an hour to the pieces he had selected. It was a bank holiday; the gallery would be overrun with tourists and Stephen was ill at ease with hordes. They made him claustrophobic. Surprisingly, when he arrived, the queue was a mere trickle. He bought his ticket and, within minutes, was crossing the cobbled courtyard. From there, he mounted stone stairs to the cool, sparsely furnished galleries and into the room where he had last encountered his sketches.

A handful of foreigners were bunched together in front of the drawings, discussing them intently, blocking them from view. Stephen strolled to the window, preferring to wait at a distance. Doubtless they would move on swiftly, most visitors did. He leaned against the wall and glanced out. His eyes lit upon the two stone sphinxes and then travelled down to the cobbled courtyard.

Seated on one of the stone benches was a woman. She had not been there when he had arrived, he was sure of it. He would have noticed her immediately. Her face was hidden from his view. It was her slender torso, leaning in a curve over her knees that he was feasting on. Was she examining the cobbles or was she in pain? The arc of her silhouette was exquisite, swan-like. Stephen was reminded of a Modigliani. The precision of her form set off the boldness of her colours. She was dressed entirely in black, her skin was pearly white and her hair was a coarse and flaming red. Stephen was transfixed by her. Head tilted, locks swinging, she ogled the ground in a semi-circle around her feet. She must have dropped something.

He turned to inspect the room. The tourists had drifted on. The art was free for him now, but he did not move from the window. He threw a cursory glance at the sketches and then greedily turned his attention back to the courtyard.

Simultaneously, the woman sat up, stretched her arms above her head and swung around, directing her gaze upwards. She seemed to be peering right at him. It was as though Stephen had called her, so precisely had the lifting of her head followed the crooking of his. Her beauty took his breath away. Jesus, she was sexy. Lavish red hair, alabaster skin swathed in black. What age? Mid-thirties probably, like Lyndsay, but her clothes and style were younger, more striking than his wife's. Black high-heeled shoes, sheer black stockings and a thigh-length skirt. She was feminine and sexy with an attitude that he rarely saw in women outside of Paris.

Stephen had never been easily ruffled. He cultivated control and stoicism, decreeing such qualities essential for his business, but the way this woman was looking up at him agitated him. He wanted to go to her, or drink her in from a distance. He couldn't decide which. If she never released her eyes, he might never shift. He had been rendered immobile by this woman's gaze.

Nonsense! Utter ludicrous nonsense! Fanciful chocolate-box piffle, not worthy of an intelligent adult. Chiding himself thus, he swung from the window to focus on 'his' sketches, drawing strength from their visceral power. Then he became aware of his body. It was trembling. This was insanity. Raising his right hand, he held it out before him and observed the tremor. He needed lunch and, uncharacteristically, a stiff drink. Stephen rarely drank at lunch. An occasional glass of a fine Meursault or a distinguished Pomerol with a meal – certainly not spirits – but at that moment he needed a bloody large Scotch. His pleasure in the artwork had been done for. He realised there was little point in staying longer. He had better find a bench, a cool spot in one of the alcoves, and get a bloody grip on himself. Feeling foolish and irritated by his skittish behaviour, he strode manfully forth.

The redhead wasn't in the courtyard nor had he bumped into her on the stairs. He'd glanced into every room on his way down, hoping he might – she ascending, he descending, a perfect opportunity to manoeuvre an introduction. Outside, the benches were empty, the courtyard deserted. She had never existed! She had been an apparition, an angel glimpsed for a few fleeting moments.

The wooden entrance doors of the Hôtel Salé creaked, frightening the life out of him. Christ, he was jumpy. They were closing up for lunch. Fearing that he was about to be thrown out and because he always enjoyed an opportunity to exercise his French, Stephen enquired of the young man who'd sold him his ticket less than twenty minutes earlier, '*Pardonnez-moi, suis-je le dernier? Attendez-vous de fermer pour l'heure du déjeuner?*'

'No, we're open during the lunch hour on Saturdays, sir,' the attendant replied in English.

'Do you know if there is a good restaurant near here?' Stephen was not at home in this neighbourhood, having ventured to the *quartier* only to reacquaint himself with his beloved Picassos.

The attendant stared at the cobbled yard, considering the request.

Surely to God, thought Stephen, the question must have been posed a hundred times before. The fellow must know the neighbouring restaurants. 'I'll find one myself,' he said. 'There must be dozens hereabouts.'

The keeper looked dismayed, having failed to furnish an answer and Stephen, as he departed, was taken aback by his own gruff behaviour. What in heaven's name had come over him? He was behaving like an oaf. Even a Parisian, assuming the young employee was Parisian, had been cowed by his bad manners.

After a couple of minutes he came across a bar, situated on a corner, facing a delightful garden. The interior looked smoky and cramped so Stephen settled himself at the only free table outside, wishing he had bought a newspaper at the kiosk he'd passed on the way.

He hadn't been in a bar as down at heel as this since his student days. He preferred the elegance of more classic establishments such as the Deux Magots over on the Left Bank or Harry's Bar in Venice. It wasn't that he was a snob, although Matt would argue that he was, it was simply that he moved in other circles. In any case, he abhorred seediness and the seamier sides of life. Red-light districts, whores, that sort of carry-on held no fascination for Stephen. Petty crime was vulgar. Illicit acts needed to be brilliantly masterminded and executed before Stephen would applaud them. He was uncomfortable with low-life.

'Large Scotch, please.'

The waiter, an inoffensive looking fellow, nodded and moved to the next table, while Stephen settled back in his chair welcoming the warm spring sun on his face. He was feeling calmer. Pollen spores drifted listlessly on air currents. Tall spreading plane trees, reaching out from across the street, softened the light and offered dappled respite from the lethargy of the hot city.

What had happened back there in the museum? Something had taken a strange grip and panicked him. A second's hysteria? Could he blame it on business pressures? His dinner engagement of the previous evening with his Argentinian client, known as *El General*, had been most instructive. Now that he'd met the man face to face and spent several hours in his company, Stephen felt better able to appraise him. This señor (whose extraction was almost certainly neither Spanish nor South American though he spoke the language faultlessly) was ruthless and greedy – most importantly, greedy – and, as such, a potentially dangerous bastard. The operation was going to require patience and kid-glove handling. Nonetheless, Stephen's programme had been accepted without a word of objection or criticism. *El General* had been appreciative of the discretion and meticulous attention to detail Stephen had brought to the table. He was satisfied; Stephen's strategy was tight and thorough, and all risks had been minimised. So, if it wasn't fatigue, if he wasn't stressed and, unlike Lyndsay, wasn't het up about Matthew's puberty, what had happened back there in the gallery?

'*Avez-vous du feu, s'il vous plaît?*'

'*Je ne fume pas.*' Stephen's response was dismissive until his attention lighted on black suede stilettos, black stockinged calves. 'Wait!'

He was almost afraid to look into her face but when he raised his eyes and they travelled the length of her, he saw that she was glorious and as slender as a piano key in her black dress contrasted against her opalescent skin. She was marginally older than he had originally estimated. Thirty-eight perhaps, forty even. And lovely.

'You were in the courtyard…!'

She waited, cigarette at the ready, saying nothing.

'I was at the window. I saw you in the courtyard. I don't smoke but I can arrange a light. Waiter!'

'Please, don't go to any trouble.'

'Waiter!' She regarded him with frank interest. It was almost too much to bear. Her eyes were olive green, flecked with amber. Her ivory skin was freckled. Could she be Celtic? Only then did it dawn on him that they had switched to English. So, she was not French, after all. 'Are you Irish?' She shook her head. His Scotch arrived. He was profoundly grateful for it. 'Would you like a drink?' She sat down opposite him, a tantalising touch away. 'What would you like?'

'No, thanks. I'm only after a light.'

'Waiter!'

The waiter, busy at another table, looked over. Stephen waved for matches and then returned his attention to the woman opposite. Her staring disconcerted him.

'I'm Stephen… Stephen Potter. And you?' She bowed her head, making no attempt to answer him. 'You're English then, not Irish?' he quizzed. What the hell did it matter? Talk for the sake of it was not a mode of behaviour Stephen usually employed.

She smiled. 'Not since a long time.'

The matches arrived. Stephen snatched them, determined that he should be the one to light her cigarette. 'Sure you won't have a drink?'

'No thanks.' Lighted match in hand, he leaned towards her and was tempted to brush his fingers against hers but thought better of such an impertinence. 'But I'll smoke my cigarette while you drink your whisky. To keep you company, if you like, Mr Potter.'

'Not since a long time, you said. What does that mean?'

'I live here. I don't consider myself English any more.'

'Why?'

'Why what?'

It was his turn to appraise her. She had turned her attention in other directions, gazing along the street, smoking languidly, as unconcerned as a black cat in the sunshine. A thoroughly preposterous thought crossed Stephen's mind – was he falling in love? Neither said a word. Utterly and hopelessly in love.

The last question, hers, remained unanswered. Her identity, where she came from, such facts mattered not a jot. Only later, after she had vanished, were they of frenzied consequence. But for now, alongside her, imbibing her, he begged time to stand still. He wanted this moment to last for eternity. Perfumes, patterns, rhythms were seducing him. He was being reborn. The world beyond his being was exploding, he was waking to its light, weakening under its heat, and at its source was this Titian goddess.

She turned her head and smiled. Her expression was warm and generous, her eyes blazing. The mistress of secrets as yet undisclosed. She ground the butt of her cigarette into the ashtray and even that, a gesture that he loathed, had sex in it. 'I have to go,' she said.

'Lunch?' he offered feebly. 'Have lunch with me.'

'I couldn't.'

'You didn't tell me your name.' He was rising as she rose, keeping step, desperate to hold onto her. Furious to touch her, to fuck her, to plunge into her.

'Gin,' she offered, smiling with green eyes, such gold-tinged green eyes.

'You want a gin?'

'No,' she grinned. 'Gin's my name.'

'Gin! Where do you live?'

'I must be on my way.'

'Yes, of course.' Helplessly, hopelessly, he allowed her to depart, permitting her to slip beyond his reach. Watching her step away from him, he feared he might never set eyes on her again yet he felt incapable of running after her, of begging.

Stephen lunched at the Crillon. He could not have faced eating alone in a public restaurant, robbed of her. He ordered a bottle of Margaux to accompany his gigot of lamb and drank the greater part of it. His share and hers. On the plane to Gatwick he downed the offered glass of champagne and followed it with a neat Scotch. The only element of the day for which he felt grateful was the fact that he hadn't parked his car at the airport. He sunk into a taxi and closed his eyes. He was drunk in a low-key, aching way. His head, resting against worn, slippery leather, was splitting. He felt irritable and bereft, trying to come to terms with what had happened. Circles ran in his mind, in an attempt to formulate a plan. How to find her again? What to go on? She lived in Paris. He would soon be living there, too. Had she said Paris? Or had she said, 'here'? It had been *here*, nothing more specific than that. She had given him nothing.

And then, seconds later, he thought of how to forget her. She was fifteen minutes in his life. A quarter of an hour in the company of a great-looking woman, a heavenly creature. There was nothing more to it. If he could convince himself of that he could forget her. But better still, if he could only find her again.

Both alternatives were futile and enervating. Gin was a curious name, an abbreviation of Gillian? He repeated the name over and over again, trying to find a key in it, a clue, building a mantra out of it. His desperation was pathetic. Something he might have expected of Matthew, or any adolescent, not of himself.

He had to put this thing back into perspective. His marriage no longer gratified. It was about to end. He had sons he cared for, two healthy boys. His business was risky. He mistrusted his current client, 'el General', and the financial stakes involved were probably making him edgy. He was craving sexual excitement, a little romance in his life. It had nothing to do with this particular woman...

I live here. I don't consider myself English any more.

Gin. It was the gentleness of her that had so flayed him. The elusiveness. No, it was her blatant backbreaking sexuality. She was a devil, not a goddess. Her name had a carnal ring to it. Prohibitive.

He was drunk. It would be a relief to arrive home. Home! He had forgotten to phone from the airport to say that he was on his way. It was something he always did. He had long since stopped thinking of Churdle Heath as his home. Paris, the apartment he had seen that very morning, that was to be his future.

When Stephen walked through the door, Lyndsay was taken aback by his appearance. 'You look terrible,' she said. 'Has something happened?'

'We need to talk,' he snapped and passed on through into the drawing room.

Stephen listened to his wife's footsteps crossing oak floors. There was never a perfect moment, or an appropriate one, for the decision he was about to impart. Somewhere deep within her she must be expecting this, he argued silently. Not today perhaps, but...

Lyndsay, in the hallway, steeled herself, trying to decide what to do for the best. She thought of the fax, of Stephen's infidelity and knew in her heart that something wretched was brewing. The ticking of the grandfather clock and the creaking of Stephen's leather chair punctuated the silence. Lyndsay slipped through to his study, switched on the answering machine and returned to face him. She seated herself in the fireside chair opposite him. Her tone was gentle, nothing accusatory, but steadfast in its certitude. 'You have something to tell me?'

Stephen, face to face with the moment he had been waiting for, found himself impotent. He shifted his position, dropped his eyes and crossed his legs. 'Something…has been hanging over us for a while…you and me.' He drummed the arm of his chair with agitated fingers. 'Lyndsay, we need to put some distance between us.'

Lyndsay swallowed nervously. This was worse than she had been expecting. 'Are you saying you want a separation?' she asked softly.

Stephen made no immediate response. His silence stabbed at the core of her. 'I'm taking a flat. Just for a while, see how things work out.'

'You've taken, or you are going – ?'

'I've found a place.'

'Found? Oh, God, I see.' Lyndsay stared blindly at the carpet. She wanted the man before her, whose gaze she could feel upon her, to lean forward and take her in his arms. She wanted to turn back the clock to a moment when life had been radiant.

'I shan't want anything from here. I shan't break up the home.'

'Shan't break up the home! Jesus, Stephen, the home is not the furniture! It's not held together by cars and fax machines! You…we…are the home.' She rested her cupped hands over her mouth in an oxygen mask of fingers. Her face was marked with feather-thin lines of tension. 'This doesn't sound like a request for a trial separation. It sounds like the first step, early negotiations towards a, fingers crossed, amicable but certain divorce.' She waited for confirmation. Or denial. Neither came. 'I've been appalling to live with,' she said flatly, 'since Harry died.' The excuse sounded pathetic.

'We've grown apart, Lyndsay.'

'You don't think that it might just be stress, or...?'

Stephen shook his head. 'That's too easy,' he said. Pain and confusion registered in Lyndsay's features, the woman who had borne him his two sons. It was tough to behold but it would be cowardly, crueller to retract. 'I'm going to go. At least for a while. Who knows, later...'

Lyndsay looked into his strong face. His dark hair was greying at the temples. He was incapable of completing the sentence. She knew he did not believe what he was about to say. 'Is there someone else?' She wanted, above all else, that he be truthful. If he admitted it then, perhaps, there was a way forward, a step towards a new communication, a more mature understanding.

Again, his hesitation. 'No,' he responded tightly.

Lyndsay reflected a moment, gathering broken threads of thoughts into a stream of sense. He was lying. A woman was pulling him away. Passion had decided him. She had neglected him. She needed to sit tight, remain patient and calm and be there for him when he came back. 'Where is this flat?' She asked in a tone that was as neutral as she could manage.

Again, there was a hesitation on his part, and then eventually he told her, 'Paris.'

'Paris!' The word stung as mordantly as if he had cited the mistress herself. Way back in the early days Paris had been their city. Now he had chosen it as his refuge from her. Oh Christ, the woman was probably French. A tantalising, sexy French mistress! 'What about the boys?'

Their eyes met for a fleeting second. It was too much for Lyndsay. If she did not go she would break down. To weep now would be demeaning. She could not, would not, beg him to stay.

He was a liar. She thought about the fax and bit back the desire to mention it, to lose her temper, to accuse him outright of his infidelity. She forced dignity not to abandon her. Withdraw before anger or bitterness took the upper hand.

'Dad!' It was Matt on the stairs.

'I'll be in the kitchen,' she said and rose to leave, brushing past her son in the hallway.

4

Lyndsay gazed at the television screen in numbed silence. The local news was announcing a full-scale police investigation into the previous night's vandalism at the Churdle Heath Bird Sanctuary. Osprey eagles, two pairs, breeding in the county for the first time in a century, had been attacked with an insecticide spray. One male bird was reported to be suffering shock and mild damage to the eye. Lyndsay's stomach turned as she recalled the blood-curdling screech, which had woken her in the night and then a cry from down the hall drew her attention back to the present: Matthew's voice. He and Stephen were locked away in Stephen's den watching a soccer match live from Barcelona. She left father and son to their sport and drifted out of doors.

It was a bright, starry evening. Lyndsay frequently strolled about the garden after sunset, but tonight she was particularly grateful for the time alone.

'I've found a place,' he'd said. His manner had been brusque and withdrawn. He hadn't even bothered to ask after Paul.

Lyndsay felt almost paralysed with shock. She had fought against a hurt which made her want to rage at him and accuse: I took your blazer to the cleaner's this morning and found a fax from Amanda confirming a suite at the Crillon booked in the name of Mr and Mrs Potter, so I know bloody well you were with someone. Don't lie to me; don't deny you're having an affair. At least, have the decency to speak the truth!

Fortunately, she had kept her anger and hurt to herself. She had stayed silent and maintained her dignity. And later, when Matt had reminded his father that the match was on television, the atmosphere had brightened.

Stephen is having an affair, he believes he loves her – whoever she is – and so he is taking the necessary steps. It may end in a divorce or it may not. I have to let this thing run its course, she silently repeated. Monitor it, if she could, from a distance. If the affair was meaningless it would peter out naturally and she would forever regret her furious outbursts. Possibly, probably, this woman was no more than a passing fancy. She had to remain sanguine and level-headed.

Wasn't she well placed to know about ugly rows, screaming matches, deceit and violence? As a child, she had witnessed it all. No one knew better than she where unleashed passions and scenes of jealousy ended. They served nothing.

She kicked off her sandals, scooped them up and waded barefoot through thick, velvety grass. It was springy underfoot and slid softly between her painted toes while the warm, late evening air caressed her. She was trying to calculate how many weekends Stephen had not returned home on the Friday evening. Until recently, he had never stayed away between Fridays and Mondays. Blossoming flowers surrounded her. Spores bursting from their cases spilled seeds all across the receptive earth. She paused and stood perfectly still. Nature was abundant, and fecund. Lyndsay spent her life working with it – nurturing, breeding, and cultivating it – but she had lost her inspiration. She was tired. Since her father's death she had grown introspective. A pair of stripped-bark eucalyptus trees, both growing tall and strong, flanked her. Their perfume was invigorating.

Had Stephen been involved before? Someone special? Had he ever considered leaving home before but made the sacrifice and stayed, for the boys' sake? Should she suggest to Stephen that they go away for a weekend? Or was it too late for that? She inhaled deeply, alone in her domain. The night-scented soapwort, the southernwood, the heady tea rose and the lilacs were a drug to her.

She must not allow herself to become obsessed by Stephen's affair. His request for a separation was not irreversible. They had spent too many years together to throw away their marriage for a passion. And what of the boys? If not for her sake, surely he would be drawn back for those two. She had to be patient, she told herself.

She stood in the grass and listened to the slumbering sounds of late evening, attempting to find comfort in them. A tawny owl hooted, frogs croaked down beyond the swimming pool and she fancied she heard the high-pitched, ultrasonic call of a pipistrelle bat searching for insects. She had always felt so safe in this space, so reassured by it, by nature's fertility and her humble contribution to it. What was to become of her and all that surrounded her? What was to become of her life with Stephen and, above all else, the family? It had been a long while since she and Stephen had made love. Could she blame him if he looked elsewhere for affection? It was up to her to woo him back.

The distant voices of diners from the Lamb and Flag strolling to their beds or preparing to motor back to the city carried on the breeze across the cowslipped pastures and fields. Mingled with the fragrance of flowers she smelled cows and dung and the sweet dark soil. All of it buoyed her and yet…she couldn't picture a life without Stephen. Since her father's death she'd been a rotten wife. Men needed affection, constant attention, reassurance of their worth. They were boys, always boys. Wasn't she well placed to know?

She thought of Marion and Arthur Finch not two miles away, caught together in their torn web. The desultory mood Marion had left behind her had been difficult to shake off. Just as the heart-rending cry of the blinded osprey would not leave Lyndsay be. For some inexplicable reason it felt connected to her own life, a portender of worse to come.

Marion had been too drunk to drive. Lyndsay should have been more forceful about detaining her, but Marion had refused the offer of coffee and Lyndsay, bored with her whining, hadn't insisted. She had allowed the boozed woman to leave, tear-stained and miserable. She could hear the Jaguar's tyres spinning against the neatly raked gravel and Marion at the wheel, squiffy and disconsolate. The truth was that in her heart Lyndsay judged Marion. She felt no compassion. She was repulsed by the woman's lack of dignity, and by her self-pity. It reminded Lyndsay of her own mother. This realisation appalled Lyndsay. Was that why Marion disgusted her? Was that why her inability to express sympathy towards a neighbour's predicament had left her feeling shabby and ashamed? Now, Lyndsay regretted her hardheartedness towards the stupid woman. As she'd driven away, Marion had carped, 'You don't begin to understand what it feels like to be returning to an empty home. You're too damned fortunate for your own good, Lyndsay.' Marion's parting words had touched a nerve.

Lyndsay had always been gratefully aware of her good fortune. But hadn't she earned her claim on it? She had served her father and supported him with ferocious care, in spite of everything. Everyone had a past. She had worked remorselessly to put hers behind her, to bury it. A secure family life had been the only goal she had ever sought to achieve. The world she had created with Stephen was harmonious and normal. She had a right to it.

Lyndsay was sitting beneath the ornamental cherry tree at the same teak table she and Marion had sat at earlier. Cupped between her hands was a glass with the remains of her white wine. She lifted the glass, swallowed the last mouthful, and decided she would take a dip in the pool.

And then the distant light in her late father's cottage caught her eye. It must have switched itself on only moments before.

Stephen had arranged for the installation of a time switch soon after Harry's death because Lyndsay hadn't been able to abide the bleakness of her father's empty home, in darkness, across the lawns.

She rose, leaving her glass on the table and her shoes hanging from the back of her chair, and set off, barefoot, for the cottage. There, she bent for the key hidden beneath a loose paving to the right of the front door. So many months had passed but still Lyndsay hadn't cleared the place out or locked it up.

Once inside, she crossed to the table in the living room and sat down. The space had grown unfamiliar even though nothing much had changed since Harry's death. It was still sparely furnished, yet busy with her father's clutter. Columns of his ageing, well-thumbed sheets of music were stacked in rows all around the borders of the floor. Two saxophones in their cases stood upright, hogging the only easy chair in the room and on top of the television was a silver, art deco picture frame. Lyndsay had given it to her father years ago as a birthday present.

In it, she had placed a treasured photo of him dressed in bow-tie and evening suit, saxophone in hand, standing proudly on a stage, singing into a microphone. Lyndsay still remembered the evening the photo had been taken. She had been eleven years old. It had been the first dance Harry had ever allowed her to attend. She'd worn white cotton ankle socks, practical canvas sandals, a neatly pressed frock, ironed by herself, and two tortoiseshell hairslides to keep her long sandy hair from tumbling across her eyes. Seated alone at a table in a corner of the ballroom, proud of his charisma, she'd watched her father at work. From his great height on the stage he'd played his popular dance music and led his quintet, creating waves of joy, while clusters of dancing couples had swirled hither and thither, locked in one another's arms, laughing and relaxed. The crowd's lightheartedness had been strange to behold. It was a mood so in contrast to her own feelings and the atmosphere in the cheerless terraced house where she'd lived as a child. It had been a matter of months after her mother's shocking death and after her sister, Rebecca, had gone.

Even as an eleven-year-old girl, staring up at her father, idolising him, terrified of losing him in the same abrupt way she had lost her mother and sister and of being bereft in the world, Lyndsay had somehow understood that his life had been destroyed. No one else would have guessed it. He had buried his guilt in his music, like the practised performer he was. She recalled that when he'd lifted his saxophone and begun to play the look in his eyes had grown quieter. But the loss of his eldest daughter had broken his heart.

After Harry's death, when she and Stephen were in the cottage dealing with the essentials, she'd noticed that Harry had removed the photo from its frame and replaced it with a photograph of Rebecca taken when she was barely thirteen. Rebecca, Lyndsay's long departed sister.

'Who's that?' Stephen had asked when he saw Lyndsay puzzling over it.

'My sister.' Looking at it, she remembered how potently she had grown to hate even the memory of her.

'Pretty girl.'

'Yes.'

Her father's dying words had been, 'I'll see Rebecca.'

Lyndsay shivered now. It was chilly in the cottage. Once upon a time she'd whiled away hours in this room with him, listening to him improvise on his saxophone. Old favourites he'd played when she was small. Evergreens, he used to call them.

All of me, why don't you take all of me, can't you see I'm no good without you.

She had enjoyed rediscovering with him his vast collection of 'thirty-threes', stacks of discontinued long-playing records, (vinyls, Matt and Paulie called them) and helping him with the annotation of his diaries; notes for the book he had always intended to write, but never had; tales about his adventures on the road as a musician. Those last few weeks before his death had been precious. Harry had spent much of it with Lyndsay and the family. Even once the cancer had taken hold he had insisted that Matt cross the lawns for his clarinet lessons, along with all the encouragement the boy could possibly want for the music he was composing. And during the final days, Harry had continued to delight the boys with his fantastic stories, regaling them with tales from his past. He'd cracked his jokes as he always had, played the fool, raised his glass with appreciation and no one would have detected his anguish. Except Lyndsay.

Now, once more within the glow of his sitting-room, she glanced about, searching for a sign of his presence, attempting to reach out to him, to pour out to him her sorrow and her fears about Stephen's departure. He was there somewhere, she was sure of it, but she couldn't feel him. The first few months after his death she'd felt his presence everywhere but not now, not anymore. In the years after her marriage to Stephen, Harry had grown mellow. He had seemed at peace. The violence had been eaten away.

Slowly now, she lifted herself to her feet, ready to leave, regarding the saxophones standing sentinel in their upright cases. 'Oh, Dad…' She missed listening to him practise his tunes while she was working in the garden, missed him recounting the jokes he'd heard in the pub at lunch-time. Most of which were utterly foolish, but they had always made her giggle.

A week or two before his death she had asked him, 'What's wrong, Dad?' He had looked so weary and frail and there had been such sadness about him. 'Tell me, Dad, please,' she had implored.

'I was to blame,' he had mumbled eventually.

He had shuffled to the chair that housed his saxophones and had settled himself between them. The light beyond the room had faded, the sky had grown black. Lyndsay had been grateful for the darkness. She had crossed and knelt at his feet, curling up on the ground in front of him. Like a small animal sheltering, burying herself there, she had pressed up against him and clutched ferociously at both his legs.

'For what, Dad?'

'I need her forgiveness.'

'Who?'

'Rebecca. If only she were alive…'

A tightness like a band had taken hold around Lyndsay's head.

5

The following Friday was a warm spring day. Stephen announced at breakfast that he was driving to Tonbridge. Matt asked his father to hire some videos for him, which Stephen agreed to do, and so Matt scribbled him a list.

Lyndsay flirted with the idea of suggesting to Stephen that she accompany him. She thought they might lunch in a pub somewhere on the country side of town, take time to talk, but a week had passed since she'd discovered his infidelity, since he'd returned from Paris announcing his departure, and, all week, his mood towards her had been cold. He'd spent the best part of most days on the telephone in his den. Evidently, he didn't want to discuss the pending separation and she elected for not broaching the subject, harbouring the hope that if she sat tight, his resolve might thaw.

'You won't have time to watch all those films, Matt, before you go back to college on Sunday. Why don't you drive in with your father and choose the ones you really want?'

If she didn't feel up to proposing her own company, she saw no harm in putting father and son together, but Matthew didn't fancy it and Stephen said that picking up a few tapes was no trouble. Lyndsay was baffled. Matt would be back at college in a couple of days and this was a perfect opportunity for father and son to spend time with each other. Was Stephen intending to talk to his sons, to inform them of his plans?

'Please take Matt with you. It'll get him into the fresh air for a morning,' she suggested as Stephen slipped into his jacket and she casually brushed his shoulder. 'He's spending far too much time in his room. And it'll give the pair of you a chance to talk.'

'He's old enough to make up his own mind, Lyndsay. Stop nagging.'

Was there a particular reason why Stephen insisted on going alone, a lunch date with his lady friend? Suspicion raised its ugly head again. Choked by confusion and bottled-up emotions, Lyndsay returned to her chores and left them be.

Mid-morning, she set off down the garden to the greenhouses. There, she checked temperatures, adjusted thermostats and windows, and watered dehydrated plants. Friday was also 'Tom's day'. Tom, the gardener, was Dennis' father but he bore little if any resemblance to his son. Amiable, hardworking, a divorcee whose wife had left him, he was now in his mid-forties and had been unemployed since his arrival on the housing estate three years earlier. Once a week he came by to lend her a hand, frequently bringing Dennis along with him, but today he arrived alone and Lyndsay was relieved. Tom took care of the physically demanding jobs; hedges to trim, logs to chop, wind-damaged branches to lop and the driving of the diesel mower to maintain a velvet finish to the lawns.

Once Matt had returned to his music upstairs and Stephen had been gone long enough not to return for something he'd forgotten, Lyndsay stole into his den, also his office. Throughout the past week she had taken to paying furtive visits there. In fact, it was becoming a minor obsession; every time Stephen disappeared out of the house, Lyndsay was in there, hunting, scavenging, searching for evidence.

His desk diary was filled with ink-scribbled notes and records of flight details and hotels. Drawers were heavy with envelopes each bearing coins of different currencies. She found a stack of airline tickets, restaurant guides, museum guides, handbooks on particular artworks, even a pocket atlas, but nothing to hint at a new or hidden life. Lyndsay sighed. There were so many ridiculous questions driving her crazy. Crazy because she wanted details of this someone else and crazy because she would never have believed herself capable of such crude and petty detective work. She wished he would just sit down and discuss the situation with her. Stephen's manner and attitude had changed markedly. He was holding back, growing cold. And she felt helpless, unable to curry favour, at a loss as to how to seduce him back. Their marriage was becoming a wall of silence.

While Lyndsay was digging through one of his bureau drawers she heard Matthew's footsteps on the stairs. She froze guiltily and then reminded herself of how many times a day, over the years, she had wandered in and out of Stephen's office, without a second thought, collecting used coffee cups, checking the answering machine, the faxes, leaving messages on his desk. It was perfectly reasonable that she should be in there, even if what she was doing was not.

'Going out, darling?' she called.

'Yeah.'

'Matt!' Lyndsay hurried out to the hall and caught up with him at the front door. She wished he didn't always look so morose and didn't always bury himself in his room. If there was something troubling him why didn't he confide in her, as he used to? 'Did you see the postcard from Paulie?'

'Yeah.'

'He's been learning to ride.'

'Knowing him, he'll probably fall off and break his arm!' Matt almost allowed a grin at the prospect of his younger brother's imagined misfortune.

Lyndsay smiled, recognising fraternal jesting. 'How about we drive over to see the ospreys and then disappear somewhere for a spot of lunch?'

She remembered how, one spring, Matt and Paul had been particularly thrilled when they'd witnessed one of the eagles plunge spectacularly, feet first, into the cold reservoir lake and rise with a huge wriggling fish between its talons.

Matt scuffed the carpet with the toe of his left trainer, his head was bent and his right hand was on the latch. His body language was telling her that he wanted to be on his way and that she was detaining him. He regarded his mother and shrugged his shoulders.

'Wouldn't you like that?'

'I'm not hungry.'

'Well no, I didn't mean – '

'See you later.'

'Where are you off to?'

'The village.'

It was where he always went. To the post office, to buy stamps to dispatch his precious music cassettes. Firing off his letters and tapes to managers. Never venturing further. Cycling home to write new tunes, his passionate obsession. He was desperate to succeed, in a silent brooding way. Was it normal to be so intense? She wished he had some friends his own age in the neighbourhood. She wished Stephen hadn't been so bloody snooty about the Hampton boys, Duncan and Thomas, sons of tenants in a farmhouse about five miles south of Churdle Heath.

'Will you be back for lunch?'

'I'm not hungry, Mum. If I want something I'll handle it.'

'Are you all right, sweetheart? I mean, you spend so much time in your room. We've hardly seen you…?'

'Don't fuss, Mum, please.'

There had been a time, a couple of summers back, when Matt had enjoyed hanging out with the Hampton lads. But Stephen had made it known that he preferred his son to find more suitable companions. At first, Matt had ignored his father. Until one evening, returning late after an all-day fishing expedition with the brothers, Matt had mentioned in passing that a boy from the local estate had accompanied them. Stephen had been furious. He'd kicked up an almighty fuss, accusing Matt of keeping bad company, describing the lads as uncouth, yes, that had been the adjective he had used and Matt had rounded on his father, screaming wildly at him while Lyndsay, in the background, had been stunned. She had never before seen Matt provoked to such a burning rage. It had troubled her profoundly, reminding her of her own childhood. He has my father's temper, she had thought. God forbid it might lead him to the same violence. Eventually, spent of all fury, Matt had run for refuge to his grandfather's cottage where he'd buried himself for the night. Relations between father and son had been prickly for the remainder of the holidays, but Stephen had got his way and Matt had terminated his friendship with the Hampton twins.

'See you, Mum.' And with that Matt was now out of the door and across the gravel forecourt without a glance back.

Matthew had grown practised at keeping things to himself, especially since his grandfather had died. Was silence his defence, his means of fending off his mother's over-protective streak? That would be Stephen's explanation. It seemed a lifetime since he'd said to Lyndsay, 'Hey, Mum, listen to this.' And she missed that. She missed his companionship, sharing those small triumphs with him, as well as his secret anxieties. Instead silence had become Matt's guard, and his music. He gave his life to his music, endlessly practising tunes he'd written and put on tape to send to the record companies. These days, if she ever asked him to play a song for her, he would shrug and mumble. 'It isn't ready yet.'

Should she call his housemaster and ask for an appointment, or was Stephen's appraisal accurate? Was this normal adolescent behaviour in a boy of almost sixteen? Or was Stephen – acquainted with only the bare bones of a family history scarred by brutality – so enamoured elsewhere that he had lost interest in the welfare of his family?

With her hands in her pockets, Lyndsay walked through into the drawing room and watched from the window as her son wheeled his bike from the shed and cycled down the drive towards Quigley Lane. He was pedalling rapidly, singing with the blackbirds. He seemed to have so many secrets. She wondered if it was possessive of her to want to share them all.

Alternatively, she could telephone Paul. He was in Brighton with the family of his best friend, Richard. She could suggest that he and Richard spend the last part of Whitsun at Churdle Bridge Farm. She could use the nature reserve as the incentive. 'A rare opportunity… The birds will be gone by the summer holidays.' On the other hand, Paul was probably having a whale of a time where he was. Why should he be hauled back simply because she was feeling neglected? She gave up on the idea and returned to the kitchen. The only sound in the empty house was the ticking of the grandfather clock in the hall. Neglected. Lyndsay hated that word. It sent a shiver down her spine for, even now, after all these years, she could hear the echo of her mother's voice screaming it down the stairs. Lyndsay shuddered. How terrified her mother must have been, terrified of being abandoned.

Once all the chores had been completed, Lyndsay elected to get out of the house for a while. She drove to the village, intending to pass directly through and go for a walk at the nature reserve. Even if Matthew was no longer interested, she would enjoy watching the ospreys.

The grounds of St Joseph's, the medieval church in Churdle Heath, were modest in size. The cemetery that housed no more than a hundred graves and headstones was fenced by a yew hedge that was encompassed by a stone wall almost as ancient as the church itself. The yew was trimmed regularly and stood no taller than the wall, which meant that any passerby, except a small child, could look over into the churchyard.

As Lyndsay approached the village, the grounds of the church appeared deserted. Sometimes an ageing local was present, placing flowers at the resting place of some long-departed relative, or a gaggle of tourists would traipse aimlessly around, but not today. Today, the dappled resting place was still and silent. In contrast, diagonally across the street from the church, clusters of the first of the season's open-air diners were seated on wooden benches outside the Lamb and Flag, drinking local ale or wine and laughing. Lyndsay turned away from the spectacle. The sense of neglect and loneliness she'd experienced earlier, watching Matt cycle down the drive, returned. She glanced back towards the empty cemetery and then slowed, for there was a familiar figure over at the far end, sitting on a stone bench beneath the weeping silver pear tree. Lyndsay loved that tree, in fact she rather coveted it for its magnificent blue hue, but today what drew her attention was not the tree itself. It was the silhouette of Mrs Bharjee. She was dressed in a dusky blue sari, the colour of the branches that gave her shade.

The presence of the young Indian woman there was so unlikely that, at first, Lyndsay thought she must be mistaken. She had never seen her outside the post office before and the local churchyard seemed the strangest of places to encounter her. Lyndsay braked. Something about Mrs Bharjee's demeanour was disturbing. Her head was bent. Yards of flowing silk hid her features but Lyndsay could tell that the young woman was dabbing her face with a handkerchief. Had she something in her eye or was she crying?

A car rounding the corner behind Lyndsay honked its horn, giving her a start. Lost in her observations, she had unknowingly drawn to a halt in the middle of the street. She accelerated obediently. Mrs Bharjee was now hidden from view behind the church. Lyndsay glanced across to the post office, directly facing her. It was closed. The clock on her dashboard read ten to one. The post office closed at half past twelve for lunch.

What was Mrs Bharjee doing in the churchyard across the street from her home? Where was her husband? Mrs Bharjee never went out and if she did, surely it would not be alone. This sighting of her troubled Lyndsay. She wondered if somebody had offended her, or if she had been the victim of some racist insult. She glanced back at the church, deliberating about whether or not to stop.

It was then Lyndsay noticed the bicycle lying on the ground beyond the honeysuckled lych-gate, a few paces along the church pathway. She hesitated. The driver of the car behind her was growing irritable, hooting incessantly.

'All right!' Lyndsay glanced in her rearview mirror. Behind her was a queue of cars stretching back around the corner and out of sight. 'Blast!'

The car honked several times in quick succession.

Flustered, Lyndsay edged forwards, scanning the street for somewhere to stop. Parked vehicles, owned by the Lamb and Flag lunch-timers, lined both sides of the narrow high street. Business was flourishing but it left nowhere to pull up.

From behind her once more came the low angry horn. There was nothing to be done. She pressed her foot hard on the accelerator and sped out of the village towards the nature reserve. She had an idea that the bike might have been Matt's, but he couldn't have been in the post office buying stamps or envelopes because it was closed. She couldn't work out why his bike, if it was his bike, was ditched on the path leading to the church portal. Perhaps he had stopped to assist Mrs Bharjee. No, Lyndsay would have seen him, unless he was inside the church. She hadn't brought her mobile and she couldn't recall if there was a phone box along this route to ring the house and find out if he was there. He might have ridden home by the bridle-path... Oh, Lord, she was being over-protective again.

At the T-junction that led to the Lingfield road she found a telephone booth and rang her own number. There was no reply. She had forgotten to switch on the answering machine. She gave up on her proposed walk and drove home by the main road, thus avoiding the snarl-up in the village.

Stephen's car was not there. He must have decided to lunch in Tonbridge. She wondered whether he was alone or if he had a prearranged date.

As Lyndsay slipped her key in the lock, the telephone began to ring. She tossed her bag down on the hall table and hurried to the kitchen. On her way through, she called up the stairs, 'Matt, pick up the phone, please!' The ringing persisted. Lyndsay hurried to get to it. 'Hello?'

It was Amanda Graeme, Stephen's personal assistant, who had written the fax of the previous week, who had made his booking at the Crillon, which meant that she was party to Stephen's infidelity. She might also know about Stephen's intention to leave home and about his newly leased flat.

Lyndsay's response was frosty. 'Stephen's not here.'

Although Lyndsay knew that Stephen would never in a million years have discussed his personal life with Amanda, in the day-to-day running of his affairs, any assistant would have gleaned plenty. It was quite conceivable that Amanda knew certain details of Stephen's life better than Lyndsay herself. After all, she had served him loyally for sixteen years. Two months longer than Lyndsay and Stephen had been married.

'When will he be back?'

'He didn't say. Is there a message?' Lyndsay was edgy and defensive.

'Please tell him that I've made the Geneva booking for Tuesday morning. It's the flight he requested. Amex will deliver his ticket to him later this afternoon.'

Lyndsay jotted this on the pad by the phone. A part of her longed to interrogate Amanda, to cunningly win her confidence and coax out of her anything she might know, such as the identity of Stephen's mistress. 'Any other message?' There had never been any jealousies between these two women – nor intimacy.

She heard Amanda light up a cigarette, one of her menthol Kools, and then proceed to the list in hand. 'Er...actually, I'd expected him to be there. I'll call later, or...'

'Do you want to fax the rest through?'

'There's a... I'll try later.'

Was Amanda hedging, holding information back? Lyndsay respected how protective Amanda was about Stephen and his armoured reserve. She also knew that Amanda prided herself on her efficiency and discretion. No personal assistant was more adept at keeping mum. Even an executive as recondite as Stephen could demand no more. So, it came as quite a shock when Amanda said suddenly, 'Pity you weren't able to go to Paris, after all. I got the feeling Stephen was looking forward to it. He was certainly keen for me to confirm the booking.'

Lyndsay placed her pencil on the table in front of her and took a deep breath, hoping that Amanda hadn't heard the catch in her throat. 'Yes,' she replied, 'wasn't it?' She was wary because she was flummoxed.

Amanda must have misread Lyndsay's tightlippedness, believing it to be a signal to steer clear of personal matters because she instantly returned to the business in hand. 'The confirmation from the German bank for the payment-on-signature funds came through. The advance will be calculated in Euros though, not Swiss francs. Does Stephen want the monies redirected to another account or continue en route for the Swiss bank? Otherwise, there's nothing urgent. I'll handle the rest before I leave.'

Lyndsay was cursing. She had let slip a perfect opportunity. 'Matthew's home,' she said by way of reintroducing a personal note into the conversation. 'So, much as I love Paris...'

'Well, there are going to be plenty more opportunities. Oh, remind Stephen, please, that I'll be leaving early today and I'm away this weekend.'

'I will.'

'I better get back to work. Say hello to Matthew from me. Bye.'

'Bye.'

Lyndsay stared at the notepad in front of her. Had she really turned her insides out over a foolish fax, misinterpreted its meaning, because she had been too tired to think straight? She'd uncovered no evidence of infidelity amongst Stephen's belongings because perhaps there was no other woman. And yet, she couldn't feel relieved or elated by this news. Stephen had told her that he was moving out. That was a fact. She left the kitchen, went to the hall and collected her bag.

'Matthew!'

No reply. She ascended the stairs. Before going to her own room she popped by Matt's and knocked. There was no response. She stuck her head in and regarded the infernal mess. No Matt. She closed the door. He wasn't back. Where had he got to? He must have decided to visit the bird sanctuary, after all.

After all – a change of plan. Amanda's words had been, 'Pity you weren't able to go to Paris, *after all*.'

Which meant that for Stephen there had been a change of plan, but not on her account because she hadn't been consulted in the first place. So why, if Stephen had been intending to invite her to Paris, had he changed his mind? The booking was in the name of Mrs Potter, but that didn't mean...

'Stop!' she cried aloud. She was torturing herself. If Amanda thought for one second that Stephen had another woman she would never have mentioned the Paris trip, unless she was discreetly trying to warn Lyndsay of the situation, as one woman alerting another. Lyndsay was growing tired of the nagging questions inside her head. She'd give Stephen his message, mention Amanda's reference to Paris and insist that he sit down with her and discuss the separation. Ignoring it, in the hope that he would change his mind or that it would go away, was not going to resolve anything. If Stephen had plans, she'd better know about them.

Neither Matt nor Stephen returned for lunch. Lyndsay made toasted cheese sandwiches for herself and Tom, which they ate in the garden under the cherry tree. She had been intending to have a private word with him about Dennis meddling with the heating in the greenhouses the previous Saturday but when it came to it, she decided to give it a miss. Tom was such a dedicated, caring soul. He would have been mortified by what he would have taken to be a criticism of his only son. Since his wife had upped and left, he had struggled against all odds to bring the boy up decently. He thought the world of him. In any case, Lyndsay had too many other more pressing matters on her mind. So, after Earl Grey tea, she weeded the paths, sold four plants to passing customers, left the nursery in Tom's capable hands and set off for the nature reserve. She promised herself a long leafy walk. It was twenty-five to three. Tom could lock up when he left at four. He had his own keys.

6

The car park was deserted. Lyndsay closed her sunroof, changed into walking shoes and set off. As she cut across the lot, her attention was drawn by the presence of a second, discreetly parked car. It was tucked beneath a shady oak on a muddied clearing behind the empty and boarded up ticket hut. Parking was free, except during the busy summer weekends. The car, a rusting Ford, appeared at first glance to have been abandoned, but as she approached she saw that the windows were misted, and the chassis was rocking slightly. A courting couple. The outskirts of the reserve were renowned for such activities. She heard a cry and hesitated. Then, arrested by the proximity of naked desire and curious to observe who in this day and age must copulate in the discomfort of a motor car, she lingered. Sprays of long hair, writhing back and forth, swept clean the glass and all but exposed the pounding couple's steamy privacy.

'Aah! Aah!'

A lorry followed by a car on the road behind her rattled by in quick succession. The woman's cries, throaty, yelping ululations, continued while a simultaneous moan, male and brutal, stilled the movement in the car. Lyndsay, shocked, not by two strangers' blatant lust but by her own prurience, recoiled. As she did so, she heard the fall of feet pounding against earth and turned to see the back of a figure slipping behind a clump of trees; the fleeting silhouette of a jogger in a dark track-suit speeding off into the woods.

A wooden rubbish bin and several discreetly installed picnic tables were to her left as she hurried away in the opposite direction, penetrating the curtained afternoon light. The temperature was noticeably cooler in the heart of the forest. Wafting on the breeze were the distant cheepings of the breeding ospreys. The calls were clean and shrill, and melodic. They satisfied her.

Every year until this one, Matt and Paul had accompanied her here and together they had buried themselves in the copse to observe the great birds. As she lost herself deeper into the woodland, Lyndsay wished her sons were with her and she wished that the terror taking hold inside of her would go away. She didn't know why she could still hear that night-shrouded screech of a week ago. Why had it branded its echo within her and stained her waking thoughts? Superstitiously, she feared some horrible deed. Some act of violence biding its time, but creeping inexorably towards her.

Ambling beneath towering, broad-branched oak trees, shadows snaking her face, Lyndsay kicked agitatedly at dark, springy leaf mould, begging the increasing sense of foreboding to give her some respite. After a quarter of an hour, she arrived at the sign that welcomed visitors to Churdle Heath Bird Sanctuary. Although she had passed this way a hundred times and knew the text by heart she stopped to read it once again. On the wooden display, which stated conditions of entry to the habitat, were sketches of the birds, such as the little ringed plovers and sand martins, which frequented the sanctuary. The osprey and its mating habits held pride of place. Leaning closer, Lyndsay realised that someone had hacked at the drawing with a knife, disfiguring the eagle's face. She was at a loss to understand such meaningless petty vandalism.

The air smelled rich with young leaves and damp spring growth while the silence punctuated by the cries and squawkings of resident and visiting birds both thrilled and pacified her.

Scattered clumps of fading wild bluebells fringed one of the tracks to her left. She craned her head and stretched skywards, indulging her solitude within the beauty of the whispering wood, ridding herself of dark thoughts. From a distance, she heard a musical whistle and recognised it as the mating trill of a visiting wood sandpiper. Any day now, it would be flying north to its breeding grounds.

She moved on, steering a path towards the wooden observation hides built some years back. They were sited by the long reservoir, known to be the richest feeding ground for the ospreys. It was a mile or so further along the track and offered the possibility of observing the breeding birds without disturbing them. She had advanced only a few yards when an unexpected rustling to her right startled her. As she turned, a lone male, tall and muscular, loomed from out of a bank of trees.

'Hello there,' he called.

Lyndsay froze, wary of his approach, recalling both the savage orgasm she had eavesdropped on not half an hour earlier and the retreating dark-clad figure, and then she relaxed. She had seen this face before but couldn't place where.

As he drew close he grinned broadly. It was a wide-open, reassuring greeting. 'I'm Ralph Beresford.' His Australian accent was broad and friendly.

'I didn't expect to meet anyone. There was a car back there, but...' she stammered.

'My truck's parked up the track a bit. You wouldn't have spotted it.'

As he held out his hand she read the label on his jacket.

'You're the new warden?'

'That's right. I've only been at the reserve a week.'

'Lyndsay Potter.'

'We've met already, just about.'

Lyndsay studied him, enjoying his good looks. 'Yes, but where?'

'I was outside the church. You were parking, crossing to the post office,' he explained.

It thrilled her, his recollection of an incident so inconsequential. 'That's right!'

'Are you out rambling, or hoping to get a peep at the eagles?' he asked.

'The birds.'

'Mind if I accompany you? I was heading that way anyway and it's probably safer.'

She nodded her accord although she felt vaguely disarranged by it, having been looking forward to a solitary hour or two, a speculative afternoon. With Beresford at her side she would feel obliged to talk. Still, when he set off, she followed happily.

On the narrower parts of the trail he walked ahead, working as they proceeded, bending to scoop up twigs or weeds from the track. He examined everything and she watched him, searching for some kind of conversation opener, though he seemed perfectly at ease with the silence.

'What brought you to England?' The question was addressed to the back of a shaggy blond head.

'A bit of lecturing.' The response was called over his shoulder. He was striking his route purposefully.

'And to Churdle Heath?'

'An unlikely neck of the woods to find someone like me, eh?' he laughed. 'I'd heard about this osprey flock and its annual visit to the Weald. I knew the Society were keen to encourage breeding and were looking for someone acquainted with raptor colonies. They contacted me when I first arrived in England a year ago but I wasn't free. Then, last week when the nests were invaded, the RSPB called me in. It's a challenge…and a peaceful place to get on with my work.'

'Which is?'

'A hodge-podge of studies, really. I'm a zoologist by trade. Just finished a couple of years in Africa. South of the Sahara close to the equator, up in the plains of east Africa and the west coast.'

'Doing what?'

'Oh, I'm putting a book together.'

Ahead of them the roofs of the watching huts could be glimpsed through a clearing in the trees. A hungry bird squawked and dropped into the distant water. Lyndsay would have liked to ask him about his book but she felt shy.

'Where are you from?' he asked, without looking at her.

'Kent. Born and bred.' It sounded dull in comparison, an ordinary life. And yet... 'You?' she said, preferring to shift the conversation away from herself.

'Originally? South of Darwin on the coast. Do you know it?' She shook her head. 'It's a great place. Nature rules. When I was a boy I was fascinated by eagles. Back there, though, we never came across groups larger than pairs. I used to spend hours rock-climbing, watching them in their nests. I can't understand why anyone would want to harm them. I've been asking myself if the intruder knew that ospreys are more sensitive to environmental poisoning than other raptors. Or was the insecticide just a coincidence? Something they had to hand.'

The track widened marginally and Beresford slowed his pace.

'Weren't they trying to steal the eggs?'

'Possibly. But it wouldn't be the whole story. Who goes out of their way to spray poison in the face of another living creature? It's too violent for regular egg thieves. My guess is it was an act of frustration, of self-loathing or hate. Vengeance against the birds' freedom, their power.'

Lyndsay, alongside him now, threw him a sideways glance. She was intrigued by him and by his evident passion for his subjects. He was strikingly tall; she was obliged to tilt her head to meet his gaze. His mouth was full and his eyes were acutely blue and prepossessing. They were eyes that had studied ecospheres a million miles away from hers. She noticed that, as he walked, one or other of his arms was stretched out, brushing against the passing foliage and the barks of trees. As he moved through the nature he appeared to be fusing with it, contacting it. She had never seen anyone do that before.

All of a sudden a piercing rattle of calls rang out. Their distress scratched through the afternoon calm. Lyndsay was reminded again of the scream she'd been woken by. Her flesh went cold. 'What was that?' she cried. The notes degenerated into a single high-pitched scream.

'Don't be scared,' Beresford said kindly, 'it's only a blackbird defending its territory.' But almost before he had finished speaking, another sound broke out, way off amongst clots of distant treetops, a breakneck, rhythmical screech, quite dissimilar to the previous call. Confused, Beresford paused to take bearings.

'What's that?' she murmured.

'I'm not sure… A kid screaming, I think.'

Instantly, the unfamiliar call was drowned by a chorus of bird cries, the harsh skraaking of a jay, a yellow wagtail tweeping, swallows twittering, moorhens kr-r-oking; a cacophony of whining, screeching, hooting unrest, reaching from across the acres, ripping through the tall oaks and the still waters.

'God in heaven!' Beresford broke into a run. 'Someone's baiting them.' His left arm reached for Lyndsay, and he took her by the elbow and propelled her through the wood more by his determination than by the physical contact. Lyndsay picked up pace and kept step with him, thrilled to be in his company. His excitement and concern reached her. All at once the locale had become a danger zone.

'Jesus, that's an angry male screeching in terror,' Beresford called back to her as they approached one of the observation stages. 'We could be dealing with egg thieves but I doubt it, or vandals trying to harm the birds again. That male is still vulnerable. He's back with his mate but his sight is not a hundred per cent. Easy prey. I shouldn't have let him loose so soon, but she needs him for feeding. Once a male has been slaughtered its female is lost and alone.' Beresford was on his haunches. He was scanning the sight, getting his bearings, talking fast, more to himself than to Lyndsay. He was like an animal priming itself. 'You wait back here,' he ordered.

Lyndsay's heart was in her mouth. She could picture the slain creature, limp torso, lying motionless, seeping dark warm blood. She screwed her eyes tight shut in an attempt to dispel the image. It was too graphic. It conjured memories too close to home, memories of her mother from the distant, hidden past.

When Lyndsay returned home, it was close to quarter past five and Stephen was back. Throughout the journey she had been looking forward to recounting the adventures of her afternoon. Of how, in the company of Beresford, she had tracked the blinded osprey and they had found him safe. 'No harm's done. He must have been terrified though by some no-gooder. I'll take him in, keep him with me for a couple of days.' But Stephen's mood was so withdrawn she decided not to bother. Instead she gave him Amanda's message, the bald facts only, mentioning nothing about the Paris trip, or their separation. The timing didn't feel right.

'Where's Matt?' was all she asked. Matt would enjoy hearing of her adventure even if his father didn't care to. She could recount Ralph's description of the ospreys' eggs. 'There are five from two breeding pairs: white, handsomely blotched with purple-brown and violet markings. Later, when the young are born, their down will be chocolate brown...'

Stephen said that he hadn't seen Matt.

'Hasn't he been here at all?'

'Lyndsay! He'll come home when he's ready.'

She didn't argue. Stephen's mood was too aggressive. And as hers was cheerful for the first time in days, she didn't want to spoil it. Earlier, when Ralph had escorted her back to her car, a flock of geese had flown overhead.

'Did you ever wonder why they travel in that V-shaped formation?' he'd asked her, and she'd admitted that it had never crossed her mind. 'Waterfowl travel in groups. Upwards of ten usually,' he'd said. 'But if they fly in a straight line or abreast, the centre birds enjoy twice as much uplift as the birds at the end. With the V, the birds on the end of the two arms receive additional upwash from their companions in front. This compensates for their position. You've probably noticed that, from time to time, they switch positions. But if one of them falls behind, that solo chap has to work much harder to fly the same distance. As a group they can travel nearly twice the distance without using any more energy. Their wing power is greater.'

'Is that what your book is about?' she had ventured then, relaxed in his company.

'Energy dynamics in flocks? Yes, and other material.'

'Such as?'

'Migratory habits, magnetic fields, environmental poisoning, the effects of pollution and insecticides on predators. I'm still getting to grips with my subject,' he'd laughed, and then as an afterthought. 'And where Man stands in amongst it all. What we can learn from it.'

'Did you remember the videos Matt asked for?' Lyndsay, in the drawing room now, enquired of Stephen.

'I left them on his bed,' was his terse response.

Matt didn't return until evening and, when he did, he went straight up to his room. It was an hour later when Lyndsay called out that supper was ready. She'd made pasta *di semola di grano duro, con funghi* – and parsley and fresh cream, one of Matt's favourites, but he shouted down that he wasn't hungry. As far as Lyndsay knew he hadn't eaten all day, but she let him be.

She'd laid the table in the dining-room, lit candles and uncorked a rather fine bottle of Barolo. She and Stephen ate alone. She fancied a romantic evening, though she was aware that it was foolish, under the circumstances. Stephen was preoccupied, barely aware of what he ate or the trouble she had taken. She drank the wine and tried not to feel too hurt or disappointed.

Each and every creature they'd encountered, Ralph Beresford had treated with gentleness and respect.

Watching Stephen from across the table, Lyndsay recalled a time, years earlier, when she had found him powerful. His silence had been a strength that had intrigued her. His cool logic had excited her; his mind had been a beacon that as well as lighting her path, had thawed her timidity and given her encouragement, but not any longer. Not tonight, at least. After an afternoon in the company of Ralph Beresford, she found that she was angered by Stephen and wounded by his disregard. She judged him cold. I might as well be invisible, she thought, for all he notices me.

'You mentioned last week that you want to leave,' she blurted out, fighting back her tears.

'Yes, I'm going to Paris in the morning.'

'You're leaving this weekend?'

'If everything is ready.'

'I see.' She rose. Her limbs beneath her felt unsteady. 'Well, don't let me detain you.' Taking her glass, Lyndsay made for the door.

'Lyndsay, listen, it's for the best. At least for –'

'And what about the boys? Have you thought about them?'

Stephen sighed and lowered his head. 'Yes, of course.'

Lyndsay, at the door, waited. 'Have you said anything to Matt? Matt! Matt!'

Stephen made as if to move. 'Lyndsay, don't! Not now. I'll talk to him myself in the morning.'

'And he's supposed to pass the news on to Paul at school? Is that the idea?'

'Lyndsay, I'm not disappearing out of your lives. I'll be back regularly. I'll see the boys just as frequently. I'm still their father.'

'And what about me? Don't I count for anything?' she shouted and then checked herself, aware of Matt upstairs and within earshot overhead. The last thing she wanted was to traumatise her son.

7

The following morning, back door open to the spring weather, Lyndsay stood at the stove preparing a bouillon for the retrievers. She felt tired and bruised. Across the room, the two animals dribbled contentedly. They had just returned from their morning run with Stephen and were hungry for breakfast. Rita, the younger, bored with the wait, yawned pointedly and settled onto her mat. In a far corner, on one of the Smallbone of Devizes units was a television set. The picture was on, the sound muted. Lyndsay glanced at her watch and reached for the volume control. It was seven-thirty; the news was beginning. Footsteps on the stairs warned her Stephen was descending. She took a deep breath.

'Tea's ready,' she said, affecting cheeriness, as he made for the morning papers. His clothes distracted Lyndsay's attention from the screen. The slacks and shirt were casual enough but more formal than his usual weekend wear. Her heart sank. He was definitely on his way.

A map of central Europe flashed up on the screen. Stephen settled at the table, and Lyndsay returned to the dogs' soup. This last week had been hell. She needed a resolution, but not the one on offer.

A neatly attired presenter spoke directly to the camera. 'Along with other like-minded intellectuals, he has joined forces with a group whose sole commit –'

'Must we listen to this potted précis of world politics?'

Lyndsay, abashed, explained, 'I'm waiting for the local traffic news.'

Stephen sighed into his paper.

The presenter smiled at her guest, seated awkwardly on an oversized leather sofa. 'Is it true that you advocate the use of violence against –'

'I'm driving to Dover this morning.'

Stephen's sole response was to rise from the table and press the off switch. 'Sorry, but I can't abide these muesli appraisals of world events.'

'Well, not everyone has your good fortune to be on the spot everywhere in the world!' Lyndsay snapped, regretting it instantly. She took a second and then added, 'Why don't you come along?'

'Where?'

'Dover,' she repeated. 'We could take Matt and the dogs, stop off somewhere for lunch –'

'I told you last night, I'm going to Paris.'

She felt the stab of confirmation. 'When?'

'Now.'

From where she was standing at the stove, waiting for the dogs' broth to cool, Lyndsay studied her husband, making surreptitious glances towards the well-groomed man seated at the country pine table, who was leafing through pages of the Saturday *Telegraph*. In sixteen years he had barely changed. A few grey hairs, nothing more. Still handsome, fit, attractive. He was a catch for any woman. And Stephen had spent the entire week at home. He had made no business trips whatsoever. Amanda's call had temporarily reassured her; there was no mistress. Still, their marriage was over, according to Stephen's decree. And deep down, she accepted it had cracked apart, not in any remarkable or dramatic way, but beneath the surface. Marital subsidence – her diagnosis of the situation – from which Stephen was extricating himself. While she opted for repair.

She should have read the signals sooner. Two people who have lived so many years alongside one another form patterns, habits, but she had not been paying sufficient attention. They should talk but he was no longer open to discussion. His decision had been made. Was she to blame? Why does one always blame oneself?

Since her father's death Lyndsay had had no appetite for sex. Not that Stephen had expressed desire. When he did she rarely refused him, for the sake of their marriage, and because she loved Stephen. Of course she loved Stephen. Everything they had built, who they were, was dependent upon one another. Their marriage had always been a smoothly running operation. She was content with all that Stephen provided for them, she was fiercely determined to bring up their sons well, to create an environment in which the boys were able to study and develop without fuss or trauma. Both she and Stephen believed in respectability, which they worked at, building blocks of it independently and blocks of it together. All of this counted for something. It was plain foolish to throw so much away.

In the months after Harry's death Stephen had been patient. He had accepted her physical reluctance but now the distance between them, the gap left by the lack of sex was no longer broached. Sex had become awkward and a discussion about it self-conscious, yet talking was what they had to do.

'Couldn't you at least stay until Monday? For Matt's sake. I think it would be fun for Matt if we all went to the boat later, slept there.'

Stephen was pouring tea. 'Want some?'

She could hardly blame him if he did have a mistress, a temporary substitute. 'Yes, please.' Or perhaps Stephen had stopped loving her altogether. 'Stephen, listen, I –'

'What's in Dover?' he butted in, thereby depriving Lyndsay of her attempt at dialogue.

'Plants to be cleared through customs. I should've gone last week. Anyway, why Paris? Are there business reasons?'

Stephen, who was now rifling through the pages of the *Telegraph* magazine, didn't seem to hear her. He rarely discussed his business affairs and, in the past, Lyndsay had always accepted that. She had no real interest in the world of economics. If pressed she would have been hard put to describe the exact nature of Stephen's business. She knew it was international investment, of some sort. Paul, on the other hand, had inherited his father's facility with figures.

'Do you have business in Paris? It's just that I'd understood from Amanda that you were going to Geneva from here on Tuesday.' This cross-questioning was unlike her and she knew Stephen would resent it. If there was a woman did she honestly expect him to admit it? But she felt compelled to persist, to push him beyond the limit. Inside she was angry because she was uncertain, uncertain of her own feelings as well as his.

'I have a meeting with the agents about the flat...'

'So, you're not moving in today?'

Stephen sighed.

'Will you be at the Crillon?' Her husband was a man who planned his itinerary. He was systematic, not impulsive. She wondered how long this decampment had been in the organising.

'Mmm.'

'I envy you. A weekend in Paris at the Crillon. I rather fancy it myself.' She could hear herself, the sharpness and fast-paced monologue, reining in pain. 'Delicious restaurants, galleries. Makes my offer of lunch in Dover seem very pedestrian, doesn't it?' She attempted a light laugh, hoping that he would not guess how his leaving like this had made her defenceless and confused and how very much she needed him to put his arms around her and hold her. 'I wish I were going with you.'

Stephen glanced at his wife, flitting between sink and hotplate, her back turned to him. She was trim, neat and efficient. Those qualities had suited him in the past. Her efficiency, her determination to run things smoothly, had always served him. For many years their marriage had worked for him, but now it was over. This life was at an end. It seemed trivial, dull. Compared to that redhead Gin's languid elegance... He had failed to erase the memory of that woman from his thoughts.

Lyndsay turned away from the sink and crossed to sit beside him at the table. 'Have you spoken to Matthew?'

'I tapped on his door. He's sleeping.'

'I hope you're not intending to just up sticks and go, leaving me to explain?' She picked an apple from out of the fruit bowl on the table between them and began tossing it from one hand to the other.

'Of course not,' he said perfunctorily. The more she went on at him, the further he withdrew.

For a few short hours she had felt safe. Amanda's call had been a reprisal but Stephen's decision to leave for Paris had refuelled her despair. Why was he leaving on a Saturday, if not for an infidelity? But to accuse him would be foolish and she knew it. Incapable of remaining unemotional, she steered the topic of conversation towards Matt, reiterating concerns about her son.

'I'm sure he's sensed something. Whenever I ask what's up, he shrugs and slopes off. I know you tell me his behaviour's standard, but it doesn't stop me being concerned and, frankly, I'm not sure his reclusiveness is all that normal.'

'Stop badgering him about how he's feeling all the time.'

'If he didn't need our concern, he wouldn't come home so often. Why else is he here? He sees no one else in Churdles. He chooses to spend half-term here, not with his pals, and when he comes home what does he find?' Her voice was growing loud.

'Lyndsay!'

'I think he's guessed! I think he's knows that his father...'

'Lyndsay, you are getting het up.'

'Go up to him! Ask him. Talk to him! Take him with you. He can take the train back tomorrow evening. I'll pick him up at Waterloo and drive him straight to college.'

'I'll be busy and Matthew wandering about Paris alone would be a liability.'

'That's terrific! Then I had better persuade him to come with me, although I seem to be the last person he wants to be around at the moment.'

'He's an adolescent boy. Stop nagging him!'

'Thanks!' Tears stung her eyes. 'Even if you don't want me anymore, the least you can bloody well do is show some interest in your sons!'

Stephen's response was even and controlled. 'If you carry on shouting like this Matt will hear you.'

She wanted to cut out her tongue. 'He needs to talk and doesn't know where to begin.' And so do I, she was thinking.

'He wants space and you're over-protective.'

'You're the one who always nags him, not me! Look what happened with the Hampton boys, forbidding him to go fishing with them. You're too strict!'

'That was years ago! And I was right. What are we giving him a decent education for if he fritters his time away with those louts?'

'Sometimes you are so pompous and insensitive.' Lyndsay's voice was sharp with restrained fury and trembling with pain. She paused, tears welling, grappling for some path to intimacy. 'Oh, Stephen... I don't know how to...' she snivelled softly. 'Please, don't leave.'

Reading her hurt, Stephen rose from the table and hovered a moment, messing with his *Telegraph*, hoping she might calm down. He had no desire to hurt her, but he felt incapable of moving close, of touching or consoling her. He just needed to be free. 'Don't let's argue again,' he said. 'Look, I'll try to get back tonight, collect a few things. I'll call you later when I know my plans.'

'Collect a few things?'

'Lyndsay,' he spoke with exaggerated patience. 'I am going to sign the papers and pick up the keys of a flat. I am moving out.'

This was a different man. A man she didn't know. 'But you're not sleeping there?'

'Not tonight. It's empty.'

'And if you don't get back, you'll be at the Crillon?'

He gave her a longsuffering sigh followed by a nod, and with that he was gone.

Amongst her hothouse flowers, embedded within the greenhouse's humidity and precisely controlled temperature, with no one to witness her, Lyndsay had expected tears to flow, but there were none. She was dazed and numb, breathing fast, heaving air. Instead of reassurance from the damp lusty growth she felt suffocated.

'Mrs Potter?'

'What?' She swung round to find Dennis directly behind her, uncombed hair, black bags beneath his eyes, looking like a terrified scarecrow and shivering. 'What are you doing here?' she accused, retreating. He shuffled closer, hands clutching his shirt. 'Get away from me!' she hissed, shoving past him. 'How did you get in, the gate's locked? Go home!'

Hurrying back up through the garden she heard the cooing of a woodpigeon, a pair of magpies squabbling over a stolen titbit, infuriating greedy beggars, and neighbours beyond the gate hailing one another. Inside, she slammed the back door shut and leaned against it, feeling confused and desperate. The dogs plonked themselves on her feet and got in her way; their attention made her irritable.

Upstairs Stephen was ranging from room to room; doors were opening and closing, objects were being displaced. He was packing, removing the essential parts of himself, preparing to take them away from her. Her heart was thudding, the pulse rising to her mouth. It felt so unreal.

She crossed to the telephone and furiously punched Tom's number.

Since her father's death she hadn't wanted Stephen near her and now that he was leaving she didn't know how she would bear it. Was there any sense in going up there and begging him to stay, if not for her sake then for Matthew and Paul?

'Hello?'

'Tom, it's Mrs Potter.'

'Oh, hello there.' His voice was gentle, unassuming, no hint of concern.

'Tom, I'm… I've just seen Dennis in the garden. Did you give him your keys?'

'Heaven's above, no! Hang on a minute…' Lyndsay heard the receiver being placed on to a hard surface.

How could Stephen even contemplate abandoning his family? She felt a whipping surge of hatred for the unknown woman. For whatever Stephen had said Lyndsay was convinced that there was another woman. He travelled so frequently that she had never allowed herself to dwell upon the myriad opportunities available to him. There had been occasions in the past when she had suspected that he might have betrayed her. Small details had suggested it but she had refused to look, refused to give the niggling doubts power. Stephen had been discreet; he had always come home, always behaved decently, been attentive towards the boys, always provided generously for them. And she had always been waiting, her thoughts never venturing beyond her family and her nursery business. She had never contemplated infidelity. Perhaps she should have. Perhaps she should have allowed herself the luxury of a passion.

'Hello, Mrs Potter?'

'Yes?'

'He must have taken them off the peg in the hall, where I hang them. I can't think what he would be doing.'

'Hide the keys where he can't find them, please. See you Friday.' And with that she replaced the receiver.

She listened to Stephen's footsteps to-ing and fro-ing while she, surrounded by jelly bases, chopped fruit and sugars, tried to grasp what was happening, searching for strength, for continuation within acts of domesticity. Resisting the fact that, beyond the room, her world was being dismantled.

At quarter to nine, the phone rang. Lyndsay answered it. She thought it might be Tom, no doubt shocked by her curtness, but it was a foreign gentleman requesting Mr Potter. Stephen was now in his study. Without asking for the caller's name, Lyndsay went in search of him. The sight of the room denuded of papers, books and the rest of his personal gallimaufry sent a shiver through her.

All of a sudden a memory returned, a monstrous wailing. Lyndsay heard the cry as though it were real. A woman screeching, 'If you go, I'll kill myself!' The voice rang in her ears, strangling her emotions.

'There's a call for you,' she said coldly and retreated to the safe harbour of her kitchen.

When Stephen came looking for her half an hour later, she was still there. 'I'll be on my way,' he said. He might have been heading to the off-licence to pick up a bottle of wine. Lyndsay nodded, eyes averted, while he hovered uncertainly before her. 'Are you going to be all right?' he asked.

If you go, I'll kill myself! Her mother's voice was still echoing in her mind. 'Fine,' she lied.

'I'll call you from Paris then.' Which was what Stephen always said when he was leaving for a trip and intending to return.

71

That felt like the final indignity. 'Just go, Stephen, for God's sake.' She could not look in his face.

He hesitated an instant, considering what else could be explained. 'Don't say anything to the boys. I prefer to talk to them myself. I'll have a chat with Matt when I get back.' And then, 'It's for the best, Lyndsay. We both know that. We're tearing each other to shreds.' Satisfied there was nothing else, he turned and left.

When she heard the front door close, Lyndsay followed through to the hall. She felt stunned, nauseous. Stephen's words and deeds had to be taken seriously. She walked into the drawing room and stood watching his Porsche disappear down the drive, following the swing of the curves, until it was out of sight.

'Tearing each other to shreds,' echoed in her head, drifting through the empty spaces.

They had not discussed the sordid business of allowances and settlements. The nursery brought in a small income, but it was insufficient to maintain Churdle Bridge Farm. Matthew had won a scholarship so his fees were taken care of.

How could she at this hour be worrying about something so mercenary as money? Because it helped to keep the worst of the pain at bay. It was how she had always dealt with the emotional blows of life; efficiency, practicality in the home and garden, at all costs. It was futile to cry for a marriage that had died, she told herself. That was how she must view it, but she did not believe it.

After the weekend, when Matt had returned to school, she would clear out her father's cottage. She had been postponing the chore since his death, had dreaded disposing of his belongings. Monday she would parcel everything up and send it all to Oxfam. If she rented out the cleared-out cottage it would bring in a small income. Should she insist they sell the house? Or was she panicking, jumping the gun? Stephen had assured her that he would not leave her in the lurch. Had he said that? What had he said? 'Tearing each other to shreds,' he had definitely said that.

Would she be obliged to call Amanda if she ran short of money? The thought of such a thing was intolerable. She returned to the kitchen and sat for a while gazing into space, willing the pain and confusions to go away. Eventually, in an attempt to pull herself together, she cleared away the breakfast things, scribbled notes for the baker and the cleaner, Blu-Tacked them to the back door and went in search of her road map. Every action was performed mechanically as though she were standing outside her body watching Lyndsay Potter battle against this unexpected day. When the practicalities had been organised she went in search of her car keys.

On the local traffic news the night before, there had been a warning about roadworks disrupting several miles of motorway along the M2. Because Stephen had switched off the morning news, Lyndsay had missed the latest update, so she was obliged to telephone the AA. The line was busy, and she was already running late.

Her assignment of South American rock plants, ordered two months earlier, had docked. She needed to clear them through customs and transport them to the nursery as soon as possible. She considered postponing the trip until Monday, after Matt had returned to college, or requesting they be delivered but that could take weeks. Meanwhile her precious and very splendid plants would wilt and die in some godforsaken warehouse lacking thermostatically controlled heat, expiring from a lack of heat, light and water or, if they did survive the incarceration, they would almost certainly get damaged in transit to her greenhouses. She had experienced several such costly disappointments in the past and had determined never to let it happen again. She had been looking forward to the plants' arrival. Why allow Stephen to spoil this small pleasure, too? But she felt little will to get going.

She needed to rise above this listlessness before it got the better of her. Stephen's behaviour was probably due to a mid-life crisis, his departure only temporary. The situation might never reach a divorce. These arguments were facile but they served to get her on the move.

At ten past ten there were still no stirrings from Matt's room. Lyndsay gathered up her purse and the customs documentation. She really was running late, the customs office closed at noon on Saturdays. She climbed the stairs, hurried along the corridor to her son's bedroom and knocked.

'Matt?'

There was no response. She turned the handle and pushed open the door. The room was in total darkness, which did not surprise her. No shaft of daylight could penetrate the layers of material Matt draped over his windows. Lyndsay sighed and entered.

'Matt, I'm driving to Dover. Fancy coming? I'll treat you to lunch on the way back, brunch in your case.' She spoke as she moved, negotiating a floor cluttered by detritus. She was expecting him to stir and groan and switch on the bedside light.

The room was airless and smelling stale. A foreign aromatic bouquet that she did not recognise permeated the darkness. A disc or something plastic cracked underfoot.

Lyndsay, suddenly short-tempered and impatient with her son's adolescent habits, shouted, 'Matt, for God's sake put the bloody light on!' There was no sound at all in the suddenly all-too-silent room. 'Matt!' She reached the bedside, and flicked the light on.

The chaotically unmade bed was empty. Puzzled, Lyndsay glanced across towards his bathroom. The door was partially open, the room in darkness. Obviously he was not in there. Surely, if he had gone out earlier, she would have seen or heard him shuffling about the house. She crossed to the window and lifted the layers of curtains and draped materials. Perhaps he had overheard them arguing.

There was no sign of him down by the pool. This did not surprise her as he rarely went to swim these days. Lyndsay returned to his bed and brushed the sheet with the palm of her hand. It was perfectly cool. He must have been up for a while then. She walked over to the bathroom, switched on the light and peered in. The place was an almighty tip – living evidence that this was Matt's bathroom – but there was no sign of life.

Lyndsay's mind flashed back through the events of the evening before to when she had last seen her son. He had come in an hour or so before supper. She was certain of that because she'd glanced at the clock on the kitchen wall. She hadn't actually set eyes on him though because he'd entered by the front door, which was unusual. Normally he came in the back way, grabbed a Coke or a snack from the fridge and bustled on through. Nor had he stuck his head round the door to say hello. He had gone straight upstairs to his room. She hadn't judged his behaviour odd because she had been too taken up by her own concerns. When she had shouted to him to come down for supper, he'd replied that he wasn't hungry. That had been nine o'clock or thereabouts. She hadn't heard him go out again, but neither had she heard him playing music. He may have been watching films. She swung round looking for the tapes Stephen had brought back from Tonbridge and found them, not on the bed where they'd been deposited, but on the floor in front of the video and television. He must have been engrossed in his films.

It dawned on Lyndsay now, standing in the middle of the mess that was her son's universe, that she hadn't actually set eyes on Matt since the morning of the previous day: Friday morning when he'd left for the village. Had there been something the matter when he came back, some incident that had kept him away all day and then forced him to avoid his parents? Perhaps the atmosphere at home had ruffled him. Might he have been eavesdropping, or were their raised voices inescapable?

She remembered her own childhood. How she and Rebecca had holed up together in their shared bedroom when they'd sensed trouble was brewing between her parents. They had learnt to read the heavy silence before an outbreak of violence.

Lyndsay knew instinctively that something was terribly wrong. She dumped her bag and briefcase on the bed and parked herself alongside them. Her eyes scanned the room for clues. Matt's guitar was there. Two Christmases ago, Stephen had searched the specialist shops for a top quality Spanish guitar. Only to find that it needed to be restrung because Matt was left-handed. Its case was leaning against the wardrobe. His other love was his clarinet. If his precious clarinet was still here he would not have gone far. She scrutinized the space one more time. There was no sign of it. Panic clutched her.

There had been no dispute between them for several days. He had been withdrawn and monosyllabic but they had not been arguing, nor had he fought with his father. In fact, the last conversation she recollected between them, at breakfast the previous morning, had been amicable and enthusiastic, its topics ranging from football to video films. She had also overheard Matt ask his father to drive him back to college on Sunday evening. So, he could not have been planning to go off anywhere at that stage.

Go away! Why ever was she considering such an outlandish possibility? It was not logical. Matthew had everything. There was no reason to suppose that he should want to run away. Lyndsay bulldozed this train of thought clean out of her mind. She was facing her own fears, reliving her own past.

Her heart beating terribly fast, she rose from the bed and stumbled across the room to her son's desk, reaching for the telephone, feverishly punching digits. Until she realised that, in her distress, she had been about to telephone the cottage – a dead man's home – and she slammed the receiver down.

Her hands were trembling, her breathing erratic. In the past she would have blamed her father, spoken curtly to him, held him responsible. Matt took after his grandfather. He loved music as Harry had, and he had a temper as furious as her father's. Lyndsay closed her eyes and sunk into the chair by the desk. Her knees felt weak as water.

No matter how hard she had tried to fight it, to protect the boys, to cosset them, to build a life which would not, could not, include the atrocities of her own past, it seemed inevitable.

She must contact Stephen. If she moved quickly she could catch him before he boarded the plane. What time was the flight? She had paid no attention, if indeed he had mentioned it. He must be flying from Gatwick; he only took the Eurostar when he was going directly from his office in the City. She lifted the receiver once more and dialled directory enquiries, cursing herself for having idled away so much time in the kitchen. Stephen's flight might have already taken off.

'Could you give me the number for British Airways at Gatwick, please.'

'Customer services or reservations?'

Which? Her mind was spinning. 'Er...reservations. Oh...and the executive lounge, please.'

Within seconds a bland digital voice relayed numbers. Lyndsay searched about the desk, shoving Matthew's papers this way and that in the hope of a pen. Finding a biro, she scrawled the figures hurriedly across the blank edging of a music magazine and replaced the receiver once more. She drew the magazine towards her, took a deep breath so as not to sound hysterical when she eventually got through to Stephen, and lifted the handset for the third time. It was then that she noticed the scattering of seeds lying on Matthew's desk beneath the papers. They were small plump seeds no larger than screw heads. Her knowledge of botany was sufficient to recognise them instantly. Marijuana, illegal narcotic grass seeds. Matthew was in possession of drugs.

8

From Roissy airport Stephen took a taxi, not to the Crillon, but to a lesser-known hotel, which was situated in the heart of the Marais. Le Pavillon de la Reine was a discreet choice. It was an elegant establishment overlooking private gardens and set back from the Place des Vosges. After he had checked in, he walked to the bar where he had drunk a Scotch exactly one week earlier.

The weather was hotter than it had been in England. Hotter, too, than the previous weekend. It was one of those exceptional carefree days. All around him there were couples holding hands, embracing outside any one of a dozen antique shops, seated at café tables sipping aperitifs, or enjoying the buskers entertaining on street corners. Stephen had never felt lonelier. Isolation suffused him, a sense of desolation he had never allowed before. In a desire to be free, he had walked out on everything. For what sane reason was he about to take on the rental of an apartment in a city so far from his sons? He asked himself if he would be better advised to while away an hour or two at a gallery and then take the next plane back to Churdle Heath. No, whatever paın was involved, he was making the right choice. He was choosing life instead of a marriage that was suffocating him. In time, Lyndsay would come to see it too, and they would be friends. But it was madness to believe that he would ever trace the exquisite redhead he had met the week before.

Yet she was out there somewhere. He felt certain of it. Gin was not a woman to be buried in the provinces, to ride the evening train back to the Paris suburbs. Her wardrobe, her style, her ease belied such locations. Gin was a capital-city creature and Stephen was in that city to find her, to trace any clue that would lead him to her.

He had lost an hour in crossing the Channel, so when he arrived at the Café au Parc-Royal he was too late for lunch. This second visit to the bar showed him that the place was not seedy, as he had judged it the week before, but had a welcoming air. Several of the tables were unoccupied including the one he'd sat at the previous Saturday. Stephen installed himself at that very one, choosing the same seat he had taken the last time. Once he was settled he looked from table to table and peered into the face of every person present. She was not there, but he had not expected her to be; her presence would have been a miracle.

The waiter arrived. When Stephen discovered it was the selfsame fellow as the week before he was barely able to conceal his delight, as though the man's ongoing existence brought a stamp of success to his mission. The waiter showed no signs of recognising him. Stephen ordered a large Scotch hoping that the repeated order might trigger the man's memory, but it did not.

'I was here last Saturday,' Stephen said. The waiter nodded, not in agreement but as if to imply, If you say so, sir. 'I was sitting with a woman, an Englishwoman with shoulder-length red hair. We asked you for a light.'

A couple arriving at an adjacent table beckoned. The waiter, responding to their call, excused himself with a bow. Stephen shuffled in his chair and fidgeted with the copy of *Le Figaro* he had purchased at the news-stand around the corner. The waiter returned with his Scotch. Stephen downed a generous slug.

'I do remember her,' the fellow said. 'A striking woman dressed in black.'

'Yes, that's her!'

'*Une très belle femme.*'

Stephen smiled at the description. 'I take it she's not a regular customer?'

'Alas, no, sir.'

'You wouldn't know where I could find her?'

'No idea, but worth the search, sir, if she were mine.'

If she were mine, thought Stephen. The fellow has poetry in his soul. If only Gin were his.

'She mentioned that her name is Gin,' he said, offering his sole shred of hope.

The waiter shook his head. '*Hélas, non, monsieur.*'

9

Rock music hailed from a radio wedged precariously amongst packets of biscuits piled high on a shelf. The harsh fluorescent lighting stung Lyndsay's eyes as she entered the garage shop and made her way to the till.

'Pump six?' enquired a weary eyed teenage girl with deadpan interest. The question was unnecessary; Lyndsay's was the only vehicle in the petrol station.

Lyndsay nodded and handed over her credit card. While she waited, she studied the girl with her hooped earrings and long, navy blue varnished nails.

'Sign here.'

Lyndsay squinted at the coupon and rubbed her eyes irritably. She felt both keyed-up and exhausted. Yet it still occurred to her to wonder why this girl's parents would allow their daughter to work in a garage at such a late hour. It was getting on for one in the morning and the garage was at least four miles to the nearest village, seven to a small town in the other direction and nine to the housing estate. There must be no other work opportunities available, she concluded.

'Here,' she said, returning the signed slip to the girl who looked shockingly immature. Lyndsay couldn't believe she wasn't afraid to be out here all alone. What if a stranger with malevolent intentions happened by?

The life of the night was alien to Lyndsay. She was not a nocturnal creature, preferring the daylight, the sun to the stars.

She and Stephen went out to dinner parties, obviously, but that was house to car, car to house. Perfectly safe, respectable and unthreatening. But this aimless solitary driving, cruising through deserted midnight streets, searching hour after hour, had unsettled her. What had jarred most had been the housing estate with its rows of bleak, empty streets, which boasted nothing more inviting than two graffiti-latticed, cement bus shelters and one desolate-looking pub. She'd driven past clutch after clutch of disaffected youths standing listlessly on street corners. Their cigarettes had burned like tiny beacons as she peered out at their scowling, resentful faces from behind the security of her sealed electric windows. Several had pitched empty lager cans at the purring vehicle while one had sworn at her, loudly, violently. 'What the fuck d'yer think yer fucking lokking a'? Fuck orf outavit! You fucking posh cow!'

Lyndsay was shocked. She had never driven through the estate before, had never penetrated its dead-end despair. She thought of Tom, her gardener, and Dennis, living somewhere in amongst all of this. She had never considered their existences until tonight. Never considered that so many bored youths had nothing better to do but hang out until they fell drunk and frustrated into their· beds. Another kind of person keeps these hours, she was thinking, sick with worry about where Matt had disappeared to. What was he up to, and who was he keeping company with?

Lyndsay mistrusted the habits of those who lived by night. When she was young she had been terrified of the dark. Terrified of what it brought forth. Terrified of what violence people did to one another at night. A murder by day is far more scandalously reported. A rape in the mid-afternoon is vile, flagrant and infrequent, splitting the veneer of society wide open. But at night, in the body-aching loneliness, such acts are anguished, shocking and depraved, but not uncommon. These are the hours when horrors and taboos rampage, when vice spreads its beating wings and ordinary men take on another, more sinister face.

It had been by night that someone had entered the bird sanctuary and harmed the osprey eagle. She tried to remember what Ralph Beresford had said about the attack – their afternoon together seemed weeks ago – but she was too tired, too stricken with fear to recall his words.

Somewhere out there in the night, away from the security of his room and his family and his college, Matthew was. And it was wrenching Lyndsay's guts. This turmoil, this terror, must have been what her father went through when…

'Your credit card!'

'What? Oh, yes, thank you.' Lyndsay retrieved her card and receipt from the young assistant and turned to leave. 'Goodnight.'

It was then that she fixed on Marion Finch's white Jaguar drawing up alongside the bank of pumps next to where her Mercedes jeep was parked. Lyndsay swung about in search of a fire exit. Marion would have recognised her car.

'I can't face her tonight.' She spied the sign for the toilet above the door. A temporary sanctuary while Marion paid and left. She beat a path towards it.

'Mrs Potter.' It was the assistant calling from behind the till. It stopped Lyndsay in her tracks. How did the young girl know her name? She'd never set eyes on her before. Ah yes, the credit card.

'Yes?'

'You've left your purse.'

'Oh, thank you.' Lyndsay was obliged to return to the desk. 'Stupid of me,' she muttered. Her retreat had been scuppered. As she turned, Marion was entering the all-night garage-cum-mini-market. They met by the litres of Castrol oil and bottles of French plonk. Lyndsay instantly realised, from the glazed dead look in her neighbour's eyes, that Marion was heavily tranquillized and had evidently consumed several drinks on top of it.

'My, what a surprise!'

'Hello, Marion.'

'Past your bedtime isn't it, Lyndsay?' Marion's voice was slurred.

'I was just on my way.'

'Little wifey out at this hour. Stephen must be phoning all over. Oh no, that's not Stephen's style. He's much more discreet, much more low-key. Attracting attention to himself is not Stephen's way.'

Lyndsay watched as Marion rummaged through her bag. She was swaying and unfocused. It was a pitiable sight. 'Marion, I've been intending to phone you. I wanted to apologise for the other day.'

'Apologise! What have you got to be sorry about? Wasn't you I found sucking Arthur's cock.'

Lyndsay felt herself cringe. She glanced protectively towards the girl at the desk who was changing radio stations. 'I just felt that I should have been a little more…'

'Sisterly? Oh, think nothing of it. Foolish of me to have thought you had it in you… Ice cubes come warmer!' Marion lurched towards the cash desk.

Lyndsay, chastened, did not move. Standing her ground alongside the wine bottles she watched Marion pull one crisp note after another out of her wallet and drop them over the display of chocolate bars. The young assistant waited patiently, regarding Marion. It was glaringly obvious to both observers that Marion Finch was wrecked and should not be on the road.

Lyndsay was torn between walking away from this scene and staying to help. She thought of Matthew and Stephen. Both were missing. Rather, both had disappeared and were unavailable to her for the time being, and here was Marion right in front of her and in need of help. Lyndsay had ignored her neighbour's cry once already. She waited while the transaction was completed, keeping her distance from the till so that when she spoke she would not be within earshot of the cashier.

As Marion turned, she staggered. She looked surprised to see Lyndsay still there. 'Late-night shopping?' she quipped as she attempted a balanced step.

The aisles of products on sale were arranged in such a way that Marion was obliged to pass by Lyndsay or take a circuitous and obvious detour. Lyndsay waited until Marion was alongside her. 'Are you going home, Marion?'

Marion peered at her with hazy mistrust. 'No, I thought I might hit the town! Make a night of it!' she snapped.

'Because if you are, why not leave the car here and let me drive you?'

'Any particular reason why you should be making this offer? I take it, it's not because it's my lucky night.' Marion snarled and then brayed like a donkey, cachinnating at her own sarcasm.

'Come on, Marion.' Lyndsay grasped the drunken woman by the arm and led her to her own car. 'Where are your keys?' Marion did not reply. She simply closed her eyes. Lyndsay didn't know if it was compliance, sufferance or emotional exhaustion. 'I'll check the ignition.' She was speaking more to herself than to Marion who was now slumped inside the Mercedes.

Across the range of pumps the white Jaguar was parked with its door hanging open. The keys were there. Lyndsay started it up and drove it out of the way to the farthest, most discreet corner of the courtyard then she circled back to the shop, popped her head in the door and said with a smile, 'Would you tell John that Mrs Finch left her car and that Mrs Potter, or…someone will be back for it first thing in the morning.'

The girl nodded comprehendingly.

'Arthur wants a divorce.'

Lyndsay made no comment. Once the coffee had been made, she installed herself at Marion's kitchen table, prepared to let

Marion do the talking. She had no intention of sharing her own troubles. Lyndsay did not confide in others, particularly women. She had no intimates. She had her family. That was her epicentre. From Lyndsay's point of view escorting Marion home had been a selfish gesture; listening to Marion's outpourings took her mind off her own problems and delayed the dreaded return home. It postponed the rediscovery of Matt's abandoned room, because in the deepest recesses of her being Lyndsay felt sure that Matt had not returned. And when she opened that door and looked upon the empty space, she would no longer be able to postpone the inevitable. Stephen or no Stephen, Lyndsay was going to have to do what she should have done hours earlier – telephone the police and report the disappearance of her son.

'Did he say why?' Lyndsay asked eventually. Her voice was tired. She was trying hard to sound committed to the conversation, and, yes, she felt pity for Marion. She felt the sting of loss.

Marion shrugged. 'Tired of our childless marriage. He says I've held him back, that without me he could have been someone. Made something of his life. So, he wants to leave before it's too late.' Marion stopped, unable to continue, a despairing heart. 'We met for lunch today in Chelsea...'

Lyndsay sipped her coffee. She never drank coffee at such an hour. She could think of nothing heartening to say. Poor weeping Marion looked a hundred years old, a dinosaur of dried-out womanhood, tired and left behind. 'Did he mention his girlfriend?' she asked eventually.

'Says she's the one for him. I asked him if she feels the same. You know he's fifty-eight. She's twenty-something. Two or three.'

'Give him time. He'll probably come back.' Lyndsay wondered for the first time about the age of Stephen's mistress.

'She's pregnant. Cunning little bitch. I can't compete with that. I've past my sell-by date on that score.' Marion was coming down. Exhaustion and disappointment had beaten both her and her panaceas. A childless marriage. Lyndsay felt a rush of gratitude for all that she had waiting for her back home, and then panic. 'And what were you doing out at this hour? I take it you weren't cruising.'

'Cruising?'

'To get laid.'

'Of course not!'

'So, what were you doing?' Marion's peering eyes were red and bleary.

Lyndsay hesitated. 'I was looking…for Matthew.'

Marion realigned her focus, suddenly looking sharp, alert, interested. Good old Marion Finch. No self-pitying could blunt her nose for a scandal. Local tittle-tattle was the food for her loneliness. 'Looking for Matthew. Why? Is he missing?'

'I…don't think so. No! No, of course not, he…' Lyndsay had no strength left to complete the lie. She could not even come up with a credible story.

From across the kitchen table, Marion studied her: neat, unruffled Lyndsay. 'That means he is missing. Well, well. Is Stephen also out hunting?'

Lyndsay cleared her throat attempting to deflect the conversation. Deciding that it was time to leave, she rose.

Stephen's absence was paining her. She had waited in most of the day, worked in the garden, looked out for Matt and eventually gone off on a scout around the village where she had hoped to find her son. At some point in the late afternoon, it had stupidly occurred to her that this was the first Saturday in their entire marriage, as far as she could remember, that Stephen had actually got on a plane and gone away. Leaving on a Saturday had, in her mind's eye, accentuated the perfidy. This was Stephen, who never worked away at weekends, who, until now, never worked at all during the weekends preferring to spend those days with his sons sailing on his boat. In many ways,

Stephen had been the picture of the ideal family man and now he was leaving. The realisation was dawning.

'Stephen's in Paris,' she replied. Her voice was flat and tight, terrified and uncertain. The coldness, the distance that had grown up between them had been her fault. If only she had been able to confide in him, if only she had revealed the truth to him, but she had been incapable of letting him in, of drawing him too close or allowing his stability to heal her.

'For the weekend?' Marion rose too. A past master, she knew when she was on to something.

'No, no. I don't think so. He'll…be back in the morning.'

'You don't sound very sure. Don't tell me you also have a marital crisis on your hands?'

'Don't be absurd. I'm just tired. Can't think straight. God almighty, it's twenty to two. I must be on my way. Thanks for the coffee.'

'It was you who drove me home, you who percolated it, remember?'

Lyndsay nodded and stepped towards the hallway, regaining her self-possession as she gathered up her bag and jacket, restoring distance. 'Are you going to be all right, alone here?' she asked with a touch of warmth. 'There are plenty of spare rooms at –'

Marion shook her head. 'Thanks all the same,' she said. 'I'll stick it out. It's a lonely road ahead. I better get used to it.'

This response, its clear expression of courage, took Lyndsay by surprise. She smiled, kissed Marion goodnight, a gesture it would never have occurred to her to make before tonight, and then set off for home. As she drove she recollected Marion's words: a lonely road ahead. Christ, she hoped not. She prayed that Matt would be in his room watching his videos, silent and surly if he wished, but there.

Lyndsay turned right at Lower Beeches Lane where the Hampton family lived. The sight of the farmhouse up ahead reminded her of Matthew. Not that she had stopped thinking of him for more than a second throughout the entire day. She recalled how furious he had been with his father when Stephen had nagged him about fishing with 'those two youths'. Lyndsay had secretly agreed with Matt but had said nothing, refusing to get involved in an argument between father and son. Had she been wrong to keep silent? Should she have defended Matt's right to choose his own friends? Should she have reassured him that he was not alone, that his point of view had been understood? Or was Stephen simply being vigilant?

The reality was that she had found an illegal substance in Matthew's room. She wondered where it had come from. Stephen would say, from mixing with the wrong sort.

Was Matt unhappy at home? She hoped she had not been as blind to Matt's needs as she now considered she had been to Stephen's. Maybe he was in some kind of trouble. If Stephen considered the Hampton boys bad companions what was he going to say when he found out about the drugs? She was intending to tell him, wasn't she? And if so, when? The questions circling inside Lyndsay's head were relentless.

The Hamptons' farmhouse was in darkness as she drove past, as she would have expected at this hour. She would give them a call in the morning to find out if their sons had heard from Matt. It was a slim chance.

Aside from the sleeping dogs in the kitchen, the house was empty. It had never felt bleaker. Lyndsay went directly to Matt's room. It was exactly as she had left it when she had gone out around eight. She was convinced now that, for whatever reason, Matthew had run away. Suddenly, she felt irrationally angry and upset. Not about Matt leaving home, although that too, of course, but because he hadn't cared about her sufficiently to write a note. She hadn't mattered.

Even Rebecca, her sister, had left a note. Lyndsay forced herself not to equate the present with the past. It brought about an impotence that petrified her.

Panicked by the idea of calling the police immediately because it meant facing up to the reality, Lyndsay decided that no matter what bloody time it was, she was going to telephone Stephen. He had to be informed. Sod his sleep, or anything else she might be interrupting.

Back downstairs in his semi-packed study, her hands were trembling as she rummaged about for Stephen's desk diary. She punched in the figures for the Crillon with a nervous resolve but before the connection had been made she replaced the receiver. She was tired, it was horribly late and she was weeping because she could not drive from her mind the fact that Rebecca, her sister, had also been fifteen, Matt's age, when she had fled. She, Lyndsay, had been eleven.

Lyndsay was back with her eleven-year-old self. She could see and hear the little girl as clearly as though they were beside one another. Lyndsay, standing in her green and white spotted pyjamas pressed up against her bedroom door, was watching her big sister, Rebecca, tiptoeing across the creaky, dark landing to the bathroom where their mother had disappeared to hours earlier.

Lyndsay had waited, terrified while Rebecca had knocked.

'Mummy,' Becky called through the closed door.

Their mother made no answer. The silence was eerie. It scared them both horribly because, earlier in the evening, their mother had been crying loudly. Wailing, keening. And after it had stopped, the stillness in the house had felt even more threatening.

Rebecca looked back at her small sister. 'I'm going in,' she whispered.

Lyndsay nodded, but stayed put.

From across the landing she heard Rebecca, out of sight in the bathroom, begin to scream, without understanding what it signified.

'What?' she cried out.

'Mummy's not moving. I think she's dead.'

They were alone in the house. Two small girls, side by side, waiting on their parents' bed for their father to return.

Swaying and reeking of booze, he came home in the small hours. Rebecca had been the one to tell him, 'Go and look at Mummy.'

And then, like the owl at daybreak, Rebecca went. She abandoned them. Disappeared. Lyndsay never saw her again.

Lyndsay saw weeks of uncertainty stretching in front of her: weeks of searching and waiting, of not knowing; the headlines in the papers; journalists hanging about at the gate. Lyndsay, the small girl, had hidden herself behind the net curtains and watched the comings and goings. Her father's voice in the room behind her had said, 'I have to go out. Don't open the door, little one. Don't let them in. Don't answer any questions.'

Weeks later, police officers had arrived in a black car. Men in raincoats with grave faces like the policemen the child Lyndsay had seen on television. 'We've found a girl, Mr Boyd, about your daughter's age. I'm afraid we'll need you to identify her.' She'd watched her father's face. She'd studied it hard. 'The body fits the description but... She's badly mutilated, sir.'

She'd seen the cigarette trembling between his amber-stained fingers. The power had gone out of him, like a deflated balloon. He left quietly with the men in the raincoats. She'd stayed behind in the empty house, praying he'd come back.

And then upstairs alone in his room with his saxophone, he'd played music. Hour after hour of melodic sequences which Lyndsay heard everywhere: in the kitchen, in the room she and her dead sister had shared, on the landing, the top of the stairs where she'd crouched waiting for him. He played the blues. Those haunting notes began inhabiting every corner of the house. Enclosed in his room her father had shed his guilt, exorcised his pain, and let go.

Her existence had meant nothing to him. And so she'd stepped into her mother's shoes: kept busy, ran the house efficiently, taken care of him. In this way, she had buried her own loss and grown indispensable.

Now, as dawn was approaching at Churdle Bridge Farm, alone in an empty house, Lyndsay cradled her face in her arms and closed her eyes. She inhaled deeply, breathing slowly. She'd forced herself to forget those memories, obliterate the misery, and build a new life. And now Stephen. And Matt. Her mouth was so dry she was barely able to speak but she lifted the receiver. She forced herself. She had to be strong. She had to get in touch with Stephen and she had to notify the police that her son was missing.

10

The chiming of bells drifted in through the open windows. They were announcing the celebration of the once-a-month Sunday service about to be held in the medieval church at Churdle Heath. Lyndsay glanced at the clock on the drawing room mantelpiece. It was a quarter to twelve. Seated opposite her was a middle-aged man with brown thinning hair. He was studying a photograph of Matthew. This gimlet-eyed stranger, intent upon her son's features, was wearing a beige raincoat. The sight of him in it, on this first day of June, a warm day, unsettled her.

'He's a good-looking boy.'

'Yes, he is.'

'How recent is this photograph, Mrs Potter?'

'It was taken at the end of last term, a week or so before Easter. So, it's…two months old.'

'Good. I'll hold on to it for the time being, if that's all right with you?'

Lyndsay nodded. 'Of course.'

'Mrs Potter, as far as you know, did your son have any dealings with the new proprietors of the post office?'

'You mean the Indian couple, Mr and Mrs Bharjee?'

'Exactly them.'

She shrugged. 'He went there, he frequently bought stamps from them.'

'But he never spent time with either one of them socially?'

'Heavens, no.'

'Never mentioned them to you?'

'No. I don't see what this has to do – '

'And you are absolutely certain that there is nothing about his behaviour of late that you have considered odd or out of character?'

Lyndsay visualised the grass buried beneath foolscap sheets of paper on Matt's desk and his strange, withdrawn moodiness. Were his moods drug-related? She shook her head. 'Nothing that I have been aware of,' she lied.

The Detective Inspector studied her for a moment longer than he had after her previous responses. Lyndsay felt his cool scrutiny. Unable to hold eye contact she smiled weakly and turned towards the sandstone fireplace, gazing at, but not registering, the cones and iron dogs placed there to decorate the bareness of a summer hearth.

'Have there been any arguments at home? Unexpected shows of aggression or depression?'

'He loses his temper from time to time and gets downhearted.'

'Like any teenager?'

'Yes.'

'But no arguments, nothing out of the ordinary?'

'Not really.'

'What exactly do you mean by that?'

She glanced back at the Inspector. Much about him disturbed her. The force of his stare, for one thing, as well as his obvious desire to pry into their private life, and she decided it would be best to disclose nothing of that. 'I mean, no. No arguments.'

The bells had ceased. Lyndsay listened out for other sounds. She did not want silence, she needed something to latch on to, to re-establish normality. In the silence of the room she began to identify the distant bleating of sheep from a neighbouring farm. One or two bird songs. A rogue cuckoo, a young male chaffinch. Missing was the crek-crek grating of the corncrake. It was now a stranger to the south of England, due to offensive agricultural techniques. It had been her favourite as a child. And then, bringing her back to the present and overriding the music of nature, was the sound of a familiar engine advancing along the driveway, Stephen's Porsche.

'It's Stephen! My husband's back!' she cried with visible relief, rising and moving.

Behind Lyndsay, a uniformed police officer turned and plodded towards the window – a better position from which to observe the arrival of Mr Potter.

As Stephen approached the house and saw the police car parked on the forecourt behind Lyndsay's Mercedes, he slowed. A quick glance told him that there was no ambulance present, which meant, mercifully, that an accident was unlikely. So, what was the law doing at Churdle Bridge Farm on a Sunday morning? There was no earthly reason why they would be enquiring after Stephen himself. Or was there? He pondered upon his client, the Argentinian, and then instantly dismissed the thought. If there were trouble on that score, it would not be the local constabulary knocking on the door. He turned his key in the lock and called his wife's name, careful to express no concern.

'We're in the drawing room,' Lyndsay shouted. There was nothing to read from the tone of her voice either.

As he made his way through the hall Stephen was immediately aware of how silent the house was. It was a silence broken by the regular ticking of the grandfather clock and his own footsteps on the oak flooring.

Waiting with his wife in the living room were two police officers. The older, a man in his mid fifties, balding and dressed in civilian clothes, was seated in one of the fireside chairs. This man, clearly the more senior of the pair, had not troubled to remove his coat. He rose to greet Stephen. The other standing closer to the window was a sergeant in uniform, burly and purple-faced. Lyndsay, also standing, looked anxious but relieved to see him. Her eyes were swollen and red, while her hands were clasped tensely in front of her. Each stared expectantly in his direction.

'Good morning,' said Stephen amiably.

'Inspector, this is my husband,' Lyndsay's voice was controlled and steady, surprisingly calm. 'Stephen, this is Inspector Burgess.'

'Detective Inspector Burgess, Area Major Incident Team. How do you do, sir?'   .

Stephen glanced from one to the other attempting to gauge the general mood of things. He saw the distress written on his wife's face and had registered the man's title: Major Incident Team. Lyndsay was drawn, pale as parchment and clearly in need of sleep. Surely it could not be his own absence that had provoked this gathering? 'What's happened?' he asked.

Lyndsay edged closer. 'Matt's gone,' she whispered. Her tone was colluding as though she were disclosing information that the two men were not party to when obviously they were.

'What do you mean, gone?' Stephen's question – accusation – was directed more to the Inspector than at his wife. Nevertheless Lyndsay flinched. His sharpness wounded.

'Your son has not been seen for almost two days, Mr Potter,' replied the senior man in the raincoat.

'That's utter nonsense! I only left here yesterday morning. He was here then.'

'No, he wasn't. I went up to his room about an hour after you left. There was no sign of him. I'm not even sure he slept here on Friday night. He's taken his clarinet.'

'Your wife seems to feel that's significant.'

'He doesn't go far without it, that's for sure.'

'If the clarinet were still in his room he'd be coming back!' There was a note of hysteria creeping into Lyndsay's voice. Stephen, determined to keep this unanticipated interview as cool and calm as possible, directed his attention at the policeman. 'Inspector, have your people found anything or…?'

'Mrs Potter only telephoned us this morning.'

Stephen turned to his wife. 'Is that right?' His question was a bald accusation.

'I wanted to talk to you first. I tried to reach you,' explained Lyndsay. She was breathing fast. 'I didn't want to call in the police until I'd spoken to you. I telephoned the Crillon. They said you weren't registered there.'

Stephen glanced at the Inspector who was watching him closely. 'I couldn't get a reservation.'

'I rang everywhere: the Ritz, the Meridien, Hilton. Not one of the hotels had heard of you. I was sitting here at four o'clock this morning telephoning every bloody hotel I could find a number for!'

'There was a convention on in the city. Everywhere was booked. Why don't we all sit down, discuss this calmly and see if we can't work out what's happened to Matt? I'm sure he hasn't disappeared.'

'You could have let me know!' A thin slither of fury ran through Lyndsay's words, controlled but unmistakable. Stephen didn't welcome her attitude in front of the law. He loathed scenes, considered such behaviour demeaning, particularly in front of strangers. Stephen despised public displays of emotion, but right now Lyndsay didn't give a damn.

The Inspector lit up a cigarette and looked about for an ashtray. 'Is there a…?'

'We none of us smoke,' Stephen snapped, brisker than he'd intended.

'I'll fetch one.' Lyndsay hurried from the room, glad of the opportunity to be alone for a moment.

In the awkward silence that ensued Stephen crossed to the chair Lyndsay had previously occupied. He moved slowly, allowing for the mood to settle. 'My wife is upset. I apologise for her behaviour, Inspector.'

'Burgess is the name, sir. Frankly, Mr Potter, I find it rather astonishing that she has waited so long before getting in touch with us. Two days could have taken your son anywhere.'

'There is nothing to suggest he wasn't here yesterday morning when I left. Or is there?' Stephen turned to the door and watched Lyndsay return with the ashtray and hand it to Burgess.

'Thank you, Mrs Potter. We haven't looked into it yet, sir.'

'Knowing Matthew, I doubt that he will have gone far. For one thing, he has no money, I'm fairly tough with the boys on that score, and he's happiest when he's holed up in his room writing his songs. Is it not possible that he just decided to go back to college a couple of days early?'

'Any reason why he should want to do that?' enquired Burgess.

'Well, he...'

'None that I'm aware of. I was merely throwing out explanations.'

'Mrs Potter, you were trying to say something?'

'I...' Lyndsay glanced uncertainly at Stephen. He hadn't mentioned their argument, nor their impending separation. Might the overnight trip to Paris have softened his resolve? 'I telephoned this morning. Matt hasn't been seen at the school since he left for his Whitsun holidays. The Matron assured me that there has been nothing extraordinary about his behaviour. I then called the Lewis' house. They haven't heard from him either.'

Burgess had taken a spiral notebook from his pocket and was scribbling as Lyndsay spoke. 'The Lewises are...?'

'The family of Matt's best friend, Rupert Lewis.'

'I take it he's not at Harry's. That's where his grandfather used to live. Or is that too obvious?'

'Mrs Potter tells us that she went there earlier.'

'And?'

'The cottage was empty, nothing has been disturbed. He definitely hasn't slept there.' Lyndsay's answer was muted and clipped.

Stephen sat down. The situation seemed utterly incredible. 'All right, let's suppose for a minute that he really is missing, what then?'

'As we speak, a member of my staff is interviewing locals in the village. He'll soon know if Matthew has contacted anybody in the neighbourhood. We'll find out who was the last to see him.'

'He doesn't mix much locally. There are no boys his own age hereabouts.'

Lyndsay felt herself go giddy with rage. 'There are the Hampton boys,' she said, more to nettle Stephen than because she believed Matt was with them. It then occurred to her that she hadn't called them as she had intended.

'Who are they?'

'Sons of a farming family. Matt used to go fishing with them.'

Burgess added this to his notes. 'No family friends or relatives he might have slipped off to visit?'

'No one I know of, but Lyndsay, you'd be better placed...'

Lyndsay shook her head as the telephone began to ring. She hurried from the room, preferring to answer it from the extension in the hall. 'Hello?'

It was the manager from the Crillon Hotel returning her call. 'I understand you telephoned. You have a complaint?'

'No, no complaint. I want to enquire about the reservations of Mr Stephen Potter?' Lyndsay glanced guiltily towards the three men. She spoke as faintly as she dared without risking a request to speak up.

'For what dates, please?'

She was feeling awkward. 'Last night, or – '

'One moment please, Madame.' As she listened Lyndsay kept her eyes on the drawing room. Burgess and Stephen were still engaged in conversation, paying no attention to her. At the other end of the line, from the centre of Paris, she heard snatches of French being shouted across the lobby. 'Hello, Mrs Potter? I can confirm information given to you earlier. Mr Potter is not staying with us.'

'Yes, I know, it's last weekend.'

'We are not at liberty to disclose our guests' itineraries, I apologise. *Au revoir, Madame.*'

'Thank you.' Lyndsay did not replace the receiver. She listened to the dialling tone while watching her husband. The Inspector had left his chair and was pacing about the drawing room.

'There's no one you think he might have gone off with?' she heard Burgess ask.

'Gone off with? No.'

If Stephen had not been at the Crillon or the Hilton or the Ritz or any of the numerous hotels she had telephoned, where had he slept? She couldn't believe he had slept in an empty flat.

'No scene took place here?'

'Scene?'

'A row, Mr Potter, between Matthew and one or other or both of his parents.'

'He certainly hasn't argued with me, nor with my wife as far as I am aware. This is a fairly well-balanced household.'

Burgess stared evenly at Stephen. 'He didn't witness anything that might have upset him?'

'I don't follow you.'

'Forgive me for saying so, sir, but I thought I detected a certain uneasiness between Mrs Potter and yourself.'

Foolish, Lyndsay was thinking, not to have enquired of the manager at the Crillon if there had been a conference in Paris this weekend and whether the hotel was fully booked. She would call again later when Stephen was not about, although she wondered what point there was to these jealous enquiries. Her desperation to know the truth about whether or not he had a mistress in Paris made little difference to the current situation.

'My wife is tense at present. Understandable under the circumstances, wouldn't you say? There is no reason in the world why my son should run off!'

'Are you acquainted with Mr and Mrs Bharjee?'

'Who?'

'The Indian couple who recently purchased the village post office.'

'Vaguely. What has – ?'

'Your wife tells us that you travel a fair bit, Mr Potter.'

Stephen frowned. He was not following this man's too frequent change of tack. 'What about it?'

'Is it usual for you to take off without leaving a contact number? In case of emergencies?'

Lyndsay replaced the receiver and moved towards the living room. Neither man noticed her approach.

'I explained a few moments ago. The Crillon, which is where I always stay, was fully booked.'

'I take it you were in Paris?'

Stephen lowered his head and closed his fingers together, as though he were praying. Lyndsay knew this gesture well. He was attempting to maintain perspective and control. 'I have receipts, if you want proof.'

'Sorry about that,' she said, returning purposefully, offering no explanation as to the identity of the caller.

Burgess waited for her to settle before continuing. 'What line of business are you in, Mr Potter?'

Stephen drew breath. 'Finance. International investments.'

'Working for?'

'My own company.'

'And where would that be based, sir?'

'The City.' Stephen's patience was growing short.

'Hmm. Well, I think you have given us plenty to be getting on with. I'll hold on to this photograph of Matthew for the time being, and we'll start circulating it.' As they approached the door the Inspector turned back. His eyes narrowed as he spoke. 'Oh, did I mention that Mr Bharjee telephoned us the day before yesterday to say that his wife is also missing? Curious coincidence.'

Hours passed in silence. It was rare for Lyndsay and Stephen to be alone together in the house on a Sunday. Usually one or other of the boys was home from college. In fine weather their habit had always been to drive to the coast, to Bosham, where Stephen moored his yacht. It was fine weather; it would have been ideal for sailing, but they were not going anywhere. Lyndsay telephoned the family where Paul was staying. There was no reply.

During an awkward encounter in the hall, Stephen announced that he was postponing his departure until after Matt's return. Lyndsay made no reply. What was she supposed to say? Thank you?

Needing to keep occupied, she became frantically busy in the kitchen; sponging shelves, rearranging flowers and ironing shirts. All the time she left the radio playing, tuned to a local station, in the hope of news. When, eventually, she had worn herself out, she sank into a chair and stared at the telephone willing Matt to ring, silently begging him to make contact. Then, too anxious to stay still, she resorted to the gardens where she engaged in nothing urgent.

It was a warm afternoon and she felt calmer outside. She surveyed her newly sown flowerbeds. A blackbird was filching roots from her plants to line its nest. On an ordinary day, Lyndsay would have shooed the hen bird away but today she left it in peace and wandered off to the rose garden, to deadhead a few roses and search the leaves for bites from leafcutter bees. She found none.

Matt must have overheard her and Stephen fighting. Had he grasped what was going on? Perhaps it had sent him scuttling off without a word. Maybe he was holed up somewhere, traumatised and devastated.

She visited the greenhouses, checked the thermostats and watered the African palms. In one of the large terracotta pots she came across two cigarette stubs and silently cursed the visitor who had discarded them so inconsiderately. Handwritten notices hung from the greenhouse doors and informed entering customers that smoking was not allowed anywhere within the vicinity of the plants.

Having failed to employ herself further, she paced the grounds, eyes fixed on the drive, praying that any second now she would catch sight of Matt returning on his bike. Her handsome boy cycling home, blithely unconcerned, just as if he had been to the post office to send off his precious tapes. Should she have mentioned to Inspector Burgess that she had seen Mrs Bharjee in the cemetery? And why had the news of Mrs Bharjee's disappearance been mentioned? Then she remembered Matt's bicycle.

Lyndsay had forgotten all about his bike. She hadn't been near the junk shed where it lived in days. She had not even considered it. Hope rose like a kite as she hurried across the lawns, past the pool, which no one had bothered to uncover, skirting a path round the azalea bushes, blind to their profusion of colour, thinking only of the sheds. There, she shoved open the door and stepped inside. The air smelt musty, of cobwebbed beams, dusty bricks and smudges of oil that blackened the concrete floor.

The bicycle was there, stowed in its place against the wall where Matt always left it. The sight of it, his fishing gear on the ground alongside it, made her want to weep, but her tears were dry, retching gulps of panic. She ran her fingers across the saddle searching for the warmth of him, the life in him. Some glimmer of assurance. Over and over her father's words rang through her head, pealing like the morning church bells. 'Your sister's dead. Only two of us left now, little one.'

'Oh, Christ, not again, please,' she wailed, sinking like a stone to her knees. 'Dear God, let Matt be safe.'

'What on earth are you doing in here? I've been looking for you everywhere.' It was Stephen.

'Is there news?'

'No. I thought we should talk.'

'What about?'

'Matthew, for heaven's sake! Let's put our heads together, go back over these last few days. I'm not clear, Lyndsay, why, when you found his room empty, you didn't call the police immediately.'

'Have you come looking for me to accuse me?'

'Of course not, don't be so touchy. I want us to think. See if we can't work out between us where he has gone to.'

'Stephen, yesterday morning when I told you that I was worried about him you accused me of being over-protective. Now you are accusing me of being neglectful and touchy.' Stephen stared at his wife staggering clumsily from the ground. 'Why didn't you call me?' she continued. 'You could have let me know where you were. I didn't hear a word from you! So, don't you dare to make me wrong. And why didn't you tell Burgess that you've taken a flat in Paris and you're leaving home?' Lyndsay's face within the shed was half in shadow. She was patched and puffy from lack of sleep and she was burning with pain and rage.

'Because it's none of his damned business. When you are ready to talk, I'll be in my study.'

As the door closed in front of her, Lyndsay let out a moan. Her heart was filled with antagonism towards Stephen and what had happened between them. She wondered if she was partly responsible for his incalculable coldness. In a time of such crisis they should be tender with one another, offer comfort and support, forgive each other's misdemeanours. Instead she was recoiling from him. It was as though she hated him, as though the rancour had been building within her for months, or worse, and more disturbing, for years.

The foreboding had been real. Everything she had built and created with love and industry was falling down around her, and she was powerless to halt the dissolution. She closed up the shed and stepped heavily into the early afternoon. Bright sunlight greeted her, warming her face. The sky was a clear, untroubled blue. In every direction splashes of blossoming flowers and bushes greeted her. She stared out, exhausted and demoralised, at the day before her. She was overreacting. She had been up all night and needed rest.

Returning to the house she climbed the stairs to their room where she lay down on their bed and closed her eyes. Through a half-open window she listened to the angry cawing of a pair of crows, a dog barking – not one of her own – and a child shrieking. Eventually, she dozed off.

A dream woke her. Dark, unrecollected, ominous. A woman was crying. No, it was the telephone. Drifts of staccato speech punctuated by silences rose up from the ground floor beneath her. Stephen, in his study, was listening, receiving information; a brief exchange. Her instinct was to go downstairs but she felt unable to move. She lay, trembling. If it was about Matt, Stephen would find her. If it wasn't, she had no interest in the call.

Seconds later, his footsteps climbed the stairs. An ordinary sound which, this afternoon, made her apprehensive.

Tucked away in her handbag, on the carpet alongside their bed, was a white envelope rolled up like a bandaged finger. In it was the grass she had found on her son's desk. She had not mentioned it to anyone, not even to Stephen, and certainly not to the two men who had sat in her drawing room a few hours earlier. It was evidence she had snaffled at daybreak when she'd turned Matt's room upside down.

After she had failed to locate Stephen in Paris she had been too disturbed to sleep. She had paced the house alone for a while, had considered taking the car out to tour the streets again, circling wider to visit motorways, garages, all-night cafés. She had even contemplated a trip to London, to roam clubs and bars in the hunt for her son. But it was the hour of the wolf, the hour of the moon. And so she had chosen to remain inside the house, a moidered creature, rifling her son's personal belongings, pillaging his space. Turning out drawers, lifting the mattress, opening folders, files, wallets, pockets, anything she could lay her hands on. She had been looking for clues as to his whereabouts and traces of other drugs. For a jigsaw piece that would unlock the puzzle; something to help her understand his behaviour, to assist her in coming to terms with it. Once her search was underway the boy she had uncovered had confounded her.

To dig deep into another's heart – even one's own child's – was a violation. Rooting about in another's secret garden. Matt was not hers. She did not own him. She had no right to demand cognisance of the mysteries of his heart and of his inner life. But once the trespass was underway there was no turning back and, once there, she found herself in a private world, the world of her son's sexual awakening. His fantasies about a girl whom he addressed simply as S. Who was she? A Susan? Sally? Sylvia? A girl he had met through his college? The sister of one of his pals? There were no other clues as to her identity.

Perfectly harmless adolescent yearnings, Stephen would no doubt assure her should she decide at some later stage to confide in him. But they were shocking to Lyndsay. Shocking because the discoveries were so unexpected, so prolific and so erotic. There were poems, love songs, dreams and idylls, recorded there on paper for her to read. Aside from his music, Lyndsay hadn't had the slightest notion that Matthew wrote anything. A few harmless lyrics she had thought, nothing more alarming than that. But among his possessions, squirrelled away in a plastic supermarket bag beneath disgustingly smelly sports togs, she had found journals, notebooks, reams of poems, romantic sonnets, (sonnets, Matthew!) love songs, ballads and diaries. All penned by him in his own hand. Much of it was just plain nonsense, self-pitying adolescent ramblings. Some sentiments were bawdy, others downright lewd, certain sections followed the spirit of his own pop culture, others his grandfather's jazz and big-band style. She found lines declaring everlasting love and fantastic intimacies about himself that she had barely dared to look upon.

This silent, withdrawn sphinx of a boy who had shared so little of himself with her of late was, on paper, powerfully, shockingly and brazenly articulate. She had blushed, transfixed, and then had grown jealous of the diaries that had received his outpourings, jealous of the richness of this inner life, which excluded her. Worse, it did more than exclude her; it ignored her. For Matthew's consuming preoccupations were all directed towards the same female, and she was not his mother. She was always S.

He was constant in his affections – that at least could be said for him – but she, Lyndsay, occupied not one line in this private world of his and the discovery of that provoked her jealousy. She felt jealous for another reason too, a more unsettling reason. The passion that consumed Matthew, his dreams and fantasies about his unobtainable S were shocking to her because she had had no notion that her 'little boy', her fifteen-year-old son, was capable of such fevered and devouring emotions. 'Cosmic penis ache', in the words of her son.

But what was also disturbing to Lyndsay was that she had never experienced such visceral longing, had never opened herself in such a way to anyone. She loved Stephen, of course she did. Not at this minute perhaps, but in the overall scheme of things. Her marriage had been fortunate; it was comfortable. Their sexual life together had been fine but once she had borne

107

her children, sex had not been a driving force for her. Looking back, her libido had always been a fairly low-key affair, which was understandable given the trauma of her past, the circumstances of the loss of her mother, and then her sister. And since her father had died she hadn't desired Stephen at all. In spite of this, Lyndsay had never considered that she had been missing out. She had believed that she possessed everything. But now she saw that she had been blinkered. Matthew's passion, his prose and poetry, might as well have been written in hieroglyphics for all its sentiments related to hers.

And the grass. She had never indulged in pot, nor was she curious to start now. That was not the point. The point was that Matthew was living a life about which she had no knowledge: *his* life. Not the one she had been so neatly honing for him. He was tasting, testing, making choices, and extending the boundaries – and they lay leagues beyond hers. Alongside her adolescent son, Lyndsay felt herself a novice. If she ever saw Matt again…no, no, when she saw him, she would doubtless feel cowed by his ardour and courage.

What had happened to her, to Lyndsay Boyd? She had long been in hiding, efficiently screened behind another woman, masked by the shadow of a woman she had created, the role she had been portraying, that of capable, efficient Mrs Potter.

The door opened and Stephen appeared. 'That was the police,' he said. 'Apparently Matthew was seen on Friday afternoon hanging about outside the Hamptons' house. Mrs Hampton spotted him entering their barn. She said he was behaving strangely.'

Lyndsay sat up. 'What did she mean by that?'

'Skulking, I think. But when she called him and went out to ask him what he wanted, he'd disappeared. She didn't see him leave. She has no idea whether he saw her, where he was heading or what he was hoping to find in the barn. She said he was haring along the path like a "good for nothing thief".'

'Thief?!'

'Calm down. She assured the police that she didn't believe he was trying to steal anything. She thinks he wanted to play a practical joke on her sons.'

'Play a practical joke on them! That doesn't sound like Matt!' But then it occurred to Lyndsay that perhaps it was exactly like him. In the light of all she had discovered, how could she know?

'Nothing was found missing.'

'He wouldn't have been stealing. He's not a thief. That's ridiculous!'

'Nobody has accused him of it, Lyndsay. I'm only recounting what the police officer told me.'

'She's sure it was Matthew?'

'There's something else.'

Lyndsay was alerted by the gravity in Stephen's voice. 'What?'

He crossed to the bed and perched. 'She saw him earlier.'

'When, today?'

'No, Friday. He was with the wife of that Indian in the post office. Apparently, they were in the churchyard together. Mrs Hampton said that it was clear for all the world to see that Matt and the Indian's wife had a prearranged meeting there.'

At first Lyndsay said nothing. Trying to take it in, the full significance of Stephen's words. All she could picture in her mind's eye was Mrs Bharjee in her dusky blue sari sitting beneath the weeping pear tree in the churchyard.

'But why would they be meeting?'

'I don't know. That's all she said, that Mrs Bharjee was sitting under a tree waiting for Matthew. Her head was bent so that she wouldn't be recognised, according to Mrs Hampton. And Matthew was creeping about in the shadows, hugging the church walls.'

'But why?'

'Careful not to be seen, I suppose, not to be recognised. By the time Matt finally approached the Indian woman, Mrs Hampton had rounded the corner and they were no longer visible. She has no idea how long they spent in the cemetery together, but claims that it was approximately four hours later she saw him hanging around her barn.'

Lyndsay started shivering. She pulled the duvet up around her shoulders. 'Did she say if he was all right?'

'I don't know, I didn't ask.'

She was trying not to shake. She was freezing. What instinct had warned her against mentioning to the police that she had seen the young Indian woman in the churchyard? 'What would Matt have been doing in the cemetery with Mrs Bharjee?'

'I have no idea.'

'Have the police interviewed Mrs Bharjee? Did she confirm that it was Matt she was with?'

'According to her husband she still hasn't returned. She's been missing since Friday lunch-time. Apparently, she left the shop a few minutes before meeting Matt.' Lyndsay pictured the bicycle lying on its side beyond the lych-gate. 'If Mrs Hampton's report is to be believed then Mrs Hampton and Matthew were the last to have seen this woman before her reported disappearance.'

Lyndsay stared incredulously at Stephen. She took a deep breath, more a gasping for air. 'There must be some mistake,' she said as she recalled her own sighting of Mrs Bharjee and then, moments later, that bloody bicycle ditched on the church flagstones.

'Can I get you anything? A drink, a cup of tea?'

'I'm going to telephone Mrs Hampton. Perhaps there is something else that she hasn't thought of, some detail that might give us a clue.'

'Let's leave the police to deal with her. Get some rest.' He turned to leave.

'Stephen?'

'Yes?'

'About Paris...' At the mention of the word Paris, Lyndsay saw Stephen's face tighten. 'When I didn't hear from you, couldn't find you, I was afraid.' His features were impassive. Lyndsay knew then that wherever he had gone to in his heart she was no longer reaching him. She had been excluded. After she had turned Matt's room upside down she had rifled the pockets of Stephen's suits, turned out the drawers and leafed through the stacks of papers in his study. Unlike Matthew, with Stephen she had known exactly what she was searching for: clues as to the existence of another woman, an explanation for his decision. She had found nothing, but perhaps he was just too clever for her. 'Are you angry?' she asked.

'What about?'

'I don't know. Because I got upset in front of the Inspector. Because I delayed before calling the police. Because you don't love me anymore. I don't know why.'

'You're tired and confused, Lyndsay. Let's discuss all this later when you are less emotional.'

'I'm cold, and, yes, tired too, I suppose.'

'Try to sleep.'

'Stephen.'

'What is it?'

She could not fail to detect the weariness in his response.

'I know this sounds utterly ridiculous but if Matthew is in some way connected to Mrs Bharjee's disappearance he would have still been with her later on Friday afternoon, right?'

'I honestly don't know. I had no idea he associated with the woman.'

'He didn't. And what's more Matt was here Friday evening. He yelled out to us as he went up the stairs, remember? He was in his room when I called up to him to come and have some pasta. So, he hadn't gone missing then. You heard him say that he wasn't hungry, you were in the dining-room with me when I called him.'

'Did you tell the police he was here that evening?'

'Yes, of course. It doesn't make any sense all this, does it?'

'Perhaps Mrs Hampton is mistaken. It's perfectly possible. You know, I've never been fond of that family.'

'Do you think this evidence, this testimony of hers, is malicious gossip then? A revenge of some sort?'

'Could be, I really don't know. Get some rest.' And with that Stephen disappeared.

Dusk was falling. It was beginning to rain. Normally, at about this time, Lyndsay would telephone Paul at the holiday home of his friend's parents. He loved to recount to her the details of his day; where he'd been, what he'd eaten, what Richard's mum had said about this or that. What, thought Lyndsay, is Richard's mum going to say about this? Lyndsay knew that Paul would ask after Matt. He always did. What was she going to say to him? She decided to postpone the call until after supper. In spite of Stephen's advice she felt an overwhelming urge to telephone Mrs Hampton, but she quashed it. Stephen was right, better leave it to the police.

The rain was falling fast now. Beyond the open window, the air smelled fresh and leafy.

Less than twenty-four hours earlier, Lyndsay had sat at a kitchen table opposite a drunken Marion Finch thanking whoever was out there for her good fortune. She gave a thought now to Marion, struggling through her lonely Sunday.

11

It was Ralph Beresford who found her, on his way to inspect the ospreys. The area where he discovered her, a substantial stretch forested with mature oaks, flanked the western sector of the nature reserve. At its densest, because it was cushioned with rich dark soil, the earth produced robust crops of ferns. There, cutting through a trackless tract of undergrowth, no more than thirty minutes' vigorous striding from the village, Ralph Beresford came across the body.

It was Monday morning, sunrise: the hour when the lark sings for the few. The ground underfoot was spongy, soaked by heavy overnight rains. Beresford was walking fast when his attention was drawn to something glistening in the undergrowth. He bent to investigate and found coiled strands of golden braid from off the hem of her pine-blue sari. Stripes of early morning sunlight shafting through the branches, still dripping with rainwater, highlighted the gold and caused it to glitter. When he delved deeper he uncovered yards of torn, muddied material stained with blood, and dusky limbs attached to a head and torso, which had been partially buried beneath the fretted fern fronds. Her body was stone cold, and the foxes had been there first.

Less than three hours after Beresford's discovery the telephone was ringing at Churdle Bridge Farm. Lyndsay, in the kitchen making toast, hurried to answer it. 'Yes?'

'Have you heard the news?' It was Marion Finch.

'What news?' she asked. Was this something to do with Matthew?

'Bharjee's wife has been murdered. The village is swarming with police vans.' Lyndsay gripped the phone tight. She did not know whether she felt relieved or appalled. It could have been Matt. 'I guessed something was up. She hasn't been in the shop since Friday morning and the police have been asking questions. I heard they'd quarrelled and she ran off. Bharjee will deny it, of course, but gossip on the local vine travels fast. Someone told me he'd been beating her.'

'There's no mention of it in the newspapers!' Lyndsay retorted, realising how foolish her remark was. But anything seemed better than listening to Marion and, in any case, Lyndsay's distracted logic reasoned that if nothing had been put into print it meant the story was unconfirmed. Facts could deny what had just been reported to her.

'They only found the body this morning. In any case, teenagers vanish far too frequently for the disappearance of one young girl to be of national interest, particularly an Indian,' replied Marion.

As Marion spoke, Lyndsay drew the mouthpiece away from her face and stared at it with a kind of horror. Why was Marion telephoning her with this news? Did the call imply that Marion believed Matt was responsible? 'Sorry, I have to go.' Lyndsay replaced the receiver immediately.

She leant over the kitchen unit holding tight to its corners. Stephen was working in his office. She had to let him know the shocking news, but she couldn't take a step. She was shaking from head to foot.

Even before she had made it across the hall, there was a loud rapping on the front door. It took her by surprise because they had an intercom system connected to the gate. Lyndsay, still shaking, hesitated.

'Good morning, Mrs Potter.' Inspector Burgess, not waiting to be invited in, brushed past her as soon as she opened the door. His behaviour was probably more to do with preoccupation rather than downright bad manners. Lyndsay followed as he made for the drawing room. 'Your husband's home is he, Mrs Potter? His car is out front.'

Without a word Lyndsay went to fetch Stephen. She guessed that Burgess was about to deliver the same news Marion had just hot lined through.

She was right. Sitting across from one another in the fireside chairs, like two inanimate objects, she and Stephen were audience to Burgess pacing the room. Back and forth he went, like a ringmaster, notebook in hand. 'When her body was found this morning, according to the statement given by her husband, she had been missing for close to three days, approximately sixty-six hours.'

Lyndsay felt numb. This pinched, eagle-eyed man marching to and fro in their drawing room quoting facts, reading notes, was nothing to do with them at all. His hypertension was in direct contrast to the deadness that was taking hold of her. Paul would have arrived at school by now. She must speak to him, before anyone else did.

'Of course, we cannot pinpoint the precise time of death until we have the pathologist's report, but it appears that she died, was murdered – I think we can safely assume that – mid-Friday afternoon. Probably about an hour before your son was sighted running into the barn adjoined to the farmhouse leased to the Hampton family.'

Lyndsay heard the information and understood it, her brain was not dulled, but the implication was too fantastic, too far-fetched. 'Probably about an hour before' meaning that Matthew would have had time to perform this atrocious act and then leg it to the Hamptons' barn. She had been in the nature reserve around that time with Ralph Beresford. She recalled the chorus of screechings. Had the birds given a warning? And suddenly, as though it were in some way connected, she heard again the scream that had woken her a week or more back, and pictured Matt ascending the stairs in his anorak. His skin had been dampened by exertion. The night the ospreys were attacked.

It was Stephen who eventually interrupted Burgess. His voice was strong although subdued. He did not seem disturbed by the magnitude of information being delivered to them, nor by its emotional weight. 'What was the cause of death?' he asked.

'She was clubbed on the back of the skull with a heavy blunt object. A rock would be my guess, although we haven't found the weapon yet. She was certainly sexually assaulted. She suffered facial bruisings, mildly disfiguring, but they are possibly not directly related to her death. A series of bruisings found on her upper thighs seem to suggest a struggle.'

'But it was the blow to the back of her head that killed her?' Stephen was being precise. Lyndsay couldn't think why he would want such details.

'Until I have read the pathologist's report I can only answer that it appears to have been that. It looks as though she was raped and then murdered. She was only eighteen years old, did you know that?'

Lyndsay asked herself if her age was significant. Are they relating one missing teenager to another and coming up with murder? Is that what everyone is going to do? Like Marion Finch, on the telephone before nine o'clock in the morning?

'Does Matthew smoke, Mr Potter?'

'Certainly not!'

Matt wasn't capable of violence. All he cared for was his music. And then Lyndsay remembered the force of his anger when he'd argued with Stephen and the passion hidden in those secret diaries. What did she know of the power of his emotions, or about S, the object of his infatuation?

'I was in the reserve,' she said. 'I saw a car.'

116

'Can you describe the car?'

'Not really. A couple were fucking in it. And later, we heard screaming. A child, Ralph had said, although it might have been a bird, or a young girl. It was far off. And earlier, there was a young man running, dressed in black.'

'Fucking?!' Stephen was appalled by Lyndsay's use of such a vulgar verb.

Burgess furrowed his brows and scribbled furiously. 'What time was the screaming, Mrs Potter? Describe the running man.'

'I didn't see his face.'

The London *Evening Standard* and the *Kent Evening Messenger* were the first to cover the story. It came out that same evening. All other newspapers, the national dailies, ran it the following morning. In the *Standard*, alongside the headlined report of the murder, was a single column devoted to Matthew and his synonymous disappearance. '*Matthew Potter, also missing since Friday, is wanted by the police for questioning.*' For questioning. Lyndsay could barely comprehend the words. They were letters from an alphabet strung together.

The photograph of Matt, grinning and sweating, wearing a striped sports shirt, which had been taken at the end of his last college term, which Lyndsay had loaned to Burgess to assist in the search for her son, was now plastered, like an accusation, for the world to see on the front page of the evening newspaper. Alongside it was a grainy, poorly focused, blown-up snapshot of Mrs Bharjee. The photo the *Standard* printed of Mrs Surinder Bharjee had been taken when she was sixteen, only months older than Matt was today.

Two photographs, printed alongside one another, related the teenage boy and girl, binding them in the kindredship of flight. It was exactly what Lyndsay had feared when she had listened to Marion on the phone and when she had watched Burgess, the beagle, psyching himself up for the hunt ahead. But what she had not been prepared for was the discovery of the Indian woman's Christian name: Surinder.

On Tuesday morning Stephen left for Geneva, giving precise details of where he could be reached and assuring Lyndsay that he would be back, at the latest, the following afternoon. He had wanted to postpone the trip but Lyndsay had said no. Her mind was bent on other matters and for these she needed time alone. She let him go with barely a word.

As soon as he was out of the house, Lyndsay bolted upstairs to Matt's room, heading directly for his wardrobe. This she locked with its key and then secreted the key inside the lining of her handbag. Later, she would return there. In the meantime, while Stephen was at a safe distance, she would take the opportunity to visit Mrs Hampton. For, suddenly, Mrs Hampton's statement, narrating her sighting of Matthew in the company of Surinder Bharjee in the church cemetery and, later, alone, lingering by the Hamptons' barn, was now charged with grotesque consequence. The precise timing of these two appearances and their validity were crucial, for Lyndsay knew they could be used as criminal evidence against her son.

She had still not breathed a word to anyone about her own observation of Mrs Bharjee in the churchyard nor that the Indian woman had been alone and crying. Nor, for the present, did she intend to. Certainly not before she had talked with Mrs Hampton. Lyndsay remembered clearly that when she first spotted Surinder Bharjee, she had glanced at the clock in her car. It had read ten to one. Was that before or after Mrs Hampton had passed by? In other words had Matt met Mrs Bharjee in the churchyard and then left her there alone? If Mrs Hampton had passed by before Lyndsay then that was a possible scenario and it would mean that she, Lyndsay, was the last – the last bar the murderer – to have seen Surinder alive. Not Matt, nor Mrs Hampton.

She drove to Lower Beeches, the neighbourhood in which the Hamptons' farmhouse was situated. As a precaution she took the lanes that skirted the smallest reservoir lake and the gravel-pits. She drove slowly keeping her eyes peeled, wondering if Matthew was hiding somewhere in the woods. She passed a trio of seventeenth-century cottages originally built as homes for farm labourers. They had recently been renovated and were for sale as a single luxury residence, Mill Farm. There were many such out-of-the-way dwellings which had been bought up and gentrified and were now used as weekend homes by city dwellers and high-flyers. Matt would know that. He could have broken into one such unoccupied house and stowed himself away in comfort.

Beyond the windscreen, Lyndsay caught sight of a flock of wading birds getting airborne. They reminded her of Ralph Beresford. Perhaps she should find him and talk through their afternoon together. Had he discussed it with the police? He must have done since it was he who had found the body.

As she approached the footbridge which led to the gravel-pits, from where the birds had taken off, she asked herself, if Matt looked up into the sky now would he see those same birds? She didn't know if he was close by, or if he was in pain.

There were two entrances to the Hamptons' farmhouse. A single gate gave on to a narrow flagged path and led directly to the front door porch. A pair of dilapidated wooden gates further along the lane led to the yard. These were left open during daylight hours for easy tractor access. Lyndsay swung her four-wheel drive through the double gates and parked in the yard. She felt uneasy about leaving her car in the road, unsure if someone might recognise it.

A couple of geese and a few hens strutting over and about the dried tyre tracks, foraging for food, paid her arrival no attention. She switched off the ignition and sat still, contemplating the impending visit. Now that she was here, she felt hesitant and vaguely guilty. Stephen had warned her against getting involved in police business. Aside from which she had no idea what sort of a reception she would receive. After all, this woman was the mother of the boys Stephen had judged unfit companions for his son.

Mr Hampton's old truck was nowhere to be seen, but then Lyndsay had not expected it would be. He would have disappeared hours earlier with his two lads, making for whatever area of the farm required their labour. Mrs Hampton did not own a car. As Lyndsay stepped from out of hers, the hens began to cluck in the morning sun. She rounded the house, noting the meagre postage-stamp lawn and a spindly pair of *impatiens* plants – busy Lizzies – growing in a pot perched atop a wooden barrel, stepped onto the porch and knocked.

It was only a matter of seconds before Mrs Hampton opened the door. She was clearly flustered by the sight of her visitor. 'Oh, it's you.'

'I'm sorry to disturb – '

'We've had the police and all sorts here. One more is little odds.'

'May I come in for a minute, please?'

'I suppose you'd better.' They trod, Lyndsay following, along a narrow hallway. 'Go through,' said Mrs Hampton, gesturing a parlour on the left.

Lyndsay had never set foot inside this house before and she was appalled by its shabby neglect. The carpets were threadbare, the walls were peeling and in spite of the bright, almost summer morning outside, the room was dark and cheerless.

Lyndsay's father and Mr Hampton had been drinking buddies in the Lamb and Flag, so she had heard all about the family's impoverished circumstances. She knew about their down-at-heel house but had also learnt from her father that Mr Hampton, who was employed and tenanted by a local gentleman farmer, never complained. He said that he was thankful for having kept hold of his job through the recession, never mind fussing about a bit of plaster coming off the walls. Mrs Hampton, who complained heartily, said that it was about a great deal more than crumbling plaster. Seeing it for herself, Lyndsay was inclined to agree with Mrs Hampton.

'It's about Matthew,' she began. By now the whole country knew the details so she felt no need to explain further.

Mrs Hampton, a solidly built woman in her late thirties but looking a deal older, listened silently, her hands folded in front of her. She pretended no niceties, did not offer coffee, merely looked Lyndsay full in the face and waited impassively.

'Inspector Burgess says that you think you saw Matt, and I'd like to ask you about it.'

Mrs Hampton continued to regard Lyndsay. 'I don't *think* I saw him, I *saw* him. Clear as day. Twice, at that.'

Cooking smells wafted through from the kitchen that Lyndsay could not identify but which turned her stomach. She had eaten nothing since the evening before and then only morsels. 'Would you mind if I sat down for a minute?' The atmosphere in the low-ceilinged room was suffocating, and she needed to move. Mrs Hampton gestured to an armchair. Lyndsay felt metal springs moving like water beneath her. Mrs Hampton remained standing which, Lyndsay felt, put her at a disadvantage. 'The first time you saw him was in the churchyard, isn't that so?' Her voice remained resolute but she was beginning to doubt the wisdom of the visit. She was intruding. Stephen had warned her, but she would never admit to having been here.

'Yes.'

'Do you know what time that was, Mrs Hampton?'

The farmer's wife frowned. 'I've already told the policeman. Before lunch.'

'Can you remember more precisely?'

Mrs Hampton, her face etched by hardship, puzzled over the question. She sat down, and the chair sunk beneath her bulk. Lyndsay noticed that she wasn't wearing a watch.

'Was the post office closed when you saw Mrs Bharjee in the cemetery or…?' Lyndsay prodded.

'I couldn't say. I wasn't paying much attention to the time, being in a hurry to get back with the shopping. I'd been to Tonbridge on the bus and I was hot. All I could think of was a cup of tea.'

'You thought Mrs Bharjee was waiting for Matthew. Are you sure she wasn't simply sitting in the shade to keep cool or because she wanted to be alone? If she were upset, for example.'

'Upset? Why would she have been?' Mrs Hampton grew agitated. She was being pressurised, she felt inadequate. 'The police keep asking questions, too! Ed's been moaning at me. He told me straight, "You've said too much already. You should keep your nose out of others' affairs," and, to tell you the God's honest truth, I wish I had kept my ruddy mouth shut! I can't be held responsible!'

'I'm not holding you responsible!'

'I spoke out. I thought it was for the best!'

'Mrs Hampton, please, don't get upset. You have two boys. So do I, and one of mine is missing. I need your help. Matthew could be charged with…with Mrs Bharjee's murder unless evidence is produced to prove his innocence. I have to do everything I can to protect him. Anything, anything you can remember that might help me.'

Mrs Hampton gave a whale of a sigh and lifted a half eaten bar of chocolate from the pocket of her baggy cardigan. She broke off a sizeable slab, stuffed it in her mouth and chewed it in a contentedly bovine fashion. All the while she was staring at the carpet as if she were trying to piece the images together. 'I was passing,' she said eventually, 'lugging the groceries. I saw Matthew creeping about near the church. He was pressed against the wall, making his way round towards the Indian lass. She was sitting on the stone bench, waiting in the shade for him. I thought his behaviour was a bit peculiar but, honestly, I was more surprised by the girl. First time I'd seen her outside that store. Too young she was, to be trapped inside that shop day in, day out. Married to that man more 'an twice her age. Queer that she and Matthew should be meeting, I thought. The girl spoke no more than a dozen words of English. Whatever would they have in common? What could they talk about? All your son thinks about is his music.' The frown on Mrs Hampton's thick face relaxed. She was pleased to have been able to recount the facts.

'Yes,' smiled Lyndsay. 'Did you notice what time it was when you got back here?'

'Before lunch. I can't be any more precise than that.'

'Do you have a set time for your lunch?'

'It depends whether Ed and the boys are coming back. If they do, then we eat when they arrive. I always keep something on the stove, takes seconds to heat. They weren't coming that day. Those days I please myself, stay shopping a bit longer. I don't have need of fancy schedules, Mrs Potter. Mealtimes, day, night, Sundays. My clock's simple. Not like yours. Meals on the table and up to make breakfast in the mornings.'

'What about the second time you saw Matthew?'

'I'd had my afternoon cup of tea and biscuits so, I'd say, about four hours later.'

'Will you tell me what you saw?'

'He was haring along the stony track that leads from the pastures to here. Looking all around him guilty-like, and he might have been scared. But he wasn't a boy on the run from a crime. Your Matthew's not capable of violence, least of all murder. He's a good lad. My boys like him, too.'

'I'm glad,' said Lyndsay. 'I'm pleased there are no bad feelings.'

Mrs Hampton seemed puzzled by Lyndsay's remark but she didn't comment on it. She began again, compiling her images into a coherent picture. 'I'd had my tea and was upstairs making the beds when I spotted him through the window. The path is visible from all the windows at the back of the house. I saw him hesitate and glance towards the kitchen. He was making sure I wasn't there. It didn't occur to him to double-check the upstairs rooms. When he thought he was safe and not being observed he took a deep breath – I remember that clearly because it made me smile, reminded me of my lads when they were small, learning to dive in the local pool – then, head down, shoulders hunched, he made an almighty dash for the barn. I called to him but I don't think he heard me. He's a good little sprinter, covered the distance in record time. The doors were unlocked. Always are. Too much of a business trying to close the blasted things. A shambles, like the rest of this ruddy place. After one more glance towards the house he slipped inside.' She paused to swallow and reflect. 'I never saw him come out. When I went down to see what he was up to, he'd gone. Disappeared into thin air.'

Lyndsay listened silently, measuring Mrs Hampton's story. Trying to imagine what Matt might have been doing. 'When he left home he was riding his bicycle,' she said.

'Not here, he wasn't.'

'Did he have it with him in the churchyard?'

'I didn't notice it.' Mrs Hampton broke off another piece of chocolate from her pocket. This she divided into two chunks, offering one to Lyndsay who refused it. 'If he came here to see my lads, he knows they don't get home before evening-time. Even then he couldn't be sure they'd go to the barn. Sometimes, I send them to collect feed or wood or deposit tools, but that's about all. There's nothing of value in there. Matt knows that. Hard to guess what he was after. I've been puzzling over it.'

It wouldn't have been a safe place to hide. He would have been found too easily, thought Lyndsay, but she didn't say it aloud. 'Will you telephone me if you think of anything else?'

'If you like.'

In response to Lyndsay's stirring, Mrs Hampton lifted herself up from the chair. Lyndsay dug into her bag and handed a business card of Churdle Bridge Farm Nurseries across to Mrs Hampton. 'Thank you for seeing me.'

No other conversation took place until they reached the front door and Lyndsay was outside on the step. She turned back and offered her hand to Mrs Hampton who took it awkwardly. 'If you do think of anything else, would you mind speaking to me before…?'

Mrs Hampton eyed her with suspicion. 'Before I tell the police?' The question was rather more baldly stated than Lyndsay would have liked but it was the sum of it. Not risking a verbal affirmative, she nodded tentatively. Mrs Hampton was still gripping Lyndsay's hand. Her big rough-skinned face broke into a smile. 'I'll help in whatever way I can,' she said. 'I'm feeling mighty bad about how everyone's blaming Matt. P'rhaps if I'd kept my ruddy mouth shut.'

At that moment, a male voice calling 'Mrs Potter?' interrupted their privacy.

Lyndsay swung round. 'Yes?'

Her eyes lighted upon a young man hovering in the yard alongside her Mercedes. He was holding up a camera. The photo was snapped almost before Lyndsay had answered to her name. Behind her, the door slammed and Mrs Hampton disappeared. It happened so quickly. Alarmed, Lyndsay hesitated, knowing she had no choice but to cross the balding patch of front lawn to where the intruder was waiting.

Pulling pen and pad from a pocket in his jacket, the journalist began to advance. A cigarette burned between his fingers.

'You're Matthew's Mum, right?' He was closing in, nimble-footed, facing her, bearing down upon her, blocking her path. 'I'm from the *Daily Mail.*'

'I don't want to talk to you!' Lyndsay growled while making a dash for her car. It was unlocked. She climbed in but, before she had succeeded in closing the door, he was there. A mixture of his deft-footedness and her panic had brought them head on. 'Get out of my way!' she fumed, reaching for the handle. His body was wedged against the door. The smoke from his cigarette rose between them. 'Damn you!' she shouted.

He responded by snapping his camera. It was a tight shot that closed in on eyes raging wildly at him.

Unused to the ways of the press, the flash startled Lyndsay. In furious defence she started up the engine, shoved her foot on the accelerator and reversed at full pelt from the yard. The door was still wide open. The young journalist clung fast but the backwards motion of the vehicle forced him to jump out of the way before he was dragged to the ground. Dust and pebbles and straw rose in a cloud around the moving car. Nearby, distressed geese were honking like machine guns. Narrowly missing the gatepost, Lyndsay managed to secure the door with her right hand while steering with her left. She lurched out of the driveway and on to the street, then jammed the automatic in to drive and screeched off out of sight.

A half a mile or so further along the lane she pulled over to calm herself and regain control. She lowered the window and inhaled the fragrant blossom of the creamy hedgerows. In the distance beneath a liquid blue sky were shoulders of soft green hills. It had been foolhardy to visit Mrs Hampton but Lyndsay did not regret it. She prayed though that the *Daily Mail* would not use the photos. Stephen would be livid. And what would Inspector Burgess make of the visit?

Instead of driving directly back to the empty house, Lyndsay decided to make a detour through the village. It was illogical to hope that Matt would be there but she reasoned that she might be closer to him. After all, it was to the village he had been cycling when she'd watched him disappear down the drive. As she approached, she thought over the two episodes that Mrs Hampton had recounted to her. What had Matt been looking for in the Hamptons' barn? If only Mrs Hampton had been able to pinpoint the time she had passed the church. She wished she knew what Matt had been so afraid of in the Hamptons' yard, what he had been running from.

Her arrival in Churdle Heath found it buzzing with frenetic activity. Before she knew what was happening she was snarled up between a Renault Espace and a small truck. She'd never seen so many vehicles in the village. It was crawling with journalists and camera crews. Having negotiated the first jam she was then held up behind a TV news team's camera truck. Frantic, she hurled everything out of the glove compartment in a hunt for sunglasses.

People were shouting from one side of the narrow street to the other. There were men everywhere, milling about, ties loosened, beer mugs in one hand, cigarettes in the other and cameras, two or three, hanging from their necks. A few of them sported copies of *Pub Lunch Trails*, a local publication that heartily recommended the beer at the Lamb and Flag. Empty tankards sat discarded on the pavements and the stone church wall. It was a circus.

'Damn it!' There were no sunglasses to be found.

Her car inching forward at a snail's pace, Lyndsay was growing hot and flustered, eager to be through the village before someone recognised her. How thoughtless not to have foreseen this. She pressed the button to close up the window. Curious unknown faces, jaded faces, were peering and squinting at her and then suddenly someone yelled her name with the force of a goal scored. Men and women with microphones flocked around her while video cameras began to film her through the glass. People were jostling and cursing to get at her.

'Mrs Potter, do you believe…?'

'Is it true that your son…?'

'What is your opinion about…?'

She was trapped. It was worse than a nightmare. She kept moving, trying not to endanger the bodies scrambling over the bonnet in an attempt to film her. A part of her was desperate and longed to hit the throttle and cut savagely through them, carve them up, mow them down, be shot of the lot of them, accursed journalists!

Suddenly a resounding thud on the car roof frightened her out of her wits, but it drove the journalists back, stopping them in their tracks.

'Let the lady through, for Christ's sake!'

Ralph Beresford confronted the few who did not respond to his command. Lyndsay, still inching forward in the traffic, watched in stolen snatches as he manhandled one photographer and then frogmarched another to the pavement. She was bowled over by the force of his intent. So were the reporters. She lowered the window to thank him.

'You OK or you want me to drive you?'

'I'll be fine once I get through all this.'

He was alongside her, escorting her, his fingers lightly brushing the vehicle's metal shell. The gesture reminded Lyndsay of how, in the nature reserve, he had stroked the passing shrubbery. She watched his face in the wing mirror. The purpose with which he accompanied her and how, all the while, he scanned the onlookers, wary lest the car be besieged again.

'You look like you could use a drink,' he said, without regarding her. Photographers stole shots as they travelled forward.

Lyndsay shook her head. 'Thanks, I have to get back.' She would have liked a drink very much but the crowd was too daunting. Besides, she had pressing matters to attend to at home.

'I'll ask the pub to call the police and clear this rabble away.'

The truck ahead began to pick up speed. The traffic was breaking up. To keep up with it Lyndsay would have had to outstrip Beresford. She held back an instant longer. 'Thanks,' she said again.

'Give me a yell if you need anything.' With that he sprinted across to the pavement directly in front of the post office. Lyndsay could barely bring herself to look at Bharjee's store. She did not know how she would ever look Mr Bharjee squarely in the eye again. Mercifully, the shop was closed. Beresford hung back, watching her. As she pulled away he winked and gave her a wave.

She rounded the corner, heading away from the Lamb and Flag, passing the churchyard on her right. As she did so, she glanced in her rearview mirror. Gaggles of journalists were seated at the bench tables supping ale or tucking into ploughman's, drinking in the sunshine outside the sixteenth-century coaching house. Beresford strolled into view. Apparently he was also on his way to the pub. His taut concern of five minutes earlier had disappeared, and now he was laughing and chatting animatedly, at ease with himself. At his side was Annie Welch, a barmaid at the pub. They seemed disconcertingly relaxed in one another's company. Lyndsay, recalling her hour with Beresford at the bird sanctuary, wondered whether he was recounting the same tales of wildlife and adventure to his young companion.

Quigley Lane was scattered with cars slewed to left and right, parked on the road or jutting at right angles off the pavements. As Lyndsay crossed the bridge her heart began to beat faster. The media had descended upon their home. She regretted refusing Beresford's offer of company when she counted more than a dozen vehicles lining the lane. Fortunately her access to the gate had not been blocked. Reaching for the automatic command tucked in the glove compartment she squeezed gently and within seconds the iron gates swung open. Lyndsay gunned the pedal, pressed fast on the alarm box and left a throng of excited faces locked out as she sped up the drive.

This fuss is going to drive Matt further underground, she cursed as she locked the front door behind her. Her first stop was the kitchen to let the dogs out – as a precaution she wanted them to patrol the garden – and then the answering machine in Stephen's office. There were six messages, five from newspapers requesting interviews. Lyndsay could not think how they had found the number; she and Stephen were not listed. The last was from Marion Finch who sounded mildly sozzled and rather enjoying the influx of scandalous activity. Might Marion have given out their number? Lyndsay was incensed by Marion's senseless ramblings and by the insensitivity of the media and desperate because there was no word from Matt. She had been hoping that the national coverage might have encouraged him to ring home.

Where was he? What had forced him to flee? Was he safe? She switched the machine back on, deciding to screen all calls. From the drinks tray in Stephen's office she poured herself a large, much-needed Scotch.

She telephoned Matt and Paul's college. Lengthy discussions ensued between Lyndsay, the principal, Mr Challoner, and Paul's housemaster. She settled herself on the carpet in Stephen's office and drank another tumbler of whisky. Eventually the question of Paul's immediate future was settled. Churdle Bridge Farm was not the nurturing environment she required for her son at present. Unless he expressed a desire to the contrary, Paul was to remain at college and continue with his studies on the clear understanding that he was protected from the press and not accosted by the brutal interrogations of his peers. All being well, Lyndsay would collect him for the weekend on the following

Friday. If not, Richard's mother had offered to take care of him until 'everything is back to normal'. Neither Lyndsay nor Richard's mother, when they discussed it, touched upon alternatives to this rosy conclusion. Finally, she called the college again and spoke to Paul.

'Are you all right, Mum?' he asked the instant he came on the line.

She smiled at his adult-like concern. 'Yes, sweetheart, but thanks for asking. And you?' A silence ensued. It was unusual for Paul to be stuck for a response. 'Paulie, I've spoken to Mr Challoner. Would you like to come home for a few days?'

'Before the weekend, you mean?'

'Yes, if you want to.'

'Mr Challoner says I'm better off getting on with my lessons.'

'And what do you feel?'

'I'll come if you need me, Mum.'

She did not know how to answer him. Her heart nearly broke at his sensible, loving response and she ached with such longing for both her boys. 'I'll see you at the weekend, darling. Night, night.'

'Matt will come back, won't he?'

'Of course, darling.'

Evening was falling. Lyndsay had still not eaten but she had consumed copious amounts of Scotch. She was groggy and depressed, tired from several nights of fitful sleep and woozy from unaccustomed liquor on an empty stomach.

S. The nineteenth letter of the alphabet. It had been coiling like a snake in her befuddled brain all day, squeezing its insinuations tighter. Was it the answer to nagging questions that would not go away?

She hauled herself up from the carpet and, unable to face the reality of Matt's wardrobe just yet, wandered aimlessly from room to room, settling eventually in the drawing room. There she switched on the television and stared at it in a vacant semi-focused fashion. All of a sudden, in full colour on the screen, the Hampton boys and their father were staring out at her, large as life.

They were being pressed for an interview by a magazine programme that spotlighted local news in and around Kent. The interview must have been filmed earlier in the day since both boys, dressed in work clothes, were standing alongside their father who was attaching sturdy locks to the gates. Neither boy proved responsive while Mr Hampton, his face set like stone, stared straight into the lens and growled, 'Me and my family have had our fill. We want no more unsolicited callers and no more bloody microphones shoved in our faces.'

Lyndsay whooped with delight.

In the final shot of the piece a horde of journalists were shown hanging about in the lane outside the farmhouse. Mr Hampton and his sons were setting off on the tractor for their afternoon's work. Lyndsay felt overwhelmingly grateful to them. By protecting themselves she felt that they were also protecting Matthew.

Next came footage of Lyndsay battling her way through the traffic and chaos in Churdle Heath. Beresford was nowhere in view. At the sight of her anxious face she switched off, hoping Paul hadn't seen it.

Alone in the house and unable to put off the moment any longer, Lyndsay finally climbed the stairs to Matt's room. She unlocked the wardrobe and drew out the plastic bag containing her son's secret notebooks and diaries.

She methodically arranged each of these books and journals on his bed and then settled herself amongst them. S. Somewhere within these secret outpourings must be a clue; she was convinced of it.

Much of this material she had only skimmed through. There had to be, somewhere among the reams of screed, one mention of a name – dear God, any ordinary run-of-the-mill girl's name – to identify Matt's beloved, vindicate him, and set her troubled thoughts at rest. Although Lyndsay's head was swimming from booze and fear she was now determined.

Trembling, she opened the first notebook and began to scan the words but she soon lost the sense. Letters grew shapeless until, eventually, she fell into a heavy sleep. Images of Matt flooded her dreams while the mystery surrounding his disappearance lay buried amidst bedding, poetry and prose.

12

I spent dark hours outside my love's window.

Lyndsay was on the patio outside the kitchen feeding the dogs. The warmth of the sun bounced off her freckled shoulders. Already swallows peppered the crystal blue sky; the heat had come without warning. June was heralding its arrival with the promise of a deliciously fertile summer: protracted days, soft and balmy; cowslips on the ground and purple clematis climbing the trellises; white and blue columbine growing wild among the flagstones and thyme spreading like outstretched lizards among the baked pots of herbs behind the house. There was no season Lyndsay delighted in more, but today her gardens failed to cheer her. She could find no comfort in all that she had created.

I spent dark hours outside my love's window.

When she'd staggered from Matt's bed, the house had felt colder and drabber than the Hamptons'. Her mood was not helped by a hangover that had woken her at dawn with a raging thirst and a pounding headache. She had gone in search of Evian, aspirin and the whisky bottle and had settled back in Matt's bed where, tucked beneath his duvet, she had begun to read the diaries in earnest.

S. Not Sally or Susan or some school chum's nubile sister as Lyndsay had originally supposed. The identity of the female, for whom so many erotic poems, so much prose had been penned, was none other than Mrs Bharjee, S standing for Surinder. It was written there in bold letters – *Surinder, surrender* – in Matt's handwriting. It was an undeniable fact.

The wife of the Indian whose arrival had caused whispered disapproval in the community. How Lyndsay wished that Bharjee and his young wife had never set foot in the village. She, who had been so shocked by the racism she had witnessed among her upright neighbours, now virulently prayed for them to go. And then she remembered: S stood for the woman who had been sexually violated and who lay murdered in the mortuary, waiting to be cremated. How could her heart harbour so little compassion towards the young woman? Yet it did.

Once the dogs were fed Lyndsay made herself strong black coffee and returned to her son's bedroom. She should shower and change but there was time for that later. She had to read the notebooks in their entirety before Stephen returned. Only then could she decide what to do with them; whether to burn them on the bonfire in the garden.

I want so overwhelmingly to touch you, to kiss your coral lips, to make contact everlasting with you.

It seemed a harmless infatuation, nothing more to it than that, surely. There had to be an explanation. But the 'dark hours' outside the window?

She had discovered Matt ascending the stairs in his anorak. His skin had been damp. Had he been returning from a trip to Surinder's window?

The idea of Matt lurking about beneath neighbours' windows in the middle of the night discomforted Lyndsay immeasurably. Or was his meaning, the 'dark hours' of the soul? How she hoped it was.

Had Matthew, wherever he was, heard about Surinder's murder? Where *was* he? He must have seen the newspapers. Had he known of the girl's death even before her body had been discovered? Had he witnessed something? Followed her into the wood? Taken her there?

Stop! Lyndsay's mind was scrambling again. She had to put a stop to these interminable trains of thought before they drove her crazy. But there was no one to share them with, nowhere to unburden them and so the unresolved questions returned, again and again, to torment her. It seemed risible that a little more than a week ago her greatest concern had been a doubt about Stephen's fidelity.

The writings had confirmed Lyndsay's suspicion that Surinder Bharjee was the object of Matt's passions, but up until now she had read nothing to suggest he would harm her. If Matt had been so infatuated with Surinder did it not follow that he was now devastated by the news of her death? And then Lyndsay silently posed the question that she had been forcing herself to turn away from. The question she feared to give an answer to. Could it be that her own small son, innocent, not-quite-sixteen years of age Matthew, whom she had discovered smoked cannabis and wrote poems of lurid sexual fantasies, had been party to Surinder's death?

There must be others, the police, for example, who were also asking themselves that same question. He was wanted for questioning. Without doubt, when they found him or when he came forward, he would have much to answer for. But it was unthinkable. Not Matthew! She had to find him first and persuade him to declare his innocence.

Yet, if he was innocent, she failed to understand why he did not come out from wherever he was hiding and speak up for himself, clear his name. It was just conceivable that Matthew knew nothing about Surinder's death or that, even if he did, it hadn't occurred to him that suspicion was settling upon him a little more heavily as each day passed. But for how much longer would she be able to defend his innocence? When would Inspector Burgess insist on searching Matthew's belongings?

She would burn the diaries, notebooks, every word, and the grass, every last thing – and yet, they were so close to the heart of Matthew, the parts of himself he had never exposed to her, that she could not bear to part with them.

Lyndsay's mind rolled on this way and that and then it began to track backwards in time. During the weeks after her sister's disappearance, when Lyndsay's father wasn't locked away in his room playing music, he had stared vacantly from his chair, chain smoking, his saxophone clamped between his knees. The silence in their semi-detached house had been tormenting. Alone and afraid in her bed at night, she had listened to him pacing the rooms beneath her, waiting for his eldest daughter to return, waiting for news. He barely spoke. How she had grown to hate her absent sister. Becky's absence had destroyed her father's spirit. Life had continued in this fashion for almost two months, until the discovery of Rebecca's body.

After the initial shock followed by the period of mourning, the knowledge that Rebecca was dead, that she would never be coming back, had eventually brought about peace. There was no more uncertainty, no more waiting. They became a father and his youngest girl building a new life together, never referring to the past, never speaking of it. Lyndsay did everything to make it work for them both.

'Lyndsay!'

Alone in Matthew's room, she was startled by the sound of Stephen's voice. His footsteps mounting the stairs whiplashed her back into the present and activity. Quick as a flash she stuffed Matthew's scribblings under her son's duvet and pillows.

Seconds later the door opened and Stephen appeared. 'I've been calling you.'

'Sorry. I didn't realise you were back.'

He glanced round the room. 'What are you doing in here?' He was holding a newspaper in his hand.

'Tidying up.' Lyndsay realised that the clutter scattered everywhere made this a very ridiculous lie. 'I was...trying to fathom things out.'

'Look at your clothes! Did you sleep here?'

Matthew's space, crammed with his belongings, seemed like the only hold left. And now Stephen's presence was threatening that. He was the trespasser now.

'No... I...'

'Come out of here, before you upset yourself further.' Lyndsay slid from the bed, obedient but reluctant. 'Have you seen this?' Stephen waved a copy of the *Daily Mail* at her. There, on the front page, was the shot of her cursing the journalist. To see herself look so angry made Lyndsay giggle. 'What are you laughing at?'

'I look so bad-tempered. Sometimes when Matt sees me cross like that he laughs at me.'

Stephen stared at his wife uncomprehendingly and then moved to the bedside table. On it was the depleted bottle of Glenfiddich Lyndsay had taken from his den. He picked it up and set it down again without comment. 'The article states that the photograph was taken outside the Hamptons' farmhouse, is that true?'

'I think so,' she sighed, searching beneath the bed for her shoes.

'You think so! Well, were you over there or not?'

'Yes!' she shouted. 'Yes, I was! Where the hell are my – ?'

'What were you doing there? Don't you know the entire neighbourhood is crawling with press? As I speak, there are crowds of journalists at the gate. I warned you not to get involved.'

'Is that all you care about? Not getting involved? I went over there to see if I could find out anything about Matthew!' Lyndsay shoved past Stephen and hurried from the room. Wearing one shoe, carrying another, she walked as though limping.

Stephen followed instantly. 'Lyndsay, listen to me, sitting in Matthew's room moping over him is not going to bring him back. You have to pull yourself together.' They were approaching the stairs. Stephen, a few steps behind Lyndsay, reached out to hook her by the shoulder.

'Let go of me!' she yelled, spinning furiously, stumbling, and all but losing her balance. Her shoe went tumbling down the stairs. Stephen grabbed her by both shoulders and pulled her close to him. The gesture was aggressive but it saved her from toppling. Her cheeks were flushed, tears were rising and the whites of her eyes were red from exhaustion.

'I don't want you going over to the Hamptons and discussing our son with just anybody, do you understand?' He was shouting too, in an attempt to make her see sense, stubbornly determined to quieten her outburst. Rage had never before played a part in their relationship; Lyndsay's emotions were usually reined in.

She wrenched herself free. 'You are such a snob! Matt was right. I should have said something; spoken out, taken his side, reassured him that one of us understood what he was going through. Instead I tried to keep the peace.' She was screaming like a mad woman. 'All my life that's what I've done, pleased others! Kept the peace!'

Her unhinged behaviour astounded Stephen. Lyndsay had always been so resourceful and emotionally contained. Observing her as she charged down the stairs, his eyes in line with the soft sandy crown of her head, a memory returned. It was of the very first moment he had ever set eyes on her.

She had been standing at a bus stop in Lower Sloane Street, off Sloane Square. Stephen had spotted her from his car. He considered her full of pep, a blossoming creature dressed in a floral-printed, cotton dress and flat Mexican sandals.

Lyndsay didn't clock Stephen or his yellow sports car. She was gazing into space, staring along the street that, further past the bend, led over the bridge to Battersea, while dandling a woven basket filled with dried flowers. She had been to the Chelsea Flower Show and from there had stopped at Peter Jones to buy embroidery silks. She had been intending to catch a late-afternoon train back to her father's house in Sevenoaks. The bus she waited for was destined for Charing Cross Station.

Stephen had swung his Sprite to the left into a lane by Le Gavroche. He decided to weave his way back round the block to offer her a lift. Unfortunately, he had got snarled up in the traffic in front of the Royal Court Theatre. By the time he negotiated the jam Lyndsay was boarding her bus. Stephen pulled into the kerb and watched her from across the street making her way to a seat by the window. A pretty, freckled girl with shoulder-length hair styled in a modish Sassoon cut, hugging a Moroccan shopping basket tight against her neat breasts. He continued to watch even after the bus had carried her away.

He'd been sorry to lose her, for he'd wanted to invite her for coffee.

What a fateful coincidence it had been when he spotted her again, days later. He was strolling home to his recently purchased flat a stone's throw from the square and paused a second at the display of the new Frederick Forsyth thriller in the window of W H Smith when he caught sight of her. There she was at the zebra crossing, carrying her basket again, this time thick with roses. He watched her, relishing her svelte elegance, while flirting with the idea of chatting her up when she reached the pavement, but decided instead to wait for her at the bus stop.

She'd accepted his offer of coffee with a fresh-faced smile. They strolled to the Richoux shop in Brompton Road. She ordered cappuccino and downed it as though it were a silken luxury. As he spoke, quizzing her, she lowered her eyelids towards her cup. She idled the froth with the tip of her finger, which she then sucked in a manner that Stephen had found both amusing and erotic.

Later that same summer in an orchard in Kent, when the leaves were as russet-gold as her pubic hair, he took Lyndsay's virginity.

It was strange that he should remember the details so precisely after so many years. Had it been love at first sight? Not at all. Lyndsay, with her pale, freckled complexion, had appealed to him. Her purity had challenged him. He smiled at the sweet memories. And then another insinuated herself into his mind, returning with a lethal insouciance. And the aching for Gin gripped him once more.

This was not about lust. It was not about adultery. It was not about risking a family. He did not want to dismantle his family but he felt he had no alternative. The marriage had dried up and no longer satisfied him. Somewhere, sometime, when he hadn't been paying the right amount of attention, the vitality had been leached out of it and it had grown cold. Love had died.

If Matt had not gone missing he would have been gone by now.

But he could not rush away. Lyndsay could not be ditched. His love for her may have petered out but he would not leave her to cope alone, not in her present condition. And because his son was missing, he would have to bide his time. He might be a man set on a new course, but he was not a monster.

When the divorce settlement was discussed, he would demand nothing. He would leave empty-handed save for a few personal belongings, and walk away. It was no sacrifice; he had ample means abroad. Lyndsay and the boys would want for nothing. It was a small price to pay for his freedom. The greatest loss would be his relationship with his sons. But they would work something out.

Right now, the priority was to locate Matt.

'Inspector Burgess left a message. He wants to see us,' Stephen said softly. He observed the tautening of Lyndsay's spine.

'What does he want?' Her voice was tremulous and wary. She had reached the hall but she didn't look back. 'He'd like to talk to us. That was all the message said.' Lyndsay headed directly to the kitchen, not even feigning interest in Burgess' call. Stephen couldn't see her expression. 'Has something happened that I don't know about?' he called, but Lyndsay had slipped beyond earshot. He didn't know who she was anymore. He had loved her once upon a time, but that had long since gone. When Matthew returns, he thought. When she is more herself. In the meantime he'd call in Doctor Wallace to prescribe her something, and contact Burgess.

That evening when Doctor Wallace dropped by to see Lyndsay he offered her tranquillisers, which she refused. 'They'll help. You'll feel better,' he said.

She was adamant. 'Surgeries are filled with women who no longer know what they feel, who don't understand why they are in pain, why they are unhappy. I have to stay in touch, have to be in control.' She bid them both goodnight. She was thinking about Matt. She had to stay alert, for his sake.

Burgess dropped by. His only news was that the police were intending to drag the reservoirs.

Stephen, alone with Doctor Wallace, confided that he did not understand the change that had taken place in Lyndsay since her father died. 'Her reason seems to be deserting her.' From his point of view, divorce was inevitable.

In the rooms above, Lyndsay shunted furniture to and fro, moving into one of the guest rooms. A Clarice Cliff vase toppled from an alcove onto the landing. It remained there unnoticed, lying in shards on the wooden floor.

The men sat together quaffing Scotch, ruminating on life and the vagaries of womanhood while Lyndsay stole her chance. She returned to Matt's room and carried off his writings, burying them, along with the grass, beneath the mattress in the spare room where she was planning to sleep.

When Stephen climbed the stairs she locked the door, barricading it with a chair. He did nothing to stop her, did not even call out to her, and Lyndsay guessed that he was relieved.

She was worn out, but in spite of her exhaustion, her night was restless and her dreams were sinister, animated with gruesome acts of sexual violence.

13

It was Thursday. The nursery had been closed since Monday, and the wrought-iron gates of Churdle Bridge Farm were firmly locked; Lyndsay and Stephen were receiving no callers.

The grandfather clock struck the hours, chunks of time passing without event. Life was in stasis. The early summer weather had grown still and sultry. It hung like a state of suspense over their home.

Detective Inspector Burgess dropped by, of course, but he never arrived with news of Matthew, merely to pose endless streams of questions: What was Matthew wearing on the Friday in question? What were his favourite beverages? Had they ever known him drink beer? None of which seemed pertinent to their absent son's whereabouts. Mercifully, he never quizzed Lyndsay about Matt's personal belongings, but she feared the day was not far off.

She had not set light to those precious secrets. Stephen was far too present to risk carting them into the garden and burning them. So they remained in the house, buried in her hiding place beneath the mattress. The fact was she had no desire to destroy them. She needed them. They were a part of Matt, of which only she had knowledge. She clung to them jealously, cherishing them, communing with her son.

Since Stephen and Lyndsay had moved to Churdle Bridge, newspapers had been delivered to their mailbox morning and evening: *The Daily* and weekend *Telegraph*, *Time* magazine, the *Financial Times*, *The Sunday Times*, *The Economist*, the *Kent Evening Messenger*. Now Stephen extended the order to include *The Sun*, *The Mirror*, *The Independent*, *The Guardian*, *The Express* and *News of the World*. Twice a day he returned from the gate carrying virtually every printed rag on the market. These he studied with what Lyndsay regarded as prurient fascination. She preferred to avoid the barrage of reportage, considering it essential to protect herself. Stephen, on the other hand, pursued all media assiduously. There was a television in his den, linked both to cable and satellite, which he left switched on every waking hour of the day. Lyndsay opted for not viewing the endlessly updated bulletins. With television and radio she had that choice but the constant flood of newspapers proved impossible to ignore. The printed word was everywhere, strewn across tables, sofas, beds, and even lavatory seats. There was news, gossip, stories, rumours, facts and conjecture; the Matthew Potter story besieged her.

'If you despise them, why do you follow them so avidly?'

'To keep abreast of the game,' had been Stephen's response.

But if she could not escape the media then neither could Matt. He could not remain blinkered forever, wherever he was hiding. By now he must have learnt of the murder of his beloved Surinder and the worst of the speculations about himself. So, why, for heaven's sake, did he not come forward?

Bags laden with fresh meat, rice, loo paper, milk, coffee and biscuits arrived from Tonbridge with the cleaner, Maria. Fresh vegetables from Lyndsay's own greenhouses were plentiful; she had no need to buy them in. So well stocked were they that she had no reason to leave the estate, but Lyndsay was itching to get out. Being penned in was driving her crazy. In addition to which Stephen's proximity and his silent moods were oppressive. Living at close quarters with a man who no longer wanted her or their life together caused her to feel more rejected than the prospect of his imminent departure. His emotional distance was a daily reminder.

While gathering herbs from the kitchen garden, Lyndsay noticed a slender strip of lightning high above the trees. Way to the south, where the sky was steel-grey was a storm, about ten miles inland of the coast, and heading in their direction. Lyndsay was not sorry that the warm weather was at an end for the present. Heavy rain would clear her head. She snipped sprays of frizzy parsley and coriander and paused to inhale their aromatic bouquets. As she did so a gust of wind whipped through the trees, banged the back door shut and untidied strands of her hair.

She had been hatching a plan for a couple of days. She would visit the spot where Surinder's body had been found, the scene of the crime. She wanted to lay flowers there as a token from Matthew. But such an act would have to wait until after dark.

First she would drive to the coast, curl up in a beach café, drink cappuccino and watch the storm play havoc with the sea and sky. Lyndsay loved storms with their lightning, resounding claps of thunder and turbulent, regenerative energy. Later, on her way back, she would make her pilgrimage to the nature reserve.

She hurried to the nursery in search of a plant – not flowers, she decided – something that would survive the shade in among all those tall oaks and ferns. She chose an unusual but hardy moth orchid from the mountains of Borneo and Sabah. Its silky scentedness would be a homage to Surinder's swathes of hair. She also made up a basket of scarlet-red geraniums as an offering for Mrs Hampton. She went next to one of the potting sheds in search of her gardening gloves and fork, which she hurriedly stuffed in her jacket pocket.

As she was locking up, her attention was drawn to the untidy state of the place. Several of the upper shelves had been disturbed. Canisters had been moved, some had fallen on their sides, and seed packets were tossed to the floor. There was also the remains of a cigarette stub ground into the wooden boards. She bent to retrieve it and particles of the loose tobacco fell from between her fingers. Whose could it be? Tom rolled his own cigarettes, and he was a neat worker. He always cleaned up after himself, and customers never ventured to this corner of the land.

She returned to the house feeling unsettled. Was Matthew smoking cigarettes illicitly? But if he was keeping grass in his room, she didn't understand why he would feel the need to indulge his habit in her garden shed.

Burgess had asked if Matt smoked.

Lyndsay deposited the gathered herbs on the kitchen table before she went in search of her keys, which were not on the hook inside the china cupboard where she kept them. She must have left them somewhere else, in a moment of distraction.

Stephen, who was in the dining room, reading, watched in silence as Lyndsay entered and began feverishly opening drawers, raking through papers, trawling the canteen of cutlery and clinking glasses. It was obvious she was on her way somewhere; she had a bag hanging from her shoulder and an armful of plants pressed against her breasts. Earth spilled from the pots on to the floor.

'What are you doing?'

'Looking for my keys.'

'Where are you going?'

'Nowhere in particular. Just for a drive.'

'Do you think that's wise?' He chose not to mention the plants.

'We can't stay cooped up in here forever. I'm not quite sure why we've dug ourselves in like this. We're not guilty of anything. We have nothing to be ashamed of…nothing to hide.' As she spoke these last words she gasped involuntarily and then rattled on defensively. 'What I mean is our son is missing… He's not a criminal. We are the victims.'

Stephen rose, reaching out to take hold of Lyndsay but she did not want him to touch her, nor expose her vulnerability, so she slipped from the room, beyond his grasp. He followed her, talking on the move as she hunted for her keys.

'Lyndsay, when I walked down to collect the mail and the papers this morning I counted more than a dozen journalists at the gate. I am sure you don't want to be harassed by that lot. Snapping cameras, shoving microphones in our faces every time we step outside.'

'I have to get out for a while. I need…' Lyndsay broke off to turn over cushions in the drawing room, and move to the hall to check pockets of jackets and coats hanging from the hat stand by the front door. 'Blast! Have you seen them?'

'I have them.'

'Why didn't you say so? May I have them, please.' Lyndsay held out her hand expectantly. From somewhere distant she heard the heavy clap of thunder and yearned to be on her way. Stephen did not move.

'I don't think you are in a fit state to drive.'

'Don't be ridiculous! Give me my keys, please.'

'No.' He spoke quietly. There was no anger, no passion in his voice.

Lyndsay stared incredulously. 'Give me my keys!'

'Lyndsay, you are more stressed than you realise. Your nerves, understandably, are frayed. I don't think you should be behind the wheel. It's for your own sake I've taken them and I am not going to let you have them back.'

'Give me my keys!'

'I think you are going mad!' he yelled, and then sighed at his own loss of control.

Lyndsay strode off in the direction of the kitchen. Choosing not to push past him, in case he forced her back, obliged her to exit by the back entrance. She scooped up her plants and slammed the door after her.

To reach the gravel forecourt, where both cars were parked, meant circuiting the house. She ran fast in case he intercepted her but a quick look reassured her that the front door remained closed; Stephen was leaving her be. She hoped that he had been bluffing, that her keys were in the ignition, but when she opened her Mercedes they were not. He was leaving her alone because he knew damn well she couldn't go anywhere. 'Sod him! The bloody bully!' she cried aloud.

Her gaze settled on his Porsche. She cast a surreptitious glance back towards the house. In case of an emergency, Stephen always left a spare set of his own keys in a magnetic box beneath the left rear wheel. She bent low, scratched her fingers inside the wheel-arch and found them instantly. Another clap of thunder sounded. The storm was drawing closer. She gunned the engine and, within seconds, she was spinning the gravel and roaring down the drive, plants on the seat at her side. Approaching the exit, she jabbed the remote control and the gates glided open, revealing a throng of hungry journalists.

'Shit!' Lyndsay took a deep breath, pressed the accelerator hard against the floor and swung out to the right. In her frenzy to escape, she misjudged the turn. The tyres of the Porsche screeched, the car careered, and narrowly missed a van approaching from the right.

She straightened up, regaining control. This sports car was far nippier than her sturdy four-wheel drive. Through the rear view mirror she glimpsed the knot of men and women at the gates, staring after her in disbelief, but she felt no triumph; she was shaken.

Twisting and turning along the lanes, she headed for the main road, smarting over the hostility building up between herself and Stephen. It was a while before she drew her thoughts back to her surroundings and, when she did, she realised that she hadn't hit the coast road after all. Unless she was mistaken, she had overshot a turning and was astray on the Churdle Heath side of Uckford. It was difficult to gauge where precisely because she had driven right into the bad weather and the storm was upon her. The change had been instant, from clear skies to grey blindness. She was unable to make out lights or boundaries and she knew she should pull over, but she couldn't make out the edge of the road.

An arsenal of sudden sheeting rain was falling fast, rapping against the glass. Quick as she could, in this unfamiliar car, she groped for the wipers. The whip in the wind caused even the Porsche to feel unsteady. And, lights! Lights to full beam. She was driving against a blanket of weather, but there was now sufficient glare to decipher banks of trees flanking her. From the tall oaks and dense forestry she could see she was approaching the nature reserve. Although from which direction, she had no idea.

Knowing where she was she felt calmer. She knew all these boundary lanes intimately. Still, she would be well advised to find a spot to shelter in. No other vehicles were about. Mercifully, she drew alongside a clearing, swung into it and parked.

Cocooned within the dry, enclosed space of the still vehicle, she became aware of her heart. Its palpitations beat in rhythm with the rain pounding against the roof. She flattened her cheek against the window, her flushed skin brushing cool glass. It was nigh on impossible to identify the entrance she had found herself in front of, to establish whether it was park side or reservoir side.

The police had been dragging the reservoirs. Oh, Matt!

She pushed her face hard against the glass until the pressure stung and calmed her. It was black as night out there, yet it was only four o'clock. She wouldn't be going to the coast today after all. She considered the two plants on the leather seat alongside her. If she were able to locate her position she could walk to where Surinder's body had been found and plant the orchid on Matt's behalf. There need be no anxiety about watchful eyes; not a soul would venture out in this weather. She took up the plant, got out and locked the car.

The rain pelted her, drumming like busy fingers against her bare head and jacketed shoulders. Still, the biting elements were purging. She felt invigorated, could breathe freely. If she wasn't mistaken this was the western sector of the reserve; nearby was a popular picnic area. On the path ahead, should be located half a dozen wooden benches and tables. She pulled her jacket tight across her breast and set off into the woods.

Within minutes she had reached the picnic furniture and the sign indicating three nature trails. She smiled, knowing precisely where she was. The middle route – the one she chose – would lead her to within half a mile of where Ralph Beresford had discovered Surinder's body. From there the going would be tougher for she would need to cut through a ferny tract. Even so, if she made good time she could plant the orchid and be back at the car by five. After, she'd deliver her geraniums to Mrs Hampton and then head for home.

The wind pricked against her skin like needles, but it was strangely agreeable. She was glad to be in the fresh air, elated to be out of doors; liberated.

Being incarcerated in the house with Stephen was driving her crazy. It exacerbated and confused the complexity of emotions building within her. Stephen's analysis, that Matt's disappearance was sending her loopy, might be partially true but it was far from being the entire story. Of all people, Stephen was the one she should have felt safe with, should have been able to reach out to. Instead of which she felt pain at his infidelity, his coldness, his leaving. She felt trapped and suffocated by his judgements and emotional distance, yet the idea of losing him filled her with dread and panic.

She couldn't blame him. She had hidden too vital a part of herself from him. The fact that she had never found the courage to trust him with the truth was rather bewildering to her now.

She had had the opportunity when he'd questioned her that first afternoon, all those years ago. But she hadn't seized it.

He had picked her up at the bus stop and then walked her to a coffee shop near Harrods. She'd never been inside such a place. The waitresses had worn Victorian dresses and aprons. She'd ordered two cappuccinos, one directly after the other. As she drank, luxuriating in the froth and creaminess, she'd chattered unself-consciously about the Chelsea Flower Show and the roses she'd purchased there.

'You seem keen on plants,' he'd said, laughing.

'I love nature,' she'd replied, blushing shyly because he was staring so intently. She'd found him debonair. His handsomeness had made her want to swoon. She was a naive nineteen-year-old – ten years Stephen's junior.

'Tell me about your family,' he'd asked.

'I live with my father in Sevenoaks. My mother died,' she'd whispered confidingly, 'when I was eleven.'

'An only child?'

Lyndsay had preferred to steer clear of the subject. These were jealously protected secrets. Eventually, though, she had admitted that there had been a sister, a few years older, who had gone.

'Gone?' teased Stephen. He had been enchanted by her choice of vocabulary. 'Married, do you mean?'

'No.'

'What then?'

Why was he insisting? It was too soon to confide, to share such sordid affairs with a tall, charming stranger. 'She's dead,' she'd admitted eventually.

'Your sister is also dead! Was there an accident?' Lyndsay had refused to be drawn further. 'You're very coy, I like that,' he'd whispered in her ear in the downstairs booth where they'd tarried, long after the other customers had paid and gone.

'Sensitive.' He'd rolled the word on his tongue as though it were an act of sex.

The creamy, puff-pastry horn cakes had been wheeled away on trolleys and stacked in the kitchens for the night. Lyndsay had been thinking about her train.

'I must go,' she'd murmured.

'Not yet.' His hand had brushed her cheek. 'You have beautiful skin, freckled. You remind me of a tiger lily,' he'd laughed gently. 'Or one of the fairies in *A Midsummer Night's Dream*.' He was as romantic as a prince. 'So innocent,' he'd exhaled.

From that very first encounter, she recollected now, her young self had cast Stephen in the role of saviour, her saviour. The idea of exposing her damaged life to one so suave had seemed an impossibility. If he had been acquainted with the truth, he would have been repelled, and she had dreaded his rejection.

Stephen demanded impeccable standards. Her innocence was what he'd sought. He would have been ashamed of her past, disgusted by it. She could never have come clean. She would have risked the marriage she had set her sights on, the home overrun with children and dogs she'd yearned for. These dreams had meant the world to her. She'd dreamed of gardens, of mushroom- and chestnut-picking expeditions in Wellingtons, of log fires and Agas and home-made bread. His bachelor-pad in Knightsbridge, his yellow sports car, and his regular table at Annabels hadn't mattered a hoot to that virginal girl with her bare legs, her sandals and neat, bra-less breasts. It was wholesomeness she'd craved, ordinary family values.

Later Stephen had told her that he'd believed only antiquated spinsters took an interest in growing and drying flowers. 'Until I met you. Who else, at the onset of the eighties, pots plants as a hobby?'

'It's not a hobby!' she'd retaliated. 'One day I want my own nursery!'

The deeper Lyndsay trekked into the woods the darker it became. She reached into her pockets for matches but there were none. If she had thought to bring a digging fork, why hadn't she remembered a torch? She could feel the brush of the branches either side of her. As she touched them, as they caressed her sleeves, she recalled Ralph Beresford, but she knew that it was fruitless to hanker after him.

It was drier here under the umbrella created by the overhead branches. All the same, she was sodden. After ten minutes of steady walking, the path became a dirt track and then began to lose its definition altogether. She was reaching the undergrowth. From here the going would be less easy, or so she thought, but when she arrived at the first clumps of fern a path of sorts continued. A route had been cut through or trampled out by the armies of police and journalists who'd been visiting the site. She hadn't counted on such good fortune.

Lyndsay found the area of the crime scene with little difficulty – it was cordoned off – but the precise point where the body had been uncovered was harder to locate. She dropped onto her haunches and, in the crepuscular light, began to root about the earth for the easiest place to dig. The soil was damp and soft, smelling richly of nature. Lyndsay eased her orchid from its pot and laid it gently on its side. Then she began to gouge out the moist earth.

A thorn or piece of flint sliced the tip of one of her fingers. It stung sharply, all the more so because her hands were wet and chilled. When she sucked it, she tasted blood. Its tepid viscosity clung to her tongue and made her queasy. She rifled through her pockets and found the gloves that she'd brought with her but had forgotten to wear.

She dug quickly and efficiently, like a small animal burrowing, for now that she was here, even in the midst of such lush growth, she found the location eerie and claustrophobic. It was deadly silent except for a curtain of relentless rain that seemed to be closing in around her. Grotesque and explicit images of Surinder's struggle – those shy coal-black eyes, which Matt had soliloquised about at length, frozen in terror – haunted her mind and the forest darkness. Lyndsay heard a girl's scream. She gasped audibly. No, it was a bird's cry from afar, not Surinder screaming, although she felt the spooking presence powerfully.

She grappled for the orchid and set it into the cold earth. Her trembling fingers were clumsy as she scraped, refilling the hole she'd dug. Images of graves swam before her. She wanted to be away from here and could not imagine what had possessed her to come. Her legs were numb from kneeling on the wet ground. As she gathered up her spade and scrambled to her feet, breathing like an asthmatic, she heard something. Something shuffling in the undergrowth close by. She heard it distinctly: a rustling, encircling her.

Her heart was beating as though it might explode. She was perspiring and shivering beneath her thermal jacket. She had panicked herself and was now too terrified to take a step and too terrified to stay. Had it been an animal? A badger, perhaps, foraging for supper? If she made a dash for it, would she run head on into the murderer? The murderer! Why had that possibility never occurred to her? Someone lurking near the scene of his crime, stalking his desecrated territory!

Without further hesitation, Lyndsay bolted. Low branches whipped her face. Briars ripped her clothes. She was petrified of tripping, of losing her way in the dense undergrowth, but she could not ease up. She ran on panting, tears staining her hot cheeks, crashing forwards for her life, not daring to listen, not wanting to know who was behind her. She had reached the trail, could see more clearly now, and her eyes had adapted to the darkness.

A bend in the track was up ahead. She slowed to gather breath and, as she did, she heard the awful sound of scraping, like a shovel against stones. She began to whimper, gasping for air, her reason deserting her. She heard a thud, something landing hard on wet earth behind her. It was closer than the last noise had been. She uttered a cry and sped on, tripping, stumbling, stubbing her feet against stones and stumps but never slowing for a second until she reached the car.

She dug the keys from her pocket and reversed into the empty lane. She knew her way and drove fast. Had there really been someone in the wood, patrolling the scene of the crime, or had she freaked herself conjuring scenes of murder? Muddied, scratched and drenched as she was, whatever comments Stephen made about her appearance she would never, never, own up to him about where she'd been.

She swung the wheel to negotiate a bend. Suddenly, from out of nowhere, a shadow swooped towards her, darkening the windscreen, crashing against the glass. She began to scream, believing it to be a hooded figure lunging at her. The wipers thrashed its bloodied blackness like a duster from side to side. It was a huge crow, blown in the storm, dead against the glass, tangled in the wipers. She had to get rid of it. She hit the brakes hard to stop the car and began to skid. The wipers were beating the bird's body back and forth, butchering it.

There were lights ahead, to the left of her. No, to the right. A pub, a garage, she couldn't make out which. The lights drew closer, looming like tiger's eyes, bearing down upon her. She heard the screeching of her skidding brakes, like an animal being torn to pieces.

Beyond the bloodied windscreen it was dark, it felt like night but it was still day. She had lost all sense of time, of place, of what was happening. She could not make out what to do as she rotated the wheel, this way and that and back, trying to stop the out-of-control car. She began to shout as the Porsche ricocheted with a momentum of its own. There was an almighty thud and her head was slapped against the windscreen, which splintered instantly into a crystal spider's web. Beyond it, the car's rocking body began to smoke.

The door was being wrenched open, voices were shouting.

What had happened? She had no idea. She had bitten her tongue. Sweet, sticky blood coated her taste buds.

'Can you move? Give me your hand. There's an ambulance on its way.' Someone was heaving her from the car.

Her forehead was trickling blood, snails' trails of blood. What did that remind her of? She prodded its stickiness. She had to move, escape the fumes; the smell of petrol was engulfing her. 'I have to go home,' she said. The words were difficult to form. 'Must get the car back to... Did I hit something?'

'No, there's no one, nothing there. Try to stay still,' said a commanding voice.

The air was wet and smoky. The stench of tyres, of burning rubber was overpowering. Lyndsay couldn't abide it. It made her want to vomit, and then, as the thought was formed, she was retching in the rain. 'I...must get home.'

'Let's go inside. You'll catch cold out here.'

It was a pretty country pub. She felt relieved to be walking. The wind was picking up. In the beer gardens to the left of her, trees were swaying. Chairs lay on their sides. She stood a moment to regain her balance. Only then did she realise that she was leaning against somebody: a man. He was holding her, guiding her. It was the man who had been talking to her. She was drenched. Was it blood or rain? The wind was whistling around her, but inside her head was ringing with an assortment of sounds including his soothing voice.

There was another woman. That was the phantom she had been grappling with: the shadow of a woman between Stephen and herself. 'There's another woman. That must be why there's...estrangement between us,' she repeated aloud. Her words were skew-whiff, her tongue felt heavy with the blood in her mouth. 'He's met someone. My fault. Drove him away.' She began to weep, silent sobbing tears.

'Come inside and sit,' the voice repeated.

She nodded, accepting the kindness obediently, having no will of her own. The stranger led her, his arm around her, as though she were made of glass.

Inside it was fuggy with a different, less threatening, smoke than the one she had just walked away from. Machines were popping and bleeping, flashing robotic lights. Pinballs were scuttling. Lights blinded her and the queer smell of kegged beer and toasted cheese made her want to throw up again. Somewhere out of sight billiard cues were clicking against balls. It was a soothing, stress-free sound like listening to dominos falling, or pebbles washing against one another on a beach.

'Mrs Potter? Jesus!' Another man was there.

Eyes in every direction were staring, curious to know about the accident. A chair was delivered, and Lyndsay was seated upon it, positioned half in, half out of a lounge bar. A big woman with full yellow hair arrived and handed her water. Lyndsay accepted it gratefully. She was aware of how parched her mouth felt, and how bitter. She tasted bile as well as blood. She thanked the woman and attempted to lift the glass to her lips, but her grip was too weak. She needed both hands. Her nails were encrusted with earth. The publican's wife watched on, clucking words of encouragement, smelling of a sweet cloying perfume and of tobacco. Her voice was brusque and husky. 'We've called you an ambulance, dear. It'll be here any moment now.'

'No! I have to go home.' Lyndsay tried to rise.

A hand on her shoulder pressed her firmly back in to her seat. 'Later.'

'What about the car?' Her voice was thin as frayed thread. Words stuck on her palate. Her tongue felt large and awkward.

'It'll be taken care of. Is there someone we should phone for you? Your husband, is he at an office?'

'What day is it?' The question caused a murmur of surprise.

'Thursday, love.'

'He's away,' she lied.

One of the two men reappeared. It was not the one who had hauled her from the car and delivered her here. The man's arrival allowed the publican's wife to leave. Thankful for his return, grateful to him for his willingness to take control, she was free to staff her till.

'I'd prefer to go home,' she said, to no one in particular.

The new man was wearing a jacket that was glisteningly wet. His damp hair lay dark and flat on his forehead, against skin that was burned by the sun. He drew up another chair, placed it alongside her, sat down. 'I'll come with you to the hospital, Mrs Potter, and then make sure you get home safely.'

She turned to study him. He knew who she was. 'My handbag,' she said. 'In the car.'

'No, I went and fetched it. I stowed it in my van for safekeeping. Unless you want it now, that is?'

She shook her head, still studying him. He had kindly eyes as blue as agapanthus flowers. He smiled when she stared: Ralph Beresford. His hair darkened by the rain, she hadn't recognised him. She began to weep because she was pleased to see him. Beresford laid his hand across hers. She wanted to hold it, to rest against him.

'I've been trying to phone your husband but the answering machine is on. I'd rather not leave a message... I looked in your bag for the number, I hoped you wouldn't mind.'

'Don't call him!' It was said before she had thought about it. 'I mean, not yet. I... I'm not hurt. I don't want to worry him.'

'We'll have you home in no time,' he reassured her. A blue light was dancing like a mobile bruise across his face. Puzzled, she turned to see what was outside. She hadn't heard the ambulance arrive. Two men in uniform climbed out of it and walked towards them. Lyndsay stared nervously at the men and then beyond at the spinning light above the vehicle. Its light was richer, more violet, than the petals of an iris.

'Can you walk?'

She nodded and rose unsteadily to her feet. Beresford took her lager glass of water and rested it on the patterned carpet.

'Thanks for everything,' he called out to the publican and his wife. And then more softly, 'I'll follow in my van. I'll try your husband again from the hospital.'

Lyndsay nodded as she was led away.

14

The telephone began to ring as Stephen crossed the hall. He left it since the answering machine was on, telling himself he'd play the message after he'd dealt with whoever was at the gate. It was most likely one of those infernal journalists making a nuisance of themselves again. Every hour or so throughout the day, at least one or other of them had buzzed. It was turning into a damned annoying habit. Bored, or nagged by their editors, they plagued the house. He had already called the police in Tonbridge to get rid of them but, as soon as the police were out of sight, they were back again.

'Yes?' His tone was brusque.

'Mr Potter, it's Inspector Burgess.'

Stephen glanced at the grandfather clock. It was quarter to seven in the evening. 'Have you news of Matthew?' he quizzed. Lyndsay had been gone for over three hours. Where the hell was she?

'No, but I need a word.'

Did this man never go home? Stephen sighed and pressed the button to release the gate. 'Make sure –'

'No one sneaks in after me. Yes, I know the routine, Mr Potter.'

While Stephen waited for Burgess he slipped back to his study, to the answering machine. There was no message, which didn't surprise him. It had become a frequent occurrence during these past days. Lyndsay had voted for turning the machine off. 'It might be Matt,' was her argument. Stephen had reasoned that if

Matthew wanted to relay news of his health or his whereabouts he'd leave a message, but he was beginning to revise that opinion, was beginning to come round to Lyndsay's point of view. Suppose it was their boy trying to make contact? Too terrified and in need of help. He quickly tapped 1471 and identified an Uckfield number, a public telephone box. He dialled the number and found it engaged. Stephen switched the machine off. It was better to receive the undesirable calls – the lunatics, the press or the downright inquisitive – rather than deter Matthew.

The doorbell sounded. Since last Sunday the Inspector had passed by every day to ask a whole series of apparently irrelevant questions, none of which, as far as Stephen could see, had any bearing on the case. The day before he had asked Stephen, 'Under normal circumstances Bharjee would have cremated his wife this week. Out of the question now, of course. The man must be bitter about it, wouldn't you think, Mr Potter?' Stephen had not given Bharjee's loss a second thought. He was convinced that this linking of Matthew with the Indian's wife was nonsense, a part of the hysteria that so frequently accompanies a murder hunt.

Stephen was equally sceptical about Mrs Hampton's statements. He did not believe that she had seen Matt and the Indian woman together. 'Matthew was skulking in the cemetery, keeping close to the wall, staying in the shade.' What sort of fanciful claptrap was that? An ignorant woman's fabrication. In all probability Mrs Hampton hadn't had a notion who was moving about in the shadows, and had cited Matthew because, once speculation had been seeded, she had convinced herself of the fact. Or an altogether more disturbing reading was that one of her own sons had been mixed up with the girl and she was covering for the lad, throwing the law off the scent.

Stephen had not voiced these theories to anyone, and would do so only when it was opportune, if Matthew did not return.

The fact was he had been damned sure his son would have been home by now. Clearly, his instinct had been wrong. He did not for one second believe that Matt was guilty of any crime nor did he think he had initially intended to run away. And he certainly did not believe that Matthew was dead. They would have found the body by now.

In their search for Matthew the police had dragged the reservoirs. They and their dogs had scoured fields, pastures, woods, the nature reserve and, eventually, the bird sanctuary. Many of the breeding birds had decamped. There had been an ornithological outcry. The ospreys had disappeared without trace, while their eggs had been found some distance from their nesting area, crushed. The police claimed that the damage had not been of their making. Ralph Beresford, when asked by the press, had made no comment.

Stephen believed that the media were a contributing factor in Matthew's continuing absence. The press would deny their responsibility of course, but such a hullabaloo would intimidate any boy. Nothing but a sordid drama with its soap opera coverage had driven their son underground and this was precisely why it was imperative that he and Lyndsay keep their heads down. The less the media had to feed off, the better were the odds that Matthew would resurface, and the less all of this would distress him.

Lyndsay's roaring away like a lunatic had been childish and irresponsible. Such lack of restraint left Stephen short-tempered. And now Burgess was at the door. Stephen was not in the mood for this interrogation. He preferred to be in control, calm and well balanced, when dealing with the likes of the Inspector. He would take him through to the drawing room, offer the man a large Scotch and have one himself.

'Good evening.'

'Come on in, Inspector.' Burgess removed his hat and stepped into the hall. 'Let me take that. It looks rather damp.' Stephen was referring to Burgess' raincoat, which was duly removed and, along with the trilby, left to hang on the stand in the hall. Under it, Burgess was wearing a worn, ill-fitting brown suit, which might explain why the mac always remained on.

'I drove through a hell of a storm. It blew up quite suddenly.'

'Yes, I noticed it through the window.'

'You haven't been out today then?'

'No, I had no need.'

'The sky's clearing now. I'm very fond of storms, aren't you?'

'Not especially.'

'They clear the air. Nature's way of hurling away the dead wood.'

'I never thought about it like that.'

'Rather like human tragedy. Tragedy takes a man back to the essentials, wouldn't you agree?'

'Sounds like Lyndsay's territory, not mine. Do come through.'

'Those gentlemen of the press are still outside, I see.'

'We keep our distance.' Stephen led Burgess through to the drawing room. As he walked, the police officer scanned from right to left and threw an appraising glance up the stairs. Nothing had changed. A picture that the day before had been crooked by a centimetre had been set straight. Lack of precision irritated Burgess. He liked things to be accurate, in their place. They entered the drawing room. 'May I offer you a drink, Inspector?'

'Something soft.'

'Sure?'

'I'm on duty, and driving.'

'Yes, of course. Do sit down. What can I get you?'

'A tonic water will be fine.'

Stephen walked to the cabinet and pulled open both doors. Inside, it was panelled with illuminated, peach-tinted glass. Bottles, tumblers, brandy balloons and liqueur glasses were all reflected there, creating the illusion of a larger space and a greater quantity of glassware.

Burgess made for his usual fireside chair. As he sat, he pointed to the cabinet and said, 'If I'm not mistaken, that's an art deco piece, isn't it?'

A creature of precise habits, thought Stephen, catching a dozen fragmented images of the seated man in the cabinet mirrors. 'Yes, observant of you. Lyndsay is rather fond of that period.'

'Quite an exceptional piece.'

'Yes.'

'Hard to find these days, original examples. Particularly when the walnut casing is in such perfect condition. It is an original, isn't it?'

Stephen poured the drinks. 'Yes, it is,' he replied warily.

'French, isn't it?'

'I believe so.' A tumbler in either hand, Stephen stepped with a calculated smile away from the bar.

'Purchased in Paris?'

'Before we were married, yes.'

'If I were to put a price on such a piece, hazard a guess, I would say, even sixteen years ago, it would have cost…fifteen thousand pounds?'

'I don't retain such details. Your tonic, Inspector.'

'Thank you.'

Stephen settled into the opposite armchair and watched the calibrating eyes of Burgess cost every item in the room. He sipped his malt, relishing its fine body. 'So what news of Matthew? I take it that's why you're here?'

'Matthew? Nothing new, I'm afraid. No leads. No further sightings of him. Curious, a young boy disappearing like that when his photograph has been plastered everywhere.' He downed a mouthful of tonic and then continued, 'You must be very fond of Paris, Mr Potter?'

'Paris? I'm sorry, Inspector...'

'I was curious to learn that you have rented a flat there. Not due to your recent difficulties in finding a hotel room, surely?'

Stephen, unflustered, rested his glass on the fireside arm of his chair. He was preparing a response, feeling his way carefully. He and the Inspector were in direct eye contact now. Stephen regarded the rather unpleasant parched texture of the other's flesh. He was looking at a man whose life was probably not an easy exercise; a lonely man who had never succeeded at intimate human relationships. He saw someone who might have ended up on either side of the law, someone who stalked the streets alone. What would such a fellow know of love and its driving passions? What would he understand of freedom, of the burning desire to live life to the full while there was still time? Nothing. A truthful explanation would be futile. Nevertheless Stephen's regard for him, seated there as he was in his appallingly cut suit, had increased.

For French tax reasons and Stephen's need to keep a low profile, the lease of his new apartment had not been registered in his name, so it was no mean feat to have dug up the information. Burgess' sleuthing warranted a fair and, relatively honest, response and he would give one.

Ironically, before Stephen had committed himself to anything, the telephone began to ring. Stephen allowed himself a smile. A timely intrusion, he thought. 'Excuse me,' he said, rising with cool assurance. 'If you don't mind, I'll take that in my study. Please, help yourself to another tonic.'

15

'I am sorry, who did you say you are?'

'Beresford, my name is Beresford. I'm employed by the Kentish Trust, working at the nature reserve.'

Stephen could not place the caller. He glanced at his watch. The Inspector, arriving with his unexpected coup about Paris, had caused Stephen to temporarily forget the fact that Lyndsay had not yet returned.

'I see. Is it my wife you wish to talk to because if it is – ' It was now almost half past seven. Where the hell was she?

'No, that's the point. I am with your wife.' Stephen drew breath. 'Mr Potter?'

'Yes, I'm here.'

'Your wife has had an accident.'

'A car accident?'

'I'm very sorry, yes. We're at St Elizabeth's in Uckfield. In casualty. She's been treated for shock and has been mildly sedated. I was going to drive her home but the doctors will only release her if she's in the care of a relative. Not to me, I'm afraid.'

'St Elizabeth's in Uckfield, you said?' Stephen was jotting down details as he spoke. 'Are you ringing from a callbox?'

'Yes.'

So, it hadn't been Matt afraid to leave a message. 'It'll take me about half an hour. I'll leave right away. Were you with my wife when the accident occurred?' As he asked this question he scribbled the stranger's name. He was not someone Lyndsay had ever spoken of. Or was he? The name had a familiar ring to it.

'No, I was on my way for a drink in the Cock and Hare. It's situated by a pretty hazardous bend on the A22, which was where the accident happened, less than fifty yards down the road. I heard the screeching of brakes and then the crash. I wasn't the first one on the scene but, when I recognised her, I stayed with her. I tried to telephone you earlier.'

'I see. Anyone else hurt?'

'She skidded in the rain. Hit a tree. No other cars involved.'

'That's a blessing. I'm on my way.'

'I'll hang on, till you get here.' The man's accent was Australian.

'Oh, Mr Beresford. If anyone from the press…'

'You can count on my discretion. She's had a gutful already, I'm aware of that.'

In spite of a firm refusal on Stephen's part, Burgess insisted on driving him to the hospital. No doubt, the Inspector wanted more time to cross-examine him at close range. Stephen was beginning to get acquainted with this officer's pull-the-carpet-from-under-your-feet tactics, and felt sure this was the reason for the lift and for all the infernal questions. Otherwise, why else would Burgess be enquiring about Paris? He wasn't going to be caught out in such a crude fashion. Perhaps Burgess wondered if Lyndsay knew about the flat, and if the prospect of their impending split had distressed Matt and caused him to run away. Those questions would be next; but he was ready for them.

For the first ten minutes of the run both remained silent. Stephen, who had still not given Burgess an explanation for the French apartment, spoke first. 'Fortunately, Lyndsay is not injured.'

Burgess had been biding his time. 'You said there was someone with her?'

'Yes. His name sounded vaguely familiar.'

'What is it?'

'I wrote it down.' Stephen removed a note from his pocket and leaned towards the windscreen, better to read in the fading light. Burgess glanced from the road but was unable to make out the ink writing. 'Beresford,' said Stephen eventually.

'Ah, Ralph Beresford.'

Stephen stared in surprise. 'Of course, he's the fellow who discovered the woman's body. Foolish of me not to have recognised it.'

'Friend of Mrs Potter's, is he?' Stephen resented this question. He had been asking himself the same thing. 'Your wife was alone with him in the nature reserve the afternoon of the girl's murder.'

'Is that so?'

'So she said. Tell me about Paris, Mr Potter. Your flat on the rue du Faubourg St-Honoré.'

Damn Burgess! He had deliberately chosen to follow up his enquiry about the flat now, when he was disadvantaged. Stephen took a moment before replying. 'As you have accurately discovered, I have leased a flat in Paris.'

'Through one of your companies?'

'I only have the one.'

'For yourself is it, this…pied-à-terre?'

'I am not quite sure what any of this has to do with the disappearance of my son.'

'Or Surinder Bharjee's murder? It has everything to do with it. When a member of such a tight-knit community decides to move away, flee the country unexpectedly, days after a murder –'

'I was in Paris when she was murdered.'

'No! You were in Paris the day *after* her murder. And on that very same day you signed the lease on a flat.'

'Which I had negotiated the week before. Are you accusing me – ?'

'Mr Potter, I am merely laying out facts. A habit of mine. It goes with the job. Can be infuriating, I am told. So?'

'I am leaving my wife. Going to base myself in Paris, for a while. I made this decision before my son disappeared.'

Burgess kept his eyes on the road. 'What does Mrs Potter say?'

'She's accepted it.'

'How long since her father died?'

'Ten months, I think.' Stephen paused before continuing. 'I'd planned to move out last Sunday, on the morning I returned from Paris. Instead, I came home to find that my son was missing. Under the circumstances, I decided to delay my departure until Matthew returns.'

'What does he think about this move?'

'We haven't told either of the boys yet.'

'Where were you on the Friday afternoon of Surinder's death?'

'Tonbridge. I lunched at the Golden Duck and afterwards walked to a video shop to rent some tapes Matthew had requested.'

'You have receipts, witnesses, I take it?'

Stephen sighed at the tediousness of it. 'I ate alone but, yes, I can furnish you with whatever you need, Inspector.'

'Walking out on your wife seems rather heartless in the light of all that has happened during these last few months. Is there another woman?'

Stephen hesitated before replying, 'No.'

'Do you suspect your wife of infidelity, Mr Potter?'

'To be perfectly frank, the idea has never crossed my mind.'

'She's a very attractive woman. It would not be beyond the bounds of possibility. In my experience, women under stress, suffering loss, turn to the most unlikely sources for comfort. The gentleman at the hospital with her now, for instance...'

'Excuse me, Inspector Burgess,' Stephen sighed and drew breath. He should have driven Lyndsay's Mercedes and not have allowed himself to be browbeaten into this bloody awful cat-and-mouse game. 'Might we not talk about what really concerns us both? The disappearance of my son.'

'Do you consider your wife to be mentally stable?'

'Of course.'

'When I first visited your home last Sunday, the morning you rolled up after an overnight stay in Paris and found me in your drawing room, I noticed that her responses were – shall we say – resentful.'

'Our son has disappeared. I was away, and unobtainable. She was anxious, understandably. Any woman would have been. You yourself have described her as a woman under stress.'

'Ah yes, she had been unable to reach you. No hotel rooms available. City overrun with, a convention wasn't it? Yes, I remember you saying that.' Stephen made no response. 'Why was Mrs Potter driving your car today and not her own?'

Stephen glanced towards a delivery van overtaking them: a florist shop from Royal Tunbridge Wells. Lyndsay knew the owners. Burgess was inching him into corners. 'I had the keys to her car.'

'Any particular reason why?'

'I drove it this morning,' he said after a second's hesitation, opting for the lie at the very last moment. It was out of character for Stephen to speak without due reflection. It seemed that Burgess had checked up on his fabrication about the convention in Paris, damn him.

'I see.'

Stephen sensed Burgess' misgivings and hoped he was not going to regret this second lie later. This journey was becoming interminable.

Burgess steered in silence for a few minutes. He drew a packet of Silk Cut cigarettes from his raincoat pocket and pressed the automatic lighter in the dashboard. 'Those American Express receipts you mentioned last Sunday would be most useful for our files.'

'I'll ask my assistant to organise copies for you.'

'Amanda Graeme. How well do you know your assistant?'

Stephen sighed and closed his eyes. 'If you are trying to insinuate that there is something between Amanda and myself on a personal level, you couldn't be further from the truth.'

'I never for one moment thought there might be.'

'Then why are you asking the question?'

'Idle curiosity. Do you approve of wife-swapping, nudist parties, that sort of carry on, Mr Potter?'

'I beg your pardon?'

'I believe it is practised a great deal in the Home Counties. Golf clubs, yachting circles. Never having had a wife I wouldn't know.'

This apparent random shifting of topics flummoxed Stephen. He found the veiled questions and innuendos infuriating because he could not tell where they were leading. 'I know nothing about such activities.' His voice was guarded. He lifted a hand and rubbed at his face.

'You and your wife don't mix with couples in such circles, then?'

'Of course not!'

'You own a yacht, though?'

'You know we do!'

'Moored at Bosham, I believe.'

'I furnished one of your officers with all the details several days ago.'

'Do you belong to the club there, socialise with other yacht owners?'

'Inspector Burgess, I am beginning to feel as though this journey is an inquisition!'

'Forgive me, Mr Potter. If you have friends who might have taken Matthew in, I need to know about them. We are attempting to find your son for you.'

Stephen closed his eyes. Was he growing excessively nervy, or was this man profoundly disagreeable? Burgess was trying to corner him and it had been remiss to give him the upper hand by revealing his discomfort and by unconsidered lies. 'The yachting crowd are simply casual acquaintances, nothing more. I shouldn't for one moment think that Matthew knows the surnames of any of them, let alone their addresses, any more than we do. If anyone in Bosham had been likely to befriend Matthew, I can assure you my wife would have telephoned them already.'

'You sport a very elegant watch, Mr Potter.'

Stephen dropped his arm and glanced at his watch. 'What about it?'

'A Rolex, if I'm not mistaken.'

'Correct.'

'What does Matthew wear?'

'Also a Rolex.'

Burgess said no more on that topic. 'Did your wife or your late father-in-law ever talk to you about their past?'

'What about their past?'

'Mrs Potter's sister went missing, I believe.'

'She died.'

'According to the newspaper clippings of the time she disappeared. Coincidentally, or perhaps not, it was hours after discovering her mother's dead body in a bath of blood. The mother committed suicide. Cut her wrists with a razor blade.'

Stephen glared out of the passenger window at the sodden bank alongside him. Branches lay like brittle skeletons in the roadside, debris from the violence of the storm.

'I take it you weren't au fait with all this?'

'No.'

'I am afraid, Mr Potter, it will be public information tomorrow. *The Sun* newspaper has dug it up. They are running a double-page spread on it.'

Stephen closed his eyes in disgust. 'Christ!'

'I thought it prudent to warn you. Thought you might both prefer to hear it from me. Nothing I could have done to suppress it, I'm afraid.'

'Is there likely to be information in all of this reportage that my wife doesn't already know?'

'Difficult to gauge whether a girl of that age, eleven at the time, I believe, knew the details precisely.'

'Does she know about the article?'

'Ah, that I couldn't say. It is conceivable that the newspaper contacted her for a comment.'

'I don't see how, without my knowledge. We have been alone in the house together since Sunday, except...' Stephen sighed, recalling Lyndsay's emotional state when he returned from Geneva on Wednesday morning. '...I think she would have confided in me. No one has called her today. I haven't left the house all day. It will come as a shock to her. Lyndsay was never able to talk about the sister's death. I never knew what happened.'

'Missing about seven weeks. When the body was found, she'd been brutally assaulted and murdered. I take it, if you didn't know the story, then neither did your sons?'

'I have just told you; my wife has never been able to talk about it. If I didn't know, then I'm sure the children didn't either.'

They drove in silence for a few hundred yards.

'What provoked the mother's suicide?'

'According to the report in *The Sun* she was depressed. Her medical file showed a history of depression and mental instability. Ah, here we are, Mr Potter.' Burgess turned the car off the road and swung up to the hospital barrier. 'No history of depression or mental instability amongst any members of your family, I take it?'

'Certainly not.'

'And the boys, either of them ever been treated for – ?'

'No! I suppose this accident of Lyndsay's is going to reach the papers, as well?'

'Not if I can avoid it.'

'Good.'

'On the other hand, Mr Potter, Matthew is out there somewhere. If he is following the news this could be what smokes him out, it could compel him to pick up the telephone to his mother.'

Stephen was thankful to arrive at the hospital. He was also aware that he had contradicted his own foolish statement, about being in all day. He thought now that he should have just explained to Burgess that he had kept the keys because he had been concerned about Lyndsay's emotional condition, but there was no going back on the story now. He had lied, for a second time.

16

Stephen was alone in the dining room. Scattered across the table in front of him were a dozen different newspapers with *The Sun* prominently featured. Lyndsay's story – her mother's suicide and her sister's consequent decampment and murder – were the rag's headlines, told with the crudest of sentiments. How he abhorred such crass reportage. Lyndsay's car accident had barely been covered. Any possibility, as Burgess had suggested, that the incident might pull on Matthew's heart-strings and drag him out of hiding seemed a vain hope.

Beyond the open door his wife was on the telephone. He was vaguely aware of her taut responses though he had no idea who she was talking to. What in heaven's name had possessed Lyndsay to keep such a lurid history from him? How can you live with someone for so many years and hide such intimate details? And then he considered his own life, how little about his professional affairs, and the liabilities involved, he had disclosed. But that was different. The business predicament he currently found himself in was stressful. During this enforced sojourn in Churdle Heath certain details regarding financial transactions made by him on behalf of his current client, *El General*, the Argentinian, had begun to slide out of line. Transfers of such magnitude needed slick responses and dexterous policing. The aggravation he might be subject to if schedule dates were bungled or, worse, funds sequestered hung like a shadow over him. Sooner or later, he would be obliged to leave for a few days.

On a less troublesome note, the paperwork on his flat had gone through. Everything, on that score, was in order. It was simply a question of biding his time.

Lyndsay replaced the receiver. Stephen listened to her footsteps returning across oak floors. Paul was coming home later in the day for the weekend, which would cheer her up.

For himself, he would have liked to take a late afternoon Eurostar to Paris. In his fantasy, he would telephone Gin and invite her out to lunch the next day. It seemed a lifetime since their encounter at that café on the park. Her telephone answering machine had been his only contact with her since, not that he had spoken to her or even left a message. Would she still remember him? What a miracle though to have discovered her identity!

On the Saturday Stephen had visited Paris to conclude matters with the estate agents, the day before he had found Burgess at Churdle Heath, he had been given the telephone number of a woman – 'the copper-haired woman in the courtyard' – who had signed herself Gin Millar. On that same Saturday evening he had dialled the number from his hotel room. The message – in French – was that of a female with just a hint of a foreign accent. He had recognised her enticing voice instantly. Her glorious timbre informed all callers that they had reached the residence of Gin Millar. He had left no message, but he had been overjoyed he had traced her.

Later, during one of the recent miserable evenings at home, after Matt's disappearance, with packs of journalists beyond the gates, Stephen had been so downhearted that he had dialled the number for the second time, not knowing what he would have said, whether or not he would have introduced himself, if she answered.

'I'm calling you from England. I wonder if you remember me? We met in a bar near the Maison Salé. You asked me for a light and sat across a table from me while you smoked your cigarette…' The speech had been prepared well in advance.

Would she have remembered him? Would she have been as exultant to hear from him, as he was to rediscover her? He would never know. But what a sweet delight it had been, even from afar, to listen to her recorded voice, to the inhalations and exhalations of her exquisite being, and to know that when the moment was right he would return to Paris and declare his feelings to her.

Lyndsay approached. 'That was the college secretary. Apparently they've read the piece in *The Sun* and want to know whether we prefer Paul to come home or stay there.'

'His place is here!'

She was startled by the sharpness of Stephen's response and was about to challenge him when the telephone rang again. 'Oh, sod it,' she said, and swung back out of the room. 'Hello? I can't discuss it now… Please, I'll call later… Yes, we've seen it.' She replaced the receiver once more and sighed heavily.

'Switch the answering machine on.'

'I thought we agreed that for Matt's sake –'

'We can intercept the calls.' Remaining by the phone, she felt incapable of deciding what to do. The rustling of Stephen's newspapers punctuated the silence. 'We can intercept the calls,' he repeated, more adamantly this time.

She walked through to the study, connected the machine and returned to settle herself across the table from him. 'That was Marion Finch.'

'I suppose the entire village has seen this?'

'Probably.'

'All gossiping nineteen to the dozen.'

'I know you loathe publicity and that this must be eating away at you even more than it is at me, but it's knocked us both for six.'

'Any particular reason why you never told me about all this?' Stephen's sleeve brushed a page of newspaper and sent it floating to the floor. On it was a photograph of Lyndsay's sister, Rebecca, taken a year or two before her disappearance. Lyndsay wondered where the journalists had dug it up.

'I did tell you that my mother died,' she replied uneasily.

'You never mentioned all this! Quite a few facts to have kept hidden from a husband, don't you think? Why?'

Lyndsay swallowed. 'I've been asking myself the same question.'

'And?'

'I suppose, I was afraid you wouldn't marry me if you knew. My past was…messy, not good enough. I didn't want to gamble everything that a future with you offered. I didn't dare risk it. It seemed so perfect.'

Stephen shoved the papers out of his way, clearing a space on the table. 'A rather calculated decision for one so young,' he said coldly. 'And was your father party to the arrangement of this perfect match?'

'Of course not! I loved you!'

'Hmm.'

'I know you want to leave,' she said softly. 'I've been hoping it wasn't true, that you would change your mind, that it was just some passing whim.'

'You know me better than that!'

'Sorry, sorry, not a whim, a crisis. You're restless. I feel it, the urgency of your desire to be gone and…and…oh, God…' She began to cry. The cuts on her face were smarting and she felt hopelessly incompetent, worn out. 'I've been acting like a stupid fool, behaving irrationally, but the truth is I don't know how to *be* when I'm with you anymore. I feel as though, in your heart, you have already left and the loss makes me clumsy and inadequate.' In his eyes she read his inaccessibility and anger. 'I know we've been fighting. I'm not even sure what the fights are about any more. All I know is that everything is crashing down around me, but what hurts most is the silences, the distance… I feel as though I don't measure up to your expectations. I've tried, God knows, I've tried...' Was this the reason for her fury towards him? 'Perhaps you're right,' she continued.

'About what?'

'Maybe we are tearing at each other.'

'And so it's better that I leave. For both our sakes. Before we destroy everything.' His words sounded so final; the situation so horribly irretrievable.

'What about Matt?'

'I'll stay till he returns.'

Lyndsay stared deep into Stephen's face. 'Do you really believe he'll come back?'

'Yes.'

'That he's still alive?'

'Of course.'

Their eyes met as they both considered Matthew and their united impotency in the matter.

'Will you tell Inspector Burgess about our separation?'

'He knows.'

He had been confided in. Christ! Somehow, that made it worse. 'There is someone else, isn't there? Another woman, I mean?'

'I told you, no.'

'I mean if there is, maybe we could...'

'There isn't.'

A man leaving home for no one else, for no declared reason other than a growing distance between himself and his wife was uncommon, and unlikely. To clear out on sons and home leaving everything behind, even if the wife no longer satisfied seemed too incredible. Instinct, damaged though hers was, cautioned her. He had to be lying. She had said too much, offered too much of her pain. 'I better get on,' she said, rising from the table. She must concentrate on the arrival of Paul. She would indulge him, and try and pretend that nothing was amiss.

'Lyndsay.'

'Yes?'

'I don't think we should say anything to Paul yet.'

'What about?'

'My leaving. The poor chap has enough on his plate.'

'All right. Will you fetch him from school?'

'Of course.'

Lyndsay returned to the kitchen and finished the trifle she had begun earlier while in the background, beyond the radio, she heard Stephen starting up her car. The Porsche was a write-off. He's leaving early, she thought. He's eager to get out.

Paul and Lyndsay were in the garden when Inspector Burgess rang at the gate. She was surprised to see him and took it to be a positive sign. 'You have news?' she asked: always the same opening question.

'I need a word.' Always his same guarded response.

'Paul's here.' She would have preferred not to mar Paul's weekend with the arrival of police officers, as they were attempting to keep things on as normal a footing as possible. She had honoured Stephen's request and had disclosed nothing about their failing marriage to her small son. One trauma, his brother's disappearance, was sufficient for the present.

Lyndsay put the kettle on and invited Burgess to follow her outside to the table beneath the cherry tree.

'I won't keep you long. Just a brief chat.' Burgess watched Lyndsay carefully as she placed brightly painted, china cups and saucers on to the sun-coloured mats already laid on the wooden table. Three sets, then a fourth. Paper napkins she arranged in neatly folded triangles beneath forks alongside plates.

'Stephen's in his office. Shall I fetch him?'

'Not yet. I'd like a few words with you alone, if I may?' he said.

'What about?'

'A little matter that probably doesn't concern your husband.'

'Yes, of course.'

Burgess studied her gestures, the drop of her head, the fall of her glossy, straight hair, the set of her mouth. She was uptight, avoiding his gaze. Then a cry from the pool drew his attention. 'Ah, there he is! Young Paul!'

'Yes, he's home for the weekend. Excuse me, the kettle's whistling. You'll have a piece of strawberry tart, I hope? It's home-made.' Lyndsay ran back up to the house and the barking of dogs greeted her. She disappeared inside. 'Tea's ready, Stephen!'

'I'm on the phone!'

Whatever emotion she was hiding was riding high within her, Burgess was thinking, as he turned towards the pool, to study the small boy who had just climbed out of the water and was now wrapping himself in a too-large towel. A wasp buzzed around a dish of jam, and Burgess flicked it away with the trilby cradled in his lap. Paul was now approaching. The boy sharply resembled his father: strong featured and dark. His skin was pale but not from his mother's sandy pigment. It was pale because it lacked sunlight. He weighed him up to be a studious, intelligent child.

Burgess nodded at him, attempting a smile. 'Hello, again. Home for the weekend, I hear?'

He was uncomfortable around small children, never having had any of his own. And though he liked youngsters well enough, he found them less compulsively fascinating than adults. In most cases, kids had little to hide aside from petty misdemeanors, less cause to draw veils across their souls. It was the deformities, distortions, and warps in mankind that obsessed Burgess. To plumb the depths of the inner being was both his profession and his passion.

'No word from your brother since our last chat?' Paul glanced at Burgess uncertainly and then shook his head. 'I thought he might at least have made contact with you, eh? Have you remembered anything you want to tell me about him?'

Paul was drying himself thoroughly, shuffling and shifting, taking refuge within the bath sheet, like a tortoise standing upright. He was using the activity as an excuse to keep his distance until his mother returned and retrieved the baton of conversation. He lifted his head in the direction of the house searching for Lyndsay.

'She's making tea. And your father's on the phone,' Burgess informed him.

'I'd prefer lemonade,' muttered Paul. Avoiding Burgess' gaze, he fished out a pair of spectacles from amongst a clutter of books on the table. With these in hand he scooted off barefoot up the garden, leaving Burgess alone beneath the clear blue sky.

Lyndsay, tea tray in hand, hesitated by the door, considering Burgess. What did he want? She watched him rise from the wooden seat and squint up at the reaching branches of the tree above his head, a cherry past its flowering season. On the ground about his feet lay the bruised and scattered remains of the last of the blossoms.

'Don't look at all those dead petals. Normally I would have cleared them away by now,' she called cheerily as she approached. Paul, a step or two behind her, was carrying a tumbler filled with lemonade. 'Windfalls on the grass look so untidy. The storm destroyed the last of those blossoms. And many of my young flowers too,' she explained needlessly. Burgess sat down again at the table. 'Milk and sugar, that's right isn't it, Inspector?' I'm trying too hard, she was thinking.

Lyndsay pushed the sugar bowl and jug towards his setting and then proceeded to pour. Her right hand holding the pot trembled as the tea flowed into his cup. She steadied it by clutching hard with the left. Then she divided out slices of fresh strawberry tart, again using both hands to support the knife.

With nothing left to serve, she was obliged to sit. 'Please help yourself, Inspector.'

Burgess spooned two helpings of sugar but he refused the tart. He had no stomach for it. He would have preferred a cigarette with his tea, but he refrained.

'Stephen's catching up on some business,' Lyndsay announced as though in response to a question. Paul was digging his fork into his cake, splintering it in to a mix of crumbs and mushy fruit.

'Bit of a disappointment for you, eh, Paul?'

'What is?'

'Your father always working. Why don't you go and call him?'

Paul readjusted his glasses, staring mistrustfully at the Inspector.

'Fetch some dry shorts, Paulie, and tell Daddy, tea's ready. Then you can come back for that.'

Paul rose obediently and headed off towards the house. Lyndsay sighed visibly.

'How is he taking the disappearance of his brother?'

'He misses him, obviously. You said there is no fresh news about Matthew, so, are you wanting to see me about anything in particular, Inspector?'

'Just checking up on you, Mrs Potter.'

Lyndsay tilted her face towards him. She had been crying. In the dappled light beneath the tree the puffiness was discernible. 'Me?'

'After your accident.'

'Oh, I'm fine,' she bluffed, attempting a laugh. 'A few scratches, that's all. After a good night's sleep, I was right as rain. I do hate hospitals, don't you?'

'I take it your husband has told you about the flat in Paris?'

She flinched. How much had Stephen disclosed to Burgess? 'Does it make any difference?'

'Been going on for some while? Your marital differences?'

'Why don't you ask him yourself?' Lyndsay replied sharply.

'I already have and he assured me that his decision to leave was made and you were informed of it before Matt went running off.'

'That's true.'

'Yet, during our first meeting, when I asked you if Matthew's behaviour had been normal, you told me – and I quote – "no arguments at home, nothing out of the ordinary". Were you lying to me, Mrs Potter?'

'No... I... I didn't think he knew.'

'Any other information you might like to correct, Mrs Potter?'

Lyndsay felt her body go rigid. 'We hadn't said anything to him. I didn't think he knew,' she repeated.

'Well, if you should think of anything else...' Burgess sipped his tea but his attention remained on Lyndsay.

'Detective Inspector, if you have nothing to tell us about Matthew, then why are you here? Why? You must see that your visits are distressing.'

'Well, then, let me come to the point. We have found someone – '

'Who has seen Matthew? Oh, thank God!'

'No, alas not. We have had numerous calls from people who claim to have seen him. Cranks, most of them. Naturally, we've run checks on the possibles.'

'But?'

'If I came knocking at the door, raising your hopes every time the telephone rang, Mrs Potter, you would be a nervous wreck, and I would get no work done. My job, amongst other things, is to screen such information. When I say we have found someone, I am referring to the death of Surinder Bharjee. We are questioning a man who has come forward and confessed to the murder.'

Lyndsay lowered her cup back onto its saucer. Both the relief and the anguish on her face showed how much she had been

185

reining in. She drew a hand up to her cheek and brushed at a falling tear. 'Forgive me…foolish…' Her voice petered out.

Burgess found himself moved. It was maddening, and quite irrelevant that he had played this scene at least a hundred times during his twenty-seven years of professional life. Still, she touched him.

'So, Matthew is in the clear?' Her voice was cracked and barely audible.

'Not until this man has been found guilty, no, Mrs Potter. Not yet. We need to run a few routine tests. I will hand him over to one or two psychiatrists working with us and we'll see what the forensic guys come up with on the DNA profile. It's always possible the man is deranged, or lying.'

'Could the psychiatrists tell if he was lying?'

'Yes.'

'I see.' The thought disturbed Lyndsay. She could not bear to consider why.

'The point is that once we have issued a statement to the press later this afternoon saying that we are holding someone, Matthew might feel less intimidated, less afraid of coming out of hiding. Who knows he may even be in possession of valuable evidence, which will help us put this fellow away. Information that he was previously too scared out of his wits to own up to. The Sunday papers will cover the story, I shall make sure of it. Let's hope it draws your boy out of hiding.'

'Is it someone…?'

'Local? No. A long-distance lorry driver travelling through the area. He saw Surinder Bharjee walking, and picked her up. She was about three miles outside the village, along one of the lanes which lead to the nature reserve.' Lyndsay frowned, not comprehending. 'We believe that although she was carrying no luggage, she was running away from her husband.'

'Why?' Something horrible was taking shape in Lyndsay's thoughts.

'She had been beaten. The bruisings on her face were not inflicted by the murderer, but, as we suspected, by Mr Bharjee. We have been aware of this fact for several days now.'

'He was beating his wife? Why?'

'We don't know why. He has admitted to the violence, but will give no reason for it. He did mention that Matthew was frequently in the store.'

S. Slipping into Surinder, I Surrender.
I am your captive. Your loins squeeze against me, press into me, funnelling my juice.

Love me Surinder, lift me from this life.
Take my sex, Excalibur, and give it LIFE. Lift it from the earth, flush it with power and let us ride together, soaring skywards on its silver spume.

Matthew's love object, the subject of his erotic passion. Adolescent scribblings, she had judged Matt's words. Nothing more.

Lyndsay lifted her hands from her lap and wrapped them tight around her midriff in a hugging gesture. 'I told you, he goes there to buy stamps.' Why was Bharjee beating her?

'She'd been dead almost sixty-eight hours when they dug the sperm out of her at the mortuary. Who knows, there may be more than one source of sperm. Bharjee's and...?'

Lyndsay was afraid to follow her thoughts into the dark places they were leading her. What if Matt's writings were more incriminating than mere adolescent fantasies? What if her fifteen-year-old son had actually become involved in a sexual relationship with Surinder Bharjee? Had Bharjee discovered his wife's infidelity and in a state of rage beaten her? Threatened to kill his wife's lover – did he know her lover's identity? No, he couldn't possibly, or he would have revealed it. Had all of this compelled Matthew to plot a crazy elopement with Surinder?

Anything you want, you got it.
For you my darling S I would abandon the constraint known to
the likes of my mother and father as Reason.

Then, somehow, their plans had gone wrong. Surinder had ended up dead, brutally murdered, and Matthew, in a state of shock and guilty panic, had fled. What if Matthew were found and tested? All those erotic fantasies... His sperm tested...

'He's only a boy!' Lyndsay blurted out. 'I'm sorry, forgive me, I... Your news... He's been gone so long, alone, out there.'

Burgess studied her with measured concentration from across the table. 'I shouldn't be surprised if he weren't home tomorrow night. It'll relieve you of that pack of journalists at the gate.'

'Why should it?'

'Tomorrow when the story breaks about the driver who has confessed his crime, whose name we will not disclose, Matthew will be of little interest to them. Their goal will be to unearth the identity of the anonymous murderer.'

'But Matt has gone. He's still missing.'

'People vanish all the time, Mrs Potter. Devastating for you, of course, but not national news.'

'But suppose when Matt reads that the murderer has given himself up, suppose he still doesn't come home?'

'Why wouldn't he, Mrs Potter? He's not guilty of any crime, is he? He will have nothing more to fear.'

'No. I don't know. I dread that he might never come back. And then what will become of him?'

'A youth who ran away from home; a figure in a statistic.'

'I don't follow...'

'Our nation's nomads. Impossible to keep tabs on them. They drift from town to town, sleeping in boxes, taking drugs, begging for money, stealing for it.' Lyndsay blanched, shocked by the violence of Burgess' views on this subject. And she was concealing her son's drug habit from a police officer, no matter how minor the offence might be. 'A faceless class,' Burgess continued, observing the way she bit her lip. 'Amongst these drifters crime breeds and festers. It's simple for a young fellow to slip in with them. Creep in through a crack in the ever-evolving chain and survive, if one can call such an existence survival. These days, Mrs Potter, in a society of shifting values, people vanish all the time. It's a modern malaise. But your young Matthew is different. He *will* return, I feel sure of it.'

Rebecca did not, thought Lyndsay.

'You never suspected that Matthew might be taking drugs?'

'Drugs?'

'Hashish, that sort of thing.'

She shook her head. 'No, no of course not.'

'And he doesn't smoke?'

'No.' She tried not to picture the cigarette stubs in the greenhouse and potting shed.

'You'll let me know the moment he does.'

'Does?'

'Return. So that we can call off our search for him.'

'Yes, yes, of course.'

'A fox carcass has been found in the woods. Nothing remarkable in itself, except that this one appears to have been poisoned. Had you heard about it?' Lyndsay shook her head. 'What insecticide do you use, Mrs Potter?'

'Sprays, you mean?' In her mind's eye Lyndsay saw Matt mounting the stairs, clammy in an anorak and pyjamas.

'In your nurseries.'

'It depends on the problem.'

'Powder solutions, mixed with water? Pesticide granules that you sprinkle on the ground?'

Puzzled, she nodded uncertainly. 'Sometimes.'

'What about cans of insecticides?'

'I used to. Rarely now, if I can avoid them.'

'Why?'

'I'm concerned for the environment.'

'Do you keep any in stock?'

'Yes, a few cans· still in the potting shed. I try to find alternatives.'

'Would Matt have had access to them and to the solutions you use?'

'The nurseries are only locked at night, Inspector. The potting sheds are usually kept closed.'

Burgess rose to leave. 'I wonder if I might have a quick look round down there?'

'Yes, of course.'

'The keys are…?'

'In the kitchen.'

'If you wouldn't mind.'

'Yes, of course.' Lyndsay ran back to the kitchen to find the keys, returning immediately.

'Just point me in the right direction and I'll potter about down there on my own. Might even buy a plant. Oh, one last tiny point.'

'Yes?'

'Have you visited the nature reserve recently?'

'I go there often.'

'To the spot where Mrs Bharjee was found?' Lyndsay was mute, incapable of opening her mouth. 'Crime scenes are frequently visited. It's not unusual. People go to pay their respects, to gawp, leave a flower. A species of orchid has been planted there; difficult to come by I would have said. I was wondering if you knew anything about it? I don't suppose it arrived by Interflora.'

Breaking into the silence came Paul's cry of 'Mummy!' He ran from the house followed, seconds later, by Stephen who looked harassed.

'I'm so sorry, Inspector,' Stephen called as he approached.

Burgess waved an idle hand, immediately returning his attention to Lyndsay. 'Well, Mrs Potter?'

'I planted it.'

'Its name?'

'*Phalaenopsis gigantea.*'

'That's the one.'

Stephen drew alongside them. 'Apologies, Inspector. Have you had tea?'

'Yes, and the rest. Delicious.'

'How can we help you? Or have you news?'

'Some news. Your wife will fill you in. Otherwise, I was picking her brains, trying to find out the name of a rather unusual plant I've come across.' Burgess, standing between them was smiling. 'Had a feeling your wife might know it.' He swung his body, looking disconcertingly at Lyndsay, 'Why would you have done that, Mrs Potter?'

'To pay my respects,' she murmured, trying not to notice Stephen's bemused expression.

'I see. Well, I'll have a quick peek around the nurseries and I'll drop these keys back on my way out. Enjoy your tea!'

17

Shafts of golden sunlight streamed down upon the two small girls, who stood alongside one another atop a hill. They were gazing about them in wonder. The snowy white hillside was a soft swirling skirt of blossoming daisies, swaying in the occasional breeze. The soil beneath them was springy from recent rains, but no longer damp.

'Race you down the hill,' said the older girl mischievously.

The girls were dressed in identical sundresses sewn by their mother, pinafore-styled and gaping, their soft puppy flesh peeping out from beneath.

'If you like,' replied the younger of the two. Her cotton bonnet fell over her sandy fringe and flopped against her freckled nose.

'Not running though.'

'What then, Becky?'

'Rolling.'

'Rolling?' Her powder-blue eyes lit up. The suggestion both thrilled and scared her. 'It's too far.'

'No, it isn't, Lyndsay,' said Rebecca, egging her on.

Lyndsay stared down the hill, appraising the gradient, fearing the drop. The daisies smelled rich and potent. She longed to be a part of them. To lie down, yield herself up to them, swim amongst them. To see their heads on emerald stalks tower above her, taller and prouder than life.

Rebecca read her small sister's excitement and, taking the initiative, lay down. Her hand reached up to coax her baby sister to the ground, and Lyndsay submitted. They lay like this, side by side, hands clasped, listening to the earth busy about its business beneath them. Creepy crawlies investigated the two young continents of flesh to be preyed upon or stung. Above them the sky was bright lilac and trumpet gold.

Lyndsay scratched an earwig off her face while studying a gull wheeling and piping overhead and Rebecca inched like a worm along the ground, repositioning herself so that now the two girls lay head to foot, head to foot.

Rebecca rolled onto her side. 'Ready?' she whispered.

Lyndsay, too, rolled onto her side. She closed her eyes and without answering or waiting for her big sister's command, took a deep breath and plunged, hurling herself into motion, kicking off the race, commencing the descent.

'Cheat!' squealed Rebecca from above.

Lyndsay giggled. Her head was swimming from the bumpy, circular movement. She passed over a stone or a rock. It cut into her, but not sufficiently sharply to impede her. How close was she to the bottom? Would she ever be able to stop herself? Or would she roll on forever, plummeting into the depths of the earth in a never-ending motion, falling for all eternity.

Still rolling, she opened her eyes; it was impossible to gauge anything. The sky was in full view and then hidden as she swayed drunkenly. A cloud tilted. The plant life: daisies, clover, grass and dandelions enveloped her. It felt like the best thing that had ever happened to her. She panted and cawed with joy as she rolled onwards, rolling beyond life, rolling out of herself.

Eventually she reached flat land and came to a stop. Eyes closed, she remained still, listening to her racing heart. When she finally lurched to her feet, she fully expected to encounter her sister somewhere close at hand. But Rebecca was nowhere to be seen and she was not at the bottom of the hill. She must have veered off course. She spun about in a panic, searching giddily for a familiar landmark until she found herself facing the deserted beach where they had picnicked earlier and caught sight of her parents' black Austin car. Her mother and father were standing alongside it. She could see them clearly. She called out to them but they didn't respond. They couldn't have heard her.

They were dancing. Were they dancing? Their bodies were twisting and turning. Then, all of a sudden, her mother let out a piercing cry. Something strange was taking place, something was happening between them. Lyndsay was too far away to understand. She caught sight of Rebecca. Her sister's wild red hair was flying in the slipstream. She was running fast towards them, arriving in between them, pulling them apart, shouting. Lyndsay could not make out the words, only high-pitched shrieks.

Something was wrong. Frightened and puzzled, she darted over the tufted dunes, whipping the sand into whorls, moving towards her family, calling as she went. They turned to watch her arrival. She drew near – and stopped dead – studying their faces at close range. Rebecca was screaming, tears falling. Her father was sweating, agitated, upset. Lastly, she took in her mother. Her mother's head was bent. She raised it slowly and Lyndsay went cold. Her mother's face was streaked with delicate dark lines, snails' trails of blood. Yes, it was blood. The sight of her mother looking like that was such a cold shock. It left her so swimmy and sick that she widdled her pants and then, ashamed, turned on her heels and fled.

Even when she heard them calling her name, she did not return. She lay on the ground shaking, trembling, buried amongst the daisies for what seemed like hours. Needing to pee again but fearing to move, she allowed the wee to trickle out, through her damp dress, stitched and starched and kept neat by her mother, into the accepting earth.

It was growing chilly, uncomfortably cold, but she stayed put. Until her skin felt raw and itchy and she grew too afraid of monsters and wanted to go home for tea.

That night in bed, Lyndsay tried to recall the rolling: the land beneath her, the drunken, rocking lilac sky, the angels' wings of golden light. She had been immeasurably happy. That was what she would remember. Not her mother's damaged face, nor the sight of those snails' trails of blood again. No more screaming, no more blood.

Lyndsay woke with a start about an hour after dawn, sweating yet shivering with cold. A dream had forced her bolt upright in the bed. She couldn't locate where she was. She cast about in search of Stephen, the warm cave of his arm to hide in, but then she remembered that she was alone. He was along the corridor and she was sleeping in one of the guest rooms.

She climbed from the bed and pulled open a drawer in a pine chest. With light from the dawn sky, she dug through folded layers of rarely worn clothes and pulled out a thick green sweater of Stephen's. She had bought it for him from the Dunhill shop in Harrods. She had loved to see him wearing it, to wrap herself around him in it as he crouched and stooped to prepare their log fires. Now, she slipped it over her shivering, naked body and peered at herself in the mirror. Her pubic hair curled out and over the cable stitching which edged the sweater. She touched the wool, stroking it tenderly and then herself, her hair only. The gesture was comforting not erotic. Then she climbed back into the crumpled bed, slipping her arms out of the sleeves and wrapping them around her torso while the sweater swam about her like a great woollen life-jacket. The scent was Stephen's. She closed her eyes and tried to sleep, giving power to the sweater to take away her emptiness and sense of failure.

The clock ticked softly in the silent room. Not since she was a child had she felt so alone. No, there was Paul.

Paul, a few yards along the corridor, was tucked up in bed sleeping, in his Lion King pyjamas. Her small obedient son. He was innocent and clear, oblivious to the panic and the sense of abandonment that was taking hold of her. She threw off the covers and rose up out of the bed, giddily. Thrusting the sweater aside she searched about for a robe.

She needed to see Paul, to set eyes on his sleeping shape, to reassure herself that all was well, that he was at peace. And then she would make tea. While walking the landing, she was thinking that she ought to telephone Marion Finch, but she could not gather her thoughts together to recollect why the call was necessary. It was something to do with Matthew. At not yet six o'clock on Sunday it was far too early to telephone anyone. Treading barefoot along the dimly lit oak corridor, Lyndsay thought she heard male voices in subdued dispute. An argument was taking place. Was Stephen up already, at loggerheads with Paul over something?

Or could it be that Matthew had returned and the two brothers were fighting?

'Matt!' Her call was low but urgent.

No strips of light spilled from beneath the doors of any of the rooms. Every room was closed, everywhere in darkness. She opened the door to Matt's room.

'Matt?' She tiptoed in to confirm that the bed was empty, that her eldest boy had not slid home during the dark hours of the night. How many times in these last days had she turned that handle and peered in, praying he'd be there? Praying that the whole business had been nothing more than a desperate nightmare. The stillness in the room denied her. She closed the door one more time and continued a few more steps along the corridor.

When she opened Paul's door, the voices grew instantly louder and more furious. A flickering screen reached out from across the room. Paul had fallen asleep with the television on, tuned to an all-night movie channel; a cowboy picture was in full tilt. Lyndsay switched it off and crossed to his bed.

Her small boy was sleeping soundly with his glasses hanging precariously from fingers brushing a well-thumbed copy of *Harry Potter and the Goblet of Fire*. Lyndsay folded the spectacles and set them on his bedside table. She bent down, kissed his soft warm cheek and felt happiness. The scent of him and the sight of his sleeping face were blissfully reassuring. He looked utterly peaceful. She was calmed by the realisation that there was love more than loss in his young heart. She perched awhile on the edge of the mattress and watched him sleeping. Whatever lay ahead she must consider Paul and protect him.

Lyndsay decided not to return to bed and so made her way down the stairs to the kitchen. It was too early also for the papers and the national coverage of a murderer detained. Whatever sordid chain of events had led Surinder Bharjee to be beaten by her husband and flee, whatever part Matt's infatuation had played in that final bloody comedy, he had not murdered her. Her son was not a murderer. She need never allow that damn doubt the power to haunt her again. Matthew was in the clear. Her son was innocent.

About his sexual behaviour she felt less quiet. He was smoking grass; he had been fornicating with a young married woman and writing about it, glorying in his exploding eroticism, expressing no guilt for it whatsoever. And for the pleasure of his passion it seemed that the young girl had paid with her life. The poems and journals had now become tainted with a truth – they were the testimony of Matthew's firsthand experience of sex. Lyndsay had not registered it during her earlier readings, but the more regularly she perused the material now, the more convinced she became that they were written from his personal experience.

After cups of warm tea in the fresh dawn light of a magnificent June morning, Lyndsay remembered why she had wanted to telephone Marion. Marion had mentioned that Bharjee beat his wife. Did Marion know for how long Bharjee had been beating Surinder? If Marion had inside information, which given her passion for gossip she might very well have, it could clear Matthew. Clear him of culpability in Lyndsay's mind.

Once she and Paul had breakfasted, after she had glanced through the papers, she would give Marion a call, and then, for Paul's sake, she would set aside her anxieties and give herself up to more carefree decisions, such as how they were all going to spend their day.

When Stephen came down, she might suggest they go to the boat. Lyndsay was not particularly fond of the sea, but both the boys loved sailing, Matt even more than Paul.

The boat! No one had visited the boat since Matthew's disappearance. No one had considered it! Did Inspector Burgess know that Stephen owned a yacht? The kitchenette on board was stacked with food. Lyndsay had restocked the cupboards not that long ago and the boat had not been used since. Matt could live aboard that yacht without any money. During the week there was barely a soul in the harbour, he could lie low without fear of being recognised. Why had they, family and law, not considered such a heaven-sent lair?

She hurried across to the telephone to inform Burgess, and instantly replaced the handset. When Matthew saw the Sunday papers and understood that he was off the hook, he would be ready to come home. Today was the perfect occasion to take Paul to the boat. The unexpected arrival of his brother and parents, the printed confirmation that he was no longer wanted 'for questioning', would send Matthew spinning into the welcoming arms of his family. By nightfall her two sons would be home together, eager to put the past behind them. Tomorrow would be time enough to call Inspector Burgess, not today.

She would never mention the letters, the poems and the sexual outpourings to Matt. She would deliver them back to his room right this minute and bury them exactly as she had found them, in a tatty supermarket bag beneath togs. She had accidentally ripped the original plastic bag and thrown it out. Another then, he would never know the difference. Matt would settle back into his life and soon nobody would remember he had ever been away. He would be a boy again, a young, healthy pubescent boy at college swotting for his A levels. She would never mention Surinder to him. The whole sordid business would be forgotten and life would return to the established order.

She hurried upstairs, fished the notebooks, papers and journals out of the drawer in her dresser where she had stashed them, and then walked across to her pillow where a slender collection of loose foolscap pages were hidden in the linen case. She had been reading these during the dark hours. She sped along the corridor to Matt's room. Out of habit she paused an instant at the door to confirm that he was not there but this was foolish because she now felt certain that he was on the boat waiting for her to fetch him.

Once in his room, she headed directly for his wardrobe, slinging his muddied sneakers across the floor in a feverish panic as she dumped diaries, books, loose scraps of paper, the whole caboodle, back where she had found them. The history of this virgin – or not so virgin – love had been hidden beneath stinking football socks and plimsolls, where it belonged. No one, not even Matt, need ever know that she was party to the mysteries of his heart.

From Matt's room she hastened along the corridor and knocked on Stephen's door, their bedroom. He was in the shower; she entered awkwardly. 'Stephen?' Already, the distance between them had taken away any right she felt to wander freely around his person. She called again to warn him of her presence, and made her way to her wardrobe, bending to a drawer in search of clean slacks and underwear. 'Shall we take Paul to the boat? It'd be fun, don't you think?'

Stephen entered, damp in a towelling robe, rubbing his wet hair with a towel. 'You said that Burgess expects Matt to come home today.'

'Yes, but...'

'Are you suggesting he returns to an empty house?'

Lyndsay rose uncertainly. Stephen's abrasive tone alerted her. At all costs, she wished to ward off another row. 'I thought it would be fun for Paul and...'

'And what?'

'Well, it suddenly occurred to me that Matt might be hiding there. There's food. He could keep –'

'Lyndsay, for Christ's sake! I think you are losing your mind.' Stephen returned to the bathroom.

She followed him as far as the door. 'Why? Why do you say that? Why do you have to make me wrong for everything I say or do?'

'Because the police would have found him there. You are not being logical. You are jumping like a demented grasshopper at every notion that enters your head.'

Lyndsay leaned her back against the bedroom wall. She lifted the neatly pressed clothes high above her head and flung them across the room. It was more an act of impotence than violence. And then something like defeat seemed to settle within her. 'I can't take any more of this,' she muttered. 'Why don't you just go, Stephen?' she said to his back. 'Pack a bag, and go. When Matt returns, we'll let you know. I can't take this.' Her eyes were glistening with tears, her nose was running, her heart felt as though it had been sliced, but within that pain she felt a hardening, a steely need for resolution.

Stephen approached the door, his head bent. There they stood, in dressing gowns, one showered, the other not, neither looking the other in the face. The thread that had connected them was severed. Now all that remained was anger and blame.

'If that's the way you want it,' he said, slowly lifting his head, frowning.

Lyndsay turned to him. The agony had peeled away everything. 'No, Stephen, it's the way *you* want it. I'm taking Paul to the boat. If Matt arrives, you can call us.' She gathered up her various articles of clothing and, without looking back, strode from the room, breathing deeply, letting go. Determined.

It was earlier than she had intended to wake Paul. 'Paul, sweetheart.'

'Has something happened?'

'No, of course not. We're going out for the day.'

Bleary eyed, Paul dragged himself from the hazy warm memory of his dreams and stared curiously at his mother. She smiled, handing him his slippers, barely registering his bemusement, and hastened to the door. 'Hurry sweetheart, breakfast's on its way. Herb sausages and poached eggs: your favourite.'

Fishing rods piled into the back of the four-wheel drive, home-baked bread and ham for sandwiches, mineral water for Lyndsay, cans of Coke for Paul, packed in a portable cooler, they were ready to set off when the telephone rang. Lyndsay glanced at her watch. It was still not yet nine o'clock. It must be Matt. He had seen the papers and was on his way home.

'Maybe it's Matt!'

'Run and answer it then, darling.'

Paul spun obediently on the gravel and scooted back into the house, to the extension in the hall. Lyndsay, whose heart was beating furiously, followed him inside.

'I'll fetch my mother.'

She read the disappointment on Paul's face. 'Who is it?'

Paul shrugged. 'A woman.' He handed over the receiver and made his way back outside.

Lyndsay said a bright 'hello' and watched Paul slouch back outside to the car and settle himself in the passenger seat. Dust motes swam about in the early morning sun.

'Mrs Potter?'

'Yes.'

'Sorry to call so early. It's Gillian Lewis.' It took a moment. The voice was so unlike the one she had been hoping to hear from. 'Rupert's mother.'

'Ah, yes. How are you?' Rupert Lewis was Matt's best friend at college.

'I do hope I haven't woken you?'

'No, of course not. We were just going out.'

'I take it you've seen the papers?'

'Yes.'

'Henry and I were so frightfully relieved that we thought now was the appropriate moment to telephone. Have you heard from Matthew?'

'Not yet, no.'

'Any minute now, I feel sure. The poor little chap has probably been too terrified to show his face. We have both been dreadfully anxious. I was all for calling you earlier but Henry forbade it. You know how men are. They do worry about getting involved.'

'I perfectly understand.' Lyndsay glanced at her watch. They must be on their way. It was an hour and a half's drive. She didn't want to miss Matt. If they arrived too late he may have read the news and set off for home.

'Of course, it would be a lie not to own up to having been a touch concerned. I mean, not that one seriously believed Matt was guilty, but after the stupid business of the Swatch… Not in itself incriminating but, well, we thought best not to telephone. Henry was livid when he heard, hopping mad with the college for involving Rupert, but I pointed out that Rupert and Matthew were best friends. The police had every right to know.'

Lyndsay felt a chill run down her spine. What business of the Swatch? What was Mrs Lewis talking about? She peered out through the shadows of the hallway towards the ink-blue Mercedes glinting in the early summer light. She could see Paul waiting for her, all set for the boat. Should she fetch Stephen? Should she enquire about 'the business of the Swatch'?

'Matthew's Swatch?' she asked, hoping that fresh concern was not apparent in her voice.

'Those stupid watches he and Rupert bought from one of the other lads in their class. I hope it's taught them all a bloody good lesson!' Lyndsay knew nothing of this transaction. 'When Rupert came home wearing his, Henry rang the housemaster. He thought it was stolen and that Rupert would be had up for possession. It turned out that a boy called Davis had bought a whole batch of them from a Chinaman in Macau, during a family trip to Hong Kong. Paid twenty pounds for the lot and sold them at five pounds apiece. Well, good luck to him. Matt must have mentioned it?'

'Yes, I'd...forgotten.'

'Well, when that Inspector Burgess – frightfully down at heel, don't you think? – mentioned the watch, Rupert panicked. He thought it had been stolen, after all. As it turned out, the Inspector had noticed it because it was identical to one they had found and Burgess wondered whether the one they were in possession of might not belong to Matthew.'

'I hope Rupert hasn't been troubled by Inspector Burgess.'

'Oh, three or four interviews. More than the rest of the boys I suppose, because he and Matthew are best friends. I suppose Burgess thought that if Matthew had dark secrets he'd confide in Rupert.'

'Dark secrets?' Lyndsay's interjection was too anxious.

'Rupert's not like that, though. Henry told him to make that plain so that the Inspector would stop calling him out of class.'

A burst of shouting could be heard in the background. 'That's Henry hollering.'

'I must go, too.'

'Do call when Matthew turns up. My word, you'll be relieved. Everyone will, I'm sure.'

'Bye!' Lyndsay replaced the receiver.

Why had Burgess kept the discovery of a Swatch to himself?

Stephen had bought Matthew a waterproof junior-style Rolex for his thirteenth birthday. Lyndsay was trying to recollect if during her several ransackings of his room she had come across it. No, she would have been aware of it.

'Stephen?'

'What?'

Was Burgess making furtive enquiries about Matthew that he did not want them to know about?

'Did Burgess say anything about a watch?'

'He asked about my Rolex, why?'

Matthew's Rolex was definitely not in his room. Matt must have lost it and been too scared to tell his father. Lyndsay was confused. Where had Inspector Burgess found the Swatch?

'Apparently, the police found a Swatch. They think it might belong to Matt.'

'Well they're barking up the wrong tree. I told Burgess I'd bought Matt a Rolex.'

What a frightful woman Mrs Lewis was. Was Burgess being secretive because it had been found at the scene of the murder? Did Matt buy the watch as a gift for Surinder? Was she wearing it at the time of...? Without further ado, Lyndsay crossed to the kitchen to dial the number of Matthew's housemaster.

Paul appeared at the door. 'Mum, are we going or not?'

'Paul, did Matthew own a Swatch?'

Paul shrugged. 'I don't know. I'm bored, Mum,' he said. 'And it's getting hot.'

'Two seconds, darling, promise, and I'll be with you.'

Paul sighed theatrically and trudged back across the gravel towards the car where he remained leaning against the bonnet with his arms crossed and his face in a sulk. His pose was a clear signal; he was fed up. The display amused Lyndsay. She went on into the kitchen, out of Stephen's earshot.

'Yes, hello. I'm Matthew Potter's mother. May I speak to Davis, please?'

She had been intending to ask for the housemaster, but requested Davis instead. He was probably in Matt's house, if she had correctly followed Mrs Lewis' meanderings. To her amazement, a boy answering to the name of Sebastian Davis came on the line. He confirmed that he had sold a Swatch to Matthew in the early spring.

Lyndsay thanked him for his help and was about to say goodbye when the young man added, 'Hey, Mrs Potter, when you speak to Matt, tell him we miss him.'

'I will.'

For Sebastian's consideration, Lyndsay found herself unnaturally grateful. She replaced the receiver, all too conscious of Paul. She had to think. The overriding factor was not that Matt owned a Swatch but that Burgess was in possession of it, and had kept this information from them. Why, if Matt was in the clear, hadn't he mentioned it?

Matt's absence felt overwhelming.

18

The fine weather had brought the day-trippers out in droves. By the time Lyndsay had negotiated the tailback of Sunday traffic at Bosham it was close to midday and both she and Paul were grumpy. For the latter part of the journey he had been sulking because Lyndsay had told him that they would not be taking the boat out of the harbour.

'I don't see the point of going if we don't sail,' he had whined.

'We'll have a picnic on deck, enjoy the sunshine. You can do some fishing, if you like.'

'Big deal.'

'Paulie, be reasonable, sweetheart, please. You know we can't sail the boat without Daddy.'

'Then why didn't Dad come?'

Prior to this, Paul had been chatting quite happily, mostly about school, about what this master thought about that, what another had remarked about something else; the usual preoccupations of a boy his age, only instead of Lyndsay's well-practised, enthusiastic questions and encouraging suggestions she had barely responded and now Paul was expressing his discontent with a major sulk.

The car park was jam-packed. Lyndsay drove around in circles for more than ten minutes until her frustration got the better of her. 'Why isn't there just one bloody place to park the damned car?'

Paul searched his mother's face for an explanation and then turned away to gaze out of the window. Eventually, when they found a space, he was up and out like a jack-in-the-box, hell-bent on claiming his fishing gear and racing to the boat.

'Hang on a minute.' Lyndsay was grappling with her handbag, which had fallen from the armrest and spilled its contents under the front seats of the car. Paul paid no heed. He was already hauling his rucksack from the seat behind him. 'Paul, I said hang on a minute!'

'I'll go ahead,' he said. 'Connect the electricity.'

What if Matthew were on the boat and in some kind of emotional state or sick? She did not want Paul to find him first.

'Paul, why don't you go to the newsagent's and buy us some ice-cream to eat with the fruit?' She fished for her purse and scooped up handfuls of loose change from the floor.

'Why can't I...?'

'Go on, Paul.'

'What flavour?'

'Anything you fancy.'

Paul accepted the money, but he hadn't given up. 'Why can't I come with you to the boat, ditch my stuff and then go for the ice-cream?'

'Paul, please!' she snapped. 'Stop being so difficult!'

Her small son stared at her and then, without a word, stomped off. Lyndsay cursed her scolding response. The prospect of encountering Matt, in the light of all she had discovered about him, was more unnerving than she had anticipated. Trembling, she lifted bags, drink coolers and baskets from the boot. Yes, she was afraid of facing her son – cowed by his passion, by who he had become – but what she dreaded more than anything else was his not being there.

She surveyed the domestic chaos spread out on the ground at her feet. It was impossible to carry it all, single-handedly, in one trip and Paul was not there to stand guard because she'd dispatched the little chap to the shop. Two gulls, alerted to the prospect of provisions, circled and swooped low, piping their melancholy call. She shoved half the contents back into the car, locked it, and scooped up the first armfuls of bags.

In the past, no matter what the hurdles, she had always managed.

Several weekend yachters pootling about on their boats paused to watch her trek along the jetty. Several called out a greeting while others glared, their attitude obvious. A few addressed comments to partners and friends while Lyndsay nodded and soldiered on.

She and Stephen had ventured out so occasionally since all of this had blown up that she had not been in a position to observe the reactions of neighbours and strangers. Apart from sitting in the pub with Ralph Beresford after her car accident and waiting for Stephen at the hospital, she had barely crossed paths with anybody and on that particular evening she had been too shocked to notice reactions. Her arrival in Bosham was causing heads to turn.

Stephen's boat was moored at the far end of one of the jetties. As she neared their yacht, a tall Dutchman with silver hair stepped forward to greet her, Joop Dekker. Joop and his Swiss wife, Inge – once a wizard in the oil-shares market – were their yachting neighbours. Elegantly turned out in Armani sportswear, smiling broadly while puffing on his pipe, Joop was a reassuring sight.

'Good morning, my dear.' His accent was as thick as the rind in home-made marmalade.

'Hello, Joop.'

Joop's style and manners were from the old tradition. He was more British than most of the British boat owners in this south coast harbour, most of whom passed their weekends getting sozzled aboard one another's vessels and roaring hale and heartily about off-shore tax schemes. It was one of the reasons

Lyndsay had never really taken to sailing; she couldn't abide the crowd. Owning up to this fact, that she had never cared for an entire section of Stephen's acquaintances, momentarily eased the pain of her failing marriage.

'You are folding beneath all of that. Let me give you a hand.'

'Thanks,' she said. 'How are you both?'

During their weekends down here she had frequently been bored. Joop and Inge were about the only two she was comfortable around.

'Couldn't be better, my dear. Where's Stephen?' As Joop spoke he gathered her entire load in his arms.

'He stayed at home. It's an outing for Paul.'

'We've seen the papers. No good pretending we haven't. We considered calling, then thought best to leave you in peace.'

Lyndsay smiled, busy now connecting the mains water. Beyond the harbour, the sea looked calm. 'Joop, just dump all that.' She needed to go aboard alone. If Matt was there she wanted to be the one to find him, to wrap herself tight around him and reassure herself that her boy was not damaged. She wanted to understand, to share what the loss of Surinder meant to him. She wouldn't ask, of course, and he wouldn't have to tell. But if others were present, mother and son would be obliged to play a different scene.

'Let me help you. I'll haul down the gangplank.'

She believed she could sense his presence already. 'No, I can manage. I have a couple more loads to collect from the car. You could keep an eye on these for me, if you like.'

Joop frowned. 'Then give me the car keys and let me carry whatever's left.'

Gratefully, she tossed him her keys, pressed the switch that connected shore-based electricity to the boat and climbed aboard.

Her heart was pounding. Stephen hid the key to the lower deck beneath the mainsail rigging. She lowered herself carefully and planed her fingers along the varnished wood in search of metal, wanting so hard for it not to be there.

The key was there.

Lyndsay rose slowly, unlocked the door to the lower deck and descended the narrow wooden staircase. The air smelt mildly musty as she would have expected of a boat that had been closed up for several weeks. Its creaking emptiness sounded as melancholy as the birds circling overhead. She coasted across to each of the cabins and opened them up, one by one, taking stock of everything as she moved about below.

No bed had been slept in, no cushion was out of place, and no cutlery was in the sink. Matt was a past master of untidiness. If he had been there, there would be evidence, even if he had tried to cover his tracks. She hurried over to the cupboards where the tins were stored. Not a baked bean was missing! Even if, after seeing the Sunday papers, he had set out for Churdles this morning, signs of his decampment would be apparent. He had not been here, not even for an hour.

And she had been so certain. Illogically, desperately certain.

Until this moment Lyndsay had believed that sooner or later Matt would come home. She had stored her faith in it. Now, suddenly, for the first time, an alternative future was panning out, and it was one that did not include Matt. It was a future where his voice never sounded, never shouted up and down the garden. In which his clarinet never offered up the tunes he spent his life writing; a life where only a memory of Matt existed, growing ever more distant and out of reach.

'Matt, please, wherever you are, I beg you to come home.'

All at once, it was feasible that Matt had gone for good. If, after reading the papers today and being reassured that no finger was pointing at him, he did not make contact, she might be forced to accept that she had lost him.

As she had lost her mother and sister.

But the loss of Matt was more terrible. Matt had been her hope. She had built the foundations of her normality on him. The prospect of losing her eldest son might send her crazy. She had no courage for this. Her reason for living would vanish. She berated herself for every cross or disinterested word she'd ever spoken to him.

'What's up?' She turned and saw Paul standing at the foot of the stairs. She hadn't heard his footsteps. He stared at her whilst cradling tubs of ice-cream. 'They've started stocking Häagen-Dazs. I got one chocolate chip and one fudge. Has the fridge been switched on?' His question was perfectly casual as though he had understood right away that his previous enquiry and Lyndsay's mood were best not pursued.

'Should be. I connected the current.'

He crossed to the refrigerator and pulled open the door. 'Mrs thingummy in the shop said that the police had been there asking questions about Matt.'

Lyndsay peered behind her. 'When was that, Paul?'

'Dunno, she didn't say. She just said she told them that she hadn't seen him. How dumb can a police force get?' He sounded disconcertingly like Stephen. He had many of his father's traits. Paul was less artistic, less sensitive than Matt, therefore less easy to damage. He dreamed of becoming a scientist or a mathematician. For an eleven-year-old boy, he had a common sense about him, a junior business head on his shoulders and a great deal of resilience – unless she was misreading this son as well. She loved him in another way; saw very different qualities in him. Did she value him less? Not at all, she treasured him for his soundness.

Paul had never been her bright young hope as Matthew had been. The knowledge of Matt's life growing within her had brought her and Stephen to marriage. It had legalised them, given fruit to their union, whereas Paul had represented something more to do with solidifying the marriage and home

they had created. This was only Lyndsay's point of view, of
course. She had never discussed it with Stephen. She had never
really considered it in such terms before. Would Stephen have
proposed to her if she had not been pregnant? Yes. It had seemed
inevitable that they would marry. The discovery that an
unplanned baby was on its way had had no bearing on their
decision. It had shifted the inevitable forward a few months was
all.

'Why do you say that, darling?'

'What?'

'About the police?'

'It's obvious. If – '

But Paul was given no opportunity to explain. Joop was calling
from above, arriving with Inge. 'Here we are!' he shouted,
unloading Lyndsay's baggage and descending the stairs.

'Tell me later,' Lyndsay whispered to Paul in a conspiratorial
way. She was on her feet and making her way up the steps.
'Hello, there!' she called brightly.

'Mum,' he said quickly before the others had descended and
before she was beyond earshot.

She turned her head. 'Yes?'

'If you want to go home now that you've seen Matt's not here,
that's fine with me. It's no fun fishing without Dad in any case.'

Lyndsay stared at her son, astounded.

Lyndsay and Paul drove the first leg of the journey home in
silence, both lost in the world of their own thoughts. Beyond the
windscreen, night was falling.

'Are you tired, sweetheart?'

'Not specially.'

'Did you enjoy today?'

'It was good, thanks.'

'What did you mean this morning, Paulie, when you
commented upon the stupidity of the police?' Paul had to think

back. 'You were referring to the newsagent's wife. The lady who said that she'd been questioned...'

'Oh, that. Nothing, except that Matthew wouldn't go there, would he?'

'Wouldn't go where? To the boat?'

'To the newsagent's. If he had stowed away on our boat he wouldn't have gone to the one shop in Bosham where everybody knows him. Not if he was in hiding. It stands to reason.'

'I see.' They cruised on without speaking. 'What are you thinking about?' she asked after a while.

Paul glanced at his mother. Her attention was on the road. 'I miss him.'

'Me, too,' and then, 'Paul, did you and Matt share secrets?'

'What sort of secrets?'

'I don't know.' Lyndsay was thinking about Surinder, about the police believing that Rupert Lewis might have known the mysteries of Matt's heart. 'Anything.'

'About girls, you mean?'

'Girls?' Lyndsay cast a glance sideways towards her son. Sometimes he struck her as so much older than eleven. 'Yes, if you like.'

'He didn't have any dirty magazines.'

Lyndsay was so taken aback by this answer that she nearly burst out laughing. 'What makes you say that?'

'I looked in his room once, when he was out, but I didn't find any.'

'You looked in Matt's room? What made you do that, Paulie?'

'Because he has a filthy temper sometimes.'

Cars, their headlights illuminated, sped past the windows. Lyndsay was barely aware of them. Had Paul found anything in Matt's room connecting him with Surinder? She did not dare to ask him. 'I don't understand.'

'It's not important.'

'Please, Paul, try to explain. Did Matt hurt you?'

'Once, when I asked him if he'd ever seen a girl naked he told me to mind my own business and then another time when I asked him whether he looked at sexy pictures, he told me I was a pain and should go to hell. I guessed that meant he did, but that he didn't want to own up to it, so I looked.'

Lyndsay had pulled the car over into the slow lane. 'Did you find anything in his room?' she ventured. She wanted to halt the car, look her son in the face and demand whether he had read Matt's writings, or found the grass. She assumed that Paul would not know what the seeds were. All of a sudden Paul burst out laughing. 'What are you laughing at?'

'Nothing.'

'Must be something. Something you saw in Matt's room?'

'Nothing, I've forgotten.' Lyndsay wanted to ask if Inspector Burgess had questioned him. 'Mum, why did you expect Matt to be on the boat today? Dad knew he wouldn't be. That's why he didn't come with us, isn't it?'

'I didn't, not really.'

'Yes, you did. That's why you were crying. It's why you sent me to buy ice-cream. You were trying to get rid of me.'

'Not get rid of you, Paulie, never that.'

'But you expected him to be there?'

'I was hoping. To hope is not the same as to expect. Hope's opposite is despair. My hopes were dashed. It made me…want to cry a little bit.'

'You sound like Mr Tanhorn.'

'Who?'

'My Latin master. He's nicknamed the "Reverend Preacher of Semantics". He drives us all bonkers with boredom.'

'Oh, dear!' Lyndsay, her eyes still on the road ahead, smiled quietly. Thank heavens for this boy, she mused, wondering if he had sensed that something was wrong at home, although she did not think so. She prayed not. Didn't he have enough to contend with, holding his head high at school, while the world thought ill of his brother? She admired his youthful resilience. 'What were you laughing at just now?'

'About Joop and Inge.'

'Are they so funny?'

'They're always taking their clothes off.'

'Are they?' asked Lyndsay incredulously.

'Matt says they're nudists. He saw them once when he was snorkelling. They were out on the cave island. Joop was fishing. He was smoking his pipe and he looked lanky with no clothes on. Just a pipe and a willy!' Paul giggled at the image. 'Inge was nude too. Matt saw her. He said lots of foreigners are nudists.' Paul sighed. 'I wish he'd come back.'

'He will.'

'Yeah, when they stop fussing.'

'We must believe it,' she answered softly.

'I do.'

'That's my boy.' But I'm not so sure I do, she thought.

'Did we go to the boat today because you wanted to take me out or because you were hoping to find Matt there?'

'Does it matter?'

'Which? I want to know.'

'A bit of both. And now, you sound like Ins—'

But before she could say it Paul roared, 'Inspector Burgess!' and they both began to giggle.

'He asked me about dirty magazines and nudists.'

'Who? Inspector Burgess?' Lyndsay felt outraged. 'When? What did you tell him?'

'Last week, when he called me out of class. He said he'd heard that lots of the boys at school looked at dirty pictures and masturbated. He was trying to suss out if Matt did. Then he said some of your sailing friends were…funny.'

'Funny?'

'He must have been talking about Joop and Inge being nudists. Asked me if I knew how Matt felt about those people. If I thought it had affected him.'

'Good Heavens, what did you say, Paulie?'

'I said Matt only cared about his music.'

Was Burgess trying to imply that the boys were being perverted by the company their parents kept? She considered the Swatch. Was he trying to frame Matt?

Burgess had been right about the journalists. They had disappeared. Lyndsay had almost forgotten the peace of being able to open the gate without a barrage of questions and faces peering through the windows.

As they approached the house along the curving driveway, the only sound was the barking of dogs.

'Dad would have called us if Matt had come home, wouldn't he? On your mobile.'

'Yes, I think so, darling.' So, all day, Paul had been hoping and waiting as much as she. She loved him all the more for it. It gave company to her disappointment.

When they entered the house, Stephen came through to greet them. There had been no word from Matt. Not that she had honestly expected news, or so she kidded herself now, to ward off the surging swell of misery. She tugged at the sleeves of Paul's sweater, folded and tucked beneath her arm. The ache within her was overwhelming.

So, the Sunday papers had not winkled Matt out of hiding as Burgess had predicted. He had been mistaken. Or was he lying? If Matt had seen the news then he must be reassured. He had nothing left to fear, no reason to remain in hiding. So why, oh why, had he not come forward?

19

On Tuesday Paul returned to school. Stephen also left – at dawn – to go away on business until Thursday. Their parting had been cool. For both, the distance was a breath of fresh air. Save for herself and the dogs, the house was deserted, the day gloriously sunny.

Lyndsay dug out Matt's bike from the dark privacy of the shed, and wheeled it to the drive, pressing it tight against her hip. She took it to keep company with her son. This was nothing she would have owned up to, although a faith in telepathic communication was becoming essential to her, in this time of loss. Matt's precious bike and writings were her companions. She deemed them channels of contact between mother and child.

She pedalled along the country lanes, flying past fields speckled with cowslips and ox-eye daisies, inhaling perfumes of clover and columbine, en route for the village. Once there, she dismounted and circled the churchyard on foot. Beyond the wall, in the cemetery, a lawnmower whirred. Once a month, a young gardener employed by Tonbridge Council came by in his beaten-up truck, to weed the stone-paved walkways, cut back the grass and dandelions and gather up the discarded ice-cream wrappers. Lyndsay knew him by sight and waved.

She slowed her pace, while reconstructing in her mind's eye what she had seen on that fateful Friday now twelve days earlier. Perhaps she was treading the same well-worn paving stones Mrs Hampton had trodden. Leaning against the wall, she peered towards that distant corner of the garden where the weeping pear tree gave its smoke-blue shade. There had to be a clue somewhere.

Aside from the gardener, Lyndsay had expected the grounds to be deserted. Certainly, she had not bargained on the raincoated spectacle of Burgess prowling amongst moss-covered tombstones in the afternoon sunshine. But there he was, traipsing to and fro, scouting right to left, scratching at illegible headstones and ancient family vaults. His presence sent a shiver down her spine.

He had not communicated with them since his visit of the previous Saturday, and Lyndsay had taken his silence to be heartening news. The unnamed suspect, the lorry driver the police were holding in custody, must have been charged by now. All suspicion against Matthew would have been allayed. Her son's continuing absence, 'devastating for you, of course, but not national news', was of no further interest to the criminal investigation. Burgess had said as much himself.

So what was he up to now? Lyndsay hung back, observing him.

She hadn't the least desire to speak to him but she was keen to know what he was doing there. Was he retracing Matthew's footsteps or hunting for a fallen article on the ground? She rested the bike against the wall. Burgess was scrutinising the graves, searching for something on the tombstones.

Lyndsay mistrusted and resented him. Matthew had not come home as he had forecast, and for what reason had he not disclosed that he was in possession of a Swatch identified as Matt's? She was beginning to suspect him of playing a double game and judged herself naive for not having cottoned on to it sooner.

Did Burgess believe Matthew was guilty of murder? Clearly, he was searching for some clue or other. Was it evidence against her son? Was this where the Swatch had been found? She wondered why Burgess had not returned the watch, if it belonged to Matt. There had been nothing in the papers during the last couple of days to confirm that a charge had been made against the lorry driver. Lyndsay concluded that Burgess was a crafty player and vowed then and there to assist him only as far as she was legally bound. She felt a sudden relief that she had never mentioned the grass or Matt's writings. No information was safe with this man. Was it too far-fetched to fancy that Burgess might actually know where Matthew was?

Someone calling out her name from behind broke her concentration. Startled, she swung the bike away from the church wall and stepped around it clumsily. Had the call drawn Burgess' attention? Would he realise that she had been spying on him?

Across the street, dressed in working clothes and muddied trekking boots was Ralph Beresford, making his way from out of the Lamb and Flag. Lyndsay flushed at the sight of him – and because she felt Burgess' eyes boring into her back. She wheeled Matt's bike towards Beresford who approached the kerb's edge, and waited for her.

'How are you?' His smile was easy, wide and convivial.

'I meant to write you a note, to thank you...' It had crossed her mind on several occasions to make contact. Bashfulness had stalled her, not thoughtlessness.

'Oh, please, don't worry.'

She arrived at Beresford's side. He was taller than she'd remembered, but the memory of riveting blue eyes had not deceived her. Lyndsay blushed beneath their intensity and industriously rubbed the sleeve of her blouse against chrome handlebars. Such a gaze disarmed.

'I was going to call you, to see how things are working out and to –'

'Everything's fine.'

'Fine?'

'I mean…under the circumstances.' She smiled shyly. A hazy image of herself weeping in this man's arms came flooding back to her and she was confused as to whether, in a state of shock, she had blathered out confidences which would have been best left unsaid. Yet, looking at him now, she knew he would not betray her. She felt confident of that.

'Matt seems to be off the hook. That's good news. And you don't look like you crawled out of the smoking remains of a car.'

'Thanks to you.' Her eyes lingered on him longer than they should have and she was, again, alive to the scent of him; a woody, ferny aftershave, strong and unfussy. Verbena perhaps. It had stayed in her memory from their afternoon together at the bird sanctuary. Inhaling it anew she felt a longing that quickened her pulse.

'I'm happy to see you. I wanted to wish you well before I head off.'

'Are you leaving? But you're writing a book.' For a moment she had felt rooted and at peace.

'I am, but not here. They fired me.'

'Fired you? Why?' Lyndsay exclaimed.

'I didn't find the culprit who attacked the ospreys, didn't manage to protect them. And now they have deserted the sanctuary…all five eggs smashed…'

'But that isn't your fault!'

'Good afternoon Mrs Potter, Mr Beresford.'

Lyndsay, facing away from the cemetery, had been blind to Burgess' approach. For a few brief moments he had been expelled from her thoughts. She felt outraged by the news of Ralph's dismissal and longed to offer assistance. Would he really desert Churdle Heath? She wondered how she could best repay his kindness. She resented this intrusion.

'I was coming to see you, Mrs Potter.'

Lyndsay felt a cold anger rise within her as Burgess studied her with calibrating eyes. 'Really?'

'I'll be on my way. Glad to see you're in one piece, Mrs Potter.' As Beresford strode off, Lyndsay felt a crucial part of herself go with him.

'Do you have news about Matthew, Inspector?'

'Alas, no. I was just paying a visit to your local churchyard.'

'Really?'

'You saw me. Have you visited it?'

'Of course.'

'I suppose you attend church here, do you?'

'I don't go to church, Inspector.'

'Not a churchgoing family? Your father?'

'My father is dead, Inspector Burgess, as you know!'

'I was talking about during his lifetime. I was wondering whether he attended this church?'

'We are none of us churchgoers and neither was my father.' Suddenly, there were a million questions she needed answered by the other man who had just walked away.

Burgess, frowning, pivoted his attention back towards the cemetery as though he were mulling over some vital fact. 'Your father, is he buried here?'

'No, he isn't.' Lyndsay took a step. She was anxious to be on her way. Burgess was breathing down her neck again. Whatever defence she prepared, he came at her from another angle. 'It's true, Inspector, that I saw you in the churchyard. Were you looking for something? Another possession of Matthew's? Aside from his Swatch, I mean.' She felt a surge of relief. The Swatch had been mentioned. Prudent or not, she had got it off her chest. A minor triumph alerting this appalling man to the fact that she had not been entirely duped.

What insane hand of injustice could sack Ralph Beresford? Or stalk Matt the way Burgess was stalking him?

Burgess narrowed his eyes. 'I was attempting to locate your father's grave. And the Swatch, identified as Matthew's, was not found in this churchyard. It was found in a clearing at the nature reserve, less than a hundred feet from the spot where Surinder Bharjee was murdered. It has been sent away for fingerprints.'

Lyndsay felt the blood drain out of her as Burgess' eyes drilled into her. She wanted to beat her fists against him, to scream obscenities, but she fought to remain calm, to return his gaze with a false defiance. 'You have your murderer, you said so yourself. He made a confession.'

'Indeed, he did.'

'Then, I don't understand. Why do you continue to insist on Matt's guilt?'

'I have never accused your son, Mrs Potter.'

'But you believe it! You believe Matt murdered Surinder because he...' She stopped dead, dangerously aware of how incriminating her next breath would have been. She had been nudging the cliff's edge. Diaries, love letters, poems would have tumbled, exposing the luxurious heat of Matt's ardour, convicting him. Lyndsay smiled crazily. Not a living soul, save her, knew of their existence. Only she was party to that private world. They, she and Matt, were safe as houses. Burgess could forage all he pleased, he would never burrow into Matt's erotic world. And then Lyndsay recalled Paul, and the vision of her small son innocently rooting for girlie magazines in his big brother's room. Had Burgess got to Paul? No, Paulie would have warned her.

'Because what, Mrs Potter?'

'Because you found the Swatch,' she lied and, to cover her tracks, she added. 'You are wasting your time. My father is not buried here.'

'Why not?'

'You saw the stones. No one has been buried here for half a century.'

'Where is he buried?'

'Why do you want to know?'

'My car is parked along the road. Show me where he is. Or I can find out for myself.' Burgess smiled in an attempt to soften his threat and to pacify Lyndsay, and then he pointed along the street that led from the village through leafy lanes to the haven of the nature reserve. Beresford had taken that direction. Lyndsay stared past Burgess' Rover. She pictured Ralph at the bird sanctuary. In the morning, she would cycle over there and find him. He hadn't specified when he was leaving.

'I see you are using Matthew's bike. We can drop it off on the way, if you like.'

'You still haven't told me why.'

Burgess glanced at his watch and Lyndsay felt the weight of his small thick arm against her back as he manoeuvred her towards his car. 'It's quarter to four. In my experience, Mrs Potter, churchyards lock their gates around five-thirty, six. If we wish to spend a bit of time at the grave we better get going. I can dispel your fears as we drive. Is it far?'

She wanted no part of this excursion.

As they passed the post office Lyndsay averted her gaze. She had not shopped there since the discovery of the body. Her stamps and stationery were now purchased in Tonbridge.

'Look at that: a stone thrown through the window. The second one, I believe. He's selling up, moving on. Did you hear?' Burgess informed her.

'No.' She was thinking about Ralph. Walking in the forest at dawn, bending to the hidden corpse of Surinder while the forest watched on. It held its breath for the lifeless girl who would never breath again, for she whose cold form had been violated and then buried beneath its foliage. She thought of Matt and the fire of his passion. What if Matt had watched on, witnessed her murder? Was that the trauma that had sent him scuttling for cover?

'Difficult at the best of times for the likes of him in a neighbourhood such as this one, wouldn't you say?' They had reached the car. Burgess strapped Matt's bicycle against the boot while Lyndsay lingered at the kerbside. Why was she agreeing to this? Because the prospect of Burgess snooping around her father's grave disgusted her. If she refused to tell him where Harry was buried he would find it out from council records.

The bicycle secured, they climbed into the Rover.

'Straight there, I think. The bike will be perfectly safe. Where to?'

'Lingfield.'

'Lingfield?' he repeated, with an exaggerated air of surprise. The car pulled away from the roadside. Lyndsay rested her cheek against the window. Her eyes danced up and down lanes and bridle-paths, hoping for a glimpse of Ralph. Where did he live?

'What do you think about them, Mrs Potter?'

She sighed. 'Who?'

'Indians. They're buying up our high streets. Moving into the countryside, settling in our villages, taking over. There is little enough work in the area, as it is. Without the likes of them, wouldn't you say?'

'I am not such a racist.'

'But your husband probably is.'

'It's ludicrous to suggest that my son killed Surinder Bharjee because she was Indian, because he has been influenced by racist attitudes.'

'I am not suggesting anything. I haven't found a motive for why Matthew would –'

'He didn't!'

Burgess did not immediately respond. Lyndsay was seething.

And then, almost as an afterthought he continued, 'In any case, it seems that whoever attacked the ospreys also killed Surinder. And, if I'm not mistaken, Matt was not in Churdle Heath on the night of the osprey attack, was he?' Lyndsay froze. She pictured her son mounting the stairs. Burgess was laying traps. Surely, he must know that Matt had been home that weekend? She chose not to deny it. It was too easy to verify.

'Of course, if he had been home, he could have had access to any one of the various products on sale in your nursery, isn't that so, Mrs Potter? Weedkillers, such as the can I took from your potting shed on Saturday, for example.'

'Matt never goes anywhere near the nurseries or the potting sheds.'

'No, he writes his music and he buys stamps at the general store.'

'The tests will put an end to all this,' she said curtly.

'Which are they, Mrs Potter?'

'The murderer's…his mental health. You said that he was being examined by psychiatrists. And his DNA.'

Burgess was making a show of concentration, studying his rearview mirror, focusing on a small car that was attempting to overtake them as they headed west. The lane was busy with oncoming evening traffic.

'Dangerous foolishness trying to pass on this stretch of road. Forgive me, Mrs Potter, what did you say?' He glanced at Lyndsay, smiling one of those menacing smiles that so irritated her. 'Ah yes, the tests… Nothing has been confirmed as yet.' She wasn't sure that she believed him. 'Did I tell you that when your friend Beresford found the body the foxes had been there?' Lyndsay shook her head. 'Scavengers, Mrs Potter. In a warm, humid spot such as the one where Surinder's body was found, semen can degenerate quickly, even go mouldy. But still we might have had a chance. If the foxes hadn't got to her.'

'I don't know what you mean…'

'We believe that after Surinder was raped, she continued to struggle. In all probability, she got to her feet and tried to run which meant that the semen recently ejaculated into her – which, given the circumstances, could have been a weak ejaculation – had worked its way out of the vagina. It trickled out, leaving few traces for us to test. Still we might have had a chance…' Lyndsay wound down the window for some much-needed air. '…but her vaginal cavity was chewed away. Due to the foxes, what little semen was left, was mixed in with her own chewed flesh and blood and her own body fluids. The cotton swabs inserted into the vagina could not give us the untainted fluid. The DNA in the semen cannot be isolated. It is permeated with her blood and other debris. So, we are unlikely to get a profile from the murderer's sperm. A tragic end, eh, Mrs Potter, for such a beautiful young girl?'

Lyndsay couldn't answer; she wanted to vomit.

'The blow that killed her came from behind her. Judging by damage to clumps of nearby fern fronds she'd put up quite a struggle and then tried to escape. She must have been running for her life, wouldn't you say?'

Lyndsay's stomach was tight. What was the point of these graphic details? 'Does all this mean you can't prove who killed her?'

'It means we are obliged to find other sources of DNA. We'll look for clothing fibres caught on branches, saliva on a cigarette stub, for example – there were burns on her inner thighs. Or a beer bottle. Details of that nature. We are not helped by the wretched rain the night before Beresford found her body, of course.'

She needed a respite from this topic of conversation. 'Why do you want to visit my father's grave?'

'Matthew was very fond of him. He might have gone to the graveside.' This knocked Lyndsay for six. The idea had never crossed her mind. 'I hope this won't prove distressing for you, Mrs Potter. You have quite enough on your plate as it is.'

'I'm fine.'

Burgess pulled up outside the gates of Lingfield Cemetery. 'Lead the way, will you, Mrs Potter?'

20

Stephen descended the stone steps that led from the Quai de Montebello to the cobbled walkway at the river's edge. There, he gazed admiringly across the Seine to the recently sandblasted Notre-Dame Cathedral. To his left a queue was gathering. He glanced at his watch; it was almost ten to the hour. A *bateau mouche*, the Parisian floating tourist bus, had been due since quarter to. From this same landing stage, he read, one could board a *bateau bus*. So, he could travel by water-bus to his destination – an enticing prospect. He had a couple of hours to kill and had been intending to walk the entire distance along the waterfront, but why not make the trip by boat? It would be delightful on such a warm afternoon. He strolled to the ticket office, requested a single to the Port de Plaisance de Paris Arsenal and enquired after the schedule.

The old man at the kiosk shook his head. 'The canal which takes you from the main channel of the river to that part of Paris is too narrow,' he explained, 'for water-buses to pass along. *Les Bateaux Mouches* also cannot go there. You must take a taxi.'

'I'll walk. I'd prefer to stay close to the river.'

'Why not take the water taxi, *monsieur*?'

'But no such service exists in Paris!' exclaimed Stephen.

The ancient fellow beamed triumphantly. '*Mais, oui*! However, there is only the one. Fortunately, the captain is a good friend of mine.'

'Then, please, telephone your friend for me.'

After a brief call, the man informed Stephen that the boat would be along in five minutes. 'Keep your eye out for it and say *"Bonjour"* to Christian for me.'

Stephen bade the old chap a good day and wandered off along the cobbled bank towards the foot of the Pont de l'Archevêché. He had no desire to wait amongst the gathering assembly of sightseers – even out of doors Stephen was claustrophobic in crowds. As he strolled he turned about, casting his gaze in every direction. He had never become acquainted with Paris from the perspective of the river, having viewed it from the quaysides on many occasions, but never before from its riverbanks. Here were the arteries of the ancient city. It thrilled him to uncover a universe so essential and yet so unfamiliar to him in the city he loved so passionately. It was as if Paris was welcoming him by exposing more intimate aspects of her nature, promising him future pleasures. Promising him future pleasures. Stephen repeated the words, running them around his tongue. How he ached to have knowledge of Gin Millar, to inhabit her. That exquisite pleasure he had dreamed of without cessation. Since the moment he had first set eyes on her; the moment she had poured herself like liquid gold into his soul and taken possession of him.

Approaching from the west he heard the chug of a motor. He swung round and saw his water taxi scudding beneath the bridge of St-Michel, then Petit Pont, Pont du Double, arriving south of the Île de la Cité. A rush of joy swept through him as he waved to attract the mariner's attention.

From a casement window of a tall seventeenth-century building on the Left Bank, Stephen caught strains of Mahler. It was the fourth symphony. The speedboat settled in the surge alongside him. Stephen climbed aboard and handed his own neatly penned copy of Gin Millar's address to the helmsman. The music high above them swept on towards the penultimate bars of the first movement, causing Stephen to smile. 'Death beckons sweetly,' he muttered to himself, recollecting a reference to Mahler's interpretation of the theme of his music.

Having glanced at the address the driver nodded and the boat took off, pounding over the water, springing on the little waves like a rocking horse in flight.

Stephen had left London on the first Eurostar of the day, while Lyndsay was still sleeping. He had intended to telephone Gin immediately upon arrival but once here he had waited, relishing the prospect of the call. It had been close to midday when he dialled her number – directly after his meeting with a Dutch offshore-investment company, which had gone rather well – and he had found her home.

'Oui, bonjour?'

'Gin? Gin Millar, is that you?'

'C'est moi.' She had sounded sleepy, but it had been too late in the day to wake her. Was someone there with her? He had never considered the possibility. If she were married then, surely, her voice-mail message would have given two names? She wore no ring. No, she was single, he felt sure of it, and unattached.

He had introduced himself. 'I'm Stephen Potter... I wonder if you remember me. We met in a bar near the Maison Salé a few weeks ago. You asked me for a light and sat across a table from me while you smoked your cigarette.' The introduction had been sung in his head a million times, now he had finally spoken it.

There had been a considerable pause, she must have been trying to recall, and then a gentle laughing. 'Yes, I remember.'

He had invited her for lunch but she had not been available. 'Dinner, then?'

'I'm not free for dinner either, sorry.' Still the warmth in her response encouraged him.

'You tell me. Whenever you have the time.'

'I'm sorry.'

He had felt panicked. 'Lunch; whenever you can make it...'

'It's not possible.'

'I have to see you. I have something for you.' There had been a silence, the length of which had unnerved him. 'Hello? Gin?'

'Yes, I'm here. But it's not poss –'

'I have to see you.'

'Why?'

'You lost something at the museum. I want to return it to you.'

'You found my earring? That's great! Why didn't you say so? Very well, Mr Potter, come by later. We'll have an aperitif – come at six.' An aperitif! So, there must be a glimmer of interest. 'Do you have my address?'

'Yes, I do.'

'How clever of you to have found me. I am not in the phone book, not traceable by Minitel.'

'It wasn't so difficult… I went –'

'You can tell me later. *A plus tard.*'

Now, it was a little after four in the afternoon and Stephen was on the river coursing across Paris in a water taxi. He was ludicrously early, but he had been restless and impatient from the moment he had climbed out of bed in England. Even the unpacked cartons awaiting him in his newly acquired Parisian apartment had failed to distract him.

Pacing the rooms, he had felt displaced, and tormented by longing, so had decided to leave early and get some air. Out in the street, a level of sobriety had returned, when he thought of his son's plight.

After his meeting in avenue Kléber with the Dutch lawyers, he'd paused near L'Etoile to telephone Gin and then Churdle Bridge Farm but, at the last moment, he had refrained from ringing home, deciding that he didn't particularly want to get tangled up in conversation with Lyndsay. Instead he'd phoned Burgess. It was laughable, to be ringing the one person who made his skin crawl and his temper short, but under the circumstances, Burgess was the least messy option and on the subject of Matthew he was the one with his finger on the pulse. The Inspector was in his office.

'I'm in Paris,' Stephen had informed him immediately. Better to be on the level with the blasted man.

'Let me jot down that address, again. And the phone number?'

'It's not connected yet. Any news?'

'Nothing in particular. You'll be back when?'

'Thursday.'

'Thursday?' Stephen detected an element of accusation in Burgess' response.

'I'm going on to Geneva from here,' he'd added. He resented the need to detail his schedule. Still, he preferred to inform Burgess of his movements rather than give the man cause to make enquiries.

'Your wife knows where you'll be?'

'Yes.'

'Stay in touch.'

From there, he had strolled to the Place de la Madeleine, drunk an espresso and then wandered around the Ralph Lauren emporium where he'd purchased loafers, sports slacks and a new check shirt. Nothing overstated, all acceptably casual. After having paid for the goods he had returned to his apartment, stopping by a bank to collect plenty of cash for his onward journey, and he had deposited the blue carrier bag that contained the suit he had previously been wearing. Before going out again, he had picked up the present he had bought for Gin.

Freshly attired, he had crossed the city to the Left Bank, to the Musée d'Orsay, where he had whiled away an hour or two with the Impressionists, then, skipping lunch and hugging the water's edge, he had walked until he'd reached the Quai de Montebello from where he had ordered his water taxi.

Desire was driving him, giving him no peace. To have her had become his living, breathing obsession.

Stephen paid Christian, the skipper, in cash, adding an excessive tip, and disembarked. The still air after the windblown journey was exceedingly balmy. He took a moment to relish it while marvelling at the man he had become. What an unaccountable change had overtaken him in so short a space of time! Recklessly optimistic, was how he perceived himself now. Stephen Potter: reborn.

He sauntered away from the canal, moving off from the smell of diesel, dawdling here and there, losing himself within the narrow streets of this eastern section of Paris, intent on whiling away the time until six o'clock. He barely noticed the post-war constructions – the cheerless blocks of faceless flats – that dominated this relatively poor yet trendy district, so taken up was he with his own contemplations. His intention to separate from Lyndsay caused him no heartache, although he felt a modicum of guilt about her evident pain and about leaving on a business trip at such a distressing hour, but it was imperative and the prospect of seventy-two hours out of England filled him with a sense of liberty. It offered a taste of future freedom. What astounded him was how constrained he had allowed himself to become in his marriage.

Soon that would be behind him. Change was the order. New beginnings. Personal risk-taking. For the first time in many a year he felt alive, liberated. Once Matt had returned – which he felt certain would be any day now – and once this Argentinian General's ill-gotten fortune had been buffed, polished and cleverly invested, he, Stephen, would retire from the investment game. Rather like air travel, the more frequently you journeyed, the shorter the odds. He had ridden the tiger; it was time to get out.

He would buy a jeep, journey across the Sahara, canoe the white rapids in Canada or climb mountains in Nepal. And what of his yacht lying idle in Bosham? He had never sailed it further than across the Channel and back. Why? Why ever not? Perhaps he would retrieve that one personal possession from his intended divorce settlement – or purchase another – and set forth to where? South America, Australia? Who could forecast to what frontiers he might venture, what seas he might navigate? The point was he would be born again, with Gin Millar at his side. When the divorce was settled, he would win the boys back, compensate, and invite them to share in his new existence. University at the Sorbonne and an economics or science degree for Paulie, and the *Conservatoire de la Musique* for Matthew.

Stephen had been so taken up with his schemes that he had failed to notice the time passing. From somewhere out of sight church bells were chiming. His watch read six minutes past six. Why did he always keep his watch five minutes fast? It was a longstanding habit, which he rectified in an instant so that the watch now read one minute past the hour. But where was he? This part of Paris was unfamiliar to him. The closest he had ever ventured to this down-at-heel district was to visit the newly constructed Opera at the Bastille.

He stepped towards the fuggy interior of a corner café where a handful of workmen sat in blue overalls, smoking, loud in discussion, sipping slender glasses of pastis. This might have been a pre-war scene. Some things never change, mused Stephen, asking for the direction of the river and nodding his thanks when one of the *ouvriers* called out a response.

Five minutes later, he was hurrying across the Place de la Bastille, sure of his direction. He strode the boulevard de la Bastille and descended to the waterfront by a temporary bridge identified by a sign that read: *Port de la Plaisance*. The chug of a small boat drew his attention. Glancing back along the canal, he saw a motor dinghy manned by water police; a routine patrol by the look of things but the sight of the two uniformed officers was a sharp reminder that not so many days ago his local reservoir had been dragged in search of his missing son.

As he passed along the cobbled strand, he noticed a number of stragglers, predominantly blacks, lazing on the grassy bank. Their lurking presence troubled him. His mistrust was aggravated when one of them rose to his feet and requested a cigarette.

Stephen shook his head briskly. '*Je ne fume pas.*'

The fellow accepted the refusal and withdrew graciously. Stephen had no aversion to immigrants as such, but he had a very serious aversion to poverty and the threat of violence that accompanied it. Was Gin safe living alone in this district? Did she have a dog? He would buy her one. No – he was intending to relocate her.

Stephen fetched up at her home, a houseboat on the Seine. It was a modest wooden affair decked out with dozens of pots of geraniums. In all his fantasies, of which there had been many, he had never dreamed of such an original lifestyle, but it did not displease him. In the light of the surrounding seediness, the robust scarlets and pinks gave an air of nobility and a breath of life to the simple abode. Stephen's delight in their splash of colour far exceeded his approval of Lyndsay's nurseries.

From the belly of the boat a female voice crooned languidly.

'Anyone home?' he called from the quay. An Alsatian on a neighbouring boat began to bark. Christ, he was nervous!

The grounds of Lingfield Cemetery were leafy, spacious and dignified. The birdsong was clear and sweet – a chaffinch, perhaps? Their path was bordered with Marguerite daisies. 'It's well maintained. Is there a full-time gardener or groundskeeper here?' asked Burgess.

'I believe so.' Lyndsay stepped onto a pebbly track that led left from the central walkway. Graves adorned with flowers and others overgrown with weeds and grass flanked her as her sandals crunched softly against the stones. She turned and saw that Burgess had slowed, and was surveying the grounds. She followed his gaze. What was running through his mind? What was he looking for, a caretaker's cottage?

A low stonewall surrounded the park. With precious little effort Matt could have gained access at any hour. There was nowhere better to hide out. She wondered where he would have laid his head if he had slept here. Lyndsay watched Burgess make a 360-degree turn scanning the graveyard for some form of shelter. There was none. Taps had been installed at various points, for watering the plants on the graves – for Matt's washing, drinking. He could have picked up a sleeping bag from somewhere and bedded down alongside his grandfather's grave. It was a macabre thought, but if he were desperate, traumatised or burdened by guilt, she reasoned that anything was possible.

Lyndsay approached her father's grave. The butter-yellow peonies she had planted a few weeks back were growing tall. If any clue, no matter how tiny, had hid itself among the grass blades, she wanted to be the one to pick it out. Had Matt been here? It was a fact – astutely grasped by Burgess – that, in times of crisis, Matt had always fled to his grandfather.

Burgess arrived at her side. Always watching, never more than a step away, probing, breathing down her neck. Bending onto his haunches he stared at the ground and the recently erected marble headstone.

'Curious.'

'What?'

'It's brand new.'

'He's only been dead a few months!'

'One name, your father's, engraved on it. Your mother and your sister are not buried here?'

Lyndsay felt her knees go weak. 'My mother was cremated. I… I don't know what happened to her ashes. I was only eleven at the time.'

'And your sister?'

Lyndsay gripped the marble stone, cold beneath her touch. She bent to the grave and lovingly removed three dead leaves and one brown curling blossom from the peony plants. This accomplished, she rose and, eyeing Burgess, stated steadily, 'My sister is buried in Sevenoaks where we lived at the time of her death.' Her point made, she strode purposefully back along the gritted path.

Lyndsay paced alongside the locked car. She would have preferred to be anywhere but in Burgess' company, suffering his nagging questions. Why couldn't his relentless interrogations, his tenacious snooping, be directed towards bringing her son back to her?

'Anyone home?'

Gin's head appeared looking relaxed and smiling. Her thick red hair was shot with gold from the evening light behind her. One solitary cloud scuffed an otherwise clear sky. The promise of a crimson sunset bled from beyond the boat's horizon. This woman, the woman of his future, rose onto the deck like a tawny angel, a dazzling angel of liberation. Once again, she was dressed all in black: tight hipster jeans with black, snakeskin cowboy boots; a cropped T-shirt covered her breasts.

'*Bonsoir*, Mr Potter, come aboard.'

The gangplank was down, so Stephen boarded without difficulty, although his heart was beating so fast he thought it would explode.

The soft jazz was unfamiliar to him but it was a velvet accompaniment to his first real introduction to her. When he enquired after the identity of the singer, Gin handed him the disc case. An arresting face with wild Afro hair stared out at him.

'Roberta Flack?' The name meant nothing to him. He studied the photograph rather than choosing to linger over Gin's bewitching features and give too much away, too soon. 'What's the song?'

'Killing Me Softly.' Gin did not speak the words, but sung them.

'So, you live here?' It was not a question, merely an affirmation of the glaringly obvious, and an enquiry to cover his awkwardness. This woman singing so freely in front of him had embarrassed him. So, too, had her habit of looking him directly in the eye, constantly appraising him. He felt clumsy and this was not a state Stephen was used to. He liked to be in control, run the show.

'Any reason why I shouldn't live here?' she laughed.

Her style was more like a student at the Sorbonne than a woman in her late thirties. But it suited her and seemed in no way sordid or seedy. In any case, what the hell did he know about the lifestyles of students at the Sorbonne? Perhaps there were many cosmopolitan women who dressed and lived this way. His awkwardness was just another example of the narrow-minded world he had buried himself in. Gazing at her now he saw that Gin would be as well-suited to a suite at the Hôtel Crillon as to this boat. The point was that she was completely at ease with herself. Her proximity brought him peace and clarity. She possessed the aura of an angel, his guardian angel. Auras, angels! What the hell was he thinking of? He was a practical down-to-earth businessman.

And yet for all her ease of manner there was a darker nature there too, Stephen felt sure of it. Standing face to face with her he felt giddy from a rush of danger. The neighbourhood in which she was living, with clots of unemployed down and outs loitering on the riverside cadging cigarettes. She was radiant but her way was marginal – even decadent. He could not define why he judged her so, but there was something about her, the fashion of her movements. He felt as though he were hanging from a tuft of grass at the edge of a precipice, as if he might find wings and fly or he might plummet. Hadn't he, for one fleeting second in the taxi from Gatwick, imagined her as a succubus and not a goddess? What was unnerving about such extreme thoughts was that given the choice: the danger of Gin or no Gin, he would devour the forbidden fruit.

'You look a little uncomfortable standing there, Mr Potter,' she said mischievously. 'Would you like a drink, a smoke, to pull up a chair?'

He concentrated on the words of the song while looking about for something to sit on. *Killing me softly with your song. Killing me softly.*

'What can I offer you? Alcohol or...'

'Scotch and water if you have it, please.'

From the quay a terrible thudding broke out, followed by a screeching which ricocheted around the port. It sounded as though some great bird was being dismembered. He looked over his shoulder and saw the swinging arm of a crane transporting a stack of cement slabs. It was late for such works.

Gin had vanished.

He glanced at his watch – ten to seven – it was ten to six in England. He should ring Lyndsay and check in.

Stephen spotted a canvas chair and carried it to where he had been standing. He sat down, crossed his legs and attempted to relax. Where had she gone? It was as if the second she was out of sight the witching returned and he was burning once more.

'I'm curious to know how you found me,' she was ascending the cabin steps with his drink.

He rose to accept the glass. 'Aren't you having a...?'

She shook her head and placed the half empty bottle of Scotch on the deck at his feet. 'Later.'

He read the word sweetly. It promised a future. There would be a 'later' for the pair of them. She was not inviting him for a polite drink and then intending to send him packing. Such boyish conclusions, such adolescent interpretations! Again, he was reminded of Matthew. Preferring not to dwell on his missing son, Stephen downed a shot of Scotch.

Gin drew up a chair and sat, but not facing him. They were side by side, both looking west, along the canal towards the Place de la Bastille. Within sight was the golden figure perched atop the monument that celebrated France's revolution. It seemed apt that he was facing liberty and a ravishing sunset.

'You have my earring?'

From the work site a drill started up, tunnelling like amplified woodworm into the evening's repose, drowning out her question.

'Doesn't that noise drive you mad?' He glanced sidelong at her profile; weak with desire to rest himself against her.

'Until last week, they were only working days. I sleep in the afternoon, I didn't notice...'

'Don't you work?'

'I work at night.'

At night. What woman works alone at night? It could not be true! He could not tolerate the possibility that he had fallen in love with...no, worse, was ready to sacrifice his entire being for...a whore. Here was the danger that he had sensed about her. Here was the dark lining within the core of one so luminous.

'Don't look so horrified, Mr Potter,' she said, glancing at her watch. 'May I have my earring?' He dug into his pocket, pulled out the small, red Cartier box and passed it over to her. 'What's this?' She seemed upset.

'I didn't find your earring,' he said. 'I replaced it.' Gin stared at the unopened box without a word. Stephen coughed. 'What line of work are you in then?' he asked warily.

21

Gin's expression had changed. There was an edge to her now. 'Well, I'm not a whore,' she said.

'No, I didn't think for one minute…'

'Then, why are you giving me these?' The question was direct and accusing. Stephen was witnessing the first flash of her anger. It made her all the more beautiful, all the more vulnerable.

'I hadn't considered your profession. It…makes no difference to me.' His heart quickened. Was he sure he knew what he was saying? In the past he had done business with men who were greedy and mercenary, partied in circles where to get stinking rich and then richer was the killing ambition, by foul means or fair, and he had felt no shame, but never, not even in youth, had he sought out professional sex. He had never bought his pleasure. Prostitutes held no allure for Stephen. In fact, they repulsed him. All sexual perversions disgusted him profoundly, they always had. Still, he loved this woman, and while the attraction was more potent than with any female before her, was he capable of openly embracing her for what she was?

Gin watched him. 'Relax! I'm not a whore,' she repeated. There was no tenderness in her tone, no acrimony either. Nothing placatory, no justification, just a simple bald denial of a fact. 'Your conclusions are hasty and crass, Mr Potter.'

'Please, call me Stephen.'

'The lady lives alone, works at night, et cetera. Her offbeat home is not in the most salubrious quarter of the city. She *must* be a tart. A rather narrow stupid judgement, don't you think?'

'Oh, come now!'

'And you have tried to buy me like a tart.'

'What?!'

'I invited you here for a drink because you said that you had found my earring. Instead you offer me these, this gift. A man I sat with while I smoked a cigarette… What am I supposed to do, jump up and down with gratitude, kick my clothes off?'

'You're being unfair!'

'Are you in the habit of purchasing twenty-four carat gold earrings from Cartier and giving them to women you have met once?'

'The earrings were to replace the one you lost.' Stephen was wounded by her irreverence. Suddenly he felt foolish and awkward under her stare. With hindsight the earrings had been a vulgar gesture. If he had been in the company of anyone else he would have walked away, but he could not. In spite of the humiliation he sat it out.

'Don't get so upset,' she said, lighting a cigarette and tossing the packet over to him.

He shook his head and passed it back and she assessed him. It was not a look of longing – how he wished it might have been – nor even of sexual interest, but nor was it hostile. She regarded him with a clinical eye; like one studying an unknown species. He took another swig of whisky. This was not going at all well, he had not anticipated any of this. He had dreamed of something more sensual, more yielding and tender.

'They were how I traced you,' he murmured.

'Bullshit! I've never been to Cartier.'

Should he tell her the truth and reveal his foolish sentiments? Would she better warm to him or would she mock him again, revile him for his nonsensical romanticism? For in the fading light of this Paris evening, after so many weeks of aching, that was how it was beginning to look. This was not the realisation of a dream, but idiotic make-believe.

'I saw you through the window at the museum,' he began hoarsely. He downed the last shot of Johnny Walker in his glass and reached for the bottle to refill it. 'May I?' He accepted her nod as encouragement to continue.

Gin lit another cigarette and slewed her chair away from the sunset so that she was facing him. The little that was left of the light glowed in sinuous looping strips behind her.

'In the café you told me your name: Gin, not much of a clue! It was a hopeless task, even if the name is unusual. The following Saturday I was back in Paris. I went to the bar. No one there knew you, so I returned to the museum. The week before I'd asked a ticket attendant if he could direct me to a good restaurant, but he'd failed to come up with a suggestion. The moment he set eyes on me again, his face lit up and he shouted across the courtyard the name of some local café or other. I thanked him and moved on, and then it hit me. If this fellow's memory was so damned good, after an entire week he'd recognised me – one man out of dozens of foreigners pestering him about restaurants – then perhaps he would remember you too.'

The glint in Gin's eyes, those wild olivine eyes, suggested that she was softening, warming to him. He was being tolerated again, for this cocktail hour at least. And her smile showed him that she was tickled by this tale of pursuit. It restored his confidence.

'I described you, your swathes of red hair, your position in the courtyard and, even before I'd finished, he said, "Ah, *la belle femme* who was searching for her lost earring"...' Gin nodded, giggling as though a jigsaw were being pieced together for her. She dragged hard on her cigarette and tossed her mane back from her face. 'You know the rest,' he said, delighted at having amused her.

'Tell me.'

'The attendant directed me to the lost property office. While I'd been in the courtyard looking for you on that first Saturday you were in the office completing a form. It included a description of the lost article: "one hooped gold earring", and with it, written in your own hand, your name, address and telephone number. I had found you.' Fate had been with me, he thought, but did not voice that sentiment.

'Hence the earrings?' she grinned.

'Hence the earrings. You haven't found the lost one?'

She shook her head. 'I thought you had it.'

'Well now you have a new pair. Will you accept them?'

'It's kind, but no thank you. Here.' She drew the small red and gold box from between her fingers and handed it back to him.

Stephen contemplated it for a moment or two, not quite knowing what to do with it. 'Why not?'

'Because it wouldn't be right.'

'Will you have dinner with me, at least?'

She shook her head again, glanced at her watch and stood up. 'No dinner, thanks. Time to go to work.'

His heart lurched. Was this it? He rose too. 'Well, if you are not…a whore,' he joked cautiously, 'what do you do?'

'I'm a singer.'

'Ah, I see. Now I understand the houseboat here. You're with the opera. You're in the chorus at the Bastille Opera.'

Gin raised one eyebrow, affecting disdain. 'Not at all. Sorry, Mr Potter, I know zilch about opera. I work in a club. I'm a jazz singer.'

'Ah, Roberta Flack.'

'Yes.'

'My son…' he faltered at the mention of his family and the memory of Matthew, 'likes that sort of music.'

'You have a son?'

'I have two. One has…is not there… Well, I'm not there either. My wife and I are separated.'

'Oh, I'm sorry to hear that.' And she did sound genuinely sorry, thought Stephen. 'Since when?'

'Er, quite recently. But it's all perfectly amicable,' he lied.

Her expression told him nothing more. 'Excuse me,' she said.

He had never hidden from any mistress the fact that he was a married man, but then he had never left home before nor given up his married status, and no other woman had ever meant so much to him. But this woman was not his mistress. He felt incapable of finding the parameters, of understanding where he stood. He watched on almost helplessly as she swung the bottle up from alongside the chair and disappeared with it below deck.

The music was switched off. Gin was preparing her departure. Their aperitif was at an end. It was almost eight o'clock. He lifted up his chair and strolled with it across the deck towards the prow of the ship, to where he had found it. Lost in thought, he sat down again and stared out across the water; it was the colour of liquidised avocado. He was facing the main artery of the Seine, towards Austerlitz. One hundred metres or so along the bank was the building site. The whining noise had died down a little.

Two African labourers dressed in soiled overalls and yellow helmets were striding about the place, another was wheeling a barrow, a fourth was waving his arms high above his head and yelling instructions, but from this distance Stephen could not make out what was being said, nor did he care. His thoughts were on Gin. He lifted his gaze to the crane. Its iron arm swung towards a stack of concrete slabs and hovered above them before beginning its descent. He idly wondered why they were all working at this hour and, more importantly, what the hell he was going to do with the evening that yawned ahead of him. After he had telephoned Lyndsay.

'Ready?'

He hadn't heard her step. He turned back to her. She was dressed in a skin-tight black leather jacket, cropped short over unchanged jeans and T-shirt. From one shoulder hung a leather overnight bag. She had brushed her hair and freshened her face, and she looked radiant.

'Of course,' he rose but stood his ground, deliberating. What now? Perhaps he should suggest that he meet up with her later, or offer to escort her to the club. She was a woman of strong will, he had already discovered that. He could take nothing for granted. 'What's going on down at that building site?' he asked not out of insatiable curiosity but rather to delay the moment of departure and because the sight of her carrying that wretched bag depressed him, digging like a hook in his gut. Was she intending to spend the night elsewhere? If so, with whom? He cursed his own short sightedness; he had found out nothing about her. Bedazzled, as on the first occasion, he had allowed all opportunity to slip through his fingers.

'They're constructing a new Metro line and an overground rail connection linking the southern part of the city with the Gare du Nord. The whole port is in chaos.'

There was a shyness that he hadn't noticed before. It added to her charm. The length of the barge distanced them: he, lingering by the prow, surrounded by the mass of a city's water; she, leaning casually against the wooden engine room. In spite of the twenty metres between them or because of it, he had an overwhelming urge to reach out to her and give voice to his feelings. Instead he said, 'But the works don't trouble you, even now when the shifts match your schedule?' He was talking for the sake of it, mouthing inconsequential small talk, and he noted by the way she lifted her thick hair away from her face that she knew it and was keen to be on her way.

'Sure, it's pretty noisy and dusty and dangerous. No more strolling along the bank lost in dreams. Got to keep a sharp eye in case a line of track flies through the sky and zaps you.' She was kidding, but she was making a move. 'I need to hit the road, Mr Potter.' She tossed her bag to shore and swung lithely up onto the gangplank, putting him in mind of some lissom jungle animal.

'Gin, I've fallen in love with you.'

Rotating on the heels of her cowboy boots, swathes of hair falling like flames onto a leather jacket that creaked as she moved, she looked directly towards him. 'What did you say?' Green eyes shot with gold, twinkling and then closing. She clasped her hands together and ran them through her hair, obviously a habitual gesture. The glint of one single earring slid into view and then disappeared. She lifted her head again and shook it. Her poise reminded him of a wild cat as she rose to her feet and leapt from the plank to shore. 'Mr Potter, sorry, but it's time to leave.'

As he followed, he tossed the box containing the earrings down the steps to the lower deck. Later, when she arrived back home, she would find them. Who knows, he thought, by then she might be ready to accept them. Ready to accept him.

22

Alone in the potting shed, Lyndsay stood scanning the wooden shelves. She reached up and along towards the corner of the top cobwebbed shelf where the cans of weedkiller were stored. She rarely used these products any more and they were never put out for sale. Burgess had taken one during his visit of the previous Saturday, which should have left five but there were only four. She was sure, almost sure, that there had been half a dozen stored there but she couldn't for the life of her remember when she had last counted them. Or was Burgess sowing seeds of uncertainty within her?

'He could have had access to any one of the various products on sale in your nursery, isn't that so, Mrs Potter? Weedkillers, such as the can I took from your potting shed on Saturday, for example.' Those had been his words.

It had been the day of the accident. She had come in here to collect a fork and had found the shelves in a state of disarray, and there had been the remains of a cigarette. Matt had already disappeared by then. But when, before that, had she been in here? She couldn't remember. It could have been a while. She was worn out. Perhaps there had only been five cans left there, not six. It was Burgess troubling her. And those graphic descriptions of Surinder's death as well as the problems concerning the DNA – why had he gone to such lengths to recount all that, turning her stomach with those images? She closed up the shed and trudged back up to the house.

For the first time that afternoon she thought of Stephen and longed for the days when he would have taken her in his arms and held her. There had been a time when his strength had been her rock. When he returned, she would tell him how much she loved him. The rows were not the reality, the steadfastness was. They would repair their marriage; find their way back to one another. She must not lose faith.

Stephen accompanied Gin to the Left Bank, crossing the Seine by way of the Île St Louis. Once in the Latin Quarter, they found the narrow cobbled lanes milling with people, tourists predominantly, tribes of them, trawling the historic streets looking for special places to dine. Here and there, as they cut through an alley or slipped down a side-street, shopkeepers and restaurant owners hailed Gin, enquiring after her well-being or wishing her a fine evening while she, in return, smiled and winked, addressing each by name.

'You're very well known here.' He felt extraordinarily good at her side – she breezed through the stir of the city with cool assurance – and for once in his life he was grateful for the press of the crowd. It drove them closer together. From this proximity his every breath was endowed with the scent of her spicy perfume. All around them Greek music sounded from the crowded tavernas.

'I used to live around these lanes before I moved to the boat. I love this *quartier*. The club where I sing is just a couple of streets away.' Since they'd left the harbour their conversation had been spare. She had asked Stephen about his sons – the boys' names, their ages and hobbies – but little else. Gin responded to his questions but sought little information. Evidently, she preferred silence.

A man pushed by carrying a live lobster on a plate.

'Won't you change your mind and have a quick bite with me?'

She shook her head. 'Thanks, but I'm going to drop in on my friend.'

Stephen nodded, affecting calm, but his heart lurched sickly. Would she deposit her bag with her friend and return there later?

Approaching them was a tramp, hobbling among the browsers and the litter, a plastic bag wrapped around his damaged foot. His complexion was fuchsia-red, his eyes marbled by booze and dead to the world. Instinctively, Stephen lifted an arm to protect Gin. The drunk drew closer, bearing down on them. Stephen moved to block his approach. He would have hit the fellow if need be, anything to keep this disgustingly ravaged creature – who at close range proved to be alarmingly young – at bay. He thought only of Gin's safety. The man growled at him, slurred something incomprehensible, and proffered a soiled palm at Gin who sunk her hand into the pocket of her jeans and passed the beggar a fifty-franc note. Stephen looked on amazed; Gin had addressed the vagrant by name. He was on the point of asking why she troubled with such low-life people when he noticed that her pace was slowing.

'My friend lives here. Goodnight, Mr Potter,' she said.

'If you won't dine with me, may I come and hear you sing?'

She drew to a halt at a crossroads of cobbled lanes. Restaurant tables, crammed tightly together utilising every square centimetre of pavement, abounded. People were eating and chattering merrily.

'Let's just say goodnight, Mr Potter.' Gin glanced skywards. A woman high above them was standing on a balcony, surveying the bustling city at play. She caught sight of Gin below and waved in an easy way.

'Is that your friend?' Stephen wanted so terribly for Gin to say yes. For there to be no sexual potential in this rendezvous of hers, no attachment to threaten his claim on her.

'Yes, that's my friend. So long, Mr Potter.'

He exhaled contentedly. 'Won't you call me Stephen?'

She smiled and her gold-green eyes lit up mischievously. 'I think I prefer Mr Potter.'

'But it's so formal.'

'It suits you,' she replied softly.

'You haven't told me the name of the club.'

'Listen, I…'

'I'll find it. You know I will.'

Gin sighed, but there was no antagonism in it. 'Les Trois Mailloches.' And she slipped like a melody beyond reach, moving towards an entrance set back from the lane. His dream was lost to him amongst the hugger-mugger of people but her scent hung in the air around him and he lingered with it, dancing with the luxury of her.

Lyndsay placed her tray of mint tea on one of the occasional tables in the drawing room, settled back against a bank of cushions and pushed the television remote control. Her need was for something light, to deaden out the day and the defeating loneliness. It didn't much matter what, just so long as it wasn't news or current affairs. *Coronation Street* was a perfect offering and not without poetry. As the image lit the set, the telephone began to ring.

'Blast!' She had considered screening calls this evening, but there was always the hope that it might be Matt, or Stephen. She muted the sound and reached for the phone. 'Hello?'

'Lyndsay…it's Stephen.'

'Yes, I know. I recognised your voice. Where are you?'

'In a restaurant on the Left Bank. How are things?'

'Fine.'

'You sound irritable.'

'I'm not irritable! I spent the afternoon with Burgess.'

'Any news?'

'No news.'

'Right, well, I'll call in the morning, shall I?'

'If you like.'

'I'll call in the morning. Have a good evening.'

'And you.'

'Bye.'

'Bye.'

She replaced the receiver and pressed herself down into the cushions. They were speaking to one another as though they were strangers. She should have told him that she loved him. Who was he dining with, she wondered.

Stephen ordered a plain-grilled steak and a half-bottle of a 1988 Pauillac. A glance around the restaurant told him that it was nothing special, although it had appeared inviting enough. At least it was not overly crowded or noisy, and it was situated within a stone's throw of the jazz club, which, after enquiry, he'd discovered was on the corner of rue Saint Séverin.

The wine was unexpectedly fine. Even so, Stephen drank only one glass. Two whiskies on an empty stomach had served him. He had no wish to befuddle his mind or dampen his ardour. He ate the food laid out before him at a leisurely pace. There was time to kill.

'Killing me softly with your song. Killing me softly.'

Gin's voice sung in his mind. Stephen's hunger for her had grown to a physical pain. Still, after her performance at the club, he would not press her to invite him back. She would be tired. Yet the aching to touch her, to lay himself against her, was tormenting. His need knew no reason. He had to have her.

When he came to pay his bill, he realised that he had left his wallet with his American Express card in his suit folded in the carrier bag on his bed. Fortunately he had plenty of cash. While waiting for his change Stephen pondered the woman on the balcony. Had she been pre-arranged or had Gin decided upon her as a delicate way of ridding herself of him? As a rule he knew where he stood, but not with her.

He traced his steps through the lanes in search of Les Trois Mailloches jazz club. She had given him no encouragement, but there might be an explanation for that. A bad marriage, a history of broken love affairs? Even so…

He had never encountered a personality quite like hers before. She was warm and sexy, yet she withheld… But at no time had she spurned the declaration of his sentiments. Or had she? Her manner had been friendly – no, polite. By neither accepting nor rejecting him she was leaving him to paddle helplessly in rapid waters and that indifference proved that she did not give a damn for him. Such conclusions sent Stephen spiralling into a well of despair.

However, by the time he reached the club he was laughing once more. His spirits were flying like a kite. He would be in her presence again soon. What a jackass he was. Just because he had fallen in love at first sight did not mean that Gin was obliged to do the same. Patience was what was required. He was charging at this like some gauche teenager trying to tug the knickers off a hot date, when what he needed was a little self-possession, a little dignity – virtues he had always prided himself on.

Stephen's thoughts turned to Matthew. When Matt was back home he would invite the boy over to Paris for the weekend, take him out to lunch and have a chat with him. Not about the facts of life, they had thrashed that out long ago, but about ways of courting a female, and elegant seduction techniques. A lesson Stephen might very well learn about himself. He giggled at the thought of Matt's probable response: chill out, Dad. Oh, to be as 'cool' as his adolescent son!

23

The sound of the phone ringing startled Lyndsay. She must have dozed off in front of the television from lack of sleep.

She switched off the set and picked up the receiver. 'Hello?'

'Lyndsay, it's...' It was Marion Finch. Marion had taken to ringing, usually at some ungodly hour, drunk and maudlin, detailing the latest turn of events in the saga of Arthur and his 'fancy bit'. Lyndsay was not in the mood. 'Did you watch the news?'

'What news?'

'They've released him.'

'Who?'

'The man who confessed to Surinder Bharjee's murder.'

'Are you sure?' Lyndsay was on her feet, zapping channels, changing systems, moving from satellite to cable and back to terrestrial coverage. No news programme showed. 'How do you know?' she cried.

'They announced it on the Kent roundup about ten minutes ago. I would have called directly but I had someone here.'

'I don't understand. When did this happen? Why hasn't anyone contacted me? Marion, I have to get off the line, I –'

'All they said was that the police are no longer holding him. They didn't report why.'

Lyndsay sank back onto the sofa. 'Marion, forgive me, I must go. Thanks for calling.' She replaced the receiver and took a long, deep breath. Had Burgess been party to this information during the afternoon? It would explain why he was in the churchyard, hunting for clues, hunting for Matt.

What had she done with Burgess' number? Why had he withheld this? She was in the kitchen, at her notepad, flicking pages, fishing through discarded messages, tracking down the number of Burgess' office when the telephone rang again. It was bound to be Marion ringing back.

'Marion, I can't talk now.'

'Mrs Potter?' It was Burgess. Lyndsay gasped at the sound of his voice. 'I've been trying to reach you...'

'That's damned well not true!'

'Your line has been engaged.'

'For two minutes. Two short calls since I came in. Since you dropped me off! Why didn't you tell me this afternoon?'

'They hadn't picked him up then. I was radioed exactly nine minutes after I left you.'

'Picked him up?' She was confused. 'But I thought you released him.'

'Matthew. We are holding Matthew.'

'Matthew.' Lyndsay felt her whole body go weak. 'Is he all right?'

'He's in Dover.'

'Give me the address. I'll collect him. Hold on a minute, please! Damn, where's my pen? I'm leaving right away. Oh, thank God you've found him! He is all right, isn't he?'

'I am with him, Mrs Potter.'

The solemnity of Burgess' delivery sent a shiver down her spine. 'You are with him? Why you?' But the questions were redundant. She knew the answer. 'Put him on the phone.'

'He's not in this office.'

'I want to talk to my son!'

'Hold on.' Lyndsay heard muffled instructions, no clear words. Her mind was racing with Marion's news and now this. 'Someone's fetching him.'

'What about the lorry driver, the tests on that man you were holding?'

'His story didn't hold water. Each account he gave was marginally different. Three psychiatrists agreed that the fellow may be unhinged, but he has not committed murder. But the overruling factor, the evidence which forced us to release him, is that his DNA did not match anything.'

'The results are back already?' Was it possible, or had the whole story been a bluff?

'If we speak nicely to the DNA lab, they'll run them in a hurry. Under certain conditions.'

'Wait, I don't understand. You told me this afternoon that you wouldn't be able to make DNA tests, that –'

'I said the semen was probably too damaged. There are other factors, other clues to trace.'

'And Matt?' She was out of her depth. Not so long ago, a few hours earlier, it had all seemed straightforward. Matt's innocence had been assured.

'Nothing to be alarmed about, Mrs Potter, it's just routine. A few questions… It doesn't mean –'

'Fuck you!' Lyndsay's words lacked rage. They were born of exhaustion. She was not in the habit of using such language. 'I need to speak to him.'

'Someone's fetching him.'

An image flashed into her mind: Matt accompanied by a police constable being escorted to the telephone. 'I want to see him. I want to be with him. I'm leaving now.'

'We'll send a car.'

And then she felt her resolution returning. 'I prefer to make my own way. Just give me the address.'

'Matthew's just walked in. I'm putting him on.'

Lyndsay gripped the receiver tight. She heard footsteps and then rustling as the phone was handed from one to the other. Breath baited, she hung on. There was the sound of coughing; it was her son's. 'Matthew? Matt, darling, it's Mummy. Are you all right?'

'I'm fine.' His voice was flat and unreceptive. It was hard to read anything into it, except tiredness.

'Oh, darling, I… We've been so worried. Where have you been?'

'Mum, I've got to go. Here's…' His voice trailed away as though he hadn't the energy to continue or he had no idea where he was, or to whom he was passing the phone back. She heard a few incomprehensible words spoken by Burgess and then footsteps again. Was Matt being led away to a cell?

'I'm coming to collect my son right now, and I'm bringing Stephen's lawyer with me.' How was she going to get in touch with Stephen? There was no phone in his flat; he had no connection yet. Why hadn't she thought to ask him for the name of the restaurant?

'Mrs Potter, Matthew has been picked up for crossing the Channel as a stowaway and for attempting to enter France illegally. Nothing more serious than that.'

'Illegally?'

'Travelling without papers, possession of marijuana. Colombian grass discovered in the seam of his jacket pocket. Routine stuff. By all means come – it's why I called you – but let me send a car. You're upset, you've had one accident already.'

'You've believed Matthew was guilty of this murder from the very beginning. All your snooping! This is exactly what you've been angling for. Just give me the address.'

Burgess sighed and read out the address. Lyndsay jotted it down and without another word replaced the receiver. She had to contact Stephen.

Should she call Alan Grater, Stephen's solicitor? She was wary of taking action without Stephen's knowledge and approval. Still, she flipped through their address book in the hall searching for Alan's home number. If Matthew was in trouble, the kind she dreaded, then, in the face of such adversity, she and Stephen must stand together. And they would need Alan's expertise. This ghastly, unwanted trauma might be the very thing to reunite the family. However, the number was nowhere to be found, and she hadn't a clue where Amanda, Stephen's assistant, was living these days. At a loss, she rang Amanda's voice mail at Stephen's office.

'Amanda, it's Lyndsay. Please ring me when you hear this. Doesn't matter how late and, if you speak to Stephen before I do, ask him to get in touch. I need him urgently. Thank you.'

She grabbed a London telephone directory and looked up Alan's office number, intending to leave a message. The line was busy. He or his partners were working late.

She hurried upstairs to dress, gathered up her bag and keys and was all but ready when the Entryphone buzzed. Someone was at the gate. Surely to God, it couldn't be the bloody press again? She decided to ignore it, but whoever it was would waylay her as she left. She ran to the intercom. 'Yes?'

'Car for Mrs Potter.'

So Burgess had radioed a car. She pushed the button to release the gate. Right at this moment she hated Burgess with a ferocious passion, but he had a point. She was nervy, tired and anxious and could concentrate on nothing except being reunited with Matthew. She would accept the lift.

Head back, eyes closed, cocooned within the purring vehicle, Lyndsay's pressured mind was drawn to Stephen in Paris and to how she was going to reach him. Was he alone or did he know people to dine with? Of course he did. Stephen had contacts all around the globe: colleagues, associates, clients, and acquaintances. Those who had peopled what he often described as his 'other lives' and then, there was the woman.

Lyndsay felt a wave of regret. Why had it gone so horribly wrong between them? What had happened to all that warm, safe love? Still, his return and the knowledge that she could count on him, if only as Matt's father, gave her security. She indulged the fancy that Stephen might be missing her, might be regretting his decision to leave, then, once the fantasy had been played out, she returned to the long-awaited moment of seeing Matthew again.

It was late in the evening and growing dark when she arrived at the police station in Dover. The place had a dreary municipal feel to it. A uniformed young female in thick flat shoes and heavy dark trousers escorted Lyndsay to the custody officer, also a woman, older and more senior than the first, thick set with grey cropped hair. The woman briefly explained the information given over the telephone by Burgess. Matthew had been picked up, stowed away on a boat, in the English Channel and was being held by the Dover police for drug possession. He was also being questioned by a senior member of the Kent Area Major Incident Team – namely, Detective Inspector Douglas Burgess – with regard to the murder of Surinder Bharjee.

The whole place was functional and dehumanised. The younger female officer escorted Lyndsay to Burgess. He was perched on an unoccupied desk in the office he had taken possession of, and was browsing through the pages of one of his spiral-bound notebooks. A clutch of files was tucked awkwardly under his raincoated arm as though he were on his way somewhere. He stood when she entered. Their greeting was brisk and formal.

'No solicitor?' he asked.

'I couldn't get through to him.'

'Do you want me to call in someone local?' Lyndsay hesitated and Burgess offered her no further time for reflection. 'Matthew's expecting you,' he said. 'Let's go.'

Within the confines of the station, Lyndsay was alarmed to find Burgess another person, professional and aloof. A calibrating mind primed to its task. No longer the irritating sleuth sniffing out the world at large, Burgess was resolute and cold. The change boded ill. This detective was homing in on his chosen target: her son.

He escorted Lyndsay, in echoing silence, along a pastel-green corridor, up one flight of stone stairs and along another narrow corridor, passing not one stick of furniture along the way, into a small, cramped room made more claustrophobic by its lack of natural light. The one window was shuttered with a black blind. It was not a cell, Lyndsay silently reassured herself, but a room, with an open door. She found Matthew with a police officer seated either side of him. They made a grim trio around the square table. Behind them a large printed notice informed them that 'video cameras are in use'. No one was speaking. Matt was twiddling his fingers on the wooden surface in front of him.

He stood up when she entered, in a bumbling rise, rocking his chair. He seemed cowed and awkward. Under the circumstances that was not surprising, but what did knock Lyndsay for six was his appearance.

She scarcely recognised him, so frightful did he look. His hair was dyed the colour of dark chocolate and shaved close to his scalp – such an amateurish cut, it looked like grass tufts gone haywire. He had obviously been sleeping rough, living from hand to mouth, starving. His skin was spangled with a mass of fine scratches, he was scruffy and unwashed and his clothes were as ragged as an urchin's and daubed with oil stains. Had he been stowed away in a ship's engine room? He was painfully thin, spotty and pale.

She tried so hard not to focus on all these external details, tried not to be thrown. Instead, she smiled encouragingly, but the instant their eyes met Matt averted his. He seemed so much older, or was that only her impression given all that she had discovered about him.

'Hello, darling.' She crossed the horrid room with its dingy linoleum floor. 'God, it's good to hold you,' she whispered, hugging him fiercely. Matthew recoiled. He barely allowed his awkward gangling limbs to brush against her. Lyndsay was mortified. There were others present. He couldn't face a scene, as she couldn't. It was humiliating to be watched over like this. 'Are you all right?' she murmured, battling against a mother's tears.

It was such a foolish question for clearly he wasn't, but she honestly did not know what else to ask. She burned to reassure him. Later, alone together, they'd communicate openly. She yearned for him to know that during his long absence she had devoured his writings and been thrilled by the figure emerging from his words. But she was only too aware that the room was a cubicle filled with custodian eyes, so she held her tongue, embraced her son once more, pressed his head tight against her shoulder and drew strength from his living, breathing frame. 'You are all right, aren't you, my darling?' she repeated, in a hushed conspiratorial voice.

Matt shrugged and stepped away. Lyndsay was acutely aware of the brush off, but wasn't sure if it was born of embarrassment or guilt.

Burgess, from behind her, butt in. 'Matthew, do you want five minutes alone with your mother?'

Matthew, eyes firmly fixed on the lino, shook his head. Lyndsay's heart sank.

'Fine. Mrs Potter, Matthew has pleaded guilty to possession of marijuana. The quantity found in the pocket of his jacket was negligible – we are awaiting confirmation from customs – so a charge of importation is unlikely, and he denies any intent to smuggle drugs into France. He also denies having rid himself of any illegal substances when he heard the police board the boat.'

Matthew glanced briefly, shamefacedly, at his mother. Clearly, he was expecting a reaction of shock, but Lyndsay, out of sight of the others, responded with a wink. Confused, Matt dropped his gaze and stared at the lino again.

Across the room, Burgess missed this silent exchange. 'We have been asking Matthew what he knows about the murder of Surinder Bharjee,' he continued.

Lyndsay felt her stomach tighten. 'Did you read about what happened to her?' she enquired tenderly.

Matthew nodded. She saw pain in his hazel eyes.

'He stated that he has never had anything to do with the Indian girl, isn't that right, Matthew? You knew Surinder Bharjee only by sight, aside from occasional, commercial exchanges during trips to the post office.' Lyndsay looked hard at her son. This could not be true. She knew it was not true. 'He stated that on the day in question there had been no prearranged meeting between Surinder Bharjee and himself. He was in the churchyard alone. His discovery of the girl there was quite by chance. And even on that occasion, although alone in the same churchyard, they did not speak a single word to one another.'

Lyndsay stared wide-eyed at her son. Matt was lying. He must be. Why was he lying? She quashed her need to ask questions. Not in front of the others. 'Then, if it's fine with you, I'd like to take Matthew home now, Inspector. Would you arrange another car for us, please?'

'I need a word with Matthew in private. A couple of tiny details I'd like to tidy up with him before he leaves.'

With a thoughtlessness born of so many anguished days, so much hidden concern, Lyndsay rounded on Burgess. 'You can't keep him here like this, you have no proof against him!' She heard the silence settle in the small room, the tinny anxiety in her voice reverberating against the flat cream walls. And Burgess' expression: a fleeting glimpse of victory.

'Mum, please...' Matthew's voice was soft and resigned.

Lyndsay knew her outburst must be ringing in the minds of these men. She had spoken like a woman who fears, knows, her son to be guilty.

'It's getting late. You're worn out. We'll book you a room at the White Hart and when Matthew and I have finished here he can join you. All being well, we'll deliver you both back to Churdle Heath in the morning.'

All being well. Burgess escorted her back along the corridor. As she'd departed, it had been she who had been unable to look her own flesh and blood in the eye.

'Not easy for you, seeing him for the first time again in here.' Lyndsay shot Burgess a glance, surprised by his unexpected softness. 'Did you lie about the car?' he asked casually as he helped her slip into her jacket, back in his office.

Lyndsay was lost. 'Sorry, what car?'

Burgess closed the door. 'You said you saw a maroon car in the parking on the afternoon of Surinder's murder. And a jogger, a figure running. We've found no trace of either, Mrs Potter. No one has come forward. Are you sure your story is accurate?' Lyndsay nodded, flummoxed by this unexpected line of questioning. 'Are you lying to protect him?'

'Of course not,' she gasped.

'Then why did you wait so long before reporting Matthew's disappearance?'

'I...'

'He returned home that Friday evening, after Surinder's murder, didn't he?'

'Yes...'

'And he confessed to you. He told you what he'd done, didn't he?'

'No!'

'Terrified, shocked. He came to his loving mother and spilt the beans.'

'No!'

'And you agreed with him to wait! Give him time to get away?'

'No!'

'A conspiracy between doting mother and son, running scared…'

'It's not true!'

'What if I told you that the can I took from your potting shed on Saturday proves his guilt?'

'What?'

'Matthew earlier admitted to the murder of Surinder Bharjee?'

'You're lying! You're lying! I heard him just now! He denied knowing her. He said so!'

'But you know that's not true.'

'I… I don't.'

'You planted that orchid for the dead girl to alleviate the guilt you feel for your son's crimes!'

'No!'

'When I informed you and your husband that Surinder's body had been found in the nature reserve, you, Mrs Potter, expressed not even a flicker of surprise. None whatsoever. Because you already knew she was dead, didn't you?'

Lyndsay's mind was scrambled. How had she learnt about…? A phone call from Marion. 'Yes, but…not from Matt! Matt didn't kill her!'

'You want to save your son, don't you?'

'He didn't…he didn't kill her,' she shouted, snatching the words from within her. They were sharp and furious, filled with fear and confusion. 'I'm certain of it.' Spittle drowned the clarity of speech. She was too tired for this. 'He couldn't kill her.'

Burgess took a step closer, hands against her shoulders, hungry to hear her. 'How can you be sure?' The force of his question, his proximity, was overpowering. He was shouting now. 'Answer me, how can you be so sure?'

'Because he was crazy about her!' she yelled, sobbing and delirious with impotence and confusion.

Burgess narrowed his eyes and sighed, allowing his arms to drop to his side. He took a step backwards. 'Fixated. Obsessed,' he confirmed with a soft certain voice. It said everything. 'He loved her too much to kill her, that's what you're telling me, is it?'

Lyndsay's words and his conclusions reverberated around the room. A motive handed to him on a plate. 'No!' she choked, a maelstrom sweeping through her brain. 'Oh, Jesus, God.' Her vision was blurred. She shook her head dumbly. 'No, no, that isn't what I mean...'

'Call your solicitor, Mrs Potter. Fetch him down here.'

24

By the time Stephen entered the club it had gone eleven, and the place was packed to the rafters and as smoky as one of young Paul's science experiments. Christ! He craned about for a glimpse of Gin, but as she was nowhere to be seen he headed for the basement. It was chock-a-block. A jazz group was in full throttle. Stephen found himself a space on a bench shared by a dozen or so others, mostly youngsters, Parisians not tourists, jazz aficionados. He staked himself a little elbow-room at the table and leaned to and fro, peering over the heads of the animated crowd. Gin was not there. He would have picked her out, no matter how numerous the throngs. He felt no great concern since a cheaply produced black-and-white poster announcing the times of her performances was on display upstairs. He had spotted it immediately, as well as her photograph at the bar and outside in the street.

The density of noise and people was suffocating. A glass of beer crashed to the stone floor and missed his new loafers by centimetres. A youth at the table adjacent to him accidentally punched him in the back with his elbow. '*Merde!*' yelled another's voice above the buzz of chit-chat and laughter. All other conversation was drowned by the jazz trio, their soft rendition of 'Smoke Gets in Your Eyes', the clinking of glasses and the scraping of furniture.

A tall dark-haired waitress dressed in high-heeled boots and a tunic dress that barely covered her breasts signalled to him for his order.

'Whisky sour,' he shouted.

She dallied, smiling in a way that said everything, then turned and elbowed her way through the crowds, back upstairs to the bar. There was still no sign of Gin.

The mood in the club was raucous. Stephen had been expecting something a little more sedate, more dedicated to the quality of the music. Under normal circumstances he would have found this insufferable and he wondered how a woman as graceful as Gin could tolerate such yobbishness night after night. Was she desperate for work?

The waitress returned. As she delivered his glass and demanded eighty-five francs her breasts brushed his shoulder. The provocation was intentional. Stephen handed her a hundred-franc note. 'Keep the change,' he said and she beamed with promise.

Scotch in hand, he turned his attention to the stage. The trio were packing up. He glanced at his watch: almost eleven thirty-five. According to the publicity, Gin's first spot was due before midnight.

Then the lights went dark, a hush fell over the crowd and a male voice coming through loudspeakers announced, '*Mesdames, messieurs, je vous présente, la bellissima*, Gin Millar.'

A blue spot lit the centre of the tiny stage and a swell of appreciation rose from the crowd as they cheerfully anticipated what they had been waiting for. A quartet of musicians ambled to their seats. The pianist struck a bunch of notes and then ran his fingers nimbly up and down the keyboard. A melody was taking shape. Several dark, melancholy notes from a tenor sax followed. Then came bass and percussion. Recognition of the number led the audience to rapturous applause. A silhouette slinked in darkness into position on the stage. Whistles and cheers broke out as she took up her position in the centre spill of light.

'Stormy weather…' Her lips kissed tight against the chrome of the mike. Her voice was deep and husky, and mellow as ruby wine.

The sight of her took Stephen's breath away. He was a boy again ready to swoon. She was wearing a floor-length, black-sequinned frock cut in curved cups across her cleavage. Her breasts were accentuated by the lighting and glittered lustrously. The skin-tight dress hugged her figure like a lovesick shadow and clung like passion all the way to her ankles. From there it fanned out to a mermaid's tail. Beneath the silvery liquid-blue lighting, her naked arms and shoulders were translucent and her Titian hair had turned to a burnt sienna. She was sexual beyond his wildest fantasies.

Seeing her up there above him, he could have come on the spot. Yet this dangerously black-swathed goddess made him nervous.

Gin was a diva of the night. She inhabited a sleazy, lowlife world about which he knew nothing. She gave meaning to this dive, and the crowd adored her. Her music, her ability to express that part of her inner self and share it with others, cowed him. He had never plumbed secrets deep within his own heart, for Stephen feared self-knowledge.

By accepting his presence in this dingy yet vital atmosphere, she was showing him that she was not for him, that she was beyond his grasp, unobtainable. He could never hope to capture her now. She lived alone and slept all day. This nocturnal world was when she came alive. He was no longer repelled by it but he was broken by it because he had lost her. His vision of a life with her had no future. It was a hallucination.

At the finish of each spot, after whistles and rapturous applause, Gin slipped from the stage and disappeared into the wings. There she remained, out of sight, until her next session. During these breaks, Stephen's waitress came by and he ordered three more whisky sours. His head felt heavy, he was more than a little drunk. The smoky atmosphere, the booze and his dispirited mood decided him. Once Gin's last number was over, her final note of the evening sung, he would slide off. Not with the sexy slip of a waitress, although she was tempting, her gaze promising the luxury of solace, her interest blatant. No, he would retreat with dignity, take refuge in his unpacked boxes and leave Gin in peace.

She would need a while to change back into her street clothes, so there would be time enough for him to depart unnoticed. In any case, it might be her habit to remain behind and enjoy a quiet drink once the club had emptied. She had told him on the boat earlier that she would have a Scotch 'later'. He guessed that was the 'later' she had been referring to. Until an hour ago he would have waited, hoping to share that moment with her, but not now. He would call tomorrow and congratulate her on her performance.

Gin's final number of the evening was 'Killing Me Softly'. The audience applauded its opening bars enthusiastically, and for one wild moment Stephen fancied Gin had included it for him. She would give him a sign, a glance from the stage. It was the whisky that had made him maudlin. His discomfort in this joint, so unlike any of his own regular haunts, had eroded his confidence.

How he waited for that look, even a fleeting glimpse, ready to receive it as a special call. But he waited in vain. She never caught his eye, never allowed those green-gold eyes to settle on him or to saunter in his direction. Was she even aware of his presence in the crowded room?

After she had taken her final bow, Stephen rose from the bench, made his way up the stairs and out into the street. It was past two. The night was mild, yet vaguely misty. A discernible scent of leaves teased the air. To breathe in the sleeping city was a joyous release after the club's fuggy claustrophobia.

He walked without heed to direction, listening to his step echoing around the narrow cobbled lanes. The area was surprisingly deserted. Would Gin walk home alone? Would she be safe? It was an idiotic worry; she made the journey every night. Perhaps someone gave her a lift. The pianist, a drummer, the club's owner? Were any of them her lovers? He wanted to turn back, to offer to escort her, to know. There must be someone. She was too beautiful to be alone. Now, out in the clear night air, clarity returned. Why had he scampered off like that? What was he afraid of? No woman had ever caused him to behave so foolishly. Gin would read his exit as impolite, as a criticism of her performance, if she had known he was there.

He could not go back now. The place would have emptied. Those, if any, who remained would be staff, regulars, musicians or friends of the musicians. To walk back in there now would be ridiculous. He would telephone her first thing in the morning and make his excuses. No, she slept late. It would be thoughtless to disturb her sleep. Well then, later in the afternoon. He would send her baskets of red roses.

Stephen had crossed the river in the direction of the Marais, close to where he had first set eyes on Gin, weeks ago.

And what of the dream he had cherished and held so dear during this time, he asked himself. Was he simply going to walk away from it and return to his loveless life in Churdle Heath?

Strolling along the rue Vieille du Temple, he fancied he might stop and have a coffee before hailing a taxi home. He had been out all day, had walked for hours, and was suddenly aware of how tired he was. He glanced into several of the café-bars searching for a convivial establishment where both men and women were drinking. This was the homosexual district of Paris – the nightlife lingered longer here – but he would not drink alone at this late hour in a bar patronised by homosexuals. He was not comfortable in their company, feeling disgust for them and their choices.

One bar was almost empty, but it was open, and appeared to have the right clientele. He found a table by the window and ordered not an espresso as he had originally intended but a large Scotch on the rocks.

He dawdled over the drink, then ordered another double, calculating the time it would take Gin to change, enjoy a nightcap with chums and return home. When he looked at his watch again it was almost three. Unless she had gone elsewhere, she would be back on the boat by now. He left a two-hundred franc note on the table and staggered out into the street.

He was very drunk – no, he was tired, it was late, he was in turmoil, not seeing straight. He was not in the habit of hanging about at night waiting for passing cabs. He could telephone from the bar, but where was he going? To his flat, of course, but directly or via Gin's boat? He didn't have a clue. His mind was a mess of befuddled confusions. A taxi approached. He flagged it down and collapsed into it.

'*Je voudrais faire un petit tour,*' Stephen told the taxi driver.

'A tour of the city, or you want to pick up a woman?'

'God, no, nothing so sordid. I'll direct you.'

First, they made for the club. It was locked up and in darkness, so Stephen requested to return north, tracking the route he had walked earlier with Gin. The taxi followed instructions, crossing bridges, cutting up through the city to the Right Bank. It had been easier on foot. Several of the streets proved to be one-way and barred vehicles approaching from the south. But Stephen was stubbornly resolute and, all the while during the frustrating course he kept his bleary eyes peeled, checking every corner, every alleyway.

Eventually, as the taxi approached the vast Bastille square, Stephen directed the driver to circle the golden central statue, twice. Decision made, he was deposited on the corner of the boulevard de la Bastille.

He pulled a wad of money from his pocket to pay the driver and, oblivious to the loss, the keys to his new apartment dropped in the roadside. As he descended to the canal bank, he realised that he was staggering. At the water's edge he paused for a moment, breathing deeply while attempting to calm his thoughts and steady his stride. He was growing feverish, excited by the prospect of what lay ahead.

To the left of him, twenty yards or so further along the bank, was the site where they were drilling for the new Metro station. In spite of the lateness of the hour, he spied activity: a diminished team working by floodlight. The noise was less intrusive than it had been earlier. Stephen peered towards the building site but his focus was blurred by booze, then he lurched to the right and, after more deep breathing, strode the short distance to Gin's boat.

He was relieved to discover that the banks were deserted. No ne'er-do-wells were loitering about or sleeping rough. He moved on through the stillness. It was not his intention to disturb Gin; he would simply stand awhile at the water's edge and inhale the night air dulcified by her close-at-hand presence. If he could not lie with her, then to dream of it while listening to the water lapping the boat where she was sleeping, to hear what she was hearing, seemed a small comfort. To picture her porcelain flesh tantalisingly close yet beyond reach was a sweet torture. While he was vaguely aware how preposterous his behaviour was, yet he felt compelled to it.

To his utter astonishment Gin was on the deck of the boat, a solitary silhouette, smoking a cigarette, gazing towards the square. Stephen was flustered. Should he call or remain in the shadows? She was – ironically – the last person he had expected to see, the sight of her was so unexpected it threw him into disarray.

At first he held back, observing her. She was barefoot, dressed in a black silk kimono, lost to her stargazing. Could it be that she was wondering what had become of him? It was half-past three. What else might she be doing standing alone staring into infinity? He crept a pace or two closer, his heart beating terribly.

If he called out the sound of his voice would startle her. Seeing her again made his longing doubly impatient. The vision of her there mocked his crazy reasoning of two hours earlier. How could he – even for one lunatic moment – deny himself the pleasure of so divine a creature?

He inched forward.

She seemed forlorn, vulnerable, in need of his strong arms about her. He regretted profoundly the excess of alcohol he had consumed. He longed to be clearheaded, and yet within sight of her how could he ever hope to be?

Without further ado he called her name but at that very same moment an appalling rumbling from the building site sounded, drowning out his voice and breaking Gin's train of thought. Unaware of him she turned, expressing an idle interest in what was going on, until she moved from the prow of the boat and headed for her cabin below deck. Stephen was no more than a metre from the gangplank now. Should he signal his arrival or climb aboard? Half a dozen steps and he would be on deck – yet an unannounced entry would panic her.

He was on the point of revealing his approach when he noticed that her lips were moving. She was talking. He froze, trying to hear but no sound reached him. There was someone with her! No, she was singing. He prayed with all his being that she was singing. He scanned the length and breadth of the boat. There was nobody but Gin on the deck. And then she disappeared below stairs.

The gangplank had been hoisted but not to its full height. Stephen reached for it and, swinging like a monkey, placing hand in front of hand, grappled the length of it until he was clambering clumsily over the hull of the barge. Releasing his hands one at a time, he tumbled onto the deck, landing unsteadily. Would she have heard him? Music was playing in the cabin. The lapping waves and the boat's sway beneath him forced him to sit a second. He was woozy, booze-clouded, out of control. But he'd made it aboard. He noticed then that he'd cut his hand and blood was dripping onto the teak deck.

The jazz played softly. Gin must've been singing with the music. He rose to his feet and stepped stealthily but unsteadily. The boat creaked. A peel of laughter rose from the cabin below. There were others! A group of friends? The laughter was followed by the sound of Gin's voice. Talking, not singing. Stephen had come too far to turn back now. In any case, he had walked away once this evening already; he would not do so a second time. He had to know.

He reached the door and crept down the wooden steps. There was a light on, not in the main living area but in a cabin to the right. The wooden stairs beneath him creaked, and he stood still as a thief.

And then, beyond the narrow cabin doorway, he saw her, supine on a bed. The lighting was subdued, he was inebriated, but he saw her clearly: Gin, naked. Wax-white naked. The black kimono at her feet like a dozing cat.

Stephen rocked on his feet, drew a breath and looked straight at her, drinking in her flame and pearl beauty, her rust pubic nakedness. He was standing in the face of ecstasy.

Languid, sexy jazz notes peeled from the cabin. He took a pace – because he had to. Had to lose himself in that autumn forest, brush his tongue against that flat stomach, feel the warmth of life suck him wetly in. His craving knew no sense.

He was drawing within range of that nakedness, his movement muffled by carpet. He was about to say her name when she began to speak, but not to him. Someone was with her, beyond his line of vision. She was laughing, joking, with a lover. What did he look like, this fucking poacher? Stephen was incensed, had to know.

Stepping too quickly, clumsily, he knocked his hip against the corner of a table. The movement arrested Gin's attention and stopped her in mid-flow. She turned and saw him, an intruder, transfixed by her, at her bedroom door.

She didn't panic, or cry out, but her companion couldn't help but notice how abruptly Gin had stopped talking. '*Qu'est-ce qui se passe,* Gin?' What is it, Gin? came the soft voice of the lover enquiring from the bathroom.

Stephen barely heard the question. Truth to tell he didn't register the other's voice at all. His eyes were locked on Gin.

It was Gin's lover who broke the moment. The tall dark-haired woman from the Left Bank who had waved from her balcony walked out of the bathroom. She was also naked but she was faster on the uptake and grabbed a chair. 'Call the police!' she ordered Gin.

A torrent of emotions flooded through Stephen. How could he have been so blind, so crassly naive? Without a backward glance he retreated, falling up stairs, bolting to the gangplank and catapulting himself onto the dockside. He landed hard on the quay and fell to his knees with a crack. His head was spinning, hands stinging, and his hip tender. Emotions choked him; tears blinded him. He stumbled to his feet and began to run, reeling, like a shot animal, blundering this way and that, his balance askew from a twisted ankle.

The surfeit of alcohol burned like fire in his stunned brain. The lights of the building site ahead drew him, and he charged mindlessly, like a moth flying towards light.

Someone called out to take care, to get out of the way. '*Attention! Attention!*'

The arm of the crane was descending. Slabs of concrete were being lowered to earth.

'*Attention!*' an Arab worker was calling. '*Attention!*'

Gin, it must be Gin! In spite of everything, she was coming after him. He spun round in search of her, staggering on his feet. Never mind what he had seen, if she wanted him, he could not resist. He did not possess the strength to say no. To hell with her past. He would give himself entirely to her.

'Gin!' he bellowed.

He couldn't pick out a figure on the boat. It was too far; his senses were short-circuiting. Was she on the shore? Stephen couldn't see her. 'Gin!' he hollered again. But there was no one there.

A second Arab labourer in stained dungarees, standing at a distance, spotted Stephen lurching about the building site. He saw what was about to happen, but it was too late to arrest the crane that dipped and swung like a great eyeless beast. No signal could have reached the operator in time. The Arab began to sprint towards Stephen, waving and shouting from across the quay, 'Get down, Monsieur, for God's sake!'

Concrete slabs transported by the crane cracked open the back of Stephen's skull while the force of the mindless, moving machine hurled his body forwards, thrusting him face downwards like a damaged doll into the river.

A deafening siren began to keen. Its strident lament seemed to pour from all corners of the sleeping city, as though Paris had been rendered senseless by this meaningless blow.

The two workmen approached the dockside, breathless from running and shouting. They gaped in horror at the blood spurting from Stephen's severed skull. It spread on the water like a russet oil slick. In the harsh floodlit pre-dawn, mingled with the aqueous grey green of the canal, Stephen's blood had taken on a coppery tone; the colour of Gin Millar's thick wiry hair.

25

Breakfast was over and the dining room at the White Hart Hotel deserted. The marmalade pots had been whisked away and the miniature cornflake packets stacked into a glass cabinet over on the far side of the room. Mustard-yellow paper napkins folded into triangles jutted from wine glasses. The tables were already laid for lunch.

Lyndsay had checked out of her room because it was too depressing for words and so here she was, staring out of the dining room window at the grey rain sheeting across the cliffs, shrouding the English Channel. The bleakness reminded her of her South American plants. Dead by now, no doubt, or withering in a customs block a mile or two along the littoral. She had been coming to Dover to collect them the morning she'd discovered Matt had gone. It seemed a lifetime ago. The customs office had sent her a form but she had been too preoccupied to fill it out.

'Poor plants,' she cried aloud to net curtains tied with velvet bows. What a dismal hotel, this was. Little better than a boarding house, and it reeked of nicotine and air freshener. A stop over for ferry folk bound across the Channel. Did the Dover Crime Squad use it on a regular basis, or was it only London-based Burgess? Where the hell was Burgess?

Lyndsay had last spoken to him at two in the morning. She had been frantic. The station night shift had been refusing to put through her calls so she had taken to ringing at half-hourly intervals until, finally, he had come to the phone.

'Where's Matthew?' she had shouted.

'We're still talking.'

'I want to see him.'

'Sorry, Mrs Potter, not right now. He's in safe hands. Your solicitor is watching over things. Get some sleep.'

'I'm coming over.'

'Stay where you are, they'll both be with you shortly.'

A minicab in Dover at two in the morning had proved an impossibility. The reception at the accursed little hotel had long since packed up for the night and the station staff had refused to send a car on the grounds that Matthew would soon be 'on his way'. Lyndsay, shattered and frustrated, had eventually fallen into a slump of a sleep, fully clothed. It occurred to her now, over a rather disgusting cup of reheated coffee, that Burgess had deliberately booked her into a hotel without night staff and beyond walking distance of the station.

After waking, when she'd telephoned again, she had been informed that the Inspector had gone off duty, so she had taken a taxi across town to the police station. She had requested a quick word with Alan Grater but was told that he was busy in the interrogation room with Matt and could not be disturbed. Apparently, they were considering a statement. The front desk had informed her that Inspector Burgess would meet her at her hotel at half-past ten, so she had taxied back to wait, wearing yesterday's slept-in clothes, exhausted, furious and terrified out of her wits. In yesterday's confusion, she had forgotten both her address book and mobile phone. It had been Burgess who had tracked down Alan Grater's listed home number.

She was on the point of asking for change for the callbox in the street – more discreet than the hotel reception phone – when she spied Burgess' car emerging from out of the torrential rain and pulling up outside the hotel. Lyndsay leapt to her feet and shoved her face against the window as Burgess dived through the weather towards the entrance and disappeared from sight. Neither Matthew nor Alan was with him.

The door opened and a sodden, exhausted-looking man entered the dining room. His expression was bleak.

'Where is he?' Her question was an accusation as much as a demand for information.

Burgess closed the door behind him and stood his ground. 'We're going to keep him for a little while longer, Mrs Potter.' He began to dig in his raincoat pockets.

'You can't continue to interrogate him, to bully him like this.'

'We are not bullying him, we are questioning him. He was taken into custody outside the country, Mrs Potter. We are entitled to detain him a while longer, which is what we are intending to do. He has not been charged. But, please, if you are in any doubt, talk to your solicitor.' His tone was grave.

'He isn't guilty!'

Burgess was rummaging in his pockets. Lyndsay presumed it was for a handkerchief to dry the falling drips from his head or for cigarettes. In fact, it was a piece of folded paper he retrieved. Approaching her at arm's length only, he handed it to her.

She accepted it warily. 'What is this?' she asked. 'Is it from Matt?'

Burgess rubbed his face, worrying away the residue rain with the sleeve of his mac. He cleared his throat. 'It's the number of a police station in Paris. There's been an accident,' he said. This time it was the softness in his voice that shook her.

She stared in dumb amazement, not because Burgess possessed such information – that did not surprise her at all – but because his tone hinted at something terrible. 'Accident?'

'There's no other way to say this… It seems he died instantly.'

Lyndsay twisted the soggy bit of paper cradled between her trembling fingers. She could not take in what she was hearing, could not bear to unfold its crumpled message. It represented too many things, too many lives in confusion. And then silently, in the presence of a man whom she no longer despised, because she hadn't the energy left to despise anyone, she began to weep. Her world, the hidden poetic one she held as her true reality, had been shattered into pieces.

26

Lyndsay passed what remained of that day's night at a police station in the eleventh *arrondissement* in Paris, gulping hot tea, while dozens of questions were fired at her. Stephen had been carrying no identification, no keys, not even a credit card. Was this a habit? Lyndsay shook her head. He was in a foreign country without papers. Why? Draped in a coarse woollen blanket, dragging it more tightly around her shoulders, her teeth chattered. She was trembling, dazed by shock and exhaustion.

'When did you arrive in France, Mrs Potter?'

'Late yesterday afternoon…as soon as I could get a plane.' Her words slurred out of control.

'Tests showed a high quantity of alcohol in your husband's blood. Was it possible that he had been intending to commit an anonymous suicide?' Again she shook her head. 'You are absolutely certain that the man pulled from the canal was your husband?' She nodded and clenched her hands so tight her nails dug into her palms. 'What was he doing at the building site at that hour?' She had no idea. Stephen had been in Paris on business. She was about to add that she suspected he might have been visiting a mistress and then, at the last moment, she buttoned back that piece of information.

An officer who had not spoken before broke in. 'Your husband recently rented a very expensive apartment in this city. Did you know about this?'

She owned up to the impending separation between Stephen and herself, confirming that Stephen had leased a flat in the rue du Faubourg St-Honoré. Denying such information would only complicate matters and she craved, above all else, an end to what was left of this bleak night.

'Was there a woman involved?'

'He said not.'

'A woman called the station to enquire about the man in the water. It was she who gave us his identity but, when she was asked to give her own name, she hung up. Do you know who that woman might be?'

Lyndsay shook her head. Was it for the boys' sake that she felt duty bound to keep the existence of another woman to herself? God only knew. She was too shell-shocked to reason. The night before she had been sick with worry for her son. And now the father of that son had been cruelly snatched from them.

Another mug of steaming tea was placed on the desk in front of her. Signatures to forms were requested. These stated accidental death; instructions for the release of the body from the morgue so that it could be flown back to England; and Lyndsay Potter, wife of the deceased, to accept responsibility for all costs. She signed.

A Renault arrived to chauffeur her to the Hôtel Crillon. They drove through streets that were eerily still. The air was thick and filmy, smelling of baking bread, damp dust from the street-cleaning vehicles and freshly ground coffee beans. The city lights were still switched on, but the early risers were venturing out of doors. For a minority – those in love or those who earned their living at night – it was time to sleep. Only once in her life had she stayed out all night. It had happened here, in this very city, with Stephen, celebrating. Lyndsay pressed her face against the cool glass. A tear stained it. Was this real? Stephen dead, gone, no more?

Back inside the lobby, memories of herself with Stephen engulfed her and with them came a profound and furious sense of waste. His life was ended for no good reason. She collected her key, made her way along endless corridors to her room, closed up her case, still open on the bed where she had left it, and picked up the telephone. There was one message from Alan Grater.

Even as he answered, she detected his exhaustion. 'Matt's released,' he said softly. And then, 'How are things?' She confirmed that the body was Stephen's. 'Jesus Christ, Lyndsay. I'm so sorry.'

'Tell me about Matt.'

'Detective Inspector Burgess is anxious to wrap this case up, but he won't pin it on Matthew. He can't detain him any longer and he hasn't sufficient evidence to charge him.'

'They haven't charged him! Oh, thank God!'

'No, and nor will they. Not unless something new comes to light. He's a tricky blighter, that Burgess. The fact of the matter is he had no right to interrogate Matt without a solicitor present. And I told him so.'

Lyndsay recalled her blathering foolishness. Burgess had been bluffing, and she'd walked right into his trap. She would deny everything, plead exhaustion. No one except Matt and she knew about his diaries and poems. There was no proof.

'Most of their suspicions seem to hang on the discovery of a Swatch they found in the woods which Matt claims he lost weeks ago. And a cigarette butt near the scene of the crime, which Matt says is not his. It could have belonged to anybody. There's simply not sufficient evidence.'

'How is he?'

'Confused and shaken. I haven't mentioned Stephen. Do you want me to, now that the identification has been confirmed?'

Lyndsay sank to the bed. She masked her face with her hand, desperate for this nightmare to go away. An insane voice within her argued that if she denied his death it might disappear. Pronouncing it gave it reality. Reason told her she had to get home and break the news to her sons. She must get on a plane and take care of the boys. 'I'll tell them,' she whispered.

'Well, I'm here when you need me. Meanwhile, I'll keep abreast of what the police are up to. They took Matt's fingerprints before releasing him, but that's standard. If necessary I'll call in a colleague of mine. He's highly regarded in this particular field, which, frankly, is not my area, but my opinion is that unless some new information or evidence is uncovered, Matt is in the clear. Burgess would have an almighty job trying to point the finger at him. And he knows it.'

'Where's Matt now?'

'I brought him home with me yesterday evening and Judy fed him a square meal. Now he's with Amanda. Looking forward to seeing you and sleeping in his own bed again.'

She thanked him – not just their solicitor but Stephen's long-time friend, and replaced the receiver.

She crossed to the window, drew back the curtain and, staring out across the famous square, watched the dawn break across the Place de la Concorde. A hazy muted glow heralded the arrival of a steamy day. It was that particular, almost tangible translucency which exists only in big cities. Cities jammed to the gills with motor engines running twenty hours a day.

If she had not argued with Stephen, had not told him to leave, he might not be dead now. But what had he been doing on the quay at that hour?

It was sixteen years since she had last seen Paris at dawn, since she had last stayed at this hotel. She had been twenty at the time and carrying her first son. Stephen had invited her here for the weekend to celebrate the small seed growing within her – little more than eight weeks old – later to be known as Matthew. The following week Stephen had proposed to her.

He had invited her, along with her father, Harry Boyd, to their local pub in Sevenoaks. He'd stood Harry a couple of vodkas and then requested Lyndsay's hand in marriage. Harry, nonplussed by such formality and by the dash of the upwardly mobile young chap propping up the bar alongside him, had raised his glass to wish the youngsters good health and then promptly cracked a joke about a man who, late for his own wedding, had ended up in the wrong church and married the wrong girl!

This view, this square, this hotel had been Stephen's favourite. There were few sights anywhere in the world he'd relished more. Stephen, who'd loved the hustle and bustle of city life, had considered it one of the most pleasing spectacles in the world, infinitely lovelier than any landscape scene. In that regard she and Stephen had been poles apart. In many regards they had been poles apart.

But Stephen gone! 'No! Dear God, this can't be true!' she begged, gripping the curtain. How would she bear it? Matt and Paulie. She had to get back to her sons.

The more determinedly she threw herself into tasks, the less chance there was to be submerged by loss. On her feet, she rang for tea and cognac, downed the cognac and began punching digits on the phone. Amanda's answering machine was on. She left a message for Matt, mentioning nothing about Stephen.

The address Lyndsay had for Stephen's flat included the code which opened the main front doors. This gave her access to the interior of the building as far as the hallway, where she found individual bells for the apartments and personal letter-boxes, but not access to the lifts or the flats themselves. For that she would need a key.

Her name, POTTER, was printed above the letter-box that serviced Stephen's flat. She was definitely in the right place. Her heart thumping as she rang his bell, she wondered what she would do if his woman answered.

Her misgivings were unnecessary for there was no response from the apartment. Why had she been so stupid as to keep so many secrets from Stephen? The writings and cannabis she had found in Matt's room should have been discussed with him. He was the boy's father, for heaven's sake. If she had trusted and confided in him all those years ago, events may not have reached such a crisis. She rested her finger on his bell and left it there. There was still no response.

She pressed her face against the wall, seeking inspiration. Her eyes lighted on the name-plate alongside her: CONCIERGE. Paying no heed to the early hour, Lyndsay rammed her finger hard against the bell. This was an emergency.

Eventually a gruff woman's voice came through the intercom, '*Oui?*'

'I'm sorry to trouble you at such an hour, *Madame. Je suis Madame Potter.*' Lyndsay's accent was execrable and she knew it. Her French had never been as fluent as Stephen's. 'I've just arrived from England.' She troubled to explain this in case the woman had met Stephen and knew that he was living alone. 'Could you let me in, please?'

'We don't have keys to the apartments,' the voice barked, plainly spoken and dismissive.

'*Attendez, Madame!*' Lyndsay took a chance based on years of knowledge of Stephen and his meticulous habits. 'My husband said he's given you a key. To clean for us.'

There was a long pause while a conversation between two people within the caretaker's apartment took place. Lyndsay could follow none of it. She grew impatient. '*Madame*, listen, there's been an accident. Something terrible has happened.'

Lyndsay's French was not sufficiently competent to express what she'd intended. The caretaker's wife, who had indeed been engaged to clean for Stephen, heard only the anguish in the Englishwoman's voice, not the reason for it.

'Wait inside by the *ascenseur*,' she instructed.

There was a buzzing and the lock on the inner door was released. Lyndsay approached the lift and waited.

Within minutes the lift doors opened and a plump, matronly woman in her sixties, clad in woollen dressing gown and slippers, smiled a perfunctory greeting and beckoned Lyndsay in. Neither spoke. The woman's hair was a rare combination of greys and tobacco-ginger streaks. It hung down her back in a plait, reaching her waist. The silence was broken by a gaoler's-size bunch of keys jangling between her thick workmanlike hands and the incessant hack of her smoker's cough.

They reached the fourth floor. Once inside the flat, Lyndsay thanked the woman. She placed a two-hundred franc bill into her hand and repeated *merci* several times over in an exhausted, grateful way. The woman pocketed the bill without comment. She padded through to the kitchen, beckoning Lyndsay to follow. There she pointed to a hook inside a cupboard. From it hung a spare set of keys. Lyndsay smiled her comprehension and the woman bid her *une bonne journée*. Her absence left Lyndsay alone amongst the unopened cartons that contained Stephen's planned new life.

She moved from room to room, investigating all the bits and pieces he had put in place, persuading herself that she was not snooping, while searching for his passport, birth certificate and other essential documents. She found a telephone and lifted the receiver. The silence confirmed that it had not been connected. On a small wooden table alongside his king-sized bed she found a notepad. She flicked through the pages but there was nothing written in it.

Freshly painted walls, scrubbed woodwork, unpacked boxes, recent carpentry, windows awaiting curtains, as well as other unfamiliar objects surrounded her. They represented new beginnings, bright possibilities and exciting encounters, all in a space that did not include her. The realisation of this saddened her and exacerbated her fatigue. She considered taking Stephen's spare keys and returning to the hotel for a brief sleep, but she was too dog-tired to move. She sat on his bed, settling against creased linen and rediscovered the scent of him. The body perfume was so familiar that it brought longing and pain to her gut. She took hold of one of the pillows and dragged it towards her. Holding it with all her might, she rocked and clenched it. How could this have happened?

Months of banked-up emotion flooded forth. She felt unprotected, rejected, and such roaring loss that she did not know how she was ever going to contain it. Her tears dampened Stephen's bedding and she wept until she was exhausted. Reaching for a tissue, a torn sheet of folded paper secreted beneath the base of the bedside lamp drew her attention. Hitching herself onto her elbows, still sniffling, she pulled the paper free.

The particulars scribbled there were not in Stephen's hand. There was a name and an address of a woman: Gin Millar. Lyndsay's heart began to beat fast. The address was at the quay where Stephen had met his death. She grabbed the phone. A swift glance at the clock told her that it was not yet eight o'clock. What the hell. She dialled the number and then remembered that the stupid line was dead.

Snatching up her coat, pulling it round her as she moved, she hurried to the kitchen to collect Stephen's keys from the cupboard. In her haste she had forgotten the scrap of paper. She ran back to the bedroom for the note that contained the address of Stephen's mistress and companion during those last moments before his accident.

She did not wait to return to the Crillon. From a callbox in the street, Lyndsay dialled the number. As the phone began to ring, she went back over the questions swimming in and out of her mind. If Stephen and this woman had said goodnight to one another literally moments before his accident, why had she not come forward? She must have heard the siren. Was she married?

Was that why she had hidden her identity? Why was Stephen hurrying along the quay? Had they had an argument? And the alcohol in his blood – why had he been drinking so heavily? – Stephen was a measured drinker. Was she the woman who had telephoned the station?

Lyndsay was on the point of replacing the receiver when a smoky voice answered, '*Allô?*'

She hesitated. What difference did these details make? And yet if she did not find answers, the questions might torment her forever.

'*Allô?*' The voice sounded disgruntled by the silence.

'Gin Millar?'

'*C'est moi.*'

'Can I speak…*parler avec vous, s'il vous plaît?*'

A pause, and then, '*Qui êtes vous?*'

'*Je suis…* Mrs… Stephen Potter's wife.'

There was a silence. A sigh. Lyndsay heard a cigarette being lit. 'What do you want?' Gin was speaking in English now. Her accent was neither French nor entirely English.

'I need…could we talk?'

'What about?'

'Stephen. You do know him?' Another pause. 'There's been an accident.'

She heard an exhalation of smoke and breath. 'Yes.'

Lyndsay had no idea what impact such a devastating event might have had on this woman. What if she were in love with Stephen? It seemed as though he had been in love with her – even if he'd denied her existence.

'Listen, I have to return to England…to my sons…'

'Ah, yes, the boys.'

'You know about them?' It felt like a straw, a lifeline. God only knew why. 'Has Stephen talked to you about the boys?'

'A little, yes.'

So she was definitely an intimate of some kind. 'Did he tell you about Matthew?' Lyndsay felt a surge of jealousy towards this woman who had shared the last moments of Stephen's life with him. 'I want to meet you.'

'No.'

'Please –'

'It's not possible.'

'Why? My husband's...' she fought the break in her voice '... I need to see you.' Again there was a sigh, and a long pause. '*Madame* Millar, please.'

'Do you know where I am?'

'Yes.'

'Then come, if you must.' And the line went dead.

The air smelled sweet. Chestnut trees were dotted amongst the familiar plane trees along the boulevard de la Bastille, but Lyndsay could not escape the signs of a premature autumn as she listened to her footfall crunch the dried and curling leaves strewn about her feet. Her tread was steady and determined, carrying her towards Stephen's mistress, telling nothing of her inner turmoil.

She descended the steps that led directly to the private harbour at the Port de Plaisance de Paris Arsenal, paused on the penultimate step and gazed out upon the grey river and then along the quay. The police report of Stephen's behaviour was bizarre, uncharacteristic. Perhaps it was the consequence of some altercation with this mistress, or was Gin Millar a whore? – although that idea seemed unlikely to Lyndsay. Nothing about Stephen's personality seemed likely to attract him to such hangouts, but then she would never have guessed at the secret, inner life of Matt. She would not claim to know Stephen any better than her son. She was learning that the hearts and minds of others would always be foreign territory. Still, it was why she was here, to try to understand what had happened to Stephen and make sense of the chain of events, if sense there was in such a cruel and fruitless death.

Still poised on the step, inhaling the stench of diesel from the boats, she trained her attention on the construction site. The highly legible sign: DANGER! blinked mockingly, but in the light of day it possessed no real menace. Open-mouthed, she gawped at the crane and pictured its blind swing. Ignorant of its deathly approach, Stephen was thinking, feeling what? It was unlikely that in those last minutes of his life, Stephen's thoughts were of her and the boys. This realisation was almost intolerable.

All traces of the accident had been cleaned away. Another shift was at work. They knew nothing of the floating corpse, except perhaps through word of mouth, nothing of Stephen's body, stiff in a Paris morgue. Nothing of the two young lives whose futures would be forever changed by a brief nocturnal incident played out against this scene. Lyndsay gripped the stone support and held it fast.

She found the woman's boat with ease and paused in front of it to gather her courage and to take a good, long look at this home. So this must be where Stephen had spent those missing nights. Lyndsay found it peculiar that anyone would choose such a habitat, but it appeared clean, generous in size and decked out with an inviting display of red and rose-pink geraniums.

She approached the foot of the gangplank. There was no one on the deck. 'Hello?' Masts clinking in the wind answered Lyndsay's call, as pleasing a sound as the clipping of shears, but there was no sign of Gin Millar. 'Anyone home?'

A head popped up from below deck. Fashioned against a backdrop of sunlight was a mass of wild amber hair. The face was directed towards Lyndsay, away from the sun, and consequently in shadow.

'Mrs Potter?' Lyndsay nodded, suddenly stricken by shyness. 'Come aboard. I'll be with you in a couple of minutes.' Gin disappeared and left Lyndsay to make herself at home.

She wandered the deck barely aware of what she was doing and began to deadhead the withered blossoms in the plant pots. It was a gesture so familiar it gave her security. Now that she was here she questioned the prudence of such a visit and what exactly it was she needed from it. She heard the other woman below, moving swiftly to and fro, clearly not daunted by the prospect of their imminent interview.

'Wanta drink?' Gin called from the cabin.

Lyndsay answered the voice, 'Are you having one?' and then checked herself for such an indecisive response.

'Large whisky and water. How does that sound?'

'Fine.' Lyndsay rarely drank Scotch, but right now she could use some mettle.

The sky had grown patchy with clouds. Here on the water she felt a light bracing wind against her flesh. She scanned the wooden deck, curious to learn something about this female. Among the range of articles was a straw broom, several weather-beaten chairs, the geraniums in their terracotta pots, black jeans and lace underwear drying in the breeze, snakeskin cowboy boots, an aluminium watering can, an old metal chest with a broken lock, a small battered dustbin, several empty wine bottles and a stack of *Liberation* newspapers, the most visible of which was thick with hardened candle grease. It was a rather bohemian inventory. Ms Millar must be younger than she'd envisaged. There was nothing however to suggest Stephen's presence here, which was reassuring to Lyndsay.

She strolled to the prow and looked over towards the Bastille while listening to ice cubes chinking in glasses and the not very evident hum of traffic. Was this a summer residence, or did Gin live here permanently?

'Grab a chair, Mrs Potter.' The voice from behind her was luxuriously husky, but there was a hint of nervous tension there, too.

Lyndsay took a deep breath and turned to face her husband's mistress. Standing several metres in front of her, barefoot, dressed in nothing except a black silk something or other, carrying a tray of drinks, was Gin. The two women regarded one another in silence. There was no denying that this woman was exquisitely beautiful.

'God,' was all Lyndsay could manage. The wind had gone from her sails.

'Here, take a swig of Scotch,' said Gin kindly.

Shaking, Lyndsay accepted the proffered glass. 'I'm...' she sighed. A well of stupid concerns befuddled her. Her lemon, tailored-linen dress felt ma'amish and square. She had been expecting to shake hands, to behave decently but, now, such formality was ludicrously out of place. Tears pricked her eyes. Words completely failed her. 'Now that I'm here, I'm not quite...' Gin was a bohemian as the inventory had suggested and a most unlikely choice for Stephen. 'You were sleeping with my husband...' Such beauty, such sexuality, disquieted Lyndsay. By comparison she felt suburban, charmless.

'No.' Gin settled the tray on the deck, dragged over another chair by hooking it around her painted toes and sat down. 'Please, sit,' she said smiling, but she was nervous and guarded too.

Lyndsay sank into her canvas seat. Silence settled; it was unnerving. She slugged at her drink.

'You're returning to England today?'

'Later, yes...' She could barely find her voice. 'Stephen's... Stephen's dead, did you know?'

'I know.'

'Oh, God!' She was losing it, giving way to emotion. 'I want to know everything.'

Gin topped up Lyndsay's Scotch. 'There's nothing to tell, Mrs Potter.'

Lyndsay tried to comprehend, to pull it together. 'You were the last person to see him before the accident?'

'I believe so.'

'You must have heard the siren?'

'Sure, we heard it but…'

'We?'

'I'm not in the habit of butting my nose into other folks' affairs. We didn't know, at first, that it was Mr Potter who'd been hurt.'

'We? Was there someone else with you as well as Stephen?' This fact affronted her. It fitted nowhere into the scenario she had built up.

'Stephen was not with me.' She handed Lyndsay the refilled glass. 'Help yourself to Perrier. You assume I was his mistress? It's why you came, right?'

'Well, yes.'

'I barely knew him.'

'You barely knew him? So, it was a one off thing?'

'Please.' Gin sipped her own drink: straight water. She was attempting to remain calm and uninvolved. 'We met casually in a bar a few weeks back. And then we met up again yesterday. You have no cause to be jealous.'

'Well, why did you meet again?'

'I'd lost an earring, he…bought me a new pair. He found my number and phoned me.'

'Why would he do that?'

'He wanted to make contact, I guess. I invited him over because he said he had my earring.'

Lyndsay sipped the burning whisky. 'I don't believe you.'

'Well, I'm sorry, that's all there is to it.' Gin rose.

She had to make sense of this. 'That's all there is to it! Stephen's been killed and – '

'Mrs Potter, please.'

'What was he running from?'

'I'd rather not discuss it. I have told you all I can.'

'Why? Why won't you discuss it?' Lyndsay glared at the elegant woman standing in front of her, knowing her time was running out.

'Mrs Potter, your husband seemed like a regular guy and I am sorry, profoundly sorry for you, that he has died in such a tragic way but none of this is my affair.' Gin took a step, but Lyndsay grabbed her by the arm.

'I want the truth!'

'I don't have the truth.'

'You were lovers!'

'Listen, you've got this all wrong.'

'Stephen's dead! I have to live with that. Help me to understand! Had you made plans? A future together? You were pushing him to get divorced?'

'Jesus!' Gin sat back down again and ran her fingers through her folds of hair. From out of the pocket of her baggy shirt she dug a pack of Gitanes. She offered the packet to Lyndsay who shook her head. Not for an instant did Lyndsay take her eyes off her. Gin lit the cigarette and dragged on it. 'This has nothing to do with me and you are making me responsible.'

'Stephen talked to you about our sons. Because he wanted you to know about his family.'

'No! He was in a bar. I asked him for a light. I should have just walked on.' Gin held a hand over her mouth. The cigarette was between her fingers so the moistness in her eyes could have been caused by smoke, but Lyndsay did not believe so. 'Mrs Potter, go home. Mourn your husband and forget me. I have nothing to do with any of this.'

'How can I walk away?' Lyndsay's voice was rising in pitch and volume.

'Please don't raise your voice,' Gin sighed and looked out across the boat to the further shore. A crease furrowed her brow.

'Listen, I admit, our marriage has been in trouble for a while. Never mind why. So, Stephen fell in love and you became lovers.

He's very charming, rich. I can see that you would have been…but then…something came to light last night which distressed him. What happened? He was running away, wasn't he? From what?'

Gin inhaled her cigarette. 'We didn't know each other. We weren't lovers! Really, Mrs Potter, this is… He was a guy in crisis, looking for love.'

'He *had* love!'

'Romance, then. Christ, what do I know? He boarded the boat last night. And found me with my lover… Her name is Marguerite.' Lyndsay stared in disbelief. 'I guess it shocked him.'

She was doing her best to cover her disapproval. 'Well, if he'd fallen for you, the sight of…with…a…would have distressed him, yes. Stephen was very conventional.'

'Look, I'm sorry. I don't want to get involved with this. With you or your family. Please, go.' Gin stubbed out her cigarette and lit another one.

'He had decided to leave. The children and me.' Lyndsay lifted the Scotch to her mouth. The glass knocked against her teeth. 'If it wasn't for you, then what was it for?'

'Himself, I guess.'

Lyndsay nodded. She placed the glass she was clutching on the tray. Then, slowly, she rose to her feet, lifted the chair and walked it back along the deck. She felt light, paper thin, as though her entrails had been flushed out of her. She could not meet the other woman's eyes.

Only as she reached the gangplank did she turn back. Gin was still smoking. Her head was turned to the left, and trails of smoke veiled her profile. A hand rested against her fractionally open mouth.

'If what you tell me is true, my husband died for nothing,' Lyndsay said simply and descended to the quay without looking back.

27

Before leaving Paris, Lyndsay was obliged to sort through Stephen's boxes in search of various legal documents. There was not a great deal to discover. In death, as in life, Stephen was inscrutable. Most of the files she stored because she had no idea what they were. At some later stage, she would entrust them to Alan. She left the rest exactly as she had found it, aside from most of Stephen's clothes, which she handed over to the concierge's wife – known to her now as Madame Berthillon – to distribute amongst whatever charities she saw fit. Monsieur Berthillon received from her sufficient funds to attend to all domestic matters and to pay the bills as and when they arrived.

For herself, Lyndsay retained an engraved, silver fountain pen she had given Stephen one Christmas and a silk handkerchief still imprinted with his scent. A box of souvenirs of his university days at Oxford and Harvard she packed up for the boys. She decided to keep on the flat itself as a mark of respect to Stephen, at least for the foreseeable future. He had settled a year's rent in advance so, when the grieving had lessened, she and the boys might spend time there and discover Paris together.

That same evening she returned to England and to her sons. Amanda collected her from the airport, accompanied by Matt. Lyndsay took him in her arms. 'Let me hold you,' she said. 'It's so good to hold you.'

In response, his greeting was confrontational. 'What's going on? Where's Dad?' .

She would have preferred to wait until they'd arrived home but, while Amanda discreetly disappeared to pick up cigarettes, Lyndsay led him to an open café area and over untouched bottles of Coke, she recalled Burgess' words to her. There's no other way to say this – was that the standard police approach?

'Matt?'

'What?'

'When I came to see you at the police station, I said that Daddy might have been in an accident. It was why I had to leave you in Dover and go to Paris, remember?'

'Of course, I remember. It was only the day before yesterday!' Only the day before yesterday. So it was. 'Mum, no one will tell me anything! Where's Dad?'

In the space of forty-eight hours, her world had spun off its axis and lodged itself in darkness. Life was still going on, but she felt unable to reach out to it. In direct contrast, in this bustling airport café with its vulgar fluorescent glare and raucous, intrusive music, people were animated and happy.

'Mum, are you listening to me? What's up?'

And here she was, face to face with her confused and very angry eldest son, preparing to deliver the same shock to his senses. 'The body the police found in the river was Daddy's.'

Matt lifted his face and peered mistrustfully at his mother as though searching for the trick in this. 'What are you saying?' he growled, but there was pleading as well as a threat in his voice, a don't-you-dare-let-this-be-true note: the seed of blame. She stretched her arm across the table, negotiating the Coke bottles, and reached out to his chewed, grubby fingers.

Give him the bare bones only, she was thinking. Details of the fateful night's incidents could come later. The existence of Gin would not be mentioned. That was an intimate affair. 'Daddy's died, darling.'

Matt dropped his head and stared intently at his disgustingly weatherworn sneakers. Lyndsay rose in an attempt to take hold of him but he shoved her away with a ferocious, defiant denial. Their clumsy grappling had sent one of the Cokes rolling across the table. Heads turned as the brown fizzy liquid hissed and bubbled like poison between them. Then, eyes blazing, nose running, Matt began to wheeze and whimper like an abandoned puppy.

When Lyndsay related the news of his father's death to Paul, in the headmaster's study, the younger boy broke down and wailed. The small bespectacled face he'd held so high, which had brazened out so much during so many long weeks, crumbled and he begged his mother to be allowed to go home with her.

Both Matthew and Paul remained away from college. It was practically the end of the school year and Lyndsay believed that their places were with one another. For herself, she needed them near her, within reach. She craved their beings and their energies around her as others might hunger for sex.

They buried Stephen in peace and with dignity. He lay in a plot in Lingfield Cemetery alongside Lyndsay's father, Harry. A heartwarming number of the local community was present at the graveside service. Trembling, Lyndsay, with her two brave-faced sons flanking her, concentrated on the vicar's sermon and the nature surrounding her. The flowering peonies on her father's grave were as radiant as the sun itself. As radiant as that woman Stephen had been besotted with and had followed to his death. The clouds, white and fast moving across a Wedgwood blue sky, promised rain and with it cleansing and fresh growth. Lyndsay bowed her head and prayed for it, although she could not perceive its form. She had no faith that things would ever be normal again. Haunted by that last, too brief phone call, all she could think of was the coldness that had grown up between her and Stephen, and the aggression and the anger that had been building. The misunderstandings, the wrong turns and the pointless loss of life.

Once, during a moment of communal prayer, while mouthing words without the faintest notion of what she was saying, her eyes began to dart desperately from face to face. She was searching for him, Stephen. He was there, somewhere. He had to be. He couldn't have just gone! But she could not feel his presence anywhere. The disappointment almost overwhelmed her.

The funeral was a friendly gathering, humming with laughter and memories. Her body was present but it was as though she were witnessing the scene from somewhere else. Everyone was in black, in glaring sunshine, shaking hands. Commiserating, consuming drinks and snacks in their garden. The boys were in suits, perfect young gentlemen. Alan was running the show. He had organised everything, had seen to it that all press were kept at a distance and well clear of the family. The newspapers more or less acquiesced. Having exploited this village episode to its limits they had moved on and found other, more recent tragedies to rake over. And Burgess, mercifully, had not dared to show his face.

In those early weeks, nature and activity cradled Lyndsay's sense of loss, as they had always done. She sought out the minutiae of daily life: the changing colours of the hedgerows in the lanes; the shedding of seasonal blossoms; cloud formations; bird songs; and the daily care of her sons: Matt, evasive and absent, and Paul who clung to her like a Siamese twin. All of these forced her to keep going, to grapple with the cycles of life. But nothing diminished her growing fury at this cock-eyed world.

She blamed herself now for having held so much of herself back, for not having shared her real self with Stephen. She had never allowed him to know who she was, what her past had made of her. All those years ago in that coffee shop in Chelsea, Stephen had been attracted to and excited by her secretiveness. She had sensed it and had allowed it to tantalise and seduce him but, she felt sure now, those secrets had eventually distanced him. The holding back had, over the years and most importantly since Harry's death, eroded the communication and finally the love that had existed between them. How she blamed herself.

Days slid by in a kind of comatose fashion. During the eight weeks that followed – groaning weeks, baggy with a sense of futility – Lyndsay felt stripped of all emotion except anger and a furious need to keep occupied. In a maniacal way she honed in on practicalities: running the house; cleaning out the cottage; caring for the nursery; deliberating about the boys' education; and then worrying over financial matters. But no matter how busy she kept herself, there was a gaping emptiness in the life she and Stephen had created together and the companionship that went along with it. There was so much she wanted to say to him, all that had remained unsaid.

And what of the future? What of the boys?

Alan, the only person entirely cognisant of Stephen's affairs, assured her that whatever she decided she was secure. If she and the boys wished to remain at the house there would be no obstacles, no reason to sell off or rent portions of land. Nine weeks after Stephen's death, when Lyndsay sat in his office and learnt the full extent of his wealth she reeled with shock.

'Where has it all come from?'

Stephen's burly-framed friend and solicitor, self-assured and unruffled, dismissed it as, 'family money, shrewdly invested'. Lyndsay felt certain this was not true. But when she tried to argue it, Alan, with his usual charm, smiled reassuringly, 'Stephen's dealings were never shady.'

She recollected the boxes of files stowed away in Paris and wondered if it wouldn't have been more prudent to have destroyed them. 'He has left some papers. Shall I – ?'

'I'll take care of them.'

'What are they?'

'Listen, Lyndsay, Stephen made his living relocating funds for the wealthy, many of whom were probably unscrupulous. From what sources their fortunes had been mined, he never made his business. He kept his own affairs squeaky clean. Stephen demanded faultless standards in life.'

Lyndsay accepted Alan's explanations – she had no strength left to debate it – and she kept her reservations to herself.

On the drive back from Alan's office, she reflected on what Alan had said. It was true that Stephen had striven ruthlessly for perfectionism. In conversation he had frequently alluded to 'standards'. Hadn't that been at the root of the arguments between Matt and his father about the Hampton boys? It had certainly been part of what had attracted Lyndsay to him. A career had meant nothing to her. She had been searching for deliverance – deliverance from the hell she had inhabited during her childhood years. She had yearned for the perfect existence, had craved security, wanting to draw a veil across her past and deny the traumas. She had wanted happiness at any price. The arrival of Stephen had promised it and, to achieve it, she would have become any woman he'd desired. The young innocent he had been so attracted to in the Richoux coffee shop; a rosy-complexioned creature with no blemishes, inhabiting a smooth clean life. A smooth clean life? There was no such article. Yet, she had given years to authenticating such an idyllic picture of herself and her family, never looking beneath the constraints of the façade.

What a bitter irony then that, in the end, Stephen had been besotted with that woman in Paris; a bohemian, a black sheep. And his fortune had been built from dubious sources. Stephen. Lyndsay tried so hard to picture him, to see him in her mind's eye, but he had become faceless. He had gone; she could not feel to where. And she was left with the task of trying to make sense of her crumbling world.

Lyndsay crossed the river by the old brick bridge and turned to the right. She was thinking that she'd occupy the rest of the afternoon caning a chair that she'd found abandoned at the rear of one of the sheds, when a figure waiting beneath the birch tree, a few yards to the left of their wrought-iron gates, caught her attention. Head bent reflectively, he was smoking a cigarette. The sight of him stabbed at the core of her. Even at such a distance she recognised that silhouette: Burgess.

Matthew's release, the absence of the Inspector at the funeral, and his ensuing silence during the weeks which had followed, had lulled Lyndsay into becoming, at least at surface level, less wary and alarmed. But now her heart churned in her gut; a part of her had been expecting him.

She stopped the car and lowered the window. 'What are you doing here?'

Burgess let drop his cigarette and ground it into the pavement with the sole of his shoe.

'I don't want you near our house. The boys are home,' she hissed.

He pulled open the door and climbed in. The engine purred softly. Lyndsay left it to idle as she stared defiantly at the closed gates in front of her. Her breathing was furious and her hands on the leather wheel were clammy.

'I'm very sorry,' he said. Because she dreaded the completion of his sentence, she made no response. 'Very bad news about your husband.'

'Is that what you came here for?'

'I'd like to see Matt.'

'Keep away from him! You have nothing against him!' she breathed ferociously.

'A query.'

'No! No! You don't have the right to take him in again unless you are charging him. And if you come near us again without evidence, I swear, I'll have you drummed out of the force for breaking the codes of practice, and for loitering outside our gates. Now get out of my car!'

'Surinder Bharjee's fingerprints have been found on Matt's Swatch.' Silenced, Lyndsay caught her breath. 'I thought you should know.'

Eyes closed, she sat pressed against the wheel as Burgess disappeared up the lane.

Should they just pack up and leave the village? Sell everything and get the hell out? Or would folk judge it as Matt's guilt? Was Matt capable of raping and killing the exquisite girl of his fantasies? When Lyndsay telephoned Alan to tell him what had happened, he said it was time to call in his colleague.

'Matt?'

Since his return and the death of his father, Matthew had spent precious little time at home. Mostly he'd passed the hours with the Hamptons but whenever he was in Lyndsay's company – which was rarely – his mood was sullen and black. She had a million questions, a million things to say to him but they were a family in the midst of grieving. Things got said by souls in pain that once said, might never be retracted. She knew that from bitter experience. And Matt was carrying a second sorrow, two losses, in his tender heart.

It was several hours after she'd found Burgess at the gate.

Matt opened his door a fraction. 'What?'

'Can we talk, please?' Before he could refuse, she pushed the door open and stepped in. No words were necessary to express her disgust at the state of his room.

'Don't start, Mum, all right.'

'I'm just checking to see how you are,' she said, wading past the mountain of clothes ditched at the foot of his unmade bed, where she perched. 'I see so little of you.'

Matt, at his desk, faced the semi-darkened window. His back to his mother, he was intent on some occupation. The room was

303

dimly lit by lamps and by an aromatic candle that flickered on his desk. Joss sticks burned alongside a photo which, as Lyndsay settled, Matt turned face downwards.

'Inspector Burgess was here earlier... Matt?'

'Yeah?'

'Are you listening?'

'Yeah, I heard.'

'He came about the Swatch you lost.' Silence. 'Surinder Bharjee's fingerprints have been found on it.' Silence. 'Matt, are you listening to me? What are you doing?'

He swung round to face her, his face angry with pain and defiance, his eyes glistening. 'Rolling a spliff, OK!'

Lyndsay leapt to her feet, crossed to her son and slapped him hard on the back of his head. Matt hunched his body against the attack, which fired her further and she began to shake him from behind and pummel the back of his shoulders. 'I don't want that stuff here, do you understand me! Do you understand me?' she shouted, knocking against him, thrusting the cigarette skins and loose grass from out of his hands. The semi-rolled joint flew in the air and scattered all over the rug and oak flooring.

Matt wheeled round and made to rise. 'Leave me alone or I'll kill you!' he yelled. Lyndsay ducked, an instinctive reaction of terror from way back. Neither made another move. Both held their ground, eyes blazing, wild grieving beasts appraising one another, his words hanging between them.

It was Matt who backed down, returning to his desk to bury his face in his arms. Lyndsay waited, hovering behind him, not knowing what to do or say. She was trembling with shock. If Stephen were here, he would give the boy a good talking to. He would demand respect. She noticed Matt wipe his eyes. Was he crying?

'Oh God, Matt, I'm so sorry.' No response. 'Matt,' she pleaded, wanting to touch him, to suck him back within her and begin from the beginning again. He was stubbornly, infuriatingly silent.

His hands lifted to his head and fingers ran through his hair as though he were trying to contain the furies beating in his brain. 'We must talk, Matt.'

'Leave me alone!'

'Shall I call someone?'

'What do you mean?'

'A counsellor or...?'

He took a deep breath and slowly blew out air. 'For God's sake!'

'Surinder's prints are on your watch,' she repeated but this time more softly.

'So what?'

'Don't you understand what that means?' He didn't answer. 'You told Burgess you didn't know her. I read... They're talking murder, Matt. Matt,' she cried, 'please...'

'Fuck off, Mum.'

She retreated silently.

The general store was closed for business. It lay silent and dark and carried a SOLD hoarding outside. R Bharjee, the Indian whose name was still painted above the shop door, had boarded it up and slipped silently away. Lyndsay, alone across the street, in front of the church wall, stood gazing across at it, thinking of Matt. Who killed Surinder Bharjee?

No one, not even after a few pints at the Lamb and Flag, seemed to be allowing themselves the indulgence of voicing that question. Except Lyndsay. A disturbing page of local history was being painstakingly turned. The sedate village of Churdle Heath had become front-page news and, in the wake of that same crime, it had lost one of its most esteemed citizens. But as each day passed the neighbourhood was endeavouring to pick up the pieces. Life must move on.

'How are you getting on?'

She turned to find Ralph Beresford drawing alongside her and attempted a smile to cover her anxieties. Lyndsay had not spoken to him since their brief meeting in the village on the day Burgess had visited her father's grave. She had noticed him in amongst the mourners at the Lingfield Cemetery on the morning of Stephen's service but there had been no opportunity for conversation. 'Slowly,' she replied. 'I heard they offered you back your job?'

Beresford had been reinstated as the warden of both nature reserve and bird sanctuary. The local council had received a petition containing over one hundred signatures and Ralph Beresford had been formally invited to return.

'Yeah, it looks as though I'll be staying. Listen, I have been wanting to have a word. There are a couple of things. Are you going to be around later?'

'Yes.'

'I'll call you, may I?'

She nodded.

At that moment, Marion Finch materialised from out of the Lamb and Flag. Sighting Lyndsay, she waved a newspaper and began her approach. Arthur had returned to Marion. On the few occasions since Stephen's death when Lyndsay had encountered her, Marion had maintained a skittish, nervy distance. Stephen was never mentioned. Matthew was never mentioned. Marion's chattering tongue wanted no part of such dark matters and that lonely, far-off night when Lyndsay had driven her home was never referred to, nor were the late-night, drunken calls. Arthur's 'bit on the side', her pregnancy, phantom or terminated, was a thorn of the past, best forgotten. Evidently that suited Marion better than the prospect of an empty old age.

'They gave him his job back, did you hear?'

'Yes.'

'The council received a petition. Dreamed up by Annabel, of course.'

'Who?'

'Annabel Welch. She's the barmaid over at the pub and a hot admirer of his. Well, good luck to her. I wouldn't kick that blue-eyed Australian out of my bed. Did you see this?' she asked, flicking through the pages of her *Daily Mail*. Lyndsay instantly stepped back, sensing malice. 'The police found an insecticide can in the nature reserve.'

'What about it?'

As Marion scanned the print, Lyndsay was observing the increasing puffiness in her face, the bloodshot eyes and the pronounced slur in her diction. 'They think it might have been the one used to attack the ospreys.'

28

'Someone said you have a cottage you might consider renting?'
Ralph Beresford's request took her off guard. Lyndsay had
vaguely toyed with the idea of offering the home she and
Stephen had built for her father to the Hampton family but had
decided finally that it was too cramped for four.

'Well, it hadn't crossed my mind.' It had been empty for the
best part of a year and its emptiness, a symptom of so much
emptiness, oppressed her. As long as she and the boys remained
at Churdle Bridge Farm it may as well be occupied.

'When the local authorities asked me to go, I gave up my flat
and bought a ticket to Darwin. So I'm looking for somewhere.'

'I don't know if it would be suitable. You know, it's very quiet
and...'

'I'm renting one of the attic rooms at the Lamb and Flag. It's
cramped, noisy and driving me crazy,' he laughed.

After wrestling with certain undeclared personal reservations,
Lyndsay invited him to come and discuss it the next day.

'Thanks.'

'You said there were a couple of things?'

'I'll tell you the other tomorrow, when we meet.'

Early the following morning, Saturday, drizzly, dismal weather
set in, closing down the view. Lyndsay was depressed by the grey
damp, which signalled the onset of winter. She was sleeping
badly. Fatigue and doubts dogged her. She made herself a pot of

strong coffee and drank it alone in the kitchen. The boys had gone off to play Quasar in a converted petrol station near Tonbridge. Ralph Beresford was due at eleven.

While she waited she studied a prospectus, trying to make up her mind about whether to register Matt and Paul at a new school for the autumn. Somewhere closer to Churdle Bridge Farm where they would not be obliged to board and where they could make a fresh start. The alternative was to sell the house, uproot and truly begin again, but that, for the present, seemed too drastic.

Ralph arrived on time. She did not invite him in. Together they descended the grassy slopes to the cottage, Lyndsay leading the way in silence. Inside, the cottage smelled musty.

They stood, the pair of them, by the bedroom window, relative strangers, separated by a respectable distance. Lyndsay was wearing a raincoat, Ralph a light wine-coloured windcheater. Both were in jeans and Wellingtons. The air was chilled and fresh, carrying with it rich, earthy perfumes from the mint ranging free in the cottage garden and the dried lavender Lyndsay had hung in ornate bunches in the empty bathroom. Paw prints from a cat autographed the wall beneath the window frame. Lyndsay wondered who it belonged to and when the animal had found its way in.

'I haven't been down here for a while,' she said.

'You've lost weight,' was his response.

Stephen's childhood had been less traumatic, less violent than her own, she was thinking as she stood in her late father's bedroom with this man who was virtually a stranger and about whom she knew so little. More than anything in the world she had wanted a loving environment for her sons. It was why she had denied so much. Denied the bloodshed, the cruelties, the suffering. Hidden the heart of herself.

Chestnut leaves were strewn across the windowsill. 'There must have been a storm since I was in here last. I'll clean it up. If you like it.'

'I can do that. No worries.' He turned his head slowly away from the window, looking about him, before staring at her quizzically. She could not guess from his expression what he was thinking. 'You all right?'

She nodded. All the furniture had been shoved against the walls. She had done it herself a couple of months earlier, in a frenzy of tidying and discarding, a few weeks after Stephen's funeral, although now she could barely recall the warm summer days she'd passed buried in these empty rooms. Her father's saxophones were Matt's now. But what was to become of Matt? Violent, inarticulate Matt.

'Has there really been a summer?'

'Hmm?'

'All the days have fused into one.'

Lyndsay gazed out at a plum tree beyond the bedroom window.

'I'll ask Tom to do that.' Weeks ago she had informed Tom that Dennis was no longer welcome at the house. She regretted her meanness towards him now. 'Poor Tom.'

'Sorry?'

'That tree, the plum, it needs pruning.'

Ralph negotiated the furniture on his approach to the window. Five-hundred metres or so further along on the other side of Quigley Lane was the vague outline of the only other house within this secluded backwater. 'Don't trouble for my sake. I rather like it as it is,' he said and left her side.

She watched him closely now, studying him, as he turned about, hands stuffed into the pockets of his mulberry windcheater. A tall, muscular man in his early thirties with dishevelled fair hair, clear and healthy skin and gentle eyes.

Lyndsay had not forgotten the periwinkle blueness of his unexpectedly gentle eyes.

'I'll give it a coat of paint though, if you don't mind.' He strolled from the bedroom where they had been standing and examined this and that in the living room, straying into the compact, tucked-away kitchen. Encrusted beer splashes had stained the tiles. She followed him through into the living area and stepped on towards the open door, waiting for him, preparing to lock the place up again, the keys weighing in her hand. 'I'd like to take it, and finish my book.'

'How's it going?'

'I had a report to write about the ospreys, and lab work to do. Their disappearance, the vandalism. Haven't had much time for my own stuff.'

'We won't disturb you.'

He smiled, but there was something in the way he looked at her. 'Are you sure you're OK?'

She wandered outside without having registered his question. The drizzling had ceased, leaving the grass spongy and damp against their booted shins. The cottage garden was turning into a wilderness. She hadn't really paid attention. She'd given up on her bouts of frenzied activity the day Burgess had come about Matt's Swatch. 'It's the only part of the grounds I haven't tended. My father didn't like me fussing about the place. And since Stephen...' Her sentence left unfinished, they began their ascent back towards the house.

'Lyndsay, have you seen anything of Burgess?'

She felt danger close at hand. 'He was here a couple of weeks ago.'

'Not since?'

'No, why?'

'He's been keeping me pretty busy.'

'Doing what?'

'He wanted to take a look at the records I made up after the ospreys were attacked and to collect the aerosol can I found in the woods.'

'It was you who found it?'

'Yes. Has he mentioned to you that it matches the canister he picked up in your shed?' Lyndsay stopped in her track. 'He's crafty, he should have told you.'

'Just because you found a rusty old can in the nature reserve, it doesn't mean –'

'Please, I didn't want to upset you.'

'Insecticides are sold everywhere.'

'There's no other nursery in the area stocks that brand. Burgess has checked. It looks as though the can which was sprayed on the osprey came from here.'

'Any child can buy insecticide sprays in a supermarket!'

'Not if they contain diazinon.'

'What's that?'

'An organophosphorus compound. You ever heard of it?' Lyndsay shook her head and shivered in the damp. 'Listen, you're getting cold. I can fill you in on the scientific details another time. It's not important. You are not to worry about the diazinon.'

As they parted, she handed him the cottage keys. 'Here. If you decide not to take it...'

'It'll do me fine. Thank you. Let me know how much you want for it and I'll give you a cheque tomorrow. If it's all right with you, I'll drop by in the afternoon with a few things. Lyndsay, is there anything I can do? I'd like to help.'

'No, thanks.' And she hurried away, avoiding his gaze. She made her way directly to the potting shed. It was locked. She dug in her raincoat pocket for the keys. It was pouring now and cold, but she didn't care. She wanted to be wet, to be drenched, for the weather to soak her through.

The wood inside smelled damp. Tom had swept up and tidied the shed out. There were no traces of tobacco on the wooden floor and only two cans of insecticide left. Lyndsay lifted one from the shelf and turned it over to read the ingredients: diazinon.

Back in the kitchen, she practically tore the telephone book to shreds looking for a number for *Which?* Magazine.

'I would like advice on all products containing diazinon, please.'

The gardening section of the magazine offered to post her a copy of their list of pesticides approved under the Control of Pesticides Regulations. They also suggested that, if the information was urgent, she could call the Ministry of Agriculture, Fisheries and Food. She looked up their number and asked to speak to someone dealing with pesticides.

'I need advice on all products containing diazinon, please.'

She was put through to a woman who informed her that she would have difficulty finding any sprays containing the ingredient. 'You might still find it in granule form, but for commercial use only.'

'Why is that?'

'It has been withdrawn from the market. Certainly for domestic use. There is one product which uses it professionally for spraying a particular fly on mushroom, would you like me to give you the name of that?'

'Any particular reason why it's been withdrawn?'

'It's highly dangerous, causes serious burning to the skin.'

'I see, thank you.' Lyndsay replaced the phone. What had Burgess said about Surinder's body? There were burns on her legs. Had Matt been in the potting sheds? When had she noticed the mess in there? She couldn't recall. Her mind was blocked, jumbled.

The following afternoon she went to the cottage. The rooms smelled of lemon-scented Ajax.

'Sorry, I should have knocked. I didn't mean to disturb,' she said, entering clumsily.

He had been bending, unpacking a paint-roller from one of several laden cardboard boxes on the ground. 'What's up?' he asked, frowning.

'I phoned the Ministry of Agriculture to find out about diazinon.'

Ralph smiled. 'I nearly called you last night. I wondered later if what I said had troubled you. The can came from here but anybody could have bought it.'

'I gave up selling insecticides ages ago. Those cans weren't kept in the nurseries.'

'It doesn't have to have been bought in the recent past. Maybe your gardener or your husband – ' He stopped mid-sentence.

Lyndsay dropped her gaze and scuffed the carpet with her shoe. 'Stephen had no interest in the nurseries. He was never down there.'

He took a step towards her and then, thinking better of it, held back. 'Listen, if you're thinking that this is pointing the finger at Matthew, you can stop worrying. Burgess is convinced that the murderer is left-handed.'

Lyndsay froze. It was as though someone had come up behind her and clubbed her on the back of the head. 'Why do you say that?'

'Just this morning, he was asking me about a form of damage to the left-hemisphere of the brain sometimes associated with left-handed people.'

'Damage?' She could not let him know what was happening.

'Burns on the inner flesh of her left thigh seem to suggest that Surinder's murderer might have been left-handed.'

Burns on her legs. Burgess knew.

'I have to go...'

Hurrying back up the hill to the sound of birds chirruping, the late summer rain stung her skin, drilled into her flesh. Lyndsay could only think of Matt, Matt who was left-handed. She was dreading the return of Burgess. He was moving closer, she felt sure, drawing in his net.

29

The boys were gathering the last of the apples in the orchard. They were with Ralph, shouting and horseplaying together. It was a warm late-autumn day, the first blue sky in a while. The trees were a riot of golds and reds and clean sharp lines. The wand flowers and the Michaelmas daisies were beginning to blossom and the air was patched with the scents of ripe and fermenting fruit. Lyndsay was kneeling on a blanket spread out on the ground close by the teak table. She was sorting through a wooden box squeezed tight with quinces, setting aside the good ones and discarding the rest into a nearby sack. All the while she was glancing towards the fruit garden to where the three males were at play, Ralph and her sons. Ralph whom she studiously avoided being alone with.

Matthew's hair was growing back. He looked a curious and unruly sight with the chocolate-dyed strands jutting above his gingery regrowth. His jeans were gashed and gaping. Lyndsay hated them and had fought with him on several occasions about them. 'Throw them out, please, Matt.'

'Get off my case,' he'd retorted.

They had been fighting a great deal, she and Matt. His loss was aggressively expressed. It flummoxed and hurt her. She didn't know how to approach him, to ease his pain, to repair the gulf between them. She had tried since Stephen's death and Matt's return to pretend that all was as it had been. She hadn't, since the incident in his room, mentioned the marijuana and she had never let on about her discovery of his writings. She was doing her utmost to treat Matt in a normal way but, in response, he behaved as though he blamed her.

Burgess had not come by. Every day she waited for him. His shadow hovered close and darkened her days.

Alongside her, the rich, cidery smell of windfallen apples, collected in baskets at the foot of the garden table, insisted on reminding her of sex, and of Stephen. A memory was stirring.

The boys shouted and yelled happily to one another. She was trying to recall what the memory was. And then it came to her: the loss of her virginity. Towards the end of their first summer together, in an orchard in Kent, Stephen had taken her virginity. The leaves on the trees had turned russet gold. 'They are the colour of your pubic hair,' he'd whispered.

Apples rotting on the ground had become one of the most erotic perfumes of all. So damaged, she'd feared his love, had trembled shyly. Yet Stephen had penetrated her with a gentleness and consideration that she could never have appreciated at the time. He'd held and loved her with male tenderness.

Suddenly, for the first time in a long while, she saw Stephen's face again. He was smiling at her, warm and clear as the day. 'Oh, Stephen!' During these last months she had been so terrified of forgetting what he looked like. Scared of letting him down, of letting him go. She saw Stephen young again as she had known him for the first time, when sex had represented so many scary things. Because no man had ever touched her there before she had not appreciated his loving control. How she longed to tell him that now, thank him for so many good times, and stop blaming herself for the rest.

She had never trusted Stephen's love because she had feared to trust. Years of repressed trauma had caused her to shrink from intimacy and of the vulnerabilities it opened up within her.

She had idolised her father, and had blinded herself to what had really taken place. His womanising had broken her mother's heart, his violence in the house had destroyed her spirit, and her mother had killed herself. Left alone with her father, Lyndsay had denied the past and had built her whole world around him. She had loved and served him because she had not been able to face the alternative. When her turn came to marry she had done the same for Stephen, loved and served him, but she had never opened herself to him in the way her mother had done. Since Harry's death, images from her childhood had begun to creep back.

Matthew was her father's kin. Was he capable of that same ugly violence? All summer long she had been wrestling with the doubt. Matthew could have taken that spray from the potting shed. He was left-handed.

'No!' Lyndsay's cry was so loud it stopped the others at their play. They stared at her, unsettled by her outburst. She struggled to her feet and withdrew into the house.

Within the cool tranquility of the kitchen she tried to regain her equilibrium. She needed to hear from Matt's own lips that he was innocent of the murder of Surinder Bharjee, she needed him to swear it to her. She wanted the truth, but she did not know how she would live with it if... In the face of all police questioning Matthew had denied knowledge of the Indian girl. Lyndsay knew this was a lie. And her fingerprints were on his Swatch.

The boy in the notebooks, the boy who played out his secret erotic life, had nurtured an adulterous passion for a young married woman. They, their flesh, had known one another. Was that same boy then capable of raping and killing the girl of his fantasies?

Lyndsay bitterly regretted ever having gone through Matt's belongings and having spied on his inner life. But there was no going back. She could not deny what she had stumbled upon in those pages. And bottling it up was driving her insane. She needed to ask him directly. Whatever had happened she would never disclose it, never inform Burgess. She would defend Matt's innocence tooth and nail. She would protect him, for she had created Matt. Whatever he might be, he was of her. But she had to know the truth.

'Are you all right, Mum?' Lyndsay was standing by the sink. She turned at the sound of Matt's voice. He was framed in the doorway with one of the dogs panting at his side. 'Mum?'

She stared out of the window to the herb pots and the flower gardens beyond. 'I'm fine.'

He stood hovering. 'Can we do something?'

'I said I'm fine, Matt.'

'Is it about Dad?'

'Just leave me!' she shouted and then with gathering control, 'Please, Matt, go back outside.'

Without another word he went away, the dog trotting at his side. She had shrunk from the opportunity.

The boys had gone to the coast with the Hamptons to Stephen's yacht. Lyndsay was alone in the house.

'Could I have a word?' Ralph's voice behind her startled her. It was the first time he had ever invited himself up to the house. She turned and saw that he was sodden from evening rain. The sight of him drenched, his hair slicked flat from the downpour, gave him a boyishness that she tried hard not to feel attracted to.

'What do you want?'

'I was on my way to the pub. I saw you at the window. Thought we might have a glass together, talk.' He drew a bottle of Brown Brother's Merlot from out of his windcheater. 'I hope you drink red,' he said. She gestured for him to come into the kitchen. 'You're very pale.'

She was edgy because she had not been expecting him. 'I'm fine.'

She was pulling glasses from a cupboard while Ralph waited a step or two behind her. As she turned she lost her balance. Ralph, to steady her, took her arm.

Lyndsay moved swiftly away to the table, uncorked the wine and began to pour. 'Here,' she said, handing him a glass.

He pulled out a chair and sat down, eyeing her steadily. 'Cheers.'

Lyndsay nodded and sipped the rich red wine. It tasted good. She sat at the table beside him, allowing her hands, cupped around the glass, to rest there.

'You're driving yourself cuckoo, you know that, don't you?'

His directness took her by surprise. 'I don't know what you're talking about.'

'I think you do. Anyone can see the way you look at Matthew. You think he doesn't know what you're thinking?'

At first she said nothing. It hadn't occurred to her that Matthew could read her thoughts, Ralph too. Were they so plainly written for all to see?

'He didn't do it, Lyndsay.'

She took another sip of wine and scribbled with her finger against the pine table. A lump caught in her throat. She feared to believe it. 'How do you know?' The question was almost inaudible.

'Until a few days ago, Burgess was convinced that whoever vandalised the ospreys also killed Surinder.' Once more came the image of Matt on that fateful night climbing the stairs. 'But Matt wasn't suffering burns during the days following the attack, was he?'

Lyndsay shook her head, puzzled. 'Not that I know of. Why?'

'When I examined the bird the next morning his feathers had traces of the active ingredient diazinon. You remember we talked about it briefly?' Lyndsay nodded. 'Most insecticide sprays contain tethramethrin and, usually, at least one other component; phenothrin, permethrin or cypermethrin. There is one that doesn't contain any of these. It only contains diazinon. As you know, this ingredient is highly dangerous and can burn the skin, which is why it's not available any more. I found it on the osprey's feathers, as well as around the poor bugger's eye.'

'What does that prove?'

'When that bird was attacked he would have fought back. The can might have got knocked, it almost certainly would have swung, been jabbed, thrust about. I strongly believe – given the hostile circumstances – that jets of spray would have landed partially onto the assailant. And that any stray drops would have left burn marks on his flesh. Also, if that bird managed to get close enough to dig his talons into the aggressor's skin, there will have been deep scratch marks.'

Ralph poured more wine.

'Thanks. Did Burgess believe that whoever harmed the bird also killed Surinder Bharjee because of the burn marks?'

'Yes, but it gave him a false lead. When I uncovered Surinder, her body, particularly her groin area, had been mauled by predating fauna. Her vaginal cavity had been eaten away and had caved in but there was enough flesh to trace markings on her thighs. Where the foxes had not eaten the flesh away, there was bruising from the violent struggle to push her legs apart and mild skin burns on her left thigh. Burgess learnt of the burns and suggested to the forensic lab that they test her vaginal cavity and legs for traces of diazinon; back to our active ingredient found in the insecticide used to spray the osprey.'

'And it matched?'

'Traces only, but it led Burgess to jump to the conclusion that the two crimes were committed by the same person. I was less convinced. The traces were minimal, in fact they barely registered.'

'So Burgess was wrong?'

'Not entirely. As I've explained, a product containing diazinon is rare. It had to be the same can, or a couple of cans purchased or stolen from the same source: your potting shed. Burgess' conclusion looked likely and it was leading him to Matthew.'

'But?'

'The insecticide can I found in the undergrowth was gnarled and damaged. The fox that got to Surinder's body – his carcass was later found – died from poisoning. I believe he chewed on or was in contact with that spray.'

'I don't understand.'

'The fox came across the can before finding Surinder's body. If my theory is right and there was a struggle between the osprey and his vandal, traces of diazinon would have covered the can. The fox was in contact with the can, licked it, chewed it, sniffed it. The minute traces of diazinon found around her vaginal cavity were, I believe, transferred there by the fox. And a fact that upholds my theory is that forensic have now isolated traces of paint from the can on her flesh. I believe it came off the discarded can which had lain in the undergrowth since the night of the bird attack.'

'So was it the fox that caused the burns on Surinder's thigh?'

'No, the markings are cigarette burns. The tip of a lighted cigarette brushing against her in a struggle. One of the Scene of Crime crew found a cigarette butt nearby. Sodden from rain unfortunately. And forensic found a couple of other traces of cigarette burns on various parts of her body and clothing which, again, suggest a struggle. That girl really fought.'

'Jesus!'

Both sat together in silence, contemplating the scene.

'That scream we heard in the nature reserve…?'

'I think it was her, yes,' he replied.

'But what if someone had heard on the news about the ospreys and copied the idea?'

'As I told you, there is only one brand with that exclusive active ingredient. That information was never released to the press. It would be too much of a coincidence for someone to copy the idea and use the same product. In any case, it was not available. Every gardening centre, hardware store, supermarket in Kent has been visited. You are the only one still carrying that product. And by the way, if you still have any cans left, I suggest you get rid of them.'

Lyndsay listened on in horror. Picturing the last fighting moments of a girl she had grown to despise because that girl's beauty and sexuality had threatened the existence of her own son. 'Does all this prove Matt's innocence?' she asked weakly.

'Whoever murdered Surinder Bharjee was smoking when he encountered her. They fought. She was raped, tried to run. If she was scarred from cigarette burns, so too might her aggressor have been. Matt doesn't smoke. He has no scars. I think you can safely assume he's in the clear.'

Lyndsay refrained from mentioning the marijuana. 'What about Surinder's fingerprints on his Swatch?'

'He should tell you about that.'

'He's told you?'

'We've talked a bit.'

'So, you're saying that he's innocent?'

'Speak to him, Lyndsay. That's what he needs. He needs your trust, and your faith.'

'Then, why –'

'Burgess had a couple of false leads. He smelled your doubt. He believed you were covering for your son. It led him to suspect Matt.' Lyndsay was thinking of Matt and the force, the joyous agonising of his passion. And of Stephen who had been her only lover. 'I'm down there, if you need me,' Ralph said, brushing her cheek. 'But I won't trouble you, if you don't.'

She wanted to be able to live with Stephen's memory and move on, as she knew he would wish her to. But she wasn't sure how.

The following day was Stephen's birthday. She was on her way to the grave to leave flowers – flowers, too, for her father. Matt was in his room. On an impulse she ran upstairs. She was thinking of the afternoon visit she had made with Burgess to the cemetery, in the hunt for Matt.

She knocked softly. 'Matt, I'm going to Daddy's grave. Want to come?'

Her son at her side in the car, Lyndsay took her chance. 'Ready to talk?' she asked, watching the wipers sweep softly to and fro. She waited. He made no response. 'OK, then it's me to start. I have a confession to make.' Matthew turned his head, studying his mother quizzically. 'When you disappeared I...missed you so badly, I went through your things. I was looking for a clue. To know if you were in some kind of trouble. I found grass and diaries, your poems...'

He turned away, gazing out beyond the glass. Lyndsay shot him a glance but she could not tell what he was thinking.

'You really loved her, didn't you?' A sigh. 'At first, I dismissed your feelings as infatuation. I suppose I didn't want to believe that my own small son could feel so...powerfully, so profoundly.'

'Why?' His eyes probed her mistrustfully, without comprehension.

'I've never felt that way about anyone. Never dared to give myself to such a degree. It told me things about you. And it made me afraid.'

'Afraid of what?'

'The power of your love. How far you might go to possess it.'

'You think I...hurt...Surinder?' At his own mention of her name Matt's voice broke. He stared out at the passing banks, soggy with rain and falling leaves. 'You've thought it all along.'

'No, I feared it.'

'Why?'

It reminded me of my past, she thought. 'Well, you lied to the police, for starters.'

'No! The only thing I said that wasn't true was that I'd lost the Swatch.'

'You said you didn't know her.'

'I didn't. I never once spoke to her, except to ask her for stamps. She seemed so sad I couldn't bear it. The only part of her that sang was her bracelets. I wanted to talk to her. I was desperate to ask what was wrong. I bought her a watch...'

'The Swatch?'

'Yes. I handed it to her across the counter. She took it without saying anything, just put it in her pocket. Her eyes stared. They were thanking me, I was sure of it, but he was out the back. She was scared shitless of him. It was obvious. I could see it in her eyes, but I didn't know why. I didn't know then that he was beating her. And then on that Friday, that horrible day, I saw her crying in the churchyard and I went in after her. I wanted to help. I hid against the wall in case he looked out the windows and saw me. I called her name and when she looked up... Oh, shit.'

'What?'

'I saw her face and I freaked. It was all covered in blood and cuts. And she was shaking. And instead of going over to her and helping I behaved like a fucking coward. I ran. I just ran and ran. I ran to the woods and lay there crying. I threw up. I felt so guilty.'

'For running away from her?'

'No, because...'

'What?'

'All the things I'd thought about her. I'd been dreaming of her and then I'd do things thinking of her.' Tears flooded his eyes. He brushed them brusquely away.

'That's nothing to feel guilty about.'

'Maybe Bharjee beat her up that day because he found out I'd given her a Swatch. Maybe he knew I was crazy about her.

Maybe he got mad and jealous. And if I hadn't run away...
Maybe I could have explained to him that she wasn't to blame.'

They had arrived at the cemetery. Lyndsay switched off the
engine, but neither moved.

'I wanted to hack Bharjee to pieces with a chainsaw. I wanted
to go to the police and have him arrested.'

'He should be arrested, for wife beating.' Lyndsay turned her
head and thought of her father. She closed her eyes, attempting
to forgive those memories of so long ago. 'Why didn't you go to
the police?'

'I went to Duncan and Tom's instead. I wanted them to help
me get her out of there. Then I heard Mrs Hampton calling me,
so I hid till she'd gone and then I ran off. Finally I came home.
But I couldn't stay in my room. I couldn't stop thinking about
her alone in that place with him. I went back to the post office.
It was about three in the morning. Some nights, I'd see her
shadow at the window, but not that night. I stayed there till it
was light, hoping to get a glimpse of her. Never in the world did
I imagine she was lying in the nature reserve, dead.'

'Why didn't you come home?'

'Dunno, I just started walking. I had my clarinet. I didn't know
where I was going. I wanted to run away, but I hadn't planned it.
It sort of happened. I thought I'd make money playing in the
streets. Then I saw the papers. There was no going back.
Because, whoever killed her, I felt it was my fault.'

'Was that the first time you'd waited outside their shop at
night?'

He hung his head. 'No, I'd go there...sometimes...'

'The night the ospreys were attacked, when I saw you on the
stairs?'

'Yeah, I'd been there then.' He waited. Both were in their
separate pictures recalling that night. 'Are you pissed off with
me?'

'Pissed off with you? No, you've taught me something very important.'

'What?'

'The power of your feelings. The authenticity of them. They are the heart of you. When I read your writings I felt…'

'What?'

'Jealous, uncomfortable. I thought, I've never felt that passionately about anyone or anything.'

'Not even Dad?'

'Yes, but… I couldn't really express it. Not like you.'

'Why?'

'Oh, it's difficult to explain. I was afraid.'

Matt stared at his mother curiously. 'Shit, look! It's bucketing down,' he said.

'Let's run and put these on the graves and go home,' she smiled and kissed her son softly on the cheek. 'There's someone I think should know all this.'

That evening, Lyndsay telephoned Burgess. 'Matt wants to talk to you,' she said. He came round once Ralph had left to take Paul to the cinema. They sat in the living room. Lyndsay was reminded of their early interviews together with Stephen. She felt angered by her own shortcomings and the twists of fate.

Burgess barely spoke. He listened and made a few notes while Matt repeated what he had told his mother in the car. As he rose to leave, he said, 'Withholding information is a crime.'

Lyndsay wanted to kill him.

She became transfixed by the rain. Whereas previously she had always buried herself in activity, she now sat for hours by the window staring out into the garden. Watching the rain beat down on her plants, seeing nothing else, doing nothing else. The heavy air, suffused with damp, seemed to contain light. A light somewhere beyond the darkness, out of reach.

The boys came and went. She fed them, laid out fresh clothes for them, dealt with the chaos in their rooms, did not shout at them, and did not chide them. They occupied themselves and let her be.

One morning, Paul told her that Ralph had seen dragons on an island near Australia, and that they were three feet tall. He asked her if they could go and see them when Matt was cleared and she was better.

'Better?' she smiled.

'Mum, will we invite Ralph to spend Christmas with us? He's teaching me about magnetic fields. The human heart has a magnetic field, he says. He says we're plugged into everyone and everything around us. We just don't necessarily know it. I bet we're still plugged into Dad.'

'I think maybe we are, darling.' Her small son was a miracle. 'Don't forget your jacket!'

When her chores were done she returned to the window, to the same chair that looked out over the back of the house. She sat there, considering every falling drop, allowing it to run its dark course, blowing in gusts against the panes until it began to resemble a flickering screen, empty of image, and into that void she poured pictures of the past, seeing them with the clarity of film. She watched them, ejected them, saw a pattern evolving, pieces of a jigsaw playing themselves out before her. She allowed herself to remember, to listen to the ghosts and then let them go.

There was her father in the room above her, playing music for the loss of his daughter, facing the suicide of his wife. The anger between her parents, tearing each other to shreds. Her father's compulsive womanising, her mother's clinging jealousy and insecurity. The violence that grew up between them traumatised the two daughters alone in their shared bedroom listening in terror to the beatings taking place in the room beneath them.

Two sisters who together witnessed such horrors that they grew incapable of communicating with one another.

Rebecca eventually fled from it and Lyndsay, to tolerate the pain had cut off, disconnected. 'Unplugged', as Paulie would have described it. She built a family life of her own which had to be perfect, at all costs. Her family became her deliverance, and her screen. But she never shared her inner self with Stephen, never opened up and trusted in his love for her, the healing power of tenderness and love.

When she'd read Matt's writings she was jealous, threatened, because she believed she'd never felt that passionately about anyone or anything. But she had, she still did, about so many things: her sons, her gardens and Stephen.

She'd turned her back on feelings, feared their power, their darkness, their betrayal. Feared herself. Her life had been built on denial, not on truth. She had idolised her father because he had been the only one left. She had never allowed herself to remember what had really happened, what had led her mother to suicide and her sister to flee. She had never allowed herself to experience the rage and pain, and the loss, the profound heartbreaking loss. Until now. For the first time she experienced feelings that had been repressed for years in her soul. And now that she had recognised and faced them, she could begin to let them all go.

One morning, one cold wintry morning, lit by a silvery-white sun, the rain stopped. The day was bare and translucent. The house creaked emptily; no fires were burning. Breath crept from Lyndsay's lips like smoke. Donning her mac and Wellingtons, she went outside: a new being emerging.

The cold air pinched her skin as she walked about the gardens, investigating and discovering. Branches, twigs and dead blossoms lay strewn about her feet. Geraniums and fuchsias hung dripping from their pots. A rat lay drowned at the bottom of the pool. Leafless trees sketched the skyline like Japanese calligraphy. The aftermath of the deluge was everywhere to behold. There was nothing left of nature but the essentials, there was no selection process to the destruction, only random devastation. No pattern to understand. Stephen's death, Surinder's murder; had they also been random acts of devastation?

The force of the wind had smashed a window in one of the garages. Rainwater had got in. Lyndsay was standing on a stepladder trying to ascertain the extent of the damage when a car approaching along the drive drew her attention. She was not expecting anyone. A customer perhaps for the nursery, although they were infrequent this time of the year. When she looked again she saw that it was Burgess. He parked his Rover and crossed the gravel to where she was now descending the metal steps. Her stomach turned over with fear.

As he drew near he pulled a small white bag from his raincoat pocket. 'Here,' he said, offering it to her. 'What is it?'

'Something for Matthew.'

'He's not here.' Lyndsay was guarded, her manner frosty.

Burgess held the bag up again then, reading her reticence, opened it. Inside was a royal blue Swatch. Lyndsay had never seen it before. She glanced at it and then up into the face of the Inspector, questioningly.

'We shan't be needing it any longer,' he said. 'Please, give it back to him.'

She accepted it warily. 'Why not?'

'We've charged someone.'

'Charged someone? I see.'

'I thought I'd bring it along myself,' he added. 'See how you are faring.'

'Fine,' was all she said, slipping the watch out of sight into her raincoat pocket. Burgess nodded, and turned back towards his car while Lyndsay stood where she was on the damp gravel.

'Inspector?'

Burgess swung back. 'Yes?'

'What about the marijuana?'

'Marijuana, Mrs Potter?'

'The traces you found in Matthew's pocket. And the "withholding of information"? Are you pressing charges?'

Burgess dropped his head and frowned considering the questions. After a moment he lifted those small darting eyes, looked directly at her and shrugged his shoulders. 'I have no recollection of anything in your son's pockets. You must be mistaken. We are all very grateful for the help Matthew has given us with our enquiries. Raj Bharjee has been charged with the rape and murder of his young wife. He has pleaded guilty to the charges.'

'And what about the ospreys?'

'We are still working on that. Good day, Mrs Potter.'

As the car disappeared from sight Lyndsay remained perfectly still fingering the negligible weight and size of the watch buried in her pocket. So insignificant an object to have carried so much import. Then she made her way down the sloping banks to the cottage.

Ralph was at the kitchen table working on his book. She couldn't help noticing how pleased to see her he was.

That evening he ate with her and the boys. She cooked a groaning bowl of spaghetti al mare and, after, they played Trivial Pursuit. When the boys had gone off to sleep she and Ralph sat silently together by the log fire in the drawing room, until eventually they began to touch.

She never closed her eyes. She watched him all the time, once the lovemaking had begun. The texture of his skin was different, more leathery and weathered than Stephen's, although he was younger. There were few words, much gentleness. He folded her to the floor and lay himself on top while Lyndsay, beneath him, felt warmth coming alive in her flesh and peace growing in her heart.

The idea of this mysterious man's power mesmerised her and now that she and he lay on the carpet entwined in one another she conceded that she had wanted him from the beginning. The longing had been there, secretly stirring. She'd feared it, the force of it, as she had feared so many feelings.

When the loving was done, he ran his hands through her hair, combing it endlessly, and she pressed her back and buttocks into him, curling and curving her body like a white shell. A small quantity of juice seeped from in between her legs. Too shy to break the silence she concentrated on that, wondering which one of them it belonged to.

'You're very quiet.' He said eventually, resting a hand against her spine.

'I'm listening,' she muttered drowsily, 'to the astonished world around me.'

When she stirred it was after two. Ralph lay sleeping on the floor at her side. Their limbs had remained meeting and mingling. Slowly, hand in hand, they crept to the door. Ralph kissed her softly on the mouth and returned to his cottage while Lyndsay crept upstairs to bed.

The following day, Lyndsay, alone amongst the tropical plants, was cleaning the banana fronds and humming happily. Suddenly, she recalled Dennis, the wild-haired boy she had banned from the grounds. And how on that May morning she had discovered him spraying himself. 'It's hot,' he'd said. Of course! She thought back to the night she had driven the streets in search of Matt, the hours she had spent cruising the bleakness of that estate, and she went in search of her car keys.

Tom's house was no different to any of the others. His street, a winding cul-de-sac, was peppered with youths huddled together on the kerbsides smoking, listening to radios, and doing drugs probably. Most of them were just out of school and jobless. Staring at blank futures.

It took a while before the door was answered. So long, in fact, that Lyndsay was about to give up when she glanced upwards and caught sight of Dennis peering from behind a curtain. Seeing her, he drew back from the window. She rang the bell again, this time more forcefully and for longer. Still there was no reply. She stepped back from the door and craned her head.

'Dennis!'

Moments later, the door was opened. Dennis looked as though he hadn't seen daylight for weeks. Dark rings beneath his eyes accentuated the paleness of his freckled complexion. His wild hair was matted and tangled. His clothes were a mess.

'Yeah?'

'I'm sorry to turn up without telephoning,' she said.

'Dad's not here.' He was about to close the door again when Lyndsay pushed her hand hard against it. 'No, it's you I want to talk to.'

'I'm a bit…bit busy.'

'It's about the birds, Dennis.'

Dennis' eyes stared wildly at her, bloodshot and nervous.

The door, which had been opened barely inches, led her directly into a small square sitting room decorated in tired peach wallpaper. The floor was covered with newspapers. Most of them lay open on the racing pages and many were scribbled with biro markings. Tom, who at work was neat and tidy, obviously gave less attention to his personal environment. She picked her way through to the centre of the room while Dennis hovered by the door.

'How are your burns healing?' she said, turning back to him. Had he understood that it had been the diazinon burning his flesh?

He drew his hands up to his chest and instinctively closed them over his T-shirt. 'May I have a look?'

He shook his head and stumbled backwards, knocking his head against the door directly behind him. 'Ow!' He lifted his hands to rub his head. His behaviour was extraordinary even for Dennis and it took a minute for Lyndsay to realise that he was doped. The bloodshot eyes, the lethargy, the lack of physical co-ordination. The realisation threw her.

'I came about the ospreys. It was you, wasn't it, that night in the bird sanctuary?'

Dennis threw his arms over his face, covering his eyes as though blacking out a nightmare. He began to cry, blubbing like a baby.

'Where were you burnt?' That day when he had come up behind her, surprising her in the nursery, he had been gripping his shirt. 'Was it your chest?' She wanted to move towards him, to help him but feared his erratic behaviour. 'Were you trying to get their eggs?'

Dennis hurled himself away from the door and leapt onto the sofa, burying his face in the worn beige velveteen, like a small animal in hiding. Lyndsay was at a loss as to what to do and thought it best to go but she feared to leave him in this distressed condition.

'Dennis, please, I am not going to tell anyone about the birds. It can be our secret. I just needed to know, to be sure.'

'No secrets with you. You're a horrid lady,' he mumbled.

Behind her, a key in the latch broke the scene.

Tom, leathery and wrinkled, frowned. He was clearly confused by her presence there in his living room. 'I recognised your car...' He looked at his son and then to his employer. 'Is everything all right, Mrs Potter?' Lyndsay nodded. 'Can I offer you a cuppa or something?'

'No, thanks, Tom, I came to see Dennis. I won't take up any more of your time.'

Tom's face fell. 'Have you been making a nuisance of yourself again? I told you to stay away. I've been keeping the keys right with me. To tell you the truth these days he barely leaves his room. He's not been feeling so bright, have you, son?'

Dennis stared up at them with his white face and heroin-ringed, empty eyes. Had he been trying to steal the eggs to make money to feed his habit?

She was unsure whether she should disclose her concerns to Tom or not. She decided to wait for a future occasion. 'No, no, everything's fine. I'll see you Friday. We can talk then. Goodbye!'

Outside in the car she sat a moment trying to restabilise herself. She was shaking like a leaf, but she knew what she had to do. She picked up her mobile phone and telephoned Alan Grater.

As days turned to weeks and weeks moved towards deep winter and Christmas shopping, the pain of the past receded. The knots were loosening, dissipating, melting with the snow flurries. Stephen's face, smiling and at peace, had however crept back to keep her company.

This brought Lyndsay peace. So, too, did the prospect of the Stephen Potter Leisure Centre. At Lyndsay's request, Alan Grater had found and purchased a sizeable plot of land close by the housing estate. Construction was scheduled to begin in the spring. The cinema, concert hall, swimming pool, gymnasium and health centre was her contribution – along with Matt and Paulie whose inheritance this affected – to their local community. The leisure centre would exonerate any blame that could have been levied against Stephen for his choice of business clients.

In any case, who, Lyndsay had been asking herself, was innocent? Was Arthur Finch, who'd built the estate that housed the unemployed, innocent? Marion Finch, who'd welcomed her husband back and, alongside him, continued to live out their lie? What about adolescents such as Dennis who turned to vandalism and heroin to alleviate their boredom and frustrations? The council, many of who were Rotary Club members, golf club buddies, for signing its permission for Arthur's estate when so many necessary community facilities were lacking? Matthew, who'd run from the churchyard on that fatal afternoon because his callow yet intense love had lacked the courage required to reach out to the object of his desire and offer her help? Those whose racism had isolated an Indian couple? Raj Bharjee, who had beaten a beautiful young wife and murdered her out of inadequacy or raging jealousy? Lyndsay and Stephen, for having blindly enjoyed so much while others struggled on with so little? In their way, each and every one of them shared in the responsibility and was unwitting accomplices to the vandalism and Surinder's murder. There was no innocent party.

On Christmas Eve Lyndsay and Matt were in the garden, trimming sprays of mistletoe, and surrounded by Christmas trees for sale. Ralph and Paulie would soon be back with the shopping. Lyndsay was rushing; there was so much to prepare. As a mark of respect to Stephen, and because she was not ready to spend Christmas alone with the boys and Ralph, she had decided to make it a more open gathering rather than a family affair. The Hamptons were invited, as well as Amanda, even Tom Carter, but not Dennis. At Lyndsay's expense Dennis was spending Christmas in a private rehabilitation centre. Later, when the leisure centre was finished, there would be a job waiting for him.

'Come on, Matt, let's get going.' In her haste Lyndsay knocked over a small flowerpot and, as she bent to retrieve the awakening buds of crocuses, she knelt on a discarded holly sprig and ripped her tights. She cursed the tear and then caught Matt's eye. He was giggling. 'What are you laughing at?' she asked smiling.

'You. You make such a fuss about everything. But you're the best Mum.'

'Oh, Matt, do you really think so?!'

Within seconds the pair of them were clutching one another, laughing and hugging.

The past is redeemed, she thought. Loss is turning to growth. A new life is finally beginning.

CAROL DRINKWATER

AN ABUNDANCE OF RAIN

Kate De Marly leaves England and a well-ordered life behind her to travel to the Fijian island of Lesa. She is excited about her reunion with Sam McGuire, the father who abandoned her as a child. On the ship she is devastated to learn the meeting will never happen – Sam is dead. His sugar plantation is now hers. Island life weaves its seductive spell over her, but there are questions Kate seeks answers to. Was her father's death an accident? Why is someone so eager to buy the land? What are the secrets threatening her own life? And then the approaching cyclone hits...

AKIN TO LOVE

Steeped in mystery, suspense and the vibrancy of the Mediterranean, *Akin to Love* is a romantic drama, a powerful tale of bitter regrets, passion and betrayal. Penny Morrison is a glamorous international star. She has written a film script which is a guaranteed success. The story is a thinly disguised retelling of her youthful relationship with the painter Harry Knowle, a man she met when she was a struggling actress visiting Crete as a backpacker. There she fell in love with Harry and discovered romantic Greece as well as the dark side of the dictatorship. When the film star Penny returns to Crete to shoot she once again finds herself under the spell of the mysterious island. And when her past catches up with her present she is forced to confront a memory long hidden even from herself.

CAROL DRINKWATER

THE HAUNTED SCHOOL

She remembered then the coach driver's description of the locals here. 'Crazy mountain folk, believe in ghosts,' he had said.

'Ha ha ha! A haunted school! That's a quaint idea. Please do show it to me. I could move in immediately…'

The tiny village of Moogalloo deep in the Australian countryside has a new schoolteacher, Fanny Crowe, sent all the way from England. Unhappy twelve-year-old Richard Blackburn wonders if she is really a friendly teacher or a wicked witch. How can she sleep in the haunted hotel – the old building that caused his mother's death? Richard is not the only anxious local. The villagers believe in ghosts and don't like an outsider meddling with their past. Can Richard alone solve the mystery of Moogalloo?

MAPPING THE HEART

Beautiful actress Eleanor McGuire has all a woman could wish for: a rich music-industry husband, a flat in Paris, a villa in the South of France and the choice of whether to work or not. And then a handsome young Frenchman who had seduced her in Brazil a decade earlier walks back into her life – quite by chance – and brings the memories flooding back. Once again Eleanor is bewitched by desire and longing. Now she has everything to lose, but love and sexual obsession drive her recklessly onwards. Throwing over everything, in an attempt to rebuild her life, she returns to Brazil where it all began. What awaits her there is a world of magic, prostitution, poverty and murder…

PAYMENT

Please tick currency you wish to use:

☐ £ (Sterling) ☐ $ (US) ☐ $ (CAN) ☐ € (Euros)

Allow for shipping costs charged per order plus an amount per book as set out in the tables below:

CURRENCY/DESTINATION

	£(Sterling)	$(US)	$(CAN)	€(Euros)
Cost per order				
UK	1.50	2.25	3.50	2.50
Europe	3.00	4.50	6.75	5.00
North America	3.00	3.50	5.25	5.00
Rest of World	3.00	4.50	6.75	5.00
Additional cost per book				
UK	0.50	0.75	1.15	0.85
Europe	1.00	1.50	2.25	1.70
North America	1.00	1.00	1.50	1.70
Rest of World	1.50	2.25	3.50	3.00

PLEASE SEND CHEQUE OR INTERNATIONAL MONEY ORDER.
payable to: STRATUS HOLDINGS plc or HOUSE OF STRATUS INC. or card payment as indicated

STERLING EXAMPLE

Cost of book(s):. . . . . Example: 3 x books at £6.99 each: £20.97

Cost of order:. . . . . Example: £1.50 (Delivery to UK address)

Additional cost per book:. . . . . Example: 3 x £0.50: £1.50

Order total including shipping:. Example: £23.97

VISA, MASTERCARD, SWITCH, AMEX:

☐☐☐☐☐☐☐☐☐☐☐☐☐☐☐☐☐☐☐☐

Issue number (Switch only):

☐☐☐

Start Date: **Expiry Date:**

☐☐/☐☐ ☐☐/☐☐

Signature: _____

NAME: _____

ADDRESS: _____

COUNTRY: _____

ZIP/POSTCODE: _____

Please allow 28 days for delivery. Despatch normally within 48 hours.

Prices subject to change without notice.
Please tick box if you do not wish to receive any additional information. ☐

House of Stratus publishes many other titles in this genre; please check our website
(**www.houseofstratus.com**) for more details.